PRAISE FOR *THE NIGHT TIGER*

"Wonderf
—NPR

"Mesmerizing."
—*USA TODAY*

"Beautiful."
—*GLAMOUR*

"Lushly detailed."
—*NATIONAL GEOGRAPHIC*

"Absorbing."
—*REAL SIMPLE*

"Engrossing."
—*REFINERY29*

"Compelling."
—LOS ANGELES PUBLIC LIBRARY

"Sumptuous."
—*KIRKUS REVIEWS* (STARRED REVIEW)

"Superb."
—*PUBLISHERS WEEKLY* (STARRED REVIEW)

"Astoundingly captivating."
—*BOOKLIST* (STARRED REVIEW)

"Richly complex . . . Gorgeous . . . Transcendent." —*SAN FRANCISCO CHRONICLE*

Praise for *The Night Tiger*

"Richly complex ... Gorgeous ... Transports us into a colonial world we more often see from the view of the occupier, in this transcendent tale about twins who share no blood, mythology and superstition, sibling rivalry, loyalty, forbidden love, and identity." —*San Francisco Chronicle*

"This is the kind of book that when you read it, you really are transported back to that time and place.... [Choo has] captured, in a very atmospheric way, the time period and the superstitions [of colonial Malaysia in the 1930s]. It's a pretty wonderful book."

—Nancy Pearl, NPR's *Morning Edition*

"Choo transports readers to colonial Malaysia and infuses the novel with magic and superstition. It's part mystery, part coming-of-age tale, and part absorbing historical fiction." —*Real Simple*

"A mesmerizing tale of murder, romance, and superstition ... So vividly told, you can practically smell the oleander blossoms outside Acton's house. This *Night Tiger* is worth a prowl." —*USA Today*

"A book for fans of Isabel Allende and for those who love a murder mystery with a beautiful backdrop." —*Glamour*

"A lushly detailed novel imbued with folklore, mystery, and romance."

—*National Geographic*

"Fans of Isabel Allende will likely soar through Choo's *The Night Tiger* at a breakneck pace, so you might want to clear your schedule before sitting down to read it." —*PopSugar*

"So engrossing you could spend a day reading this lush historical novel without staring at your phone once ... A sweeping novel with something for everyone—and incredible writing." —*Refinery29*

"A sumptuous garden maze of a novel . . . Choo weaves her research in with a feather-light touch, and readers will be so caught up in the natural and supernatural intrigue that the serious themes here about colonialism and power dynamics, about gender and class, are absorbed with equal delicacy."
—*Kirkus Reviews* (starred review)

"Mythical creatures, conversations with the dead, lucky numbers, Confucian virtues, and forbidden love provide the backdrop to Choo's superb murder mystery. Mining the rich setting of colonial Malaysia, Choo wonderfully combines a Holmes-esque plot with Chinese lore."
—*Publishers Weekly* (starred and boxed review)

"A work of incredible beauty . . . Astoundingly captivating and striking in its portrayal of love, betrayal, and death, *The Night Tiger* is a transcendent story of courage and connection."
—*Booklist* (starred review)

"[Choo] presents complex characters and multilayered stories in a vivid setting that coalesce into a richly evocative and mesmerizing tale in which myths and folklore intertwine in daily life. For fans of Kate Mosse or Isabel Allende."
—*Library Journal*

"A bravura performance."
—Washington Independent Review of Books

The
Night
Tiger

Also by Yangsze Choo

The Ghost Bride

The Night Tiger

Yangsze Choo

FLATIRON
BOOKS
NEW YORK

THE NIGHT TIGER. Copyright © 2019 by Yangsze Choo. All rights reserved. Printed in the United States of America. For information, address Flatiron Books, 120 Broadway, New York, NY 10271.

www.flatironbooks.com

Designed by Devan Norman

The Library of Congress has cataloged the hardcover edition as follows:

Names: Choo, Yangsze, author.
Title: The night tiger : a novel / Yangsze Choo.
Description: First Edition. | New York : Flatiron Books, 2019.
Identifiers: LCCN 2018030163| ISBN 9781250175458 (hardcover) | ISBN 9781250229175 (international, sold outside the U.S., subject to rights availability) | ISBN 9781250175441 (ebook)
Subjects: | GSAFD: Fantasy fiction.
Classification: LCC PS3603.H664 N54 2019 | DDC 813/.6—dc23
LC record available at https://lccn.loc.gov/2018030163

ISBN 978-1-250-17546-5 (trade paperback)

Our books may be purchased in bulk for promotional, educational, or business use. Please contact your local bookseller or the Macmillan Corporate and Premium Sales Department at 1-800-221-7945, extension 5442, or by email at MacmillanSpecialMarkets@macmillan.com.

First Flatiron Books Paperback Edition: January 2020

10 9 8 7 6 5 4 3 2

This book is for my father and mother,
who were born and grew up in the Kinta Valley.

1

THE OLD MAN IS DYING. REN CAN SEE IT IN THE SHALLOW BREATHS, the sunken face, and the skin stretched thinly over his cheekbones. Yet he wants the shutters open. Irritably, he beckons the boy over, and Ren, his throat tight as though he's swallowed a stone, throws open the second-story window.

Outside is a brilliant sea of green: the waving tops of jungle trees and a blue sky like a fever dream. The tropical glare makes Ren flinch. He moves to shield his master with his shadow, but the old man stops him with a gesture. Sunlight emphasizes the tremor of his hand with its ugly stump of a missing finger. Ren remembers how just a few months ago that hand could still calm babies and suture wounds.

The old man opens his watery blue eyes, those colorless foreign eyes that had frightened Ren so much in the beginning, and whispers something. The boy bends his cropped head closer.

"Remember."

The boy nods.

"Say it." The hoarse rasp is fading.

"When you are dead, I will find your missing finger," Ren replies in a clear, small voice.

"And?"

He hesitates. "And bury it in your grave."

"Good." The old man draws a rattling breath. "You must get it back before the forty-nine days of my soul are over."

The boy has done many such tasks before, quickly and competently. He'll manage, even as his narrow shoulders convulse.

"Don't cry, Ren."

At times like this the boy looks far younger than his years. The old man is sorry—he wishes he could do it himself, but he's exhausted. Instead, he turns his face to the wall.

2

Ipoh, Malaya
Wednesday, June 3rd

FORTY-FOUR IS AN UNLUCKY NUMBER FOR CHINESE. IT SOUNDS LIKE "die, definitely die," and as a result, the number four and all its iterations are to be avoided. On that ill-fated day in June, I'd been working at my secret part-time job at the May Flower Dance Hall in Ipoh for exactly forty-four days.

My job was a secret because no respectable girl should be dancing with strangers, despite our services being advertised as "instructors." As perhaps we were for most of our customers: nervous clerks and schoolboys who bought rolls of tickets to learn to foxtrot and waltz or do the *ronggeng,* that charming Malay dance. The rest were *buaya,* or crocodiles, as we called them. Toothy smilers whose wandering hands were only deterred by a sharp pinch.

I was never going to make much money if I kept slapping them off like this, but I hoped I wouldn't need to for long. It was to pay a debt of forty Malayan dollars that my mother had incurred at a ruinously high interest rate. My real day job as a dressmaker's apprentice wasn't enough to repay the money, and my poor foolish mother couldn't possibly come up with it by herself; she'd no luck at gambling.

If she'd only left statistics to me, things might have turned out better as I'm generally good at numbers. I say this, but without much pride. It's a skill that hasn't been very useful to me. If I were a boy, it would be a different matter, but my delight in working out probabilities when I was seven years old was of no help to my mother, who'd just been widowed at the time. In the sad vacuum of my father's passing, I spent hours penciling numbers on scraps of paper. They were sensible and orderly, unlike the chaos our household had descended into. Despite that, my mother kept her sweet vague smile, the one that made her look like the Goddess of Mercy, though she was probably worrying what we'd eat for dinner. I loved her fiercely, though more about that later.

THE FIRST THING THE DANCE-HALL MAMA TOLD ME TO DO, WHEN I was hired, was to cut my hair. I'd spent years growing it out, after teasing from my stepbrother Shin about how I looked like a boy. Those two long braids, neatly tied with ribbons just as they'd been all the years I'd attended the Anglo-Chinese Girls' School, were a sweet symbol of femininity. I believed they covered up a multitude of sins, including the unladylike ability to calculate interest rates on the fly.

"No," the Mama said. "You can't work for me like that."

"But there are other girls with long hair," I pointed out.

"Yes, but not you."

She sent me to an alarming woman who snipped off my braids. They fell into my lap, heavy and almost alive. If Shin could see me, he'd die laughing. I bent my head as she clipped, the nape of my exposed neck frighteningly vulnerable. She cut bangs in front and when I raised my eyes, she smiled.

"Look beautiful," she said. "Look exactly like Louise Brooks."

Who was Louise Brooks anyway? Apparently, a silent movie star who was wildly popular a few years ago. I blushed. It was difficult to get used to the new fashion, in which flat-chested tomboys like me should suddenly become popular. Of course, being in Malaya and on the far outskirts of the Empire, we were sadly behind in style. British ladies who came East complained of being six to twelve months behind the London fashions. It was no surprise, then, that the craze for ballroom dancing and cropped hair was finally hitting Ipoh, when they'd been in full swing elsewhere for quite a while. I touched the shaved nape of my neck, afraid that I looked more like a boy than ever.

The Mama, shifting her large bulk practically, said, "You'll need a name. Preferably English. We'll call you Louise."

So it was as Louise that I was dancing the tango that afternoon of June third. Despite the faltering stock market, our bustling town of Ipoh was giddy with the rush of new buildings built on the wealth of tin and rubber exports. It was raining, an unusually heavy downpour for midafternoon. The sky turned the color of iron, and the electric light had to be switched on, much to the dismay of the management. Rain drummed loudly on the tin roof, which the bandleader, a little Goanese with a skinny moustache, tried his best to drown out.

The craze for Western dancing had led to the mushrooming of public dance halls on the outskirts of every town. Some were grand affairs, like the newly built Celestial Hotel, while others were no more than large sheds open to the tropical breeze. Professional dancers like myself were kept in a pen, as though we were chickens or sheep. The pen was a section of seats separated by a ribbon. Pretty girls sat there, each with a numbered paper rosette pinned to her breast. Bouncers ensured that nobody approached us unless they had a ticket, though it didn't stop some men from trying.

I was rather surprised that someone asked me to tango. I'd never learned it properly at Miss Lim's dancing school, where, as consolation for being forced to leave school by my stepfather, I'd been taught to waltz and, more daringly, foxtrot. The tango, however, wasn't taught. It was too risqué, although we'd all seen Rudolph Valentino dance it in black and white.

When I started at the May Flower, my friend Hui had said I'd better learn it.

"You look like a modern girl," she said. "You're bound to get requests."

Dear Hui. She was the one who taught me, the two of us staggering around like drunkards. Still, she tried her best.

"Well, perhaps nobody will ask," she said hopefully, after a sudden lurch almost brought us down.

Of course, she'd been wrong. I quickly learned that the kind of man who requested the tango was usually a *buaya*, and the one on that ill-fated forty-fourth day was no exception.

HE WAS A SALESMAN, HE SAID. SPECIALIZING IN SCHOOL AND OFFICE supplies. Immediately, I recalled the crisp cardboard scent of my school notebooks. I'd loved school, but that door was closed to me now. All that remained was the idle chatter and heavy feet of this salesman who told me that stationery was a steady business to be in, though he could do better, he was sure of it.

"You have good skin." His breath smelled like garlicky Hainanese chicken rice. Not knowing what to say, I concentrated on my poor trampled feet. It was a hopeless situation, since the salesman seemed to think that the tango consisted of striking sudden and dramatic poses.

"I used to sell cosmetics." Too close again. "I know a lot about women's skin."

Leaning back, I increased the distance between us. As we made a turn, he jerked hard so that I staggered against him. I suspected he'd done it on purpose, but his hand made an involuntary movement towards his pocket, as though he was worried something might fall out.

"Do you know," he said, smiling, "that there are ways to keep a woman young and beautiful forever? With needles."

"Needles?" I asked, curious despite thinking this was one of the worst pickup lines I'd heard.

"In western Java, there are women who stick very fine gold needles into their faces. All the way in, till they can't be seen. It's witchcraft to prevent aging. I met a beautiful widow who'd buried five husbands, said to have twenty needles in her face. But she told me that you must remove them after death."

"Why?"

"The body must be made whole again when you die. Anything added must be removed, and anything missing replaced—otherwise your soul won't rest in peace." Enjoying my surprise, he went on to describe the rest of his trip in detail. Some people were talkers while others danced in sweaty-palmed silence. On the whole, I preferred the talkers because they were absorbed in their own world and didn't pry into mine.

If my family discovered I was working here part-time, it would be a disaster. I shuddered to think of my stepfather's rage, my mother's tears, as she'd be bound to confess her mahjong debts to him. Then there was Shin, my stepbrother. Born on the same day as me, people used to ask if we were twins. He'd always been my ally, at least until recently. But Shin was gone now, having won a place to study medicine at the King Edward VII Medical College in Singapore, where native talent was being trained to combat the lack of doctors in Malaya. I'd been proud, because it was Shin and he'd always been clever, yet deeply envious because between the two of us, I'd scored higher marks at school. But there was no use thinking about what-ifs. Shin never answered my letters anymore.

The salesman was still talking. "Do you believe in luck?"

"What's there to believe?" I tried not to grimace as he trod heavily on my foot.

"You should, because I'm going to be very lucky." Grinning, he took yet another turn too sharply. From the corner of my eye, I noticed the Mama glaring at us. We were causing a scene on the dance floor, staggering around like this, and it was all very bad for business.

Gritting my teeth, I scrabbled for balance as the salesman unleashed a dangerously low dip. Undignified, we teetered. Arms flailing, grabbing at clothes. His hand cupped my buttocks as he peered down my dress. I elbowed him, my other hand snagging in his pocket. Something small and light rolled into my palm as I snatched it away. It felt like a slim smooth cylinder. I hesitated, panting. I should put it back; if he saw that I'd taken something, he might accuse me of being a pickpocket. Some men liked to make trouble like that; it gave them a hold over a girl.

The salesman smiled shamelessly. "What's your name?"

Flustered, I gave him my real name, Ji Lin, instead of Louise. Worse and worse. At that instant, the music ended, and the salesman abruptly released me. His eyes were fixed beyond my shoulder as though he'd seen someone he recognized, and with a hurried start, he was gone.

As if to make up for the tango, the band launched into "Yes Sir, That's My Baby!" Couples rushed the dance floor as I walked back to my seat.

The object in my hand was burning like a brand. Surely he'd come back; he still had a roll of dance tickets. If I waited, I could return what I'd taken. Pretend he'd dropped it on the floor.

The smell of rain blew in through the open windows. Unnerved, I lifted the ribbon separating the dancers' seats from the floor and sat down, smoothing my skirt.

I opened my hand. As I'd guessed from the feel of it, it was a thin-walled cylinder made of glass. A specimen bottle, barely two inches long with a metal screw top. Something light rattled inside. I stifled a cry.

It was the top two joints of a dried, severed finger.

3

WHEN THE TRAIN RATTLES INTO BATU GAJAH, REN IS ON HIS FEET, face pressed against the window. This prosperous little town, the seat of British administration for the state of Perak, has a peculiar name: *batu* means stone, and *gajah,* elephant. Some say the town is named after a pair of elephants who crossed the Kinta River. Angered by this act, the deity Sang Kelembai turned them into two boulders rising out of the water. Ren wonders what those poor elephants were doing in the river, that they should be turned to stone.

Ren has never traveled by train before, although he's waited for the old doctor at the Taiping railway station many times. The windows are open in the third-class carriage despite the particles of soot, some as large as a fingernail, that blow back as the steam engine rounds a bend. Ren can taste the heavy monsoon wetness in the air. He presses a hand against his carpetbag. Inside is the precious letter. If it rains hard, the ink might run. The thought of the old doctor's careful, shaky script washing away sends a stab of homesickness through him.

Every mile that the train rattles onward takes him farther and farther from Dr. MacFarlane's rambling, untidy bungalow, his home for the last three years. He's gone now. The small room where Ren stayed in the servants' quarters, next to Auntie Kwan, is empty. This morning, Ren swept the floor for the last time and neatly tied up the old newspapers for the *karang guni* man to collect. As he closed the door with its peeling green paint, he saw the large spider that had shared the room with him silently rebuilding its web in the corner of the ceiling.

Treacherous tears fill his eyes. But Ren has a task to complete; this is no time to cry. With Dr. MacFarlane's death, the forty-nine days of the soul have begun to tick away. And this town with its strange name isn't the first place that he's lived without his brother Yi. Ren considers the stone elephants again. Were they twins like Yi and himself? Sometimes, Ren feels a tingle, like the twitch of cat whiskers, as though Yi is still with him. A flicker of that strange twin sense that bound them, warning him of events to come. But when he looks over his shoulder, there is no one.

BATU GAJAH STATION IS A LONG, LOW BUILDING WITH A SLOPING roof that lies next to the railway line like a sleeping snake. All over Malaya, the British have built similar stations that fall along familiar, tidy lines. The towns repeat themselves, with white government buildings and grassy *padangs*, clipped like English town greens.

At the ticket office, the Malay stationmaster is kind enough to pencil Ren a map. He has a handsome mustache and trousers starched to knife-edge creases. "It's quite far. Are you sure no one will fetch you?"

Ren shakes his head. "I can walk."

Farther down, there's a cluster of Chinese shophouses leaning against one another with their overhanging second floors and little sundry shops spilling out below. That way leads to town. But Ren takes a right instead, past the Government English School. He glances longingly at the wooden building with its whitewashed, graceful lines, imagining other boys his age studying in the high-ceilinged rooms or playing games on the green field. Doggedly, he keeps walking.

The hill climbs towards Changkat, where the Europeans live. There's no time to admire the many colonial bungalows built in the style of the British Raj. His destination is on the far side of Changkat, right up against coffee and rubber plantations.

Rain splatters the red earth furiously. Gasping, Ren starts to run, clutching his carpetbag. He's almost reached a large *angsana* tree when he hears the rattle of a goods lorry, engine rasping as it climbs the hill. The driver shouts from the window. "Get in!"

Breathless, Ren climbs into the cab. His savior is a fat man with a wart on the side of his face.

"Thank you, Uncle," says Ren, using the polite term to address an elder. The man smiles. Water trickles down Ren's trousers and onto the floor.

"The stationmaster told me you were going this way. To the young doctor's house?"

"Is he young?"

"Not as young as you. How old are you?"

Ren considers telling him the truth. They're speaking Cantonese, and this man looks kind. But he's too cautious to relax his guard.

"Almost thirteen."

"Small, aren't you?"

Ren nods. He's actually eleven. Even Dr. MacFarlane hadn't known that. Ren added a year, as many Chinese did, when he entered the old doctor's household.

"Got a job there?"

Ren hugs the carpetbag. "Delivery."

Or a retrieval.

"That doctor lives further away than the other foreigners," the driver says. "I wouldn't walk here at night. It's dangerous."

"Why?"

"A lot of dogs have been eaten recently. Taken even when they were chained to the house. Only the collars and heads were left."

Ren's heart squeezes. There's a buzzing in his ears. Is it possible that it has started again, so soon? "Was it a tiger?"

"Leopard's more likely. The foreigners say they'll hunt it. Anyway, you shouldn't wander around when it gets dark."

They pull up at the bottom of a long curving drive, past the clipped English lawn to a sprawling white bungalow. The driver honks the horn twice, and after a long pause, a skinny Chinese man emerges onto the covered veranda, wiping his hands on a white apron. As Ren clambers down, he thanks the lorry driver over the rattle of rain.

The man says, "Take care of yourself."

Bracing himself, Ren makes a mad dash up the driveway into shelter. The pelting rain soaks him, and he hesitates at the door, worried about the water pooling on the wide teak planks. In the front room of the house, an Englishman is writing a letter. He's seated at a table, but when Ren is shown in, he rises with an enquiring look. He's thinner and younger than Dr. MacFarlane. It's hard to gauge his expression behind the twin reflections of his glasses.

Ren sets the battered carpetbag down and reaches into it for the letter, presenting it politely with two hands. The new doctor slits the envelope precisely open with a silver letter opener. Dr. MacFarlane used to open letters with his stubby finger and thumb. Ren drops his eyes. It isn't good to compare them.

Now that he has delivered the letter, Ren feels a great weariness in his legs. The instructions that he memorized seem hazy; the room tilts around him.

WILLIAM ACTON EXAMINES THE PIECE OF PAPER HE'S BEEN HANDED. It comes from Kamunting, that little village next to Taiping. The handwriting is spiky and tremulous, the hand of a sick man.

Dear Acton,
I write with little ceremony, I'm afraid. I've left it too long and can barely hold a pen. With no relatives worth recommending, I'm sending a bequest: one of my most interesting finds, to whom I hope you'll give a good home. I sincerely recommend my Chinese houseboy, Ren. Though young, he is trained and trustworthy. It is only for a few years until he gains his majority. I think you will find yourselves well suited.
Yours, etc. etc.
John MacFarlane, M.D.

William reads the letter twice and looks up. The boy stands in front of him, water trickling through his cropped hair and down his thin neck.

"Is your name Ren?"

The boy nods.

"You used to work for Dr. MacFarlane?"

Again, the silent nod.

William considers him. "Well, now you work for me."

As he examines the boy's anxious young face, he wonders whether it is rain or tears running down his cheeks.

4

SINCE I'D PICKED UP THAT HORRIBLE SOUVENIR FROM THE SALES-man's pocket, I was unable to think of much else. The shriveled finger haunted my thoughts, even though I hid it in a cardboard box in the dance-hall dressing room. I didn't want to have it anywhere near me, let alone take it back to the dressmaker's shop where I boarded.

Mrs. Tham, the tiny, beaky-faced dressmaker to whom I was appren-ticed, was a friend of a friend of my mother's, a tenuous connection that I was grateful for. Without it, my stepfather would never have allowed me to move out of the house. However, Mrs. Tham came with an unspoken condition: that she should have free access to my private possessions at any time. It was an annoying but small price to pay for freedom. So I said nothing, even when the little traps I set—thread caught in a drawer, a book open at a certain page—were invariably disturbed. She'd given me a room key, but since she obviously had her own, it was quite useless. Leav-ing a mummified finger in that room would be like throwing a lizard to a crow.

So it stayed in the dressing room of the May Flower, and I lived in constant fear that one of the cleaners would find it. I considered turning it in to the office, pretending that I'd discovered it on the floor. Several times I actually picked up the horrid thing and started down the corridor, yet somehow I always turned back. The longer I hesitated, the more suspicious the whole affair seemed. I remembered the Mama's disapproving glance when we were dancing; she might think I was a pickpocket who'd had second thoughts. Or perhaps the finger itself held a dark magic that made it difficult to get rid of. A watery blue shadow, that made the glass vial colder than it should be.

I'd told Hui of course. Her plump, pretty face creased. "Ugh! How can you bear to touch it?"

Technically, I was only touching the glass bottle, but she was right—it was unsettling. The skin had blackened and shriveled so that the finger resembled a withered twig. Only the telltale crooked joint and yellowed fingernail prompted a lurch of recognition. There was a sticker on the metal lid with a number: 168, a lucky combination that sounded, in Cantonese, like "fortune all the way."

Hui said, "Are you going to throw it out?"

"I don't know. He might come looking for it."

So far there'd been no sign of the salesman, but he knew my real name.

"Ji Lin" was the Cantonese way of pronouncing it; in Mandarin, it would be "Zhi Lian." The Ji in my name wasn't commonly used for girls. It was the character for *zhi*, or knowledge, one of the five Confucian Virtues. The others were benevolence, righteousness, order, and integrity. Chinese are particularly fond of matched sets and the Five Virtues were the sum of qualities that made up a perfect man. So it was a bit odd that a girl like me should be named for knowledge. If I'd been named something feminine and delicate like "Precious Jade" or "Fragrant Lily," things might have turned out differently.

"Such a peculiar name for a girl."

I was ten years old, a skinny child with large eyes. The local matchmaker, an old lady, had come to call on my widowed mother.

"Her father named her." My mother gave a nervous smile.

"I suppose you were expecting a son," said the matchmaker. "Well, I've good news for you. You might get one."

It had been three years since my father had died of pneumonia. Three years of missing his quiet presence, and three years of difficult widowhood for my mother. Her frail figure was more suited to reclining on a chaise than doing other people's sewing and washing. The skin peeled off her pretty hands, now rough and red. Previously, my mother had put off all talk of matchmaking, but today she seemed especially dispirited. It was very hot and still. The purple bougainvillea outside trembled in the heat.

"He's a tin-ore dealer from Falim," said the matchmaker. "A widower with one son. He's no spring chicken, but neither are you."

My mother plucked at an invisible thread, then gave a slight nod. The matchmaker looked pleased.

The Kinta Valley in which we lived held the richest tin deposits in the world, and there were dozens of mines, both large and small, nearby. Tin-ore dealers made a good living, and he could have sent to China for a wife, but he'd heard my mother was beautiful. There were other candidates, of course. Better ones. Women who'd never been married. But it was worth a try. Crouching closer to eavesdrop, I hoped desperately that this man would choose one of them instead, but I had an unlucky feeling about it.

SHIN AND I, FUTURE STEP-SIBLINGS-TO-BE, MET WHEN HIS FATHER came to call on my mother. It was a very straightforward meeting. No one bothered to pretend that there was some romantic pretext. They brought Chinese sponge cakes wrapped in paper from a local bakery. For years afterwards, I was unable to swallow those soft steamed cakes without choking.

Shin's father was a stern-looking man, but his expression softened when he saw my mother. It was rumored that his late wife had also been a beauty. He had an eye for attractive women, though, of course, he didn't visit prostitutes, the matchmaker had assured my mother. He was very serious, financially stable, and neither gambled nor drank. Studying his face surreptitiously, I thought he looked hard and humorless.

"And this is Ji Lin," my mother said, propelling me forward. Wearing my best dress, outgrown so that my knobby knees stuck out, I dropped my head shyly.

"My son's name is Shin," he said. "Written with the character *xin*. The two of them are already like brother and sister."

The matchmaker looked pleased. "What a coincidence! That makes two of the five Confucian Virtues. You'd better have three more children so you can complete the set."

Everyone laughed, even my mother, smiling nervously and showing her pretty teeth. I didn't. It was true though. With the *zhi* in my name for wisdom, and *xin* in Shin's for integrity, we made up part of a matched set, though the fact that it was incomplete was a bit jarring.

I glanced at Shin to see if he found any of this amusing. He had sharp, bright eyes under thick brows, and when he saw me looking at him, he scowled.

I don't like you, either, I thought, overcome with anxiety for my mother. She'd never been strong and bearing three more children would be hard for her. Still, I'd no say in the matter, and within a month, the marriage negotiations were concluded and we were settled at my new stepfather's shophouse in Falim.

Falim was a village on the outskirts of Ipoh, little more than a few lanes of Chinese shophouses, their long narrow bodies sandwiched next to each other with shared walls. My stepfather's shop was on the main street, Lahat Road. It was dark and cool, with two open courtyards breaking up its serpentine length. The big upstairs bedroom over the front was for the newlyweds, and I was to have, for the first time in my life, my own room at the back, next to Shin's. A windowless corridor ran lengthwise beside the two small rooms, which were stacked in front of each other like railway cars. Light entered the hallway only if our doors were open.

Shin had barely spoken to me during the whole rushed courtship and marriage, though he'd behaved very well. We were exactly the same age; in fact, it turned out that we were born on the same day, though I was older by five hours. To top it off, my stepfather's surname was also "Lee," so there was no need to even change names. The matchmaker was pleased with herself, though it seemed like a horrible trick of fate to me, shoehorning me into a new family where even my birthday would no longer be mine. Shin greeted my mother politely but coldly, and avoided me. I was convinced that he didn't like us.

In private, I'd begged my mother to reconsider but she'd only touched my hair. "It's better for us this way." Besides, she seemed to have taken an odd liking to my stepfather. When his admiring gaze rested on her, her cheeks turned pink. He'd given us money in red packets to buy a simple trousseau for the wedding, and my mother had been unexpectedly excited about it. "New dresses—for you and for me!" she'd said, fanning the bank notes out on our worn cotton bedspread.

That first night at the new house, I was frightened. It was so much larger than the tiny wooden dwelling, one room with a step-down, earthen-floored kitchen, that my mother and I had lived in. This shophouse was both a business and a residence, and downstairs seemed a vast and hollow space. My new stepfather was a middleman who bought tin ore from small-time gravel pump miners and *dulang* washers, women who panned tin ore from old mines and streams, to resell to the large smelters like the Straits Trading Company.

It was a silent, dark shop. Prosperous, though my stepfather was tight-lipped and tightfisted. Hardly anyone came unless they had business selling tin, and the front and back were shuttered with iron grates to prevent theft of the stockpiled ore. As the heavy double doors banged shut behind us that first day, my heart sank.

At bedtime, my mother gave me a kiss and told me to run along. She looked embarrassed, and I realized that from now on, she wouldn't be sleeping in the same room with me. I could no longer drag my thin pallet next to hers or burrow into her arms. Instead, she belonged to my stepfather, who was watching us silently.

I glanced up at the wooden staircase that yawned into the darkness of the upper floor. I'd never slept in a two-story building before, but Shin went straight up. I hurried after him.

"Good night," I said. I knew he could talk if he wanted to. That very morning, when we were moving our last few belongings in, I'd seen him laughing and running with his friends outside. Shin looked at me. I thought that if this were my house and some strange woman and her child moved in, I'd probably be angry, too, but he had a curious expression, almost pitying.

"It's too late for you now," he said. "But good night."

Now as I examined the bottle that I'd taken from the sales-man's pocket, I wondered what Shin would make of it. It occurred to me that there were animals with fingers, too.

"Suppose this isn't even human?" I said to Hui, who was mending her skirt.

"You mean, like a monkey's finger?" Hui's nose wrinkled. Clearly, this idea was just as repulsive to her.

"It would have to be big—a gibbon or maybe even an orangutan."

"A doctor might be able to tell," Hui bit off her thread thoughtfully. "Though I don't know how you'd find one to examine it."

But I did have someone to ask. Someone who was studying anatomy, even if he was only a second-year medical student. Someone who'd proven, over the years, that he could keep a secret.

Shin would be back from Singapore next week. He hadn't been home for almost a year, and even then, only briefly. The last holiday he'd worked as a hospital orderly in Singapore for extra income. His letters to me, never frequent, had petered out, and I'd stopped waiting for them. Perhaps it was better not to hear about his new friends or the lectures he attended. I was so envious of Shin that sometimes a bitter taste would flood my mouth. Yet I should be happy for him. He'd managed to get away.

Since I'd left school, my life had been a complete waste of time. A scheme to train as a teacher had fallen through when my stepfather discovered that new teachers could potentially be dispatched to any village or town in Malaya. Out of the question, he said, for an unmarried girl. Nurse-training was even more unsuitable. I'd have to sponge-bathe strangers and dispose of their body fluids. In any case, I didn't have the money. My step-father offered the cold reminder that I'd been permitted to stay on at school at his expense, long after most girls had dropped out. His opinion was that I ought to stay decently at home, clerking for him until I got married; it was only grudgingly that he'd even allowed my dressmaking apprenticeship.

THERE WAS A KNOCK AT THE DRESSING-ROOM DOOR. I TUCKED THE glass vial into my handkerchief.

"Come in!" Hui sang out.

It was one of the doormen, the younger one. He pushed the door open with an embarrassed air. The dressing room was dance-hostess territory, though at the moment only Hui and I were there.

"You know that salesman you asked me about the other day?"

I was instantly alert. "Did he come back again?"

His eyes shied away from the dresses draped over the backs of chairs, the traces of spilled powder on the dressing table.

"Is this him?" He held out a newspaper, folded open to the obituary section. *Chan Yew Cheung, twenty-eight years old. Suddenly, on June 4th. Beloved husband.* And there was a grainy photograph, obviously a formal portrait. His hair was slicked back and his expression serious, the confident smirk laid aside, but it was the same man.

I pressed my hand against my mouth. All this time the stolen finger had been weighing on my mind, the man himself had been lying cold and stiff in a mortuary somewhere.

"Did you know him well?" asked the doorman.

I shook my head.

The obituary was a small notice, but the word "suddenly" had an ominous air. So the salesman's prediction about being lucky had been wrong. Because according to my calculations, he'd died the day after our encounter.

With a shudder, I put the glass bottle, wrapped in my handkerchief, on the table. It seemed heavier than it ought to have been.

Hui said, "You don't think it's witchcraft, do you?"

"Of course not." But I couldn't help recalling a Buddhist statue I'd seen as a child. It was a little thing made of ivory, no bigger than this finger. The monk who'd shown it to us had said that a thief had once stolen it, but no matter how often he tried to sell or throw it away, it reappeared in his possession until, guilt-stricken, he'd returned it to the temple. There were other local tales as well, such as the *toyol,* a child spirit made from the bone of a murdered infant. Kept by a sorcerer, it was used to steal, run errands, and even commit murder. Once invoked, it was almost impossible to get rid of, save by proper burial.

I studied the newspaper carefully. The funeral would be held this weekend in the nearby town of Papan, a bit farther out from my family home in Falim. I was due back for a visit; perhaps I could return the finger. Give it to his family, or drop it in his coffin so it could be buried with him, though I wasn't sure how to manage it. What I was certain about, however, was that I didn't want to keep it.

5

Batu Gajah
Wednesday, June 3rd

THE PERSON WHO REALLY RUNS THE NEW DOCTOR'S HOUSEHOLD IS A taciturn Chinese cook named Ah Long. He's the one who takes charge of Ren, dripping wet as he is, and ushers him through the bowels of the house to the servants' quarters in the back. The outbuildings are separated by a covered walkway, but it's raining so hard that the spray wets them to the knees.

It's difficult for Ren to judge adults' ages, but Ah Long seems old to him. A wiry man with knotted arms, he offers Ren a rough cotton towel.

"Dry up," he says in Cantonese. "You can have this room."

The room is small, barely eight feet across, with a narrow window of louvered glass panes. In the blue gloom, Ren can make out a single cot bed. The household is eerily silent and he wonders where the other servants are.

Ah Long asks if he's hungry. "I have to prepare the master's dinner. Come to the kitchen when you're done."

At that moment, there's a blinding flash of lightning and a boom. The electricity in the main house flickers and blinks out. Ah Long clicks his tongue in annoyance and hurries off.

Alone in the gathering darkness, Ren unpacks his meager belongings and sits timidly on the cot. The thin mattress sags. A finger—a single digit—is so small that it could be hidden anywhere in this large house. His stomach knots with anxiety as he counts in his head. Time is passing; since Dr. MacFarlane's death three weeks ago, he has only twenty-five days left to find the finger. But Ren is tired, so bone weary from his long journey and the heavy carpetbag that he's been carrying, that he closes his eyes and falls into a dreamless sleep.

THE NEXT MORNING, AH LONG PREPARES WILLIAM'S BREAKFAST OF a boiled egg and two dried-up pieces of toast barely smeared with butter, even though there are at least three tins of Golden Churn lined up in the pantry. The butter comes from Australia by way of Cold Storage. Soft at room temperature, it's a beautiful yellow color. Ah Long doesn't eat butter himself, but he still rations it for his master.

"Like this," he explains to Ren in the kitchen. "No need to buy so much."

He resembles the toast he prepares, crusty and hard-hearted. But Ah Long is also honest, and if he's frugal with William's food, he's just as stingy about his own rations. At the old doctor's house, they ate thick slices of Hainanese white bread, toasted over charcoal and spread with butter and *kaya*, a caramelized custard made from eggs, sugar, and coconut milk. Ren can only think that this new doctor, William Acton, has a rather sad-looking breakfast.

When Ah Long judges the time is right, he pokes his pinched face through the dining-room door.

"Boy is here, *Tuan*," he announces, before disappearing back into his lair.

Obediently, Ren slips into the room. His clothes are plain but clean—a white shirt and khaki knee shorts. At the old doctor's house, he had no official houseboy's uniform and now wishes he did, as it might make him look older.

"Your name is Ren?"

"Yes, *Tuan*."

"Just Ren?" William seems to find this a little odd.

Of course he's right. Most Chinese are quick to give their family names first, but Ren isn't sure what to say. He has no family name and no memories of his parents. He and his brother Yi were pulled as toddlers from a burning tenement, where families of itinerant workers slept. No one was certain whose children they had been, only that they were clearly twins.

The matron of the orphanage named them after the Confucian Virtues: *Ren*, for humanity, and *Yi*, for righteousness. Ren always thought it was odd that she'd stopped at two of the Five Virtues. What about the others: *Li*, which was ritual, *Zhi*, for knowledge, and *Xin*, for integrity? Yet the other three names were never given out to new children at the orphanage.

"What sort of work did you do for Dr. MacFarlane?"

Ren has been expecting this question, but he's suddenly overcome with shyness. Perhaps it's the eyes of this new doctor, which pin the words in his mouth so they won't spill out. Ren looks at the floor, then forces his gaze up. Dr. MacFarlane taught him that foreigners like to be looked in the eye. Ren needs this job.

"Whatever Dr. MacFarlane wished."

He speaks respectfully and clearly, the way the old doctor liked to be addressed, and lists the chores he's accustomed to: cleaning, cooking, ironing, caring for the animals that Dr. MacFarlane kept. Ren is unsure whether or not to admit that he can read and write quite well. Gazing anxiously at William's face, Ren tries to gauge his mood. But the new doctor seems unperturbed.

"Did Dr. MacFarlane teach you English?"

"Yes, *Tuan*."

"You speak very well. In fact, you sound just like him." The expression on William's face softens. "How long were you with him?"

"Three years, *Tuan*."

"And how old are you?"

"Thirteen, *Tuan*."

Ren holds his breath at the lie. Most foreigners have difficulty telling the age of locals. Dr. MacFarlane used to joke about it all the time, but William's brow furrows, as though he's making a swift calculation. At last he says, "If you can iron, I have some shirts that need to be done."

Dismissed, Ren starts towards the door in relief.

"One more thing. Did you ever help out Dr. MacFarlane in his medical practice?"

Ren freezes, then nods.

William turns back to his newspaper, unaware that the boy is now staring at him with a frightened expression.

////

SURPRISED THAT AH LONG ISN'T LYING IN WAIT OUTSIDE THE DOOR, Ren finds his way back to the kitchen. In his experience, servants are invariably suspicious of newcomers. During his early days at Dr. MacFarlane's, the housekeeper followed him from room to room until she was satisfied that he wouldn't steal.

"You never know," she'd said long after Ren had become an indispensable part of the household. "Not everyone is as well brought up as you."

Kwan-*yi*, or Auntie Kwan as Ren had called her, had been a robust, middle-aged woman with a temper. She was the one who had run Dr. MacFarlane's untidy household with an iron hand, the one who trained Ren to cook rice on a charcoal stove without scorching the bottom of the pot and to catch, butcher, and pluck a chicken in half an hour. If she'd only stayed on, everything might have been different. But Auntie Kwan had left six months before the old doctor died. Her daughter was having a baby and she was going to move all the way down south to Kuala Lumpur, to help her out.

Dr. MacFarlane said he'd find a replacement, but months went by and the old man became preoccupied with other matters. He'd already shown signs of this before Auntie Kwan left, which seemed to give her unease at her departure. Ren, trying not to cry, had clutched her fiercely and unexpectedly. She'd pressed a grubby slip of paper with an address into his hand.

"You must take care of yourself," she said, worried.

He was prone to accidents. Once a tree branch had crashed down, missing him by inches. Another time, a runaway bullock cart almost pinned him to a wall. There were other near misses—so many that people said Ren attracted misfortune.

"Come and see me," she'd said, with a hard squeeze. And now, he wonders whether he should have done that instead. But he owes the old doctor a great deal, and there are promises that Ren must keep.

IN THE BREEZY KITCHEN, AH LONG IS MOODILY HACKING UP A chicken. Ren, standing at a respectful distance, ventures to say, "The master asked me to iron his shirts."

Ah Long says, "Laundry's not back yet from the *dhobi*. Wash the dishes first."

Ren is quick and neat, scouring the pots with a coconut brush and soft brown homemade soap in the deep sink outside. When the dishes are done, Ah Long examines his work. "The master's gone out, but he'll be back for luncheon. You can sweep the house." Ren wants to ask if there are other servants, but the look on Ah Long's face restrains him.

The house is surprisingly bare. The wide teak planks are worn smooth and the unglazed windows with their turned wooden bars look out onto the intense green of the surrounding jungle. There's little furniture other than the rattan armchairs and dining set that look as though they came with the house. No pictures on the walls, not even the indifferent water-colors so beloved by English *mems*.

Dr. MacFarlane had been an untidy man whose interests spilled into every part of his house. Ren wonders how it's possible that the two men could have been friends. He thinks back to the old doctor's dying request, counting the days again. The lorry driver's warning about dogs being eaten worries him. He'd been hoping to find the finger quickly, perhaps in a cabinet of preserved specimens. That would be the best solution. But Dr. Mac-Farlane wasn't even sure if it would be here.

"He might not have it anymore," he'd said hoarsely. "He might have given it away. Or destroyed it."

"Why don't you ask him for it?" Ren had said. "It's your finger."

"No! Better if he knows nothing." The old man grasped Ren's wrist. "It must be taken or stolen."

REN IS SWEEPING THE FLOOR WITH CAREFUL FLICKS WHEN AH LONG comes by to tell him to do the master's study as well. Pushing the door ajar, Ren stops short. In the dim light of the half-closed shutters, he sees glassy eyes and an open mouth, fixed forever in a snarl. Ren tells himself that it's only a tiger skin. The sad remnant of some long-forgotten hunt.

"Does the master hunt?"

"Him? He only collects," Ah Long mutters. "I wouldn't touch it myself."

"Why not?" Ren is uneasily fascinated by the tiger skin. Despite the indignity of being draped across the floor, its fur worn away in patches, the glaring glass eyes warn him away. Tiger eyes are prized for the hard parts in the center, set in gold as rings and thought to be precious charms, as are the teeth, whiskers, and claws. A dried and powdered liver is worth twice its weight in gold as medicine. Even the bones are taken to be boiled down into jelly.

"*Aiya!* This tiger was a man-eater. It killed two men and a woman down in Seremban before it was shot. See the bullet holes in the side?"

"How did he get the skin?"

"He's keeping it for a friend who told him it was *keramat. Cheh!* As if a *keramat* tiger could ever be shot."

Ren understands only too well the meaning of these words. A *keramat* animal is a sacred beast, a creature with the ability to come and go like a phantom, trampling sugarcane or raiding livestock with impunity. It's always distinguished by some peculiarity, such as a missing tusk or a rare albino color. But the most common indicator is a withered or maimed foot.

When Ren was still at the orphanage, he once saw the tracks of the elephant Gajah Keramat. It was a famous beast, a rogue bull that had ranged from Teluk Intan up to the Thai border. Bullets were magically deflected from Gajah Keramat's mottled hide, and he had the uncanny ability to sense an ambush. That morning, the sun's burning rays had dyed the dirt road blood red, spotlighting the men huddled over the tracks leading out of a culvert, across the road, and then into secondary jungle. Ren stopped to goggle at the excitement.

"*Tentulah,* it is Gajah Keramat." There was a hiss of agreement.

Wriggling his way to the front of the crowd, Ren saw how the elephant's shrunken left forefoot had pressed a curious mark in the damp red earth.

Later, when Ren entered Dr. MacFarlane's household, he'd related the incident to the old doctor. Dr. MacFarlane had been fascinated, even writing it down in one of his notebooks, the words inked across the page in his careful copperplate. Ren hadn't known then just how deep this interest in *keramat* animals would run.

A shudder travels up his spine now as he regards the tiger skin on the floor. Is this, then, the link between the old doctor and the new one? And is death now coming on soft feet, or has it roamed ahead, like a shadow set free from its owner? He hopes, desperately, that it's merely a coincidence.

6

Falim
Saturday, June 6th

ONE OF MY MOTHER'S CONDITIONS OF BOARDING AT MRS. THAM'S
dressmaking shop was that I would return home to Falim often. Each
time I did, I brought a treat to make up for the fact that I wasn't home-
sick at all. Today it was rambutans, the hairy, red-skinned fruit that
snapped open to reveal a sweet white interior. They'd been selling them
by the bus stop, and I'd bought a bundle wrapped in old newspaper. As
I sat on the bus I rather regretted it, as the rambutans were crawling
with ants.

Once, Falim had been full of vegetable gardens, but the outskirts of
Ipoh were encroaching every year. Already, the tin tycoon Foo Nyit Tse
had built a new housing estate as well as a grand mansion on Lahat Road
that was the wonder of the neighborhood. My stepfather's store stood in a
row of narrow-fronted shophouses, their upper stories jutting out to form
a shady five-foot walkway or *kaki lima*. Though only eighteen feet wide, it
was surprisingly deep. Shin and I had once paced out its length and found
it to be almost a hundred feet.

When I arrived, Ah Kum, the new girl that my stepfather had hired
to replace me, was penciling notes into the ledger.

"Back today?" Ah Kum was a year older than me, a cheerful gossip with
a mole beneath her right eye, like a teardrop. Some people said that such
a mark meant she'd never be lucky in marriage, but Ah Kum didn't seem
bothered. In any case, I was very grateful to her. If she hadn't started working here, I'd never have been able to leave.

"Want some?" I dumped my bundle of rambutans on the counter.

Ah Kum twisted a fruit open. "Your brother's back."

That was news to me. Shin was supposed to return next week. "When did he arrive?"

"Yesterday, but he's out right now. Why didn't you tell me he was so good-looking?"

I rolled my eyes. Shin and his female admirers. Obviously they weren't aware of his true personality, as I'd often explained to him. But Ah Kum had only started working here after Shin left for Singapore—how was she to know, poor girl?

"If you think he's so wonderful, you can have him!" I said, ducking as she swatted me. Our laughter was cut short by a footfall from the second floor. Suddenly sober, we glanced at each other.

"Is he in?" *He* could only refer to my stepfather.

She shook her head. "That's your mother."

I went deeper into the shophouse, inhaling the familiar dark scent of earth and metal from the stockpiled tin ore. Upstairs, shuttered windows opened over the courtyards, bringing light and air to the family quarters. This large upper room was used as a private sitting room, away from the business of the shop below. Sparsely furnished with rattan armchairs, a square card table for mahjong, and a few large sepia photographs of my stepfather's parents, it had scarcely changed since my mother and I had moved in ten years ago. A long rosewood sideboard was covered with school trophies and ribbons. The earlier ones were equally divided between Shin and myself, but the last few, after my stepfather decided I'd been educated enough, were all Shin's.

My mother was sitting by the railing, gazing at the pigeons as they strutted and burbled along the ledge.

"Mother," I said softly.

Over the years, she'd become very thin. Her bone structure was still lovely though, and I was struck by the delicate outline of the skull beneath her skin.

"I thought you weren't coming till next week." She looked happy to see me. I could always count on that from my mother; sometimes I thought I'd do anything to keep her smiling.

"Oh, I just felt like it. I bought rambutans." I didn't mention that I'd come home carrying a mummified finger, or that I planned to crash a stranger's funeral tomorrow.

"Good, good." She patted my hand briefly.

Glancing around, I passed her an envelope. My mother's lips trembled as she counted the money. "So much! How did you manage to get so much money?"

"I made a dress for a lady last week." I wasn't good at lying, so I always kept my statements short.

"I can't take it."

"You must!"

It had been two months since I'd discovered my mother's debts, though I'd been suspicious for a while, noting her anxiety and the small luxuries she'd given up. She even ate less at mealtimes. And especially, no more mah-jong parties with her friends. For it was mahjong that had done this.

Upon questioning, she'd broken down. It had been deeply unsettling to see my mother weeping like a child, pressing her hands against her mouth while the tears ran silently down her face. One of her friends had recommended a lady who lent money privately. She was very discreet and, most importantly, wouldn't mention it to my stepfather.

"Why didn't you tell me earlier?" I'd said angrily. "And what kind of interest rate is thirty-five percent?"

My stepfather could have repaid it. He made a good living as a tin-ore dealer—but we both knew what would happen if he found out. And so, bit by bit, we squirreled away money. She was much slower than me. My stepfather scrutinized the household accounts every week, so she had to economize without alerting him. But since I'd started working at the May Flower, I'd been able to pay down some of the principal. My mother always tried to refuse, but in the end, I knew she would—indeed, must—take it.

She hid the money away in the toe of her wedding slippers. My step-father would never look there, though he liked her to dress well. She'd wanted to sell her jewelry, but he often requested that she wear certain pieces and it would be difficult to explain where they'd gone. His atten-tion to clothes extended even to me, and growing up, I was always well dressed. My friends said I was lucky to have such a generous stepfather, but I knew it was all his own vanity. He was a collector and we were his acquisitions.

I'd never told Shin how I felt about his father. I didn't have to.

WHEN MY MOTHER AND I HAD FIRST MOVED IN, I'D BEEN AMAZED AT how strict my new stepfather was with Shin. He seemed to expect absolute obedience. At home, Shin barely spoke unless he was spoken to; he was a shadow of the boy that I came to know outside the house. In fact, I was rather surprised at how popular Shin was. Knots of children appeared every day to play with him. Since they were all boys, he didn't bother to introduce me but simply ran off. That impish, excited look on his face was never seen in the house, and soon I discovered why.

Shin had gone off one afternoon while I had to stay behind, pinching the roots off an enormous pile of fat, crisp bean sprouts. I didn't like them, but my stepfather did, and so my mother often fried them with salted fish.

While I gloomily picked away, my stepfather came home. He walked silently through the kitchen, then checked the courtyard, his nostrils turning white with anger. Shin had forgotten to bag and weigh the drying piles of tin ore. When he finally returned, his father took him to the back and caned him for every pile he'd forgotten.

The cane was four feet long and as thick as a man's thumb, nothing like the weak rattan switch that my mother occasionally disciplined me with. Seizing Shin by the collar, his father wound his arm back as far as it would go. There was a hiss, then an explosive crack that resounded through the courtyard. Shin's knees buckled. A choked cry squeezed out of his throat. I tried to tell myself that he deserved it, but by the second stroke, I was weeping.

"Stop!" I screamed. "He's sorry! He won't do it again!"

My stepfather looked at me in utter disbelief. For an instant I was terrified that he would cane me, too, but he glanced at his new wife who appeared, white-faced, behind me, and slowly put the cane down. He didn't say a word, but went back into the store.

That night Shin cried and I couldn't bear it. I pressed my mouth against the wooden wall that separated us.

"Does it hurt?"

He didn't reply, but the sobs intensified.

"I'm sorry," I said.

"It's not your fault," he said at last.

"Do you need ointment?" I had some Tiger Balm in my room, the all-purpose Chinese salve rumored to contain boiled tiger bones. It claimed to cure everything from mosquito bites to arthritis.

There was a pause. "All right."

I slipped out into the dark corridor. Though I knew my stepfather and mother were safely in their bedroom at the front of the shophouse, I had to steel myself before opening the door to Shin's small room. It was a mirror image of my own, the beds reversed against the wall. He was sitting up in bed. In the moonlight, he looked very young and small, even though we were about the same size. I unscrewed the jar of Tiger Balm, and in silence, helped him rub it on the welts on his legs. When I was done, he seized my sleeve.

"Don't go."

"Just for a bit, then." There'd be trouble if I were discovered, but I lay down next to him. He curled up like a small animal, and without thinking, I patted his hair. I thought he might object, but he only said, "My mother used to sit with me sometimes."

"What happened to her?"

"She died. Last year."

Only a year, I thought. My father, my real father, had been gone for three years. If my mother had owned a big shophouse like this, she wouldn't have had to remarry, I told myself. I imagined the two of us growing potted orchids in the courtyard, making *nian gao*, the sweet sticky new year's rice cake together as we'd done before. We would have been just fine by ourselves.

"When I grow up, I'll never get married," I said.

I thought he might make fun of me. After all, that was what girls were supposed to do. But Shin considered it seriously. "Then I won't get married either."

"I suppose you'll be all right. You'll have the business." My stepfather was keen for Shin to carry on. Although he himself was one of the smaller tin-ore dealers, others in his trade had done extremely well, and there was money to be made in reinvestments.

"You can have it. I'm leaving as soon as I can."

I snorted. "Don't want it. I'm the one who's going to leave."

He started to laugh, and buried his head under the pillow to muffle the sound. As he did so, a wrinkled piece of paper fell out. It had a single Chinese character written on it: 獏.

"What's this?" In the wavering moonlight, it was hard to make out. "Is it an animal?"

Shin made a grab for it. "My mother wrote it for me," he said gruffly. "It's the character for *mo*—you know, tapir."

I'd seen pictures of a tapir. It had a nose like a stunted elephant's trunk, and black and white markings as if the front of the animal had been dipped in ink, while the back part had been heavily floured, like a rice dumpling. It was supposed to be quite large, almost six feet long, yet difficult to see in the jungle.

"Your mother's writing was beautiful." My own mother was illiterate, which was why she'd always been keen on sending me to school and to Chinese brush-writing classes on weekends.

"She came from the north of China. That paper is for me. When I have bad dreams. *Mo* is a dream-eater, don't you know?"

"Do you mean a real tapir, from the jungle?" I wondered what sort of stories Shin's mother had told him. My own family had been in Malaya for three generations; though we still spoke Chinese, we'd also adapted to life under British rule here.

"No, the dream-eater is a ghost animal. If you have nightmares, you can call it three times to eat the bad dreams. But you have to be careful. If you call it too often it will also gobble up your hopes and ambitions."

There was silence while I digested this. I wanted to ask Shin whether this charm for dream-eaters really worked, and whether he'd ever seen one, but he'd fallen asleep, so I crept quietly back to my own bed.

////

WHEN PEOPLE WHO DIDN'T KNOW OUR FAMILY CIRCUMSTANCES DIS-covered that Shin and I shared the same birthday, they assumed we were twins even though we didn't look alike. My mother had a soft spot for him, and she'd touch our heads affectionately.

"It's good you have a brother now, Ji Lin."

"But he won't call me *Ah Jie*," I'd point out, aggrieved. It was my right to be called "older sister," even if I held that advantage by only five hours. But Shin willfully ignored this, calling me by my given name and sticking out his tongue.

In some ways it would be better if he still did such things, but the last two years, Shin had grown strangely aloof. It was inevitable, I supposed, though it stung. But I was too proud to hang around like the other girls and so miserable over being forced to leave school before my Upper Sixth, that I'd had little time to worry about this change in him. If it came down to it, however, I thought I could still rely on Shin. To be my ally, to keep my secrets. And to identify severed fingers. At least, I hoped I could.

DINNER THAT NIGHT WAS A SILENT AFFAIR, DESPITE THE LUXURY OF a whole steamed chicken rubbed with sesame oil. It sat, expertly chopped into bite-sized pieces, on a large platter. None of us had touched it; it was as mutely reproachful as Shin's empty seat. My mother asked timidly after him.

"He said he'd be out tonight." My stepfather shoveled food into his mouth, chewing methodically.

"I should have told him I was going to kill a chicken today." My mother cast a worried glance at the bird, as though Shin would materialize behind it. I stifled a snort.

"How long is he back for?" I asked.

"He has a part-time job at the Batu Gajah hospital, so he'll be here for the summer." My mother looked pleased. Actually, there was no "summer" here in Malaya. It was the tropics, after all, though we'd adopted the vo-cabulary of summer holidays as a result of being a colony. But I didn't say any of this aloud. It was always better to say less during mealtimes.

"Is Shin staying here?" Batu Gajah was more than ten miles away. I couldn't imagine that Shin would choose to spend much time under the same roof as his father.

"The hospital has staff quarters. He said it was more convenient." She glanced swiftly at my stepfather, who continued chewing in silence. He was in a good mood, I could tell. Ever since Shin had won a scholarship to study medicine, he'd been perversely proud of him. Being congratulated on such a clever son must have gone to his head.

It was odd that Shin would come to a district hospital like Batu Gajah when he could easily have worked as an orderly at the Singapore General Hospital, as he had over Christmas. I'd never been to Singapore, though I'd pored over postcards of St. Andrew's Cathedral and the famous Raffles Hotel with its Long Bar that ladies weren't supposed to go to.

My mother gave another anguished look at the untouched chicken. "Whom did Shin go out with tonight?"

"Ming, and another friend. Robert, he said." My stepfather helped himself to a piece of chicken, and with a sigh, my mother followed suit, placing it on my plate.

I looked down, embarrassed. Ming was the watchmaker's son, Shin's best friend. He was a year older than us, serious and mature, and wore thin, wire-framed spectacles. I'd been in love with him since I was twelve—a hopeless, awkward crush I'd hoped nobody noticed, though my mother's sympathetic glance seemed a little too knowing. Ming had done well at school and we'd all expected him to go on to further studies, but he'd unexpectedly taken over his father's business. And a few months ago, I'd heard he was engaged to a girl from Tapah.

Good for him, I told myself, stabbing the chicken with my chopsticks. Ming was a sincere person; I'd met his fiancée and she seemed like a nice girl, quiet and not flashy. Besides, despite Ming's kindness to me growing up, he'd never been interested. I knew that very well and had given up on him. Still, hearing his name filled me with an inky, twilight gloom.

My mother's debts, Ming's marriage, and my lack of a future were cold weights on a string of bad luck. And that wasn't even counting the mummified bottled finger tucked at the very bottom of my traveling basket.

/////

MY STEPFATHER ALWAYS WENT TO BED EARLY. MY MOTHER HAD also adopted this habit, and soon enough, they retired to their room upstairs. I washed the dishes and put the leftovers into the mesh-screened food cupboard to keep lizards and cockroaches out. Each cupboard leg stood in a small saucer filled with water, so that ants couldn't climb up. Finally, I collected the food scraps and took them into the back alley for the stray cats.

It had cooled down, though the sides of the buildings still radiated the heat of the day. The night sky was sprinkled with stars and a thin crackle of music wafted into the evening air. Somewhere, someone was listening to a radio. It was a foxtrot, a dance that I could do with my eyes closed now, humming under my breath.

The music ended in a smattering of applause. Startled, I turned.

"Since when have you been able to dance?"

He was a shadow in the darkness of the alley, leaning against the wall, but I'd know him anywhere.

"How long have you been here?" I said indignantly.

"Long enough." Detaching himself from the wall, his dim outline seemed taller, his shoulders wider than before. I couldn't see the expression on his face and felt suddenly shy. I hadn't seen Shin for almost a year.

"Why didn't you stay in Singapore?" I asked.

"Oh, so you didn't want me to come back?" He was laughing, and I felt a rush of relief. It was the old Shin, my childhood friend.

"Who'd want you? Well, maybe Ah Kum does."

"You mean the new girl at the shop?" He shook his head. "My heart belongs to the medical profession."

The neighbor's window banged shut. We were making too much noise in the alley. I headed back towards the fan of light spilling from the kitchen door.

"You cut your hair," he said in surprise.

My hand flew to the shorn nape of my neck. *Let the jokes begin,* I thought grimly. But surprisingly, Shin didn't say anything else. He sat down at the table and watched as I fidgeted, wiping down an already clean counter. The oil lamp had burned low and the kitchen was full of shadows. I hurriedly asked one question after another about what Singapore was like.

"But what have you been doing?" he asked. "Some poor woman probably has a dress that's sewn inside out."

I threw the dishtowel at him. "I sew very well. I'm extremely talented, according to Mrs. Beaky Tham."

"Is her name really Beaky?"

"No, but it should be. She looks like a tiny crow, and she likes to walk into my room and open all the drawers whenever I'm out."

"I'm sorry," Shin said, laughing. And then he really did look sorry.

"What for?"

"Because you should be the one in medical school."

"I could never go." I turned away. It was still a sore spot for me. I'd been the one who'd first thought of being a doctor, or some kind of medical aide. Anything to heal the bruises on my mother's arms, the sprains that she mysteriously developed. "I heard you saw Ming tonight."

"And Robert." Robert Chiu was Ming's friend. His father was a barrister who'd been trained in England. All his children had English names—Robert, Emily, Mary, and Eunice—and they had a piano and a gramophone in their large house, which was teeming with servants. Robert and Shin had never really got along. I wondered why the three of them had been together.

"Ming asked about you—are you joining us for lunch tomorrow?" said Shin. Was it pity in his eyes? I didn't want sympathy.

"I have to attend a funeral."

"Whose funeral?"

I was annoyed with myself for not making up another excuse. "Nobody you know. Just an acquaintance."

Shin frowned, but he didn't question me further. In the lamplight, the angles of his cheekbones and jaw were the same, yet sharper, more mature.

"I need your help," I said. Now was as good a time as any to show him the finger, without my mother or stepfather around to interfere. "It's an anatomy question. Can you take a look?"

His eyebrows rose. "Don't you think you should ask someone else?"

"It's a secret. I can't really ask anyone else."

Shin's face turned red, or perhaps it was just the low light. "Maybe you should ask a nurse. I'm not really qualified, and it's better if a woman examines you."

I rolled my eyes. "It's not for me, silly."

"Well, how was I to know?" Shin rubbed his face, now even more flushed.

"Wait here," I said. "It's in my room."

I hurried upstairs, treading softly to avoid the creaky floorboards, and slipped down the corridor to my room at the back of the house. Moonlight flooded the shutters like pale water. Nothing about that room had changed, not even the position of the bed, still wedged against the wall that separated Shin's room from mine.

When I was fourteen, my stepfather had considered moving Shin downstairs, swapping his bedroom for my stepfather's office, but it proved too inconvenient. He was afraid that Shin and I might sneak into each other's rooms, which was ridiculous. Shin never came to my room. If we wanted to whisper we crept into the corridor outside or sat on his floor, but my room was mine alone. It was the sole concession to the fact that I was a girl.

Thrusting my arm into the rattan basket that I used as a traveling bag, I fished out the glass vial, tucked in a handkerchief because I didn't like to look at it.

Downstairs, I laid it next to the oil lamp. "Tell me what you think."

Shin unwrapped the handkerchief, his long clever fingers untying the knot. When he saw the finger, he stopped.

"Where did you get this?"

Looking at his dark brows knitted together, I realized I couldn't possibly let Shin know that I'd lifted it out of a stranger's pocket while working as a dance-hall hostess. No matter how I tried to rationalize the faded gentility of the May Flower or the hardworking girls, it sounded wretched. Worse still, it would reveal my mother's gambling debts.

"I found it. It came out of someone's pocket."

Shin turned the bottle from side to side, narrowing his eyes.

"Well?" I squeezed my own hands under the table.

"I'd say it's the distal and middle phalanges of a finger. Possibly the pinky, from the size."

"Could it be an orangutan's?"

"The proportions look human to me. Besides, look at the fingernail. Doesn't it look trimmed?"

I'd noticed that myself. "Why does it look mummified?"

"It's dried out, so maybe it happened naturally, like beef jerky."

"Don't talk about beef jerky," I said gloomily.

"So how exactly did you get this again?"

"I told you, I found it." Pushing my chair back, I said hastily, "Don't worry, I'll return it. Thanks for taking a look. Good night."

As I retreated up the stairs, I felt his opaque gaze following me.

7

Batu Gajah
Friday, June 5th

SINCE HIS ARRIVAL, REN HAS LEARNED TWO IMPORTANT THINGS about his new master. First, Ah Long informs him that William is a surgeon and therefore should be referred to as "Mr." or *Tuan* Acton instead of "Dr."

"Why's that?" asks Ren.

"No idea. Is a British thing." Ah Long is shelling giant river prawns. "But that's how you address him."

The second thing he's learned is that his new employer prefers a tidy environment, worlds away from the lively and chaotic household Ren left in Kamunting. Dr. MacFarlane often left half-eaten sandwiches and banana skins in the muddle of papers on his desk. This new doctor, William Acton, places his utensils neatly on the edge of the plate. The shining surface of his desk is broken only by the archipelago of inkwell, blotting paper, and pen.

Ren has already memorized the exact position of each object and replaces it correctly each time he dusts. Maybe it's a waste of time as he doesn't know how long he'll stay here. Until his task is done—though what comes after finding the finger and returning it to his grave, Ren has no idea. Dr. MacFarlane gave no further instructions. A wave of homesickness strikes him, so intense that tears well shamefully in his eyes. Ren tells himself that he's too old to cry. Twenty-six days have passed since his old master's death and he feels a rising panic. But nobody else has died. Unless dogs count.

Yesterday, Ah Long mentioned that the neighbor two houses over had lost a pedigreed terrier: a yappy, scrappy creature, worth more than a month's salary. A tuft of fur attached to a stumpy white tail was all that was discarded. "Leopard," grunted Ah Long. Ren hopes so. Not tiger.

He gazes out of the window onto the expanse of clipped grass and gravel driveway. The white bungalow stands on a slight rise, the lawn lapping it like a grassy pool. Jungle presses in on all sides and is kept at bay by two Indian gardeners. Troops of monkeys parade past, and wild chickens, jungle fowl, scratch in the undergrowth. Ren, fascinated, watches them from the open kitchen where he peels vegetables and washes rice.

Yi, he mouths silently, *you would like this place.* Catching sight of his reflection in a steel tray that he's polishing, he nods. It's hard, even after three years, to be without his brother.

The worst part about death is forgetting the image of the beloved. It's the final robbery, the last betrayal. Yet it's impossible to forget Yi's face, for it is his own. That's the only comfort that Ren has in losing his twin.

When they first arrived at the orphanage, no one knew which child was older. The matron was the one who decided that it should be Ren, and she named him accordingly, *ren* being the greatest of the five Confucian Virtues. It means human-heartedness: the benevolence that distinguishes man from beast. The perfect man, according to Confucius, should be willing to die to preserve this. Ren thinks that if he had a choice he'd rather have died to save Yi.

Ren has a recurring dream that he's standing on a railway platform, just like the one in Taiping where he used to see Dr. MacFarlane off on his trips, only this time it's Yi who's on the train. He leans out of the window, thin arms waving wildly. When he grins, there's a gap where one front tooth hasn't grown in yet. He looks exactly the same as when he died.

Ren wants to chase after Yi's smiling face, but his feet are clamped inexplicably to the platform. He's forced to watch as the train picks up speed, its wheels spinning faster as Yi gets smaller and smaller until he's gone, and Ren wakes up bathed in sweat or tears.

Yet it's a happy dream. He's delighted to see his brother again and so is Yi. He can see it in Yi's gestures, his bright-eyed gaze. Sometimes he speaks, mouth moving as he gesticulates, though there's never any sound.

Ren thinks it's odd that Yi is always the one who is going on a journey, when it's Ren who is growing older and leaving him behind.

REN IS MOPPING THE FLOOR. HE PUTS STRENGTH INTO IT, RINSING the mop often and changing his bucket of water, as trained by Auntie Kwan. The patch of shining floor grows larger in leaf-shaped swipes, like a glossy plant spreading over the wide teak planks.

"Good." Ah Long's voice breaks in.

Startled, Ren looks up. Ah Long has the uncanny ability to materialize in all corners of the house, which has made it difficult for Ren to search for the finger. He's like a suspicious old cat, squinting in the sunlight.

"There are houseboys older than you who don't do such a good job," Ah Long says. "We had one a few months ago. Twenty-three years old and couldn't iron a shirt. Wanted to wear a uniform and serve drinks at parties."

Dr. MacFarlane seldom formally entertained. The old doctor had a reputation for collecting specimens, though, and it wasn't uncommon to find a row of local hunters patiently awaiting his return, their prizes bulging out of sacks or snarling at the end of a rope.

"Is the master married?" Ren asks. He knows that many foreigners leave their wives and children behind in England or Scotland or wherever they come from. The tropical climate here is considered unhealthy for European children.

Ah Long sniffs. "No. Better if he was."

"Why's that?" Ren is eager to take advantage of Ah Long's good mood. Normally it's hard to get more than a few words out of him.

"Then he'd stop playing around. *Aiya*, as if we all didn't realize what he's been doing!"

Ren has a vague understanding that this touches upon adult matters. Things like marriage or not-marriage, and relationships between men and women that are too difficult to puzzle out. But if William has no interfering wife or family, it increases the chance that Ren can retrieve the finger. The fact that he hasn't found it yet despite two days of quiet searching worries him.

////

THEY BRING THE INJURED WOMAN IN JUST BEFORE NOON. REN HEARS shouts, anxious wailing, and then Ah Long's determined refusal.

"*Tak boleh! Tuan tak ada di sini!*"

Ren runs out. There's a wheelbarrow propped on the drive and in it lies a young Sinhalese woman. There's a deep gash in the back of her left calf. Dark splotches of blood soak her sari.

Ah Long is trying to persuade her relatives to take her to the hospital in Batu Gajah, for *Tuan* Acton is not at home, but they insist that it's too far. Ren knows that the deeply superstitious Ah Long is afraid the woman will die in this house. He pushes his way forward.

"Bring her in!"

"Are you mad?" cries Ah Long.

Ignoring him, Ren tells the men to bring her up onto the veranda while he races into the study. The doctor keeps an emergency bag behind his desk as well as a drawer full of first-aid equipment.

"I need a basin of boiled water," he says to Ah Long.

"What if she dies here?"

Ren ignores him as he washes his hands thoroughly with soap, forcing himself to count slowly to fifteen. Next, he examines the makeshift tourniquet, a narrow band of cloth twisted tightly around the leg. The woman has fainted, and he's grateful for that. He washes the leg as best he can with the boiled water, then ties another tourniquet above the original. His head swims; there's a sick feeling in his throat. In his mind's eye, he sees Dr. MacFarlane's square hands again, repeating the steps. A stick through the knot, functioning as a windlass to tighten it if necessary. Ren cuts off the original rough tourniquet.

"What are you doing? If you take that off she'll bleed to death!"

"It's too tight and too close to the wound. She'll lose the leg."

Ren grits his teeth, willing the new tourniquet to hold. Around him people are muttering, but no one else appears to take charge. Ren checks the pulse in her ankle. Still some slow bleeding. Twisting the knotted stick, he slowly increases the pressure until it stops.

The woman is beginning to stir again, moaning as they hold her down and he syringes the wound with hydrogen peroxide. It's all he has on hand, but as the raw flesh bubbles and foams, he feels the onlookers turn away. The blood makes him dizzy. *Breathe,* he tells himself. *If you don't breathe you'll faint.*

At last it's over. The dressing he puts on top soon becomes soaked, but it's better than the glimpse of bone.

"You should take her to the hospital now," he says over the relieved chatter. "She needs stitches."

They put her into the wheelbarrow again, and he worries how she'll endure the journey. If he had some morphine, he'd give her a quarter grain. He isn't supposed to do that. The old doctor always warned him away, locking the medicine cabinet, but he's seen him administer it enough times.

Ren begins to clean up the litter of dressings. His legs are weak; his hands tremble uncontrollably. He hadn't even asked for the woman's name or what caused the injury, although he was dimly aware that someone had given an explanation. All that had consumed him was stopping the blood.

He's about to fetch water to scrub down the veranda when Ah Long says, "Leave it. Go and change." Then he realizes his new white houseboy's uniform is spattered with blood.

"Soak the clothes in cold water," says Ah Long. "If it doesn't come out, you'll have to make a new set out of your own wages." He has a curious expression on his face, both sour and grudgingly respectful.

Ren washes himself in the small bathhouse behind the servants' quarters, scooping water out of a large pottery jar with a dipper and sluicing it over his body. When he closes his eyes he can still see the blood seeping onto the wooden planks. Like Yi's blood, he thinks, oozing out from beneath his own fingers. He'd placed his hands on his brother's chest, trying to stanch the flow. But it was hopeless. Yi's body turned cold, his eyes rolled up in his head. His small chest rattled its last.

When Ren returns to the main house, Ah Long is preparing lunch for the servants. Ren has discovered that there are indeed others: a woman who helps with the laundry, the Malay driver, Harun, and two Tamil gardeners. But he and Ah Long are the only ones who live in the servants' quarters behind the large bungalow.

Since William is at the hospital, Ah Long has put together some simple noodles in broth. Shredded chicken and boiled greens are piled on top, with a gloss of fried shallot oil. Ren notices that Ah Long has given him a larger portion than usual, with extra meat. They eat in silence. When they're finished, Ah Long says, "You shouldn't have done it. If she dies after you treated her, it'll be your misfortune."

"Will the master be angry?" Ren recalls the dressings he's used, the half-emptied bottle of hydrogen peroxide. He'll boil the glass syringe; fortunately he didn't use a needle. He never had to ask Dr. MacFarlane for permission.

"He doesn't like anyone touching his things."

Ren is silent. What had he been thinking? And he hasn't even completed the task the old doctor set him. With a feeling of panic, he tallies the time since Dr. MacFarlane died. Only twenty-three days left.

"What happens during the forty-nine days after someone dies?" Ren asks Ah Long.

Ah Long, thinking that Ren is still worried about the young Sinhalese woman, says, "She won't die. At least, I hope not."

"But what happens anyway?"

"*Aiya*, the soul wanders around. It goes and looks at people and places it knows. Then if it's satisfied, it leaves."

"What if it's not satisfied?"

"It won't pass on. That's how hauntings occur."

Ren's eyes widen, and Ah Long says, "Don't worry, that's just superstition."

"Can a wandering spirit turn into an animal?"

"*Hah?* No, there are stories, but it isn't true."

Ah Long is so dismissive of the idea that Ren is somewhat comforted. In the bright sunshine, there's nothing to worry about. Today, he's saved a life. How much weight does that carry?

8

DESPITE MY ACHING HEAD, I FELL INTO A DEEP SLEEP AS SOON AS I burrowed into my narrow bed. So deep that I felt pleasantly drugged, floating in cool water down a river of dreams.

Bright riverbanks flickered lazily past, the images tiny and clear as though seen through the wrong end of a telescope. Thickets of bamboo and underbrush, sunlit elephant grass. It was the sort of landscape with tiny figures you might see from a train, and even as this thought occurred to me, I spotted a locomotive. It stood, billowing steam, at a small railway station.

Strangely, the train tracks started beneath the water, the submerged railroad ties snaking up from the white sandy bottom and climbing the bank. There was no one in the train except a little boy, about eight years old. He smiled and waved from the window, showing a gap where one of his front teeth was missing. I waved back at him. Then I was floating away again, led by the current until I woke in the grey dawn.

Pale light seeped in through the wooden shutters, and the headache that had bothered me last night had vanished. There was no sound from Shin's room, but from the faint noises below, I knew my mother was up. I dressed quickly.

"Did you make that dress yourself?" she asked when I ran downstairs.

I'd debated over what to wear to the salesman's funeral today; something formal but not conspicuous enough to make my family wonder where

I was going. The only suitable dress I had was a plain grey Mandarin-collared *cheongsam* that I'd made as part of my apprenticeship. A *cheongsam* is an unforgiving, formal Chinese dress to tailor. I'd made a mistake sewing the high collar, which wouldn't lie quite flat, but it was decent enough. I already knew what my mother would say.

"This fabric is so serious—a girl like you should choose bright colors."

My mother loved clothes and had exquisite taste. On special occasions, she dressed with great care, taking out her good shoes that she kept in a cardboard box on top of the wardrobe. In fact the whole idea of my becoming a dressmaker's apprentice was hers, though it had also met with my stepfather's approval. But I didn't see any point dressing up to please my stepfather, who only wanted us to look good to complement himself. We were a chocolate-box family, I thought. Brightly wrapped on the outside and oozing sticky darkness within.

"I'm going to the market, but you're dressed so nicely it's a pity to ask you to come," said my mother.

"I'll go." Going to the wet market had always been one of my favorite errands. You could buy almost anything there: piles of red and green chilies, live chicks and quail, green lotus seed pods that resembled shower sprinklers. There were fresh sides of pork, salted duck eggs, and baskets of glossy river fish. You could eat breakfast, too, at little stalls serving steaming bowls of noodles and crispy fritters.

While my mother was busy shopping, I picked my way between the crowded stalls looking for flowers. White flowers, the color of Chinese funerals and death. I had them wrapped in newspaper to hide them. It was hard to keep secrets in a place like Falim, and anyone seeing me walk around with a bunch of white chrysanthemums would instantly guess it was a death offering.

As I headed back first, laden with my mother's various purchases, I heard the silvery ring of a bicycle bell. It was Ming. I hadn't seen him for a while but he was the same, his thin-framed, bespectacled figure pushing a heavy black bicycle.

"Ji Lin!" He looked pleased. "I saw your brother last night."

I'd been so melancholy over Ming's engagement, avoiding him, and now here he was, wiping his glasses with a handkerchief in his usual absent-minded way. My heart gave a treacherous little flip.

"I heard," I said. "You went out to eat even though my mother killed a chicken for Shin."

Ming smiled. "We didn't know you were back. Or about the chicken, otherwise I'd have come over to help eat it." Taking my basket of purchases, he hung it on the handlebars of his bike in his quiet way. Unlike my stepfather, I'd never seen him lose his temper. If Ming was aware of my past crush, he'd always been too kind to say anything. I was glad we were still friends, I thought, as Ming helped me carry the basket into the shophouse.

Shin was leaning against the desk, talking to Ah Kum who'd dropped by even though it was her day off. Giggling coyly, she said she'd brought over some homemade pickles, though it was obvious from her glances that she was only here for Shin. I had to admire the speed at which she'd decided to make her move.

But Ah Kum was right: Shin was very handsome. Growing up, we'd taken his looks for granted and I sometimes forgot how surprising they were. His high cheekbones and nose had been inherited from his mother, a woman from the far north of China. At least, that was what everyone said, though I'd never seen a picture of her. *Lucky Shin,* I thought enviously, as I often had during our childhood. To be born a boy and win a scholarship to medical school. Good looks were just the icing on top of that. Yet he didn't look pleased. In fact, he looked distinctly irritated when Ming and I came in, our faces flushed and laughing.

"You're early," he said to Ming. "I thought we were meeting for lunch."

"I ran into Ji Lin at the market, so I decided to bring her home."

"She doesn't need looking after," he said dismissively.

I scowled at him, but he ignored me. Ming smiled his gentle smile as he helped lift the melon out of the basket. The top button of his shirt was missing, though with his usual air of bemused dignity, he didn't seem aware of it. If Ming had fallen in love with me, instead of some girl from Tapah, I'd gladly have mended his shirt.

I went upstairs to pack. It was best to leave before my mother came home and forced me to stay for lunch.

"Not joining us?" Ming looked surprised as I passed through the front of the shophouse. The bouquet of newspaper-wrapped chrysanthemums was tucked in my basket. A single snowy bloom peeked out, and Shin glanced at it sharply. He said nothing, however, as I made my goodbyes. Under the flowers, the finger was a guilty burden in my basket. I felt compelled to return it. And what better place to leave it than at a funeral?

ACCORDING TO THE NEWSPAPER OBITUARY, THE SALESMAN'S FUNERAL would be held in Papan, a nearby town. The sun broiled down from a cloudless blue sky; my only consolation was the giant rain tree that shaded the bus stop. I'd dusted my face with a little rice powder and applied a smudge of lip rouge, but feared it would soon melt off.

The bus arrived with a rattling roar. It had the body of a lorry, the sides circled with a wooden railing, and was always a bit difficult to climb up into when wearing a dress, particularly a pencil-slim *cheongsam*. I boarded last to avoid showing too much leg to anyone standing behind me. Still, I struggled, silently cursing the modest side slits that didn't allow me to take large steps. To my horror, someone lent me a hand from behind. A man's hand, from the feel of it, that slid over-familiarly down the small of my back and shoved me up into the bus. I swung round and slapped him.

It was Shin.

"What did you do that for?" He looked annoyed.

"Nobody asked you to help. What are you doing here?"

The bus driver honked his horn, and I sat down hastily on the wooden bench. Shin swung himself up and squeezed in next to me. With a jerk, the bus roared off.

I glared at him. "What about lunch with Ming?"

Ignoring the question, Shin looked pointedly at the rattan basket that I hugged on my lap. "Is it in there?"

I knew he was talking about the finger, but didn't reply. What cheek, after being so unfriendly earlier!

"That was quite a slap you gave me."

"How was I to know it was you?"

I'd reacted unthinkingly, a lesson learned from dancing with strangers. Feeling rather sorry, I peeked at his face to see if I'd left a mark.

"So are you going to tell me about this finger?"

There was no point holding out as Shin was clearly planning to follow me, so I gave him an edited version of events. How the salesman had come by my (unnamed) place of work and dropped the bottle with the finger, and how the next day he had died.

"And that's all," I said. "Now will you please go home? It's rude of you to ditch Ming."

"I didn't leave him alone. Or are you worried that Ah Kum will make a move on him?"

"He's engaged!" I snapped. "And besides, Ah Kum is only interested in you, not Ming."

He turned his head to look out of the window. I felt rather guilty. Shin was, in his own way, looking out for me.

"Friends?" I said, holding out my hand after a while. Shin could stay quiet for days but I could never hold a grudge against him. There wouldn't be anyone to talk to in that house if we didn't make up. He didn't look at me, but stuck out his right hand, and we shook, a little too heartily, to show that everything really was all right between us.

The bus deposited us on the main road in Papan and roared off in a cloud of dust. I coughed violently. Never mind the face powder I'd applied—I was now covered with white dust. Shin's lips twitched, but mercifully, he didn't laugh. We had to ask around for the address, as Papan had quite a few streets with small houses on them.

"That's the Chan house," an old lady said. She studied my grey *cheongsam* and bouquet of white flowers. "Did you mean to come for the funeral?"

"Yes," I said.

"You're too late. It was yesterday." Seeing my crestfallen face, she said, "The newspaper misprinted the date, but they told all the family ahead of time. Didn't you know?"

"We'd still like to pay our respects." Shin smiled at the old lady, and she succumbed, giving us detailed instructions. Deflecting her questions, we hurried off.

The house was a small, single-story wooden building with a guava tree in the front yard and a skinny yellow dog tied to it. There were still signs of the funeral that had taken place, though the two large white paper lanterns with the name of the deceased written on them no longer hung on the sides of the door. Ash and scraps of partly burned colored paper blew around the compound—the remains of paper funeral goods burned for the deceased. I wondered whether they had burned plenty of dancing girls and garlicky chicken rice for the salesman in the Afterlife, then felt remorse for such irreverent thoughts.

At our approach, the dog hurled itself at us, barking madly. The guava tree shook, and I nervously eyed the rope that held the animal back.

"Excuse me!" I called out.

An older woman came out, shushing the dog. She looked enquiringly at us. "Oh dear, I told Ah Yoke that the date was wrong in the newspaper! Are you here to see her?"

I had no idea who Ah Yoke was, but I nodded. We took off our shoes as the woman showed us into the front room of the little house, dominated by a family altar wreathed with joss sticks and offerings. I placed the bouquet of white chrysanthemums on the altar. Bowing, we paid our respects to the deceased, the same portrait used in the newspaper obituary. The salesman stared out of the picture, stiff and formal. Chan Yew Cheung had been twenty-eight years old, to which had been added, as was customary, three more years to increase his life span. One year from the earth, one from heaven, and one from man. Soberly, I thought that even with the borrowed years, his time here hadn't been very long.

Setting down two cups of tea, the woman said, "I'm his aunt. Were you friends of Yew Cheung? It was such a shock. He was always so strong—I never thought I'd outlive him." Her face creased, and I was afraid she was going to start crying. I felt more and more uncomfortable.

"What happened to him?" asked Shin.

"He went to see a friend in Batu Gajah, but it got late and he still hadn't come home. Ah Yoke was upset. You know how she can be. The next morning a passerby found him. He must have slipped and fallen into a storm drain. They said he broke his neck."

"I'm so sorry," I said. And I was. I hadn't liked the salesman much, but sitting in the house where he had lived, on a rattan armchair that he must have used, I felt a cold shadow settle on me.

"Actually, I didn't know Mr. Chan well," I said. "He was a customer at our shop and he happened to leave something behind. Then I read he'd passed away and thought I should return it."

"In that case, you'd better talk to his wife." She got up and parted the curtain of wooden beads in the rear of the house. "Ah Yoke!" she called. "This young lady has something from Yew Cheung."

There was a long pause. Shin and I shifted uncomfortably in our seats. The aunt had just begun to say, "She's very upset, as you can expect—" when a woman rushed into the room, hair wild and face swollen with crying. She flew straight at me.

"Bitch!" she shrieked. "How dare you come here?"

Shocked, I could barely block her with my arms, even as she slapped and scratched hysterically. Shin leaped up and dragged her off me. She fell in a heap on the floor and started to scream. It was a horrible noise, like a pig being slaughtered.

The aunt said, "Ah Yoke, what's wrong with you? I'm so sorry! She's been like this since yesterday. Are you hurt?"

Shaken, I put my hand to my throat. Ah Yoke was still lying on the floor. Her screams had died down into whimpers. "Give it," she said. "Give it back to me."

"What does she want?" I asked, horrified.

"Ah Yoke," said the aunt, "you're mistaken. This young lady works at a shop. She's not one of Yew Cheung's girls." Darting a quick glance at me, she said, "You're not, are you?"

I shook my head. "I only met him once."

"See?" The aunt was patting Ah Yoke's head. "She didn't know him. And look, she came with her young man today."

Ah Yoke continued to sob and writhe on the ground, her hands clenching and unclenching. Her body contorted unnaturally, her movements like a snake. She didn't seem human anymore. I felt dizzy; if not for Shin's grip, I'd have fallen to my knees.

"You'd better go," the aunt said quietly. "Yew Cheung was my nephew, but he wasn't a saint. He played around. And yesterday, you know, there were some girls here. Bar girls and prostitutes. They wanted to pay their respects, but they shouldn't have come. I guess she mistook you for one of them."

Shame colored my face. A dance hostess wasn't anything to be proud of, either. I'd made my own troubles when I took the finger, and now I had to get out of them myself. Taking out the glass bottle, I set it on the floor.

"Do you recognize this?" I asked Ah Yoke.

She sat up slowly, her long black hair straggling over her face like drowned strands of riverweed. "It's his," she said dully.

"Was this what you were looking for?" I said.

Shaking her head, she started to cry, making no attempt to brush away the tears running down her white, swollen face. It felt indecent to watch her; her face was so raw and naked. I stood up, but she snatched at the hem of my skirt.

"Did he give you anything else? A gold pendant?"

"No."

Oddly, she seemed to take heart at this. "Last week he bought a pendant for another woman. That's what I wanted to know about. Not this." She jerked her head towards the finger. She hadn't touched it once. Her eyes were puffy, the lids painfully pink. "It was his good luck charm. Since he had it, his sales record improved a lot."

"When did he get it?" asked Shin. She stared at him as though registering his presence for the first time.

"Three . . . maybe four months ago. He got it from a friend. Actually, I think he stole it." Ah Yoke made a face as though there was a bad taste in her mouth.

"I'd like to return it to you," I said. In that neat little wooden house, amid the utterly ordinary furniture and daily objects—a crocheted doily on the table, a palm-leaf food cover to keep off the flies—the withered finger looked even grimmer and out of place. I glanced at the aunt and realized that she didn't look surprised. *She's seen it before*, I thought.

Ah Yoke shook her head wildly. "Don't leave it with me!" I was afraid she was going to start screaming again.

The aunt hustled us to the door. "You'd better go now."

"But what about the finger?"

She tucked it firmly into my basket again. "Do whatever you like. Or give it back to whoever he got it from."

"And who was that?" asked Shin.

"He told me it was a nurse at the Batu Gajah hospital," said the aunt, in an undertone. Shin's ears pricked up at this. "That's all I know. Now please leave."

We walked back to the bus stop in silence. It was past noon now, and the glare from the road was so dazzling that I wanted to cover my eyes. My face was tender where Ah Yoke had attacked me. Shin stopped under a large tree.

"Wait here." Crossing the road to a small shop, he returned with an enamel mug of water and a bottle of iodine. He tilted my face to examine it. I closed my eyes. His hands were cool and deft.

"You're going to have a black eye and some spectacular scratches."

I winced. One of Ah Yoke's flailing elbows must have caught me in the eye. "I suppose that serves me right for slapping you on the bus."

Shin didn't laugh but continued to study my face. I pulled away.

"Don't look at me," I said. "Is it very bad?"

"Those scratches should be disinfected."

Obediently, I stood still as he rinsed his handkerchief and cleaned my face. How was I going to explain this to Mrs. Tham, let alone show up for work at the May Flower? If I skipped work, I wouldn't be able to make the next payment for my mother; my stepfather would skin us alive if a debt collector showed up at the house. I calculated furiously. At five cents a dance, could I make up the shortfall?

"Stop thinking so hard," said Shin. "You'll wear out your tiny brain."

I opened my eyes indignantly. "How rude! When I beat you at almost every exam in school!"

In answer, he just wiped harder.

"You're wiping off all my face powder," I complained.

"Makeup won't improve someone like you, if that's what you're worried about."

He applied iodine to the scratches and it stung. Or perhaps it was my pride.

"I'm quite popular, thank you." I thought about some of my regulars at the May Flower—the ones who were at least putting in a credible effort to dance. Mr. Wong, the optometrist from Tiger Lane who only liked waltzes; old Mr. Khoo, who'd told me his doctor had advised him to get some exercise; Nirman Singh, the tall skinny Sikh whom I was certain was a schoolboy although he vehemently denied it. They'd all find other girls to dance with this week. Maybe they'd prefer them.

"So what are you worried about?" Shin rinsed his handkerchief with the last of the water.

I shook my head, unwilling to involve him further. "I need to get back to work."

"You're not going home?"

"Mother will only worry if I show up like this." It would raise uncomfortable questions in Falim, with its network of gossip. Everyone knew about my stepfather's temper.

Shin returned the mug to the shop, and we caught the bus back without speaking. There were too many people around, in any case, to discuss the bizarre events of that morning. Self-conscious about my scratched face, I kept my eyes on my lap. Shin got off at Falim, but not before slipping the glass bottle with the dried finger into his pocket.

"I'll take care of it," he said, forestalling my objections. And with that, he jumped off.

A sense of unease descended upon me; I shivered as a plump woman carrying a live chicken squeezed in. It was a white rooster with yellow eyes, the pupils angry dots. At Chinese funerals, a white rooster was released into the graveyard at the end of the ceremony. Of course, this lady might just be taking it home for dinner, but the sight of the white bird on Shin's recently vacated seat filled me with dismay. As though the chill, liquid shadow haunting me had passed onto Shin.

9

ON RAINY DAYS, THE NEW DOCTOR, WILLIAM ACTON, WRITES letters. They're all to his fiancée, Iris, though he knows she hasn't read a single one.

Dear Iris, I think of you every day. The rain peters out and a weak sun appears. William puts down his pen.

On days when it doesn't rain, he goes for long walks early in the morning with a pair of binoculars, ostensibly for bird-watching. William hesitates before taking the familiar detour through the neighboring rubber estate. He's been secretly seeing a local woman, the wife of a plantation laborer. Her name is Ambika, and she's Tamil, with smooth brown skin and long curling hair that smells like coconut oil. There's a raised scar—a keloid—on her left breast in the shape of a butterfly. How many times has he pressed his lips against it? He finds it beautiful, although Ambika covers it up.

William always pays her, yet he thinks she likes him. At least, her smile is warm, though she never refuses his money. He thinks their meetings are a secret, and perhaps they are to the European community and even her husband, who drinks too much.

At least one other person knows, however. One of William's former appendectomy patients—a Chinese salesman. It was pure bad luck that he caught Ambika and William together a few weeks ago when his car broke down near the rubber estate, leading him to cut through for help. They sprang apart as soon as they became aware of the intruder and the salesman said nothing, but he'd given William a look. That was the worst part, the knowing in his eyes. For unlike other locals, he knows William's name and exactly where he works. Talk is bad for William, especially after what happened in England. To make matters worse, Ambika recently asked for more money. When William hesitated, she gave him a sullen stare, an expression that she'd never shown him before.

Walking through the rubber estate, he admires the neat rows of slender trees, imported from South America. Each tree has thin cuttings on its trunk and a small cup into which the milky latex sap drips. Before dawn, the tappers make their rounds, emptying each cup into a bucket. Ambika is one of them, though it's her husband who takes the buckets to the processing center afterwards, making this a convenient time to meet her. Checking his watch, William quickens his pace.

But the familiar lean-to, with its corrugated metal roof, is empty. It was the same when he stopped by a few days ago. Where has she gone? With no one to ask, he has little choice but to continue on to work at the Batu Gajah District Hospital, where the staff thinks he sometimes takes the long walk for exercise.

In his office, William is out of sorts. He pulls out the letter he started that morning.

Dear Iris,

I've inherited a new Chinese houseboy. His name is Ren and I'd put his age at ten if not for the assurance that he's almost thirteen. He comes to me from poor MacFarlane. Hard to believe he's gone—I still remember when we went to Korinchi to look for tiger-men, harimau jadian, *as the natives call them.*

Malaya, with its mix of Malays, Chinese, and Indians, is full of spirits: a looking-glass world governed by unsettling rules. The European werewolf is a man who, when the moon is full, turns his skin inside out and becomes a beast. He then leaves the village and goes into the forest to kill. But for the natives here, the weretiger is not a man, but a beast who, when he chooses, puts on a human skin and comes from the jungle into the village to prey on humans. It's almost exactly the reverse situation, and in some ways more disturbing.

There's a rumor that when we colonials came to this part of the world, the natives considered us beast-men as well, though nobody has said that to my face.

William scratches the bridge of his nose.

Of all the things MacFarlane has presented me with over the years, this houseboy has to be one of the strangest. After all, a boy isn't a pet or an animal. He seems grateful for the work and has tidied my study obsessively, opening every cupboard—

A knock on the door. Time to make the rounds at the wards and afterwards there's an incisional hernia surgery.

LATER THAT AFTERNOON, WILLIAM RETURNS TO FIND A SURPRISE visitor waiting in his office. She sits on the edge of his desk swinging a sandaled foot. William is moderately acquainted with Lydia Thomson, the daughter of a rubber planter, although he has the feeling she'd like to change that.

The papers on his desk are disarranged, whether through her choice of seating, or because she's been looking through them. William, tired from hours of standing in surgery, has difficulty adjusting his expression from irritated to pleasantly neutral.

"What can I do for you, Lydia?" he says, pulling out a chair for her.

They're on first-name terms, as almost all the foreigners in this little town are. Batu Gajah—no, the whole of colonial Malaya—is full of Europeans who've fled half a world away for some personal reason or other. Many are lonely; Lydia is clearly one of them. Gossip says she's here to find a husband. She isn't too old, perhaps twenty-five or -six, though she's entering the dangerous years. Still, she's one of the local belles, volunteering often at the hospital

"You forgot your notes from the panel," she says.

They're both on a local committee to combat beriberi, that elusive disease that sickens Chinese laborers in the tin mines, swelling their limbs and causing heart congestion, though less prevalent, as Lydia pointed out, among Malay or Tamil workers. She's been passionate about educating them, trying to get them to eat less white rice. "It's lack of vitamin B that causes it," she explained earnestly at their last meeting. William, gazing at the stoic faces of the locals, wondered whether Lydia understands how much white rice is a status symbol. Afterwards, an older Chinese man had nodded at him and said, "Your wife cares a lot."

"She's not my wife," William said, smiling.

"Then you should make her yours. A good woman like that."

It's a common misconception, given that they've been thrown together recently. He's squired Lydia to a charity auction. Driven her home after a couple of dinners, though he should be careful not to flirt too much with Lydia. It's his weakness; old habits die hard. Now, looking at her in his office, William wonders what Iris would think of all this.

"I don't need the notes." He's been too familiar with her, he realizes belatedly.

"Oh, it was no trouble at all! I'd stopped by to pick up my father's medicine," she says.

"And how is he?"

"Much better, thanks to you."

William is too conscientious not to explain to Lydia that the routine gallbladder operation he performed on her father would likely have turned out well under any circumstances, but she keeps smiling at him no matter what he says. The cleaning lady appears with two teacups on a tray, a digestive biscuit tucked into each saucer. Suppressing a sigh, William hands Lydia a cup.

"Were you very busy today?" she says brightly.

"Not really. Though I've been presented with a mystery."

"What is it?"

"Apparently a patient came to my house this morning and received medical treatment from an orderly. Though I haven't got an orderly at home."

"Oh." Lydia frowns.

William was surprised to see the young woman, an attractive Sinhalese girl, on his afternoon rounds at the hospital. She explained in a mixture of halting Malay and English that she'd been taken to his house for treatment that morning. No, she couldn't remember who it was, as she'd fainted. Someone in a white uniform. Her uncle, who'd brought her in, would know, though he'd already gone home. William examined the wound, resulting from a heavy iron *cangkul*, or hoe, that had slipped and cut the back of her calf. It was deep and must have bled a lot. She could have died if it hadn't been stanched.

Lydia's voice recalls him to the present. "Did you solve your puzzle, then?"

"No. I wasn't home at the time."

He has nothing against her. In fact, she's proven both diligent and practical, campaigning for powdered milk to be distributed to local children. But for some reason, she always makes him feel guilty. Perhaps it's her coloring. She has the same light hair, the same fine skin as Iris, though Iris's eyes were grey, and Lydia's a bright, frenetic blue.

"But I actually saw you this morning, walking in the rubber estate. You seemed to be looking for someone."

Blood rises, a hot guilty brand on William's neck. She couldn't have seen anything. Not this morning, anyway. He hopes Lydia will finish her tea and go away, but she says, "I hear you have a new houseboy—the one from Dr. MacFarlane's household." Seeing she's piqued his interest, Lydia continues. "Apparently the old doctor took him in because the locals thought he was cursed."

"Cursed?"

"Some superstition or other. And then there were all those deaths afterwards in Kamunting."

"What sort of deaths?"

"In the past year, at least three people were killed by tigers. Though some people were saying it must have been the same animal."

"A man-eater." William leans back in his chair. He's not sure whether Lydia is really interested in him, or simply finds him a challenge. Sometimes her flirting seems almost malicious.

"They say it's a ghost tiger, which can't be killed by bullets and vanishes like a spirit. All the victims were women. Young women, with long hair." Aware of William's scrutiny, two spots of color appear on her cheeks, an unexpectedly girlish blush. "You must think I'm very silly," she says. "It's all superstition anyway."

"There are no such things as ghosts, Lydia."

As I should know, he thinks to himself.

/////

THE NEXT MORNING IS SATURDAY, AND WILLIAM CALLS REN INTO his study. Nervous, Ren carries in the midmorning tray with a bone china teacup and a plate of Marie biscuits.

"Ren," says William. "Would you mind sorting this for me?"

With dread, Ren sees that the medical kit he used yesterday is spread out upon the desk. Rolls of bandages, bottles of iodine, chlorodyne, and tinctures, and a mess of metal implements. The half-empty bottle of hydrogen peroxide stands reproachfully to one side. Quickly, he rolls up the dressings and sorts the bottles by usage, as Dr. MacFarlane taught him. Poisons and emetics in the inner compartment, to reduce accidents. Scalpels and scissors that need frequent sterilization in another. The thick hollow needles are already in a vial of alcohol. His hand trembles as he picks up the glass syringe he boiled the other day.

When he's almost done, William says, "I see you know what you're doing."

Ren lifts his eyes, but as usual, the doctor's face is hard to read. He doesn't seem angry, however.

"Were you the one who treated that woman yesterday?"

"Yes, *Tuan*."

"You did a remarkably good job. I think she'll keep the leg."

Ren shifts uncomfortably.

"Was there already a tourniquet?"

"Yes, but it was too tight and close to the wound."

"So what did you do?"

Ren describes his actions, forgetting his nervousness as William listens intently. It's a rare feeling that he hasn't experienced since the old doctor died.

"Next time," says William, "you must tell me if you treat anyone. And I think I'd better oversee you. Can you read?"

Ren nods.

William raises an eyebrow. "Is that so? Tomorrow is Sunday. If you want to spend your half-day off going over basics, I shall be free in the afternoon."

/////

AFTER THE BOY HAS GONE, WILLIAM WALKS OUT AND LEANS ON THE wooden veranda railing. Branches shiver as a troop of monkeys passes, their whoops piercing the still morning. A flash of black and white as an indignant hornbill takes flight. William slings his binoculars around his neck and walks down the steps, over the clipped lawn that's the gardener's pride, and farther into the undergrowth. He recalls MacFarlane's letter, the trembling handwriting promising he'd find the boy interesting, and wonders what else there is to discover about Ren.

Although William could have found a house closer to the European quarter in Changkat, he doesn't mind the bungalow's isolated location. There's an old elephant trail not too far from the house though he's never seen any elephants. It rained the night before and the red clay is soft underfoot.

William halts abruptly. There in the mud is a tiger pugmark. He's never seen one so close to the house before. It's so fresh that a blade of grass, trodden into the print, is still green. Tigers are rare near town, though there are still many in the deep jungle. A skillful tracker could probably estimate the animal's age and physical health, but from the size and squareness, William guesses it was a male.

A surveyor for the Federated Malay States Railways once told him how a tiger had carried off one of his best coolies. The workers slept twelve men to a camp house, their bedding laid out on the floor. This particular man, strong and well-built for a native, was sleeping in the middle of the row. The door was left open to let in the breeze. In the morning, he was missing. Tiger prints were discovered and tracking them for a quarter of a mile led to the recovery of his head, left arm, and legs. The torso and entrails had been devoured. In the night, the tiger had silently entered, picked its way over the sleepers, and selected the best specimen.

WILLIAM KEEPS NO DOGS TO WARN HIM OF ANY APPROACH AND NOW regrets it. He has an old Purdey shotgun in the house, but it isn't loaded.

He ought to warn Ah Long and the boy not to wander from the house in the evening. Turning back, he sees Ah Long on the veranda.

"*Tuan!*" he shouts. "Hospital!"

William is the medical officer on call this weekend. He hurries up the steps. "What is it?"

Ah Long's Malay is bad and his English even poorer. He should have the boy take messages in future, but for now, Ah Long is the bearer of news even he can express clearly. "Someone is dead."

Out of the corner of his eye, William sees Ren staring, white-faced, at him. He looks terrified.

HARUN IS OFF DUTY SO WILLIAM DRIVES HIMSELF. THE INCIDENT has taken place at the same plantation that he walked through on Friday morning; the message was brief and only mentioned that a body had been discovered. Most local deaths are caused by malaria or tuberculosis, though snakebites and accidents are also common.

The manager of this estate is Henry Thomson, Lydia's father. As William pulls in, he sees a small knot of people. Thomson's thin figure hovers near the tall bulk of a Sikh police officer and his Malay constable. The officer introduces himself as Captain Jagjit Singh, an inspector in the Federated Malay States Police. His English is excellent, and William guesses that he, like many police officers in Malaya, was recruited from the Indian Army to supplement the dearth of trained officers.

"The body was found past noon," he says. "Looks like an animal attack, but we can't rule out foul play. We couldn't get hold of Dr. Rawlings, and I'd like to establish a cause of death before we move it."

They're walking now, heading deeper into the rubber estate. Distracted by the sameness of the trees, William wonders whether he's ever passed through this portion of the estate.

"Who found it?" he asks.

"One of the rubber tappers."

Thomson has been silent, his thin, worried face looking down at the dry leaves on which they tread, but now he says, "I'm not sure if it's one of my workers. We'll need to do a roll call."

"What makes you think it might be foul play?" asks William.

Captain Singh hesitates. "It's hard to say. There's not much of it left."

////

ARRIVING AT THE SCENE, A DIP IN THE GROUND COVERED BY UNDER-
growth, they see the squatting figure of a Malay constable left on guard.
He stands up hastily with a look of relief. Thomson excuses himself. "I
don't need to see it again," he says.

William walks over. A slim arm protrudes from under a bush. It has a
greyish pallor; a line of ants crawls over it. Pushing his way into the bush,
William lifts the low whiplike branches out of the way.

"Has it been moved?" he calls over his shoulder.

"No."

William stares down at what was once a woman. Two outstretched arms
are still attached to a torso. Part of a green blouse wreathes one shoulder.
Beneath the thin cotton, the punctured rib cage shows the shattered white
ends of bone and a hollow bloody darkness. Rubbery-looking skin is beginning to peel from the edge of the wounds. From the pelvis down, there
is nothing.

"Where's the head?" says William, fighting back his sickness. There's
a sickly sweet carrion smell rising from the body and the shimmering wrig-
gle of maggots. Their size, and the fact that it takes eight to twenty hours
for them to hatch in this tropical climate, puts the time of death somewhere around Thursday night or Friday morning.

"We haven't found it yet." Captain Singh stays carefully upwind from
the smell. "We're still searching in a quarter-mile radius."

William forces himself to look at the body again, but his mind is
already made up. "It's an animal. Those deep punctures on her torso
look like tooth marks. The cervical spine has been severed. Her shoulders are also marked. It probably got her by the neck and suffocated her
first."

"What do you think then—leopard or tiger?"

Leopards are far more common in Malaya than tigers, outnumbering
them by at least ten to one. William knows several residents whose dogs
have been eaten by leopards.

"Tiger, maybe. The spacing of the bite marks looks a bit large for a leopard. Also, it takes a certain amount of jaw strength to break the spine. You should ask Rawlings—I assume he'll be doing the autopsy?"

Rawlings, the hospital pathologist, is also acting coroner, the one who will weigh and measure out the sad secrets of this body. William takes a handkerchief out of his pocket and holds it over his mouth. The pressure alleviates his nausea.

"No tracks," says Captain Singh.

William looks at the ground, thickly carpeted with dried leaves. In the absence of bare earth, it will be hard to find pugmarks.

"I think she was killed somewhere else," he says. "There isn't enough blood—perhaps this part of the body was taken for a second meal."

Tigers, he knows, will return to a carcass repeatedly, even when the meat has gone high. It may be difficult to find the other body parts, as a tiger's range can cover many miles. His thoughts leap to the fresh prints near his bungalow.

"I'll get a tracker and some dogs," says Captain Singh. "But something about this doesn't look typical. Doesn't it strike you that not much has actually been eaten? Tigers tend to go for the abdomen first, not the limbs. But here the torso is largely intact." Like many Sikhs, he's a tall, rangy man, made even more imposing by his white turban. His sharp amber eyes are fixed on the corpse.

William takes a final look himself and stiffens. On the left breast, the greyish skin is still intact and there, unmistakably, is a raised keloid scar in the shape of a butterfly. He knows this mark intimately, has paid money to run his fingers over it, and not even the handkerchief pressed desperately against his face can save him now.

William lurches out of the undergrowth and vomits by the side of a tree.

10

I RETURNED TO THE DRESSMAKER'S SHOP WITH A SCRATCHED FACE and the beginnings of a black eye. I'd hoped to let myself quietly in, but Mrs. Tham opened the door at the rattle of my key.

"Your face! Ji Lin, what happened to you? Did you get into a fight? Have you seen a doctor?"

I told her that I'd slipped and fallen. It wasn't a very good story, and I waited, holding my breath, for the questioning to start again, but surprisingly she stopped. Studying me, she said. "You went home to Falim, did you?"

"Yes."

"Did you see your stepfather?"

A look of pity crossed her face, and I understood that she, too, had heard the rumors about my stepfather's temper. I felt like giggling hysterically. Of all the things that had happened this weekend, he was the least to blame for once. And the truth was, he'd never laid a hand on me. He didn't need to.

From the very beginning, I'd discovered that it was beneath my stepfather to discipline a girl. That was my mother's job, and at the slightest sign of his displeasure, he'd merely glance at my mother for her to bite her lips and softly reprove me. At first, I hadn't understood the cost. Singing loudly or whistling were offenses. So was talking back to him. They resulted in my mother emerging from discussions with him, white-faced and holding her wrist gingerly. Bruises on her upper arms where hard fingers had dug in. These were never as spectacular as the punishments meted out to Shin, and my mother never referred to them. But both of us learned to dread the vertical line that appeared on his forehead, in the exact middle of his brow, and the whitening of his nostrils.

I suppose you could say he thought what he was doing was right and just, and boys needed to be whipped into shape, and wives should learn their place. I didn't know and, frankly, I never cared to understand my step-father. I only knew I hated him.

Peering into my small mirror, I was dismayed. My left cheek-bone was swollen, and there were several long scratches across my face. And as promised, I was developing a nice shiner. Glumly, I ran the numbers through my head again. At five cents a dance ticket, which meant three cents to me, I was still short seventy-five cents this month for my mother's debt. But there was no way I could work like this, despite the knot of anxiety in my stomach. Rather than going in and facing stares, it would be better to ask Hui to tell the Mama that I couldn't make it on Wednesday, so the next day after work, I went to visit her.

Hui sometimes worked evenings at another place, but I was fairly certain I'd find her at home. She didn't live too far, which was how we'd become friends in the first place. Hui had brought a dress to Mrs. Tham's shop, and I'd been given the task of altering it. It was a pretty frock—light frothy turquoise that looked like sea foam. I'd asked her what she wore it to.

"Tea dances. Have you ever been to one?" she said.

I hadn't, although I'd taken dance lessons before.

"You look like you'd be good at it," she'd said, and between this and our idle chatter, I'd made the mistake of taking the hem up a little too high for Mrs. Tham's conservative guidelines. Laughing, Hui said it didn't matter and that shorter was better. Later, I found out why, but by then we were already good friends.

Hui lived on Panglima Lane, the narrowest street in Ipoh. Cramped houses pressed against each other and strings of laundry hung overhead like gaily waving flags. Thirty years ago, it was notorious for its brothels, gambling, and opium dens, but now it was mostly private homes. In Cantonese, it was called Second Concubine Lane. I'd often thought it would be a terrible place for a rendezvous because the houses were so close to each other. You could practically see across from the upper floors.

"Hui!" I called out as I arrived.

"Upstairs." Her landlord, an old man who chewed betel nuts and looked like a vampire because of his crimson-stained mouth, gestured towards the front room. I found Hui lying on her stomach in bed, leafing through a newspaper. She was wearing a thin cotton slip, her bare face shiny with face cream.

Her eyes opened wide when she saw my face. "Whom did you fight with?"

"How did you know?" I set two portions of *nasi lemak*, coconut rice wrapped in a banana-leaf packet with curried chicken and sambal chili, on the table. Hui's room was larger than mine at Mrs. Tham's, and littered with pots of rouge, face powder, and magazines.

"Those scratches—I've seen girls fight. What happened?"

I explained yesterday's events as we started to eat.

"So it was the widow who did it," she said, opening her packet of *nasi lemak* appreciatively.

I sighed. "Well, I can't blame her—she was so upset."

"I told you not to go! I hope you weren't alone."

"My brother went with me."

"I didn't know you had a brother. Does he look like you? Because if he does, I want to meet him." Hui had been delighted by my fashionably short hair, helping me apply the unfamiliar pomade that kept its sleek shape.

"We don't look alike at all. He's my stepbrother so we've no blood relationship."

"Oh," she said, wrinkling her nose. Hui knew a little about my stepfather, although I tried not to discuss my circumstances at home. "Is he horrible?"

"No, he's apparently quite a catch. At least, according to the women in Falim." I rolled my eyes and she burst into a fit of giggles.

"But listen," she said, "I meant to tell you that it's better that you don't come to work for a while anyway. On Sunday there was a man asking for you by name. Not Louise, but your real name."

My spirits sank. The only customer that I'd inadvertently revealed my name to had been the salesman. "What did he look like?"

"Chinese. Ordinary. I told him that there wasn't anyone here by that name."

I wanted to hug her. "And then?"

"He left. Maybe he was looking for the finger. Did you leave it with the widow?"

"She wouldn't take it." Remembering that scene in the little wooden house, with Ah Yoke writhing and sobbing on the floor like a snake with a woman's face, I felt deeply uneasy.

"So who has it?"

"My brother." What was Shin planning to do with it anyway?

Hui sighed. Warm evening air wafted through the open window and you could hear bicycle bells ringing and the click of passing feet. "Where do you find such reliable men? I'm sick to death of the ones I meet."

I hadn't thought about it in that light before, but I supposed she was right. "We were close when we were younger, but not so much now. He's turned into a womanizer."

Hui gave a shriek of laughter. "I'm sure he can't be that bad."

I had to smile. "He's working in Batu Gajah for the next few months."

"Batu Gajah?" Hui waved the newspaper at me. "Did you hear about this? They found a body on Saturday. There's a man-eater on the loose."

It was a small article: a paragraph or two that must have been rushed to press. *Body found in Batu Gajah rubber plantation. Headless female torso discovered by estate worker.*

A tiger. From time to time, the newspapers carried gruesome reports of people strangled by pythons, taken by crocodiles, or trampled by elephants. But tigers were different. Referred to as *datuk,* an honorary title, there were charms spoken to appease a tiger when venturing into the jungle. A tiger that devoured too many humans was said to be able to take the form of a man and walk among us.

It had nothing to do with Shin or me, but I felt the cold touch of that shadow again, the one that undulated in the watery depths of my fears, as though it was searching for something.

////

By Friday, only my black eye lingered, having turned greenish-yellow. Fortunately it wasn't swollen anymore, and I decided that with the judicious application of makeup, I'd be able to make my afternoon shift at the dance hall. Besides, I really needed the money. The numbers kept scrolling up and down in my head in red ink—a horrible shortfall. Missing a payment might result in the loan shark sending a nasty reminder to my stepfather's house. I convinced myself that the risk of some man looking for me about the finger was minimal, and anyway, perhaps he'd already crossed the May Flower off his list.

It was a slow afternoon. The sun was baking down outside, and in the dim coolness of the dance hall, iced drinks were doing a brisk trade. I sat out a couple of dances, chatting with some of the other girls. Hui didn't work on Fridays, but I'd made friends with Rose and Pearl. Rose was a widow, and Pearl never said, but I suspected she'd run away from her husband. Of course, those weren't their real names, either. If I'd had a choice I'd rather be called May or Lily, something pretty and light unlike my serious Chinese name, but I was stuck with Louise. In fact, patrons referred to me by my hairstyle. "I want the one who looks like Louise Brooks," they'd say, pointing at me, and I'd stand up and smile as though it were my birthday.

It was my fifty-third day of being Louise. In Cantonese, fifty-three was a homophone for "cannot live." Another day with an unlucky number, and nine days since I'd danced with the ill-fated salesman Chan Yew Cheung. Rose had just finished telling us how she'd stayed up all night because her little girl had a bad cough, when she suddenly said, "Oh, he's back!"

A customer was scrutinizing us. He had a narrow face with a crooked chin, as if his head had been caught in a vise. Guessing he was the man Hui had warned me about, I got up in alarm, but he was too quick for me.

"May I have this dance?"

I hesitated, but the Mama's eagle eye was on me. I'd no reason to refuse, though my stomach twisted with dismay. Surprisingly, he was a good dancer. We went around the floor a couple of times; I was beginning to think my suspicions were unfounded when he said, "You must be Ji Lin."

"I could be, if you wanted," I forced a smile. "But I'm afraid my name is Louise."

"I'm looking for a girl who picked up something last week. A family heirloom of mine."

For an instant, I was tempted to come clean. I'd already fulfilled my obligation to the salesman's family. But I no longer had the finger; if Shin had destroyed it, this man might be furious. Hedging, I said, "What does it look like?"

"It's my ancestor's finger from China that's been in our family for generations. My friend borrowed it last week. He said he'd lost it here."

"A finger?" I tried to look surprised, even horrified. He watched me carefully. I wondered if he was lying. According to the salesman's wife, her husband had possessed the finger for the last three months. "I'll ask around for you."

"Let me know," he said, staring intently. "You can leave a message for me here." He scribbled down the address of a coffee shop on Leech Street together with a name: Mr. Y. K. Wong.

"If you find it, I'll give you a reward. For sentimental reasons." He smiled his sharp-toothed smile.

After that, he danced with several other girls, who later confirmed that he'd asked them the same questions: if they were called Ji Lin, and if they'd picked anything up, though nothing about missing fingers. I recalled the way he'd made a beeline over to me as soon as he'd entered and a shiver traced the back of my neck.

"I'm surprised you came in today," said Rose, fanning herself vigorously during an intermission, while the band drank soda water and mopped their brows. Despite the face powder, her forehead was almost as shiny as the parquet dance floor, and I was sure that I was no better.

"I need the money."

"If that's the case," said Rose, "want to make extra?"

I shook my head. "No call-outs."

Call-outs were when a man would book a girl outside the dance hall, ostensibly to take her shopping or to eat a meal. They were lucrative, but everything came, of course, with a price. I'd explained to the Mama from the very first that I wouldn't do them. The incident today with Mr. Y. K. Wong, if that was really his name, reminded me just how vulnerable I felt with a stranger. And we hadn't even been alone—we'd been dancing in full view of dozens of people.

"It's not a call-out. I have this client who asked me if I could find a few girls to dance at a private party. And he promised, no hanky-panky."

"There's no such thing as a private party with no hanky-panky."

Rose smiled. "What a grandma you are! I wasn't too keen, either, so I told him we'd have to get the dance-hall Mama's permission—to put him off, you know. But he went and asked her and she said yes!"

"She did?" I had a hard time believing this.

"Well, she'll get a nice commission, and she said she'd send one of the bouncers with us and hire a car. They want four or five girls because there are lots of bachelors and they want to dance. It'll be in Batu Gajah."

I paused. "At the hospital?" If it was, I couldn't go. I'd no intention of revealing my seedy part-time job to Shin.

"No, a private residence in Changkat."

I'd heard of Changkat, a prime residential area situated uphill of Batu Gajah. "Does that mean they'll be foreigners?"

"Do you mind?"

Most of the customers at the May Flower were locals though there were always some Europeans in the mix. Not as many as at the glamorous Celestial Hotel, but a fair smattering on any given afternoon. They were mostly planters or civil servants, servicemen, and policemen. I'd danced with a few myself, though to be honest, they made me nervous.

But that explained the Mama's swift acquiescence, as well as the extras like a bouncer and a hired car.

"Hui will come, too, and it pays double."

That would be enough to cover what I'd missed. And if Hui, who was always so canny about taking care of herself, was willing to go, then I would as well.

By the time I'd finished work, the orange sun was low on the horizon. Pearl and Rose did the evening shift, so I was alone when I left by the May Flower's back door. I didn't know how they managed to stay on their feet for so many hours, but they would dance on till past midnight.

Pearl had a son, and Rose two little girls. Did the children wait for them to come home, watching the oil lamp burn down in the darkness? If my mother hadn't remarried, that might have been my fate as well, though I couldn't imagine her working in a dance hall. She was too timid, too gullible. Even now she'd managed to run up debts from simply playing mahjong. I wondered, for the hundredth time, whether she'd really lost all those games or had been cheated.

When it was all paid off, I'd save up and train to be a teacher. It didn't matter what my stepfather thought. I was sure that eventually he'd rather have me out of the way than deal with a spinster at home. Besides, I'd said I wouldn't get married, even though my mother had started nudging me towards matchmakers. The promise I'd made with Shin, so long ago when we were children whispering in his room, still held true. I didn't see what marriage could do for me, especially if the one I'd wanted was going to marry someone else.

But there was no point hoping for Ming anymore, though in my most evil moments I imagined his fiancée deserting him. Or perhaps he'd suddenly realize he'd made a terrible mistake and propose to me instead. I pictured him coming up the dusty street on his heavy black bicycle, his unruly hair standing up. "Ji Lin," he'd say, looking embarrassed yet serious in his bookish way, "I have to talk to you." And I'd come running—no, walking demurely down the stairs—and listen with a beating heart. But at this point, I always ran out of steam even though I managed to think of lots of quite good things for Ming to say. It simply wouldn't happen. He'd never looked at me the way I'd seen him gaze at his fiancée.

The May Flower was on the outskirts of Ipoh, quite far from Mrs. Tham's. Having just missed the bus I decided, despite the falling dusk, to walk partway. It was dinnertime, and I could smell fish frying, hear the scratchy sound of a radio playing Chinese opera. Crossing the street, I narrowly avoided a bicycle that swished past. Out of the corner of my eye, I saw a man follow across, though the light was too weak to make out his face.

Hui and the other girls had warned me to expect the occasional customer who'd wait outside. Pearl said once a man pursued her all the way home, and her mother had threatened him with a kitchen knife.

"And did he leave?" I'd asked.

"She chased him off, shouting that my husband was a pork butcher!"

We'd laughed about it then, but right now I wished heartily for pork-butcher relatives of my own. Whoever was following me did so at a cautious distance. When I walked faster, he did, too. When I stopped, he slipped behind a pillar. I ducked under a hanging bamboo *chik*, or blind, into a dry-goods store, crowded shelves packed with glass jars of sweets, cast-iron woks, and wooden clogs. It was almost closing time as the shopkeeper, an elderly man in a white singlet, informed me.

"Please," I said, "do you have a back door? There's a man following me."

I must have looked frightened for he nodded. "Go through, past the kitchen."

I hurried through the long shophouse, apologizing to his startled family who were sitting down to fish soup and fried tofu. The back door led to a narrow alleyway between the shophouses. The wise thing, of course, would be to leave as quickly as possible, but it was too good an opportunity to pass up. Silently, I peeked round the corner.

My pursuer stood staring at the dry-goods store. The shutters were now being closed, and he was clearly puzzled as to why I hadn't emerged yet. I recognized him right away. As I feared, it was the young man with the narrow face who'd asked me about the finger: Y. K. Wong. My shoulders tensed. One way or another, I'd better not return to the May Flower for some time.

Cutting back to the dusty street behind, I hailed a trishaw, leaving my pursuer still waiting fruitlessly in front of the store. I hoped he'd stay there a good long time. Listening to the crank of pedals, the wheels humming in the falling velvet dusk, I closed my eyes and wished fiercely that I could leave this place. Leave everything and start over somewhere else.

To my surprise when I got home, Mrs. Tham was waiting for me in the front room. She looked both excited and a little put out, an expression that I recognized with a sinking feeling.

"Where have you been?" she asked.

"Just finishing up." It was no later than my usual time on a Friday.

"One of the rules of this house," she said, her little bird face alight with indignation, "is no male visitors. I can't imagine what you could have been thinking, Ji Lin, to tell a man to come and wait for you here!"

I flinched. I'd left the mysterious Mr. Y. K. Wong standing in the street at the other end of town. How was it possible that he'd found the dressmaker's shop? It was like witchcraft; the man was a demon. Or perhaps he had a twin, a doppelgänger that heralded death.

"He stood outside for the longest time. I thought he was waiting for a customer, peering into the shop the way he did, but finally he came in and asked for you. When I said you were out, he left right away. Though I must say he was very good-looking."

"Oh," I said, understanding dawning. "Was it my brother?"

"Your brother? You don't look anything alike."

Not wanting to explain any further, since Mrs. Tham had obviously heard bits and pieces of my family history and was eager to ferret out more, I simply said, "People often say that."

"If he was your brother, why didn't he say so?" she said indignantly. "Making me worry like that!"

I'd no idea, to be honest. Had my mother given Shin this address? And why was he here so late in the evening? There were too many mysteries today.

11

REN IS WAITING ANXIOUSLY AT THE DOOR WHEN WILLIAM RETURNS. *"Selamat datang,"* he says. *Welcome home.* That is the correct way to greet his master; servants should be lined up at the door for arrivals and departures. Ren had always done it for Dr. MacFarlane. The old doctor used to joke he didn't feel right leaving home without Ren's quiet goodbye. Today, Ah Long has joined him, his usually taciturn face animated as he takes William's medical bag.

"Tuan, is it a tiger?"

"Probably," says William. "I want the doors locked at night. And don't go out in the evening or early morning alone. That goes for you, too, Ren."

Ren nods. He thinks the new doctor looks ill. His face has a fish-belly pallor and his eyes, behind the thin-rimmed glasses, are bloodshot. There are so many questions that Ren wants to ask, but he hesitates, wondering how to broach the subject.

Ah Long asks, "Who died?"

"A plantation worker." William passes a hand over his eyes. "I need a bath and a drink. A whisky *stengah,* please."

William goes off to the tiled bathroom, where he'll rinse himself off with a bucket dipped in a pottery jar of water. Ah Long turns to Ren.

"Know how to make one?"

Ren looks dubious. Dr. MacFarlane drank things from bottles, but he never asked Ren to mix them for him.

"Now's a good time to learn. Watch me."

Stengah comes from the Malay word *setengah*, meaning "half." Ah Long fetches a block of ice from the cold box in the kitchen, where it's kept buried in sawdust. Chipping away with an icepick, he fills a tall highball glass.

"Don't make the ice too small," he warns. "Otherwise it melts too fast."

Next, he fills the glass one-third full of a medicinal, tea-colored liquid that he pours out of a square bottle. It has a picture of a man in a tall black hat with white trousers. *Johnnie Walker Blended Scotch Whisky* reads a label that seems to have been slapped half-heartedly on the bottle.

"Why is the label crooked?" asks Ren.

"It's not crooked. It's just like that. Now watch carefully!"

Using the soda siphon, a glass bottle encased in metal wires that Ren has never dared to touch, Ah Long dispenses a stream of sparkling soda water into the frosty glass. The sharp whiff of carbonation makes Ren wrinkle his nose.

"The water and the whisky should be about the same amount." Ah Long cocks his head, listening. "He's probably done now. Take it out on the veranda."

The wide, teak-planked veranda runs the length of the bungalow, shielded from the sun by hanging bamboo *chiks*. On extremely hot days, Ren wets them with water so that the evaporation will cool the veranda. William sits in a rattan easy chair. He wears a cotton singlet and a sarong, a loose piece of checked cloth sewn into a tube and worn rolled at the waist—Malay clothing that many Europeans have adopted at home, though they'd never dream of appearing like this in public.

Like Ah Long, Ren doesn't wear shoes in the house and his soft-footed approach is so silent that William doesn't hear him. He's sunk in thought, an expression of misery on his face. Ren has never seen his new master display much emotion before and wonders if this is a sign that he's a truly compassionate doctor. A spark of hope ignites in Ren. Maybe he can ask him about the finger—though Dr. MacFarlane said not to tell anyone.

"Whisky, *Tuan*," he says.

William picks it up and drains half of it, making a face.

"May I ask, why do you think it was a tiger-killing?" Ren is so polite, so quiet, that William can't be irritated with him.

"Leopard is a possibility, but most likely it's a tiger. We won't know for certain until the autopsy is performed."

"Will the tiger come back?"

"Don't worry." With an effort, William focuses on the boy. "Man-eaters are rare. Most tigers avoid people—it's usually old or sick animals that prey on humans." The ice in his drink clinks as he tilts it.

"Tigers who kill people can be divided into two types: man-killers, who kill once or twice because they're disturbed or threatened, and man-eaters, who routinely hunt humans as prey. It's too early to know what kind of animal we're dealing with here, so we shouldn't panic." He speaks deliberately, as though he's making a case to an invisible audience.

"Will there be a tiger hunt?" Ren asks.

"There are always people who want to go on a tiger hunt. Reynolds and Price at the Club, probably. Idiots who can't shoot straight to save their lives. The last bounty paid for a tiger around here was seventy-eight dollars."

Seventy-eight Straits dollars is an enormous sum to Ren, more than he can ever dream of saving. He wonders how William is so knowledgeable and asks him timidly.

"Oh, I was quite mad about tigers when I first got here." Sinking deeper into his rattan easy chair, William is unusually talkative today. "That's how I got to know MacFarlane; he had some interesting beliefs."

Ren decides to be bold. "He believed many things. About spirits and men who could turn into tigers."

"Ah yes. The famous weretigers of Korinchi." William gazes through the trees to an invisible destination. "He and I actually went looking for them. Did you know that the Malays are often suspicious of men from Korinchi, because they're believed to turn into tigers? There was a case in Bentong years ago when a tiger was killing buffaloes. Cage traps were set and baited with stray dogs, but they didn't catch anything."

Ren shifts his feet, listening intently. The afternoon shadows are growing long, the green silence broken only by the humming of insects.

"One evening, an old Korinchi peddler was traveling through the jungle when he heard the roar of a tiger behind him. Terrified, he ran until he came across a tiger trap. He crawled in and let the heavy door fall behind him. The tiger prowled round, but unable to open it, went away.

"Early the next morning, a crowd of people heard his shouts for help. The peddler asked them to release him, but they said, 'The tiger was here last night, and now you are in the tiger trap.' Paw prints leading towards the cage had been partly obliterated by the crowd. It was impossible to tell whether the beast had gone away, or had entered the trap and turned himself into a man. In desperation, the old man begged them to recognize him as the trader they had known for many years. The villagers, however, were unable to decide whether he was a man, or a monster who, if released, would devour them."

"So what happened?" asks Ren.

"They put a spear through the side of the trap and killed him."

William falls silent. Ren, still holding the tray, is filled with questions. "Do you believe that a man can become a tiger?"

William closes his eyes and steeples his fingers. "The conditions for a man to become a tiger seem to contradict each other. He either has to be a saint or an evildoer. In the case of a saint, the tiger is considered *keramat* and serves as a protective spirit, but evildoers are also reincarnated as tigers as punishment. And let's not forget the *harimau jadian*, who aren't even men, but beasts who wear human skins. They're all contradictory beliefs, and so I'd classify them as folktales."

He opens his eyes again. They're disconcertingly sharp, as though he's snapped back from wherever it is that he's gone. "You shouldn't worry about today's incident. The last thing we need around here is a superstitious panic. Forget it. God knows," he adds under his breath, "I wish I could."

William unpacks himself from the rattan chair and stands up, stumbling slightly. Ren feels profoundly relieved. The tight band of worry around his chest dissipates; he tries not to think that there are only twenty-two days of the soul left. This new doctor is so reasonable, so sane. Everything he says makes sense. Obediently, Ren follows him into the house.

12

SLEEP WOULDN'T COME TO ME THAT NIGHT. WHEN I THOUGHT ABOUT the mysterious Y. K. Wong, with his narrow jaw and thin eyes, my head tightened. Who was he, and why had he tried to follow me home? I didn't buy his story about an ancestral heirloom. That single finger made me uneasy, like a missing piece from a set of five digits. A reminder of unfinished business. On and on my mind ran, like a mouse on a wheel, but the wheel turned into a giant snake that turned to engulf me. And then I was panting, struggling breathlessly as I fell and slipped and slid down the tunnel into the world of dreams.

UNLIKE THE FIRST DREAM, I DIDN'T COME FLOATING DOWN THE COOL river. This time I burst out on the riverbank, thrashing through bushes and sharp-bladed *lalang*, to find the river running next to me. The sunlit water, clear and shallow at the edge, grew mud-colored towards the middle.

And then I saw it. The same small railway station with deserted benches, the same stalled locomotive, only this time the train had stopped a little farther, as though it was about to pull out of the station. The carriages were empty: there was no one inside, not even the little boy who'd waved at me so happily last time. When I reached the station, however, he was sitting there on a bench. He smiled, a quick flash that showed his missing front tooth.

"*Ah Jie*," he said, politely addressing me as "Older Sister." "I didn't think I'd see you again so soon."

"What are you doing?" I sat down next to him.

"Waiting."

It was cool and peaceful under the station's thatched roof. "What for?"

He swung his short legs. "For someone I love. Is there anyone that you love, *Ah Jie*?"

Of course there was. My mother, Ming, and Shin. Even Hui and my school friends, though I'd avoided them recently out of pride—many girls from school had gone on for teacher training, while others had married— and I'd been so bitterly disappointed at my lot that I couldn't bear to face them.

"Because if there's someone that you really, really love," he said seriously, "it's all right to wait for them."

Sitting next to him, my anxiety melted away. The breeze from the river was pleasant, the sunlight sparkled off the water like fish scales.

"If you see my brother, please don't tell him that you've met me."

"Do I know your brother?" My head felt heavy. I could barely keep my eyes open.

"You will when you see him." The little boy turned, his eyes widening in alarm. "Please don't fall asleep! If you do, you'll fall through."

"Fall through to what?" I was having difficulty understanding him.

"To the level below. This is Station One, you see. Oh please don't! Wake up!"

He was making quite a racket. The banging got louder and louder until I forced my eyes open blearily.

"Wake up! Ji Lin, wake up!" It was Mrs. Tham, hammering on the door of my room.

Light streamed in through the slats. Disoriented, I found myself lying in bed. Mrs. Tham burst in, her feathers ruffled. Something was up; she was positively simmering with excitement.

"He's downstairs. Your brother, that is. I think he's come to take you home to Falim."

"He is?"

"I told him I knew that he was your brother and why didn't he say so yesterday? He's waiting for you in the front room."

"Is my mother all right?" Fear gripped me. Something must have happened, otherwise why would Shin come to fetch me away?

I'd always been afraid of receiving a message like this and the terror must have shown in my eyes, because Mrs. Tham said quite kindly, "No, there's nothing wrong. That was the first thing I asked him. It's just a family get-together to celebrate."

Our family almost never had get-togethers, let alone celebrations. If we did, they were stiff affairs in which my stepfather's friends were invited over and the men would sit and talk for hours while my mother and I served them endless cups of tea. Shin knew perfectly well how I felt about them; I couldn't imagine that he'd come to fetch me away to such purgatory.

"If it's a special occasion," said Mrs. Tham, "why don't you wear something nice? Show your mother what you've been learning."

Despite her fussiness (or perhaps because of it), Mrs. Tham was a talented dressmaker and a shrewd businesswoman. Sending me off nicely dressed was good advertising for her shop. Now she was busy inspecting the clothes I'd made, twitching them off hangers and muttering, "No, not this one. Maybe this one. Here. Show the other girls in Falim what Ipoh clothes look like."

It was a Western-style frock, a deceptively simple yet elegant design that Mrs. Tham had copied from a magazine picture. She had good taste, I had to admit.

"And if anyone asks you about your dress, be sure to give our shop's name!" she said on her way out. "Oh, and fix your face!" she hissed, pointing significantly at my eye.

I washed up and packed a simple overnight kit. What could possibly be happening at home? Pulling back my bangs, I stared gloomily at the small round mirror above the washstand. My black eye was still vaguely purple and yellow. I couldn't possibly show this to my mother, so I did my best with a little pan-stick makeup and a smudge of kohl.

I could hear Shin's low voice in the front room of the shop. Clutching my rattan basket, I stood hesitantly in the doorway. It was embarrassing to be so dressed up early in the morning, but Mrs. Tham jumped up, dislodging her little dog, Dolly, from her lap, and greeted me with a cry of delight.

"Isn't it lovely?" she said, turning me to one side and then the other.

"This pattern turned out so well. And your sister is as good as a professional mannequin. I always like her to model my dresses."

I signaled Shin with my eyes. *Time to leave!* But he was enjoying himself at my expense.

"I can't tell," he said. "Make her twirl a bit more."

To my horror, Mrs. Tham actually started to spin me around. Dolly barked hysterically.

"No, no. He's just joking. And we have to leave now."

"But Mr. Tham has just gone to the coffee shop to buy some *char siew bao!*" she said, forcing me to sit down. I glared at Shin as he bit back his amusement.

"Now!" said Mrs. Tham, fixing us both with a beady eye. "Which one of you is older?"

"I am," I said quickly.

"We were born on the same day." Shin hated being my younger brother and would deny it at every opportunity.

"So you're twins!" Mrs. Tham looked pleased. "How nice for your mother." I was about to tell her that Shin was my stepbrother but she chattered on relentlessly. "Twins are special, I suppose. Especially boy-girl dragon and phoenix twins. Do you know that the Chinese believe that boy and girl twins were husband and wife in a former life? And that they couldn't bear to be separated, so they were reborn together?"

That seemed both silly and rather tragic to me. If I loved someone, I wouldn't want to be reincarnated as his sibling, but it wasn't worth arguing with Mrs. Tham. She had an uncanny knack of sucking you into her orbit. Shin, too, seemed to have had enough. Smiling, he said that it was time to get going as we'd miss the bus.

"So why are you here?" I asked him as soon as we were away from the shop. "Did anything happen at home?"

"No."

I had to run a little to catch up with Shin's long stride, as he suddenly seemed to be in quite a hurry and was heading in the wrong direction for the bus.

"We're not taking the bus," he said. "We're taking the train. Don't look so worried—it's nothing to do with home. In fact, they think I'm in Batu Gajah."

It was half a mile to the railway station from Mrs. Tham's and Shin showed no sign of slowing down as we turned up Belfield and took a left on Hugh Low Street.

"What's the hurry?" I asked as we cut in front of a bullock cart, narrowly avoiding a cyclist who rang his bell angrily at us.

"It's later than I thought." Shin seized my traveling basket, and there was nothing to do but hurry after him.

Though I'd taken a train only a few times in my life, everyone knew the railway station. Famously known as the Taj Mahal of Ipoh and designed by a British government architect who'd come to Malaya by way of Calcutta, it was an enormous, sprawling white building that looked like a wedding cake or a Moghul palace. Domes and minarets topped curved archways that led to marble-tiled corridors, a hotel for travelers with a bar and café, and tunnels and stairs that went up and down and led to railway platforms.

Shin headed straight into the station. Breathless, I caught up with him at the ticket window.

"Two tickets to Batu Gajah," he said, sliding the money across the counter.

I was filled with unreasonable excitement and delight. Why were we going? Not wanting to ask too many questions in front of strangers, I squeezed Shin's arm instead, my face bright.

"Honeymooners?" said the ticket seller, looking at my smart frock.

I dropped Shin's arm as though it burned. A crimson stain appeared on the back of his neck, all the way up to his ears, but he didn't say anything.

"Platform Two. Ten minutes till the train leaves," said the ticket seller. We ran down the marble stairs under the tracks to the other side and then into the train that was already beginning to blow steam.

"It's a third-class carriage, I'm afraid," said Shin.

I didn't care. I was so excited that I had to stop myself from jumping up to look at everything, from the hard wooden seats to the windows that slid up and down. Amused, Shin put my basket on the rack above the seat and I noticed for the first time that he'd brought nothing with him.

"Were you in town last night?" I asked. "Mrs. Tham said she saw you."

"I stayed with a friend."

I wondered who it was—maybe a woman—but felt I shouldn't pry.

"So why are we going to Batu Gajah?" I'd been there once to visit one of my mother's relatives. It was a pretty little town, sleepily satisfied with its position as the center of colonial administration for the Kinta district. "It's not because of the finger, is it?" My face fell.

The train gave a final, ear-splitting whistle. "Of course it's because of the finger," said Shin. "Don't you want to find out where it came from?"

I considered telling him about narrow-faced Mr. Y. K. Wong, but couldn't explain without mentioning the dance-hall part. Instead, I nodded.

"Anyway," said Shin, "I went down to Batu Gajah early on Monday. They're a bit short-staffed and were glad enough to have me." He was looking out of the window, but I understood, without his saying anything, that Shin couldn't stand being in the same house as his father. No doubt that was why he'd stayed in Singapore during the last holiday break.

"How is it?" I asked.

"I'm bunking with another orderly—he's friendly enough. The first thing I did was to look up that salesman, Chan Yew Cheung. His aunt said he'd been close to a nurse at the hospital, so I tried to find out if he'd been a patient. Unfortunately, the patient registrations are locked up in the records department. But I lucked into something else."

"What? The nurse who gave it to him?" Knowing Shin, that would be a fairly easy job.

"No, the pathology department. It's run by a doctor named Rawlings. They're fixing up that part of the hospital, and there are boxes of records and specimens to move. He asked me to work overtime and finish it this weekend. It's just donkey work, but I jumped at it. Also, he said to get some help. I said I knew someone who'd do it for cheap."

"Is that me?" I asked indignantly.

"Don't you need a part-time job?"

For a heart-sinking moment, I thought he must have found out about everything—my mother's debts, my dance-hall work—but he was only joking.

It wasn't as though I didn't trust him; I knew he had a soft spot for my mother. But I was sure, down to my very bones, that getting Shin involved would be trouble. One of these days, either he or my stepfather would kill the other. It had very nearly happened a couple of years ago.

THAT EVENING, I'D BEEN OVER AT A FRIEND'S PLACE FOR DINNER. On my return, I was surprised to find all the neighbors standing in the street in front of the shophouse. The fading light dyed everything in cold blue shadows. Not a time to be out chitchatting, as I noted in alarm. Someone was saying that they ought to call the police but my mother was begging them not to. It was just a family disagreement, she said, and it wouldn't happen again.

I rushed over, anxiously scanning her for telltale signs of injury. But she seemed unhurt and in fact, when I slipped into the shophouse, it was my stepfather who was holding a bloody towel to his face. I'd never seen him with any kind of wound and, for a treacherous instant, was pleased to see a mark on him, even if it was just a bloody nose.

The interior of the shophouse was completely silent. That frightened me more than anything. "Where's Shin?" I said, though it took all my nerve to speak to my stepfather. He said nothing, only glared in silence.

Dropping my schoolbag, I ran through the house. Past the hanging pendulum scales, past the silent piles of raked tin ore. My breath came in short gasps; my side hurt. I wanted to call out to Shin but my mouth was sealed with terror. If he didn't answer, then he must be severely injured. Or dead. My stepfather's beatings had tapered off over the years: Shin had learned to watch the mood, to be careful what he said and did. Why, only a few weeks previously my mother had said she was glad that Shin had grown up so well, which was her way of saying he wasn't getting into trouble with his father, but I'd had my doubts. I never trusted that man.

I ran through the long, long house. It was dark, and no one had lit any lamps. I could barely see into some of the corners; the shadows were so thick that they gathered like soot, soft and blurry. Or perhaps it was the tears in my eyes. There was no sign of Shin. Gasping, I took the stairs two at a time, flinging the bedroom doors open though I didn't really believe he was upstairs. Not if he was hurt. Or maybe he really was dead. And still in the front room, my stepfather sat like a gargoyle, alone.

I ran to the back again. All the way to the kitchen, searching. We'd had favorite hiding spaces to play in—the cupboard under the stairs, the narrow space between the water jars—but Shin was too big now to fit in most of them. At last I went through the kitchen again into the last court-yard, the one with the high wall that led to the back alley. And there I found him, huddled behind the chicken coop.

I could barely make out his shape in the dim blue twilight, propped up against the back wall. His legs, so much longer than when we were children, stuck out in front as though he were exhausted.

"Shin!" I hadn't noticed the tears running down my face until they dripped off my chin.

"Go away." His voice was hoarse.

"Are you hurt?" I tried to help him up, but he shook me off.

"Don't touch my arm. I think it's broken."

"I'll get a doctor."

I jumped up but he grabbed my ankle with his good hand. "Don't!"

There was a crack in his voice, something so sad and despairing that it made me stop. I put my arms around him then, as though he was a child again. His shoulders heaved with harsh gasps as I cradled him. He buried his face in my neck. A shudder ran through him. His hair was matted and sticky, with sweat I hoped and not blood. *Please, no blood.*

I hadn't seen Shin cry for years. We clung to each other behind the chicken coop for a long time. It smelled pungent, and there were bits of straw and other nameless soft unpleasant things on the ground, but I couldn't see them and maybe it didn't matter in the dark. Twice I heard my mother come looking for us. The second time I called to her softly and said that Shin was all right, just to leave him alone for a bit. When she'd gone, he pulled himself away.

"I'll kill him," he said quietly.

"Don't! You'll go to prison."

"Who cares?"

"Well, I do!" Part of me believed Shin was quite capable of killing his father in a fight. He was already taller than him; it was surprising that he seemed to have had the worst of it today. Whatever had made Shin hold back, I was grateful. Because one day, just like today, I'd come home and one of them would be dead. *But please, let it not be Shin.* Though the alternative was just as bad. Shin would be locked up forever. Or hanged.

"Stop crying," he said at last. "I won't, all right?"

"Promise me."

He sighed. "I promise. Don't lean on my arm. It hurts."

I got up. Shin slowly untangled himself from behind the coop and crawled out as well. My eyes had adjusted to the dimness but it was still hard to see. Everything looked strange and wrong, as though the kitchen courtyard was an entirely new country. Shin's left arm hung at an odd angle.

"Told you. It's broken." He sounded so matter-of-fact that I felt like crying again.

"What happened?"

"He took a stick to me. The carrying pole."

The carrying pole was used for heavy loads. Strong and heavy, and flattened to balance on one shoulder, it was a deadly weapon when rival Chinese clans fought gang wars. If my stepfather had really hit Shin with it, he must have lost his mind. He could have maimed him. I was so furious that I wanted to scream, report him to the police. I wished that all the doors and windows would burst open and the roof fly off, so that the neighbors would see exactly what happened in our house.

"You said not to kill anyone," said Shin, reading my expression,

"They don't hang girls," I said, though I wasn't really sure. Perhaps they did. Or maybe they drowned them, like witches. I didn't care. I was so angry that my hands trembled. And yet, I was terrified. I hadn't dared to raise my voice to my stepfather, even when I was searching the house so desperately.

"What happened? Why did he do it?"

But Shin only shook his head.

I NEVER DID FIND OUT WHAT HAPPENED THAT NIGHT. THE MORE I asked, the more Shin retreated into silence. My mother was no help, either.

She said they'd already been fighting when she came home and it was best forgotten.

Shin stayed home from school for a week to hide the bruises, telling the doctor who splinted his broken arm that he'd fallen down the stairs. My stepfather also had injuries. Besides the bloody nose, he had a twisted elbow and, my mother suspected, a cracked rib though he too said nothing. I think in his own way he was sorry. He probably realized he'd gone too far, but I wouldn't forgive him. I would never forgive him.

In fact, the thought crossed my mind about actually poisoning him. I even went so far as to check out all the detective novels I could find in our school library. It was no good though. They only let you take two books out at a time, and besides, where on earth was I going to find a trained snake, as in *The Adventure of the Speckled Band*? Anyway, if my stepfather were poisoned, the most likely suspect would be my mother.

Strangely, after that incident Shin and my stepfather came to some understanding that I wasn't privy to. They left each other alone. I thought at first my stepfather was feeling guilty about the whole affair and perhaps he was, but I noticed that he gave Shin more leeway. Shin, too, started making a noticeable effort at school. His grades had always been good but now he studied as though he was possessed, surpassing me. He rarely had time for me anymore; it was around then that the two of us began to drift apart.

13

THEY'VE FOUND THE HEAD. IT'S THE BIGGEST NEWS AT THE BATU Gajah District Hospital on Monday morning, as Leslie, the fresh-faced doctor who's the closest thing to a peer that William has here, informs him.

William's initial horror at Ambika's death has been subsumed by guilt and fear. The woman he embraced so many times is now no more than a piece of meat, discarded by a carnivore under a bush. Over and over, he's questioned whether not identifying her was the right thing. His conscience whispers he's a coward, an assessment that he's forced to agree with.

He wonders if anyone is waiting anxiously for her to come home. Her husband, a habitual drunkard, may not miss her, but perhaps there are children, though she's never mentioned any. And then there's the nagging matter of the Chinese salesman who stumbled upon him and Ambika in the rubber estate. What bad luck, to have one of his own patients discover them. He inhales sharply. As long as William isn't the one to identify the body, nobody will make the connection between them.

"I think her name was Amber-something," says Leslie. He has red hair, bleached to straw by the fierce tropical sun, and so many freckles that his face is a mess of dots. But William stares at him with intense relief, as though Leslie is the most beautiful person he's seen all day. *Thank God. Thank you, thank you.* William's own verification is no longer needed. How fortunate that they found her head, otherwise who knows how long the torso would have remained unclaimed in the mortuary?

"Apparently there's something odd about the body."

Alarmed, William says, "Did Rawlings do the postmortem?"

"He did. And then when they found the head on Sunday he had to do it all over again."

"So what does he think?"

Leslie glances up, "Why don't you ask him yourself?"

Turning, William spots the stooped, familiar figure of Rawlings, the pathologist. Rawlings is enormously tall and storklike, and to make up for this, he lowers his head on its skinny neck when speaking.

William hurries after him, despite Leslie's plaintive cry of "We need to talk about the party at your place!"

"Later," says William. He's completely forgotten about the monthly party, a much anticipated social event where people dine on canned food sent from Europe—peas, lobster, tongue—drink too much, and congratulate each other on having a wonderful time out in the Colonies. It's his turn to host, and he must remind Ah Long to lay in extra wine and spirits and discuss the menu. William would rather eat fresh local food than something that has died and been sealed in a can, like a metal coffin. He shudders at the thought and quickens his pace to catch up with Rawlings.

The hospital cafeteria is an open, airy space with a thatched roof and a poured concrete floor. The daily menu includes both Western and local food. Rawlings stands in line at the counter and demands a *kopi-o*, strong black coffee with sugar, and a slice of papaya in his deep bass. Queuing behind him, William asks for the same.

"I heard you've identified the body," William says as they sit down. There's no need to say which one; there aren't many unknown corpses in Batu Gajah.

"You were first on the scene, weren't you?" says Rawlings. Taking out a penknife, he slides the slice of papaya neatly off its skin. Rawlings is a vegetarian, and William can't blame him. He'd become one too if he had to spend his days examining corpses.

"Well, the police were there first," says William. "Looked like a tiger or a leopard got her. What did you think?"

Rawlings squeezes half a lime over his papaya, and William does, too. He's read somewhere that if you mimic people, they're more likely to open up to you.

"I saw your notes," Rawlings wipes his mouth. "And initially, I was inclined to agree with you. From the marks on the body, I'd say it was a tiger. The puncture wounds are too far apart for a leopard's jaws."

"Why do you say 'initially'?"

"Tell me, was there a lot of blood at the scene?"

William casts his mind back to that clearing between the rubber trees. The thick, rustling layer of dried leaves on the ground, the clove scent of the Malay constable's cigarette. The piece of flesh that was once an attractive woman.

"No. I assumed she was killed somewhere else."

"The skin at the edges of the puncture wounds had no indication of hemorrhage or marginal erythema. No arterial bleeding, either, not even where the spine was snapped and the body separated."

"No bleeding," says William slowly. "So she was already dead before the animal got her."

"Yes. Tigers are scavengers, too. When we found the head, it raised further questions."

"What do you mean?"

"They did a search for the other body parts in a half-mile radius. The inspector used dogs and they found the head and one leg. That's not unusual in large animal kills, by the way."

William fights to keep his composure, fixing his eyes on a spot behind Rawlings's left ear.

Rawlings says, "The head was very interesting though. Do you want to see it?" He half rises, but William raises a hand.

"Not before lunch, thanks."

"It was almost untouched. In fact, the whole body gave me the same impression: that the animal was starting its routine—that is, removing limbs, disemboweling the torso—and just stopped."

William covers his mouth. The ripe orange papaya flesh that yields under his spoon is so fleshy and sensual that vomit rises. He thinks about Ambika's generous smile, her smooth shoulders sliding under his hands and then it all dissolves into a mask of blood and yellow fluids. He wants to cry.

"Are you all right?" Rawlings stares at him, hooded eyes narrowed in concern.

"Stomach problems," William lies.

Rawlings continues, "Without the dogs, we'd never have found the head. What's interesting is that it looked like there were traces of vomit in the mouth."

"So what does that mean?"

Rawlings steeples his fingers. "The first possibility is that the poor woman was killed by a tiger, perhaps by mauling the throat or suffocation. It's hard to say because we don't have a neck anymore. But then the tiger left its kill and returned much later—maybe a day or so—for the rest of the postmortem injuries. What kind of animal does that?"

"Perhaps it was disturbed," says William. There's a sick tightening in his gut; a bad feeling that he's going to hear something that he'll regret.

"Very few things will disturb a tiger feeding except for humans or another tiger, which would have then eaten the kill. And there haven't been any reports of people driving away a tiger. We could have waited to see if the animal came back."

"She was *human*. A person. We couldn't leave her out as bait!" Without realizing it, William has raised his voice and a few heads turn.

Rawlings looks at him with surprise. "It's not like it hasn't been done before. There were several cases in India when man-eaters were ambushed when they returned to the corpse."

William has often been accused of being cold and unfeeling, but he thinks that compared to Rawlings, he's a mess of emotions. If he isn't careful, people will be suspicious. Swallowing hard, he looks down into his coffee cup.

"In any case, I'm not keen on that theory. It's much more likely that she died out in the rubber estate and was scavenged by a tiger. Death could be due to natural causes. Another possibility is someone killed her."

"It's a long shot to murder," says William in dismay. "She could have been bitten by a snake. Or any other number of things."

Rawlings waves his hand dismissively, then leans forward. "You know what I think?"

"What?"

But Rawlings changes his mind, sitting back. "I can't confirm it yet. But I'm writing it down as a suspicious death. This will go to the coroner's court."

This isn't news that William wants to hear—far better if Ambika were simply the unfortunate victim of a tiger. He recalls how she'd recently asked for more money and wonders if Ambika had other lovers. His chest constricts. If that's the case, they'll start looking for everyone associated with her.

"One way or another," says Rawlings, "the tiger in this case behaved very strangely. The locals will be full of gossip that it's a ghost tiger or something foolish like that."

"Keramat," William says automatically. "A sacred beast."

Rawlings snorts. "Sacred beast! Exactly."

William stares across the room, thoughts unspooling like loose threads. Besides the salesman, who else has seen him with Ambika?

He needs to be careful.

REN IS MAKING AN OMELET. IT'S A TRICKY, DELICATE TASK, REQUIRING patience over a charcoal fire. Since finding the body over the weekend, William has been nauseated and out of sorts. He can't stomach rich food like chicken in coconut gravy or fried pork chops. Returning early today, he requested an omelet and Ren volunteered to cook it.

Omelets were a favorite of Dr. MacFarlane's and Auntie Kwan taught him how to make them fluffy and meltingly soft. Ren tips the omelet carefully onto a plate; the secret is to take the eggs off the heat before they're completely set. Looking up, Ren breaks into a smile and amazingly, so does Ah Long.

"You can serve it yourself," he says.

Ah Long sprinkles finely chopped green onions on top and fans out a few tomato slices on the side. Setting it on a tray with a starched white napkin, Ren trots off with it. All the way down the long, polished wooden hallway and upstairs, where he knocks at the master's bedchamber.

Like all the other rooms in the house, the airy, high-ceilinged room is painted white and is quite bare except for the four-poster bed in the center, hung with mosquito nets. The slanting afternoon sun, green and gold through the treetops, gives Ren a sudden feeling of déjà vu. It's just like the old doctor's room, back in Kamunting. Except it's not Dr. MacFarlane sitting at a table by the window, but William, who is writing a letter.

"Thank you," he says, with a guilty start as Ren sets the tray down.

"Did they find the tiger yet?" Ren asks.

"Not yet. It may be miles away by now." William takes a bite. "Who made this?"

The worried look returns to Ren's face. "I did, *Tuan*."

"It's very good. I'd like you to make all my omelets from now on."

"Yes, *Tuan*." Emboldened by this, Ren asks, "May I have permission to take leave soon?"

"Where do you want to go?"

"Back to Kamunting. Just for a few days."

William considers this. Ren has been working here for only a short while. By rights, he hasn't accumulated enough leave to go anywhere, but he looks so hopeful. "To see your old friends?"

"Yes." Ren hesitates. "And to pay my respects to Dr. MacFarlane's grave. I'd like to go before the mourning period is over in twenty days."

"Of course." William's expression softens. "You may take three days off if you like. Check with Ah Long about the dates—there'll be a dinner party here. You'd better wait until afterwards. Do you need train fare?"

Ren looks confused at this offer. William sighs. "I mean, I'll pay for your trip. Put some flowers on poor MacFarlane's grave for me."

DISMISSED, REN WALKS BACK TO THE KITCHEN. SINCE THE GRUE-some discovery of the body, Ren has frantically stepped up his search for the finger. He has now explored every room and opened every drawer in the house. Sometimes he thinks that Ah Long suspects him, as more than once, the cook surprised him with his silent approach. He's like an old, grizzled cat, a resemblance even more pronounced when Ah Long sits on the kitchen steps, slitting his eyes against the sun. Still, Ah Long hasn't said anything.

Ren has the uneasy feeling that the finger isn't in this house. Has never been, perhaps. There's no way to explain it, just a tingling twitch of cat whiskers. When Yi was alive, he often felt this sixth sense. People said it was magic, but Ren knows it's because they were a matched pair. Chinese say that good things come in pairs, such as the character for double happiness, cut out of red paper and pasted on doors for weddings, and the two stone lions that guard temples. As children, Ren and Yi were perfect doubles of one another. Seeing them, people would break into smiles of delight. Twins, and boys—how fortunate! But all this came to an end when Yi died. If a chopstick breaks, the other is discarded. After all, half of a broken pair is one: the unlucky number of loneliness.

Dr. MacFarlane once explained radio signals to him, saying they needed both a transmitter and a receiver to work. Ren immediately understood what he meant. He and Yi always knew where the other was, so much so that the matron at the orphanage would send one boy on an errand and keep the other with her. At any delay, she'd ask the remaining twin how far away his brother was. It was a useful skill, though no more marvelous than Pak Idris, the blind Malay fisherman by the Perak River who caught fish by hearing them underwater.

"What is it like?" Ren had asked.

"Like pebbles dropping," he'd said. "Like a mirror, in which the fish are reflected."

A mirror full of fish. Over the years, Ren has often thought about that phrase. What were the fish like to Pak Idris, who couldn't see them? Were they like stars, moving in a dark firmament, or a field of flowers blowing in the wind? With Yi's death, Ren has lost his beacon in this world. He no longer has a good sense for distances, nor does he know what's happening in a different location. Instead, his ability has dwindled so that he can only sense imminent events, like the crack of a branch that collapses just as Ren leaps out of the way. There have been many near accidents. Too many, perhaps.

Sometimes Ren thinks that he hasn't lost his long-range ability at all. The signal is faint simply because Yi is so very far away. But where that is, he can't say. He's crossed over to another country, the land of the dead. In Ren's search for the missing finger, his invisible cat whiskers have twitched only once in this house—at the tiger-skin rug in the study. But that's not surprising, given the old doctor's obsession with tigers and which, as Ren feared, William seems to share to some extent. Hurrying down the hallway, it occurs to Ren that there's one more place to search: the Batu Gajah District Hospital. The place where William has an office.

Time is running out: there are only twenty days left before Dr. Mac-Farlane's forty-nine days of the soul are over. If by then he can't find the finger, he'll have failed. How will his old master rest? Ren remembers Dr. MacFarlane's last days, the shivering fevers. And then the dreams, the waking nightmares in which the old man would cry for mercy, or crawl slavering on all fours. If Auntie Kwan had still been with them, she would have taken charge, but in the end there was only Ren.

A gust of wind shivers through the house, banging all the doors simultaneously. To Ren, peering out of the window at the top of the stairs, the trees are a waving green ocean surrounding the bungalow. It's a ship in a storm, and Ren is the cabin boy peeking out of a porthole. Clutching the windowsill like a life buoy, Ren wonders what secrets lurk in the jungle surrounding them, and if his old master is in fact doomed to roam this vast green expanse forever, trapped in the form of a tiger.

14

A SHRILL WHISTLE SOUNDED. UP AND DOWN THE TRACK, DOORS began closing as steam billowed over the platform. It was so exciting that I glanced at Shin, laughing. He raised his eyebrows and grinned back. There was a jerk, then a bigger jolt as the train pulled slowly out of Ipoh Station. The platform slid away. People waved at departing passengers and I couldn't resist waving back.

Shin rolled his eyes. "You don't even know them."

"Why not?" I said defensively. "The children like it."

I remembered my dream of the little boy at the train station. That had seemed so real, though it had been nowhere near as grand as Ipoh's palatial white railway station, now rapidly receding behind us.

The trip to Batu Gajah was fifteen miles or about twenty-five minutes, Shin told me. Sometimes though there were wild elephants on the track, or *seladang*, the huge jungle oxen said to stand six feet at the shoulder. Cool air rushed in from the open window, and I closed my eyes blissfully.

"That's a yes, then?"

Shin's glance burned through my lashes, making me feel self-conscious. Had he noticed the makeup I'd applied to hide my black eye? Well, it didn't matter if my hair looked like a bird's nest. It was only Shin.

"Yes to what?"

"To cleaning out the pathology storeroom this weekend."

I opened my eyes. "As long as I get paid, too. But what makes you think we'll find anything?"

"That finger definitely came from the hospital," said Shin, "If you unscrew the bottle cap, it has the same mark as the other specimens in the hospital pathology lab. We should look through the records and see if there's anything about amputated fingers."

"Where's the finger?"

In answer, he patted his pocket. The gesture reminded me of the salesman, and my spirits sank. That shadow again, staining the bright day. Why was Shin so enthusiastic about tracking down its owner, anyway? Perhaps we could just quietly replace the finger in the hospital. It occurred to me that I should also do some research for myself—tour the hospital, talk to the staff. I didn't want to admit it to Shin, but if I couldn't go to medical school, maybe I could become a nurse or a clerk. Anything was better than my current dismal prospects.

"You're plotting something, aren't you?" Shin said with a snort. "I can tell—you're so predictable."

"Nobody else says that," I said crossly, thinking of the starry-eyed schoolboys and old men who lined up to dance with me. Nirman Singh had claimed that I was "shrouded in fateful mystery," though I was fairly certain he was talking about the real Louise Brooks and not me—and also that he was all of fifteen years old and shouldn't be spending his pocket money at a dance hall.

"Whom have you been keeping company with?"

I'd forgotten how sharp Shin was; it was the flip side of being on good terms with him again.

"No one."

Shin was watching me with a thoughtful expression. "Do you like boarding at Mrs. Tham's?"

"Well, you've seen what she's like," I said. "But it's not that bad."

"How much does she pay you?"

"She doesn't pay me anything—I have to pay her. For my apprenticeship, you know."

A muscle twitched in his cheek. "That's ridiculous. You're working there for free."

"Actually she's supposed to pay me a little for helping out, but there's also my room and board and the teaching fees, so it's all a wash."

"And you're happy with it?"

I debated telling him that of course I wasn't happy. Two years ago I'd have said so with no reservations, but now the thought rolled around the tip of my tongue, like a glass marble that would fall out and shatter on the ground. Why ruin the first nice day we'd had in a long time? So I said nothing.

THE RAILWAY STATION AT BATU GAJAH WAS MODEST: A SIMPLE rectangle with a thatched *attap* roof and a few wooden benches that faced the tracks on both sides. I gazed at it with uneasy déjà vu. Surely, I'd been sitting on one of these benches just last night in my dream. There was no river in sight, though according to the elderly Malay gentleman across the aisle, the railway line actually did cross the Kinta River.

"But you won't see it until you pass this station." He himself was going south to Lumut.

"We're getting off here," I said regretfully.

"Goodbye," said the old man. And then to Shin, "Your wife is beautiful. Very modern and stylish."

"We're siblings!" I said hastily.

Shin was quiet as we got off the train. It was the second time that someone had mistaken us, and I was afraid he'd found it irritating.

"Of course I'm annoyed," he said. "Who wants to be related to you?"

Relieved, I burst out laughing. Shin rolled his eyes. "You're supposed to get offended, like other girls. Not snort like that."

I fell silent. One of the reasons I was popular at the May Flower was because I wasn't afraid of joking around with the customers, but was that how decent young women behaved? Ming's fiancée had been so soft-spoken, so genteel—the sort of girl who wouldn't be caught making stupid jokes by the roadside.

The walk to the Batu Gajah District Hospital was uphill to the European quarter of Changkat. Oleander shrubs with their pink and white fluffy blooms and pointed oval leaves were everywhere, as were fragrant frangipani trees, the graveyard flower of the Malays. The English were mad about gardening—we all knew that from our history books—and had carried their passion to every corner of the Empire.

By the time we arrived at the hospital, it was almost eleven o'clock in the morning and quite hot. The hospital was a series of tropical white and black Tudor-style wooden buildings connected by shady verandas and clipped grass lawns. Glancing up, I noticed that the terra-cotta tiles on the roofed walkways had come all the way from France and were stamped underneath with the name of their maker: SACCOMAN FRÈRES, ST. HENRI MARSEILLE.

Shin led me past the administrative offices to the back of one of the outbuildings. Taking out a key, he unlocked a door. "Here we go. We'll have to get this into some sort of order."

It was a large room, airy and high-ceilinged. Tall windows let in the light from behind stacks of boxes and filing cabinets. Specimen jars were jammed next to cartons overflowing with papers, while five-gallon glass carboys stood on the floor amid a litter of old medical journals. Staring at this mountain, I was no longer surprised that Dr. Rawlings, whoever he was, had suggested that Shin commandeer some extra help.

"Are we supposed to do all of this today?"

"Well, it's a good chance to check if they have any missing fingers," said Shin. "They wanted it moved, and I've done most of that. We just need to organize the specimens. Want to have lunch first?"

I glanced at the jars of gruesome-looking specimens. Bits of entrails floated in murky baths, together with bottles of rattling vertebrae.

"No," I said. "Let's start now."

What was the purpose of this collection anyway? Shin said he'd no idea. Despite doing all the heavy lifting, he was in a good mood. I could tell from the way he whistled in the corridor as he trundled boxes over. We got along best when there was a job to be done, just as we'd done the housework swiftly and efficiently when we were younger. If we were both hired as janitors, I thought, there would be no disagreements between us.

MY MOTHER WAS AN EXEMPLARY HOUSEWIFE; ON THIS, MY STEPFA-ther could never fault her. She was obsessively clean, taking the wooden bedframes outside to pour boiling water over every cranny, so that we never had bedbugs.

When we first moved to the shophouse, she was reluctant to ask Shin to do housework. He was a boy after all, though he was willing enough. She poured out her affection on us, softhearted to the point of foolishness even. Stray dogs and beggars made a beeline for her, and more than once she gave away our dinner and had to beg us not to tell my stepfather. I'd hold out, bargaining for something better, but Shin always capitulated. I could read him easily; the quick nod, the hopeful expression. He was hungry for affection.

I think my mother would have liked more children. Certainly, my stepfather was disappointed in that. Several times the local midwife was called in because my mother had miscarried. But no one would ever tell me exactly what had happened or why.

The matchmaker had made such a fuss about how Shin and I were destined to be siblings, how we were practically twins since we were born on the same day and were named after two of the five Confucian Virtues, that I felt sure that the other three children—Ren, Yi, and Li to give them their rightful names—must be waiting impatiently to be born. I pictured them jostling each other in the dark, waiting to be let out into the world. But they never came. And each bloody episode increased my fear that they would steal my mother away with them.

I'd told Shin about this when we were talking quietly one night. He was lying on the floor in his room and I was sitting in the narrow corridor, the open doorway between us. This was just in case my stepfather should suddenly emerge from his room. We must have been about thirteen at the time, and he'd become increasingly strict. I could no longer set foot in Shin's room, and he, of course, was never allowed in mine.

The moon was very bright that night, a sharp slice of white. It was too hot to be in bed and the only relief was the cool wooden floor planks.

"Do you think they'll have more children?" I asked.

"No. It's harder when you get older." From time to time, Shin would display a kind of calm rationality that I envied.

"But I'm afraid."

Shin rolled over and propped himself up on his elbows. "Of what?"

I told him my fear of losing my mother and how I couldn't help thinking there should be three more of us, like the matchmaker had said.

He was quiet for a while. "That's rubbish."

"Why?" I said, stung. "Is it any more rubbish than what you said about the *mo* and dream-eaters?"

Immediately, I was sorry for my words, since I knew how Shin treasured that scrap of paper from his own mother. But he only said, "I haven't had bad dreams in a long time. I don't think I dream at all in fact. Besides, all this talk about three more siblings is stupid. Why should there be any more?"

"Because there are only two of us right now."

Shin sat up abruptly. "Don't count me in. I'm not really your brother, you know."

Climbing into his bed, he turned his back on me. Rejected, I retreated to my own room. It worried me sometimes that perhaps he was just putting up with me. That he'd wanted a different kind of sister, not someone who argued with him all the time and outscored him on tests. Whenever I felt bad, I thought about numbers. In Cantonese, two was a good number because it made a pair. Three was also good because it was a homophone for *sang*, or life. Four, of course, was bad because it sounded like death. Five was good again because it made a complete set, not just of the Confucian Virtues, but also for the elements of wood, fire, water, metal, and earth. In any case, it didn't matter how prickly Shin was. Whether he liked it or not, he was still the only brother I had.

THE DOOR OF THE PATHOLOGY STOREROOM OPENED ABRUPTLY. Thinking it was Shin back with another load, I said without turning round, "Don't put it there. Put it on the other side."

Silence. An odd tingling alerted me that something was wrong. I turned to see a stranger in the doorway. A foreigner. Tall and raw-boned, he wore glasses. The rest—pale face, pale hair, pale arms burned unevenly by the sun—looked like all the other Europeans to me.

"I'm looking for Dr. Rawlings."

Shin had said that Rawlings was the resident pathologist, but I'd no idea whether he was here on a quiet Saturday or not. The man gave me a sharp look. His colorless eyes pierced like needles behind the glass lenses. I feared they would soon see that I wasn't hospital staff at all.

"If he comes back, please tell him that I came by. My name's William Acton."

15

REN GETS HIS CHANCE TO LOOK FOR THE FINGER AT SATURDAY lunchtime, when William announces that he's going into town and will drop by the hospital. Ah Long immediately asks if he will pick up supplies: tinned goods, washing powder, and brown shoe polish.

Glancing at Ren, who's holding the car door open, William says, "Hop in. You can take a list to the store, can't you?"

Ren's eyes widen at this unexpected opportunity. William shouts over his shoulder at Ah Long. "I'm taking the boy. Anything else you need?"

There's a brief scramble as lists are made. Ah Long presses a cent into Ren's hand. "Buy something for yourself," he says gruffly. "Sometimes he drinks at the Club. If it gets late, stay with the car. He'll come home by morning one way or the other." His wiry figure, stiffly disapproving, waits on the gravel driveway.

"*Selamat jalan,*" he says to William. Good travels.

Harun, the Malay driver, is a plump, comfortable-looking man with three children of his own, and he smiles as Ren climbs excitedly into the front passenger seat, clutching a rattan market basket lined with old newspaper in case of spills. William sits in the back. Ren keeps quiet though he'd love to ask Harun about the car. There's an intimidating array of switches and dials on the Austin's dashboard, and Ren watches carefully as Harun changes gears.

"Swing by the hospital first," says William. "I have to drop some paperwork off."

The hospital. Ren squeezes the basket handle.

As they motor closer to town, the trim lawns and gravel drives of other bungalows come into view. Ren knows a few of the houses now, but they are so far apart, so secluded by the lush jungle, that he never hears the neighbors. Ren can tell which houses have European wives: they're planted with neat beds of cannas and ginger flowers and surrounded by hibiscus and oleander shrubs. There are oleanders behind William's house, too, but Ah Long always tells the gardener to cut them back. The soft twigs ooze a milky sap that will blind you, he says darkly, and a decoction of leaves will poison stray dogs.

Rounding a bend, the breeze through the open windows whips a sheet of crumpled newspaper out of Ren's basket, into the backseat where William catches it deftly in one hand.

"Sorry, *Tuan!*" Ren glances back, but his master, staring at the paper, lets out a sharp exclamation.

"Is this last week's paper?"

Guiltily, Ren nods. Are they not allowed to use it? There's an odd expression on William's face. The sheet of newspaper that's transfixed him is the obituary section, with rows of black-and-white photographs. Ren says, "Did someone you know die?"

William bites his lip. "A patient of mine."

"Was he an old man?"

"No, quite a young one. Poor fellow."

After a long moment, William passes the crumpled paper back to Ren who stuffs it back in the basket, but not before glancing curiously at the page. The only listing for a young man is a Mr. Chan Yew Cheung, salesman. Twenty-eight years old.

William closes his eyes, fingers loosely knotted in his lap. Long, white fingers capable of stitching up a wound or amputating a limb. He hums lightly. Ren wonders why his master looks relieved, even happy.

As the car turns in at the hospital, Ren feels an electric thrill as though a faint, far-off radio signal is connecting. It shivers through his body the same way that he and Yi used to connect. The finger is here. He's suddenly sure of it. William picks up a leather briefcase and gets out. Quickly, Ren jumps out, too.

"May I carry your bag, *Tuan?*"

William stops to look at him. "Do you want to see the hospital?"

There are two sections, explains William. This part is the district hospital for locals, while the European wing exclusively for foreigners lies across the street. William nods at the receptionist. Doors open, people smile. Trailing in William's wake, Ren wonders whether all Europeans are treated like this or perhaps it's the combination of being a surgeon as well.

There's a strict medical hierarchy, Dr. MacFarlane used to joke, with general practitioners like himself at the bottom of the heap. But Dr. Mac-Farlane was very skilled, Ren thinks. He treated patients that everyone else had given up as hopeless, like the *orang asli* hunter who came in with an infected arm and the Chinese storekeeper's baby with convulsions. He doctored them all, often with surprising results.

"I'm going to stop by the wards, since I'm here," William says. The long corridors, tiled in a checkerboard of brown and cream, smell like disinfectant. "Do you want to see your patient?"

Ren is confused. What patient?

"The woman whose leg you treated. It just so happens that she came in again."

Of course Ren wants to see her, though he feels suddenly shy. The ward is empty except for an old man asleep with his mouth open, and the young woman who's sitting up in the next bed. Ren is surprised at her appearance. She looks nothing like she did lying in a wheelbarrow with her leg dripping blood all over the driveway. Now, her honey-colored skin is fresh and her hair neatly braided. She has a dimpled face that's exactly heart-shaped, and when William asks to see her leg, she colors.

"This is Ren," he says. "The person who treated you at my house."

Ren notices that he doesn't say "my houseboy" or "my servant" and feels obscurely proud.

"So young!" she says. Her name, according to the patient manifest, is Nandani Wijedasa, and she's eighteen years old, unmarried. Her father is a clerk at the rubber estate near their house, and she was readmitted this morning for fever and pain in the leg.

William gently pulls up the loose hospital-issue pajamas with a reassuring smile. The wound is smaller than Ren remembered, though still a shocking gash on the back of her smooth calf. Sutured with black thread, it looks tender and puffy.

"We'll need to open it up again and irrigate it, maybe debride the tissue and then reclose it. When you go home, keep a gauze pad soaked in carbolic on it to prevent infection. You must keep the wound clean, otherwise you might get blood poisoning. Do you understand?"

He looks directly at her and a spark jumps between them. Ren's cat sense hasn't been this strong since Yi's death. What's the meaning of this? But he knows, without even raising his head, that something is happening between William and the young woman Nandani. Some kind of attraction that makes the doctor linger as Nandani bats her long curling eyelashes.

Ren isn't the only person to think so. A foreign lady has come in, pushing a trolley with novels and back issues of *Punch* and *The Lady* for patients to read. Her eyes, an astonishing electric blue, fix on William's back.

"William—what brings you in today?"

Turning, William says, "Hello, Lydia."

Sunlight streaming into the ward picks out the gold in her pretty curls, and Ren wonders whether her hair is fluffy all the time or if it has to be steamed and pressed, like a sponge cake.

"One of your patients?" Lydia gives the Sinhalese girl on the bed a quick stare.

"Not mine." He glances at Ren, who gazes shyly at the crack in the floorboards next to Nandani's bed.

Drawing William aside, Lydia threads her arm through his. "Leslie said you're hosting the next get-together for the younger doctors."

"It's just a group of bachelors talking shop. Not very interesting, I'm afraid." He turns up the charm.

Lydia looks both hopeful and plaintive. "Can I come?"

"Only if you don't mind hearing about tropical diseases."

"Not at all! I want to help as much as possible—sometimes people don't know what's best for them."

While they talk, Nandani touches Ren's sleeve. "Thank you." Her smile is warm and Ren is very glad that she's alive and not lying dead in a wheelbarrow full of blood. "Are you studying to be a doctor?"

"I'd like to."

"You will be a good doctor." Her eyes drift to William. "Is your master kind to you?"

Ren realizes, with a feeling of surprise, that yes, William has been good to him.

"He's nice," she says. There it is again, that invisible spark between her and William. It flies out with a tiny sizzle, so that Ren half expects to see it flare in the air.

William turns round to Nandani again. "Where do you live?" he asks. Shyly, she tells him her address.

He writes it down in the little notebook he carries in his breast pocket. "You're quite close to my place. If you stop by, I'll look at your leg again next week. No need to come to the hospital."

Behind William, Lydia sorts her book trolley industriously.

Ren can't sense anything from her at all. Perhaps because she's an unknown quantity—a foreigner and a lady—and he has almost no experience with this combination. She and William make a well-matched pair. They're both so tall, with light eyes and skin mottled from the fierce sun, not smooth and evenly colored like Nandani's. Ren feels sorry for the foreign lady; she's trying so hard. Why doesn't William like her?

DONE WITH THE WARDS, REN TROTS ALONG NEXT TO WILLIAM. He's giddy with his cat sense, that long-lost sensation of feeling the invisible, as though he's regained a limb or an extra set of eyes and ears. What is it about the hospital that's so special? William says he'll stop by pathology to see his colleague Dr. Rawlings. He has a question for him about an autopsy report. Ren knows that pathology means organs and bits of dead people and animals, a good sign that it's where the finger is. Buzzing with excitement, he's confident that even with his eyes closed, he'll finally be able to locate it.

As they navigate the covered walkways, lined with beds of day lilies on one side, Ren discovers he can read William now in a way he never could before. William's interest is like a taut string. It snaps around, but mostly it's drawn to women. Nurses passing, a lady visitor bending over a bed. Certainly, William doesn't pay attention to the things that Ren notices, like the spider behind the door, or the perfectly round pebble under the lilies that Ren would like to put in his pocket but doesn't dare to because it's probably hospital property.

As they draw nearer the pathology department, the twitch of invisible filaments grows so strong that Ren is tense with excitement. It's never been like this before, not even with Yi. They turn a corner. William pats his breast pocket, then rummages in his trousers with annoyance. "Ren, go back and fetch my fountain pen. The ward sister will have it."

With a wrench, Ren watches as William crosses to another building, opens the door, and goes in. Something in that room is calling Ren, drawing him, even at fifty feet, like a magnet. He must enter that room.

But retrieving William's fountain pen is an order he can't disobey. The name of the pen, William has explained, is that of the highest mountain in Europe, Mont Blanc. The white, rounded star on the pen represents the snow-covered peak, and it has an engraved nib made out of real gold. It's the pen he uses to write letters every day. If he doesn't find it, William will be very unhappy.

Rushing back, Ren gets confused and takes a wrong turn. It's hard to filter out the flood of signals that assail him. *Like a mirror full of fish,* he recalls the blind fisherman Pak Idris saying. *You must know their song.* Though what he senses right now is more like fireflies darting in the darkness. They move in odd and random patterns of people's interests and emotions, and Ren thinks that if only he can find a still, quiet place, he'll able to sort them out. But first, he must retrieve the pen. The ward sister on duty tells him that she's given it to Matron.

Matron, like most of the senior staff, is a foreigner. A sharp-faced Australian woman, she's all elbows and briskness and looks doubtfully at him when he finally arrives at her office. "This is an expensive pen. You'd best not drop it." Her white, starched headdress stands out like stiff wings. Clutching the pen, Ren hastens anxiously back to the pathology storeroom. At one point he breaks into a run, only to meet angry glares from adults. No need to ask for directions. The wires are humming in his head, singing. As he races around the last corner, he cannons into William.

"Did you find it?" he asks.

Dazed, Ren stares at him. The pen. He produces it triumphantly.

"Splendid!" William looks pleased, but whether it's because he's regained his fountain pen or something good has happened in that room,

Ren can't tell. In fact, William is in a far better mood than he's been all week. Ren peers past him. The door is now ajar, but the dazzling sunlight makes it hard to see the dim interior. There's a lean shadow in the doorway. A man perhaps—it looks too tall for a woman. Is this the Dr. Rawlings that William spoke of?

Electricity runs through him. Ren's thoughts become jumbled, incoherent. His cat whiskers sizzle. He must go back, to the room that William has just exited, but instead he sways on his feet.

"Steady," says William, marching Ren over to a bench. "Did you not eat lunch?"

Ren shakes his head. Neither he nor Ah Long planned for him to go on this surprise excursion into town.

"Let's get you something then. There's a café in town with decent coffee."

Tears of frustration prick Ren's eyes as he's led all the way back to the front of the hospital where Harun is waiting for them, squatting next to the parked car in the shade. As the car pulls away, he looks back at the hospital. It isn't that far from the Kinta Club where William is planning to go later. Perhaps Ren can return quietly by himself. In fact, he must.

16

THE FOREIGNER, WILLIAM ACTON, STOOD IN THE OPEN DOORWAY OF the pathology storeroom. "I haven't seen you before. You're not a nurse are you?"

"No, I'm just helping out." I recognized the flicker of acquisitive interest in his eyes. It made me nervous. Where was Shin?

"I see," but he didn't move from the door.

I stood there awkwardly, holding a jar with part of an intestine in it. He took his glasses off and rubbed his face, a gesture that made him look oddly naked and unwell. His skin was grey under its tan and there were rings under his eyes. He could have been anywhere from twenty-five to thirty-five though his movements seemed quick enough.

"Do you work for Rawlings then?"

I nodded. He smiled then. It was completely unexpected and lent his face a haggard charm.

"I suppose you won't tell me your name?"

"Louise." That at least I knew how to answer.

"Well, Louise, you don't seem very squeamish about these specimens."

"I'm not," I said coolly.

"Some of them were actually contributed by me."

Despite myself, I was curious. "You've donated your own organs to science?" I thought people only did that after they were dead.

The foreign doctor smiled again. "I meant patients of mine. Let's see—I think I did an unusually large gallstone and a couple of fingers."

"Fingers?" I was instantly alert.

"One was a vestigial sixth finger removed from an Indian patient. Another actually belonged to a friend of mine. We've got quite a collection of digits here, at least a dozen if I recall."

He crossed the room, pointing out a large jar of murky fluid. "This should be dumped. A lot of the older specimens are fixed in alcohol, which really ought to be changed once a year. We only keep them if they're medically interesting. And of course, some people take their own parts back to be buried with them."

He leaned in, and I took a step sideways. I was wary of standing close to men. Working at the May Flower had taught me their long reach, their surprising strength, and how difficult it was to twist away if you were seized by the waist. But there were no glowering bouncers right now, nor the Mama with her eagle eye. It was just the two of us alone in this room. If I screamed, would anyone come?

But perhaps I was being overly suspicious, as he kept talking about various specimens. He seemed to know quite a lot about them.

"How long do you keep them for?"

"No idea. They're mostly curiosities—the orderlies like to bring the trainee nurses in after dark to give them a thrill."

I couldn't resist asking, "Is it hard to become a nurse in this hospital?"

"Have you gone to school? You sound like it."

Briefly, I told him about having finished my School Certificate and how I wanted to do something else.

"I see." He rubbed his chin, appraising me again. "It's not a very standardized system, nothing like what we have in Britain. Here it depends on the hospital. Batu Gajah District Hospital trains local girls to fill positions. Lectures on nursing are given by senior nursing staff and some of the doctors, and there's a state examination."

"Are there still vacancies for trainees?" The hopeful note in my voice embarrassed me, but he looked pleased at my interest.

"You'd have to find out from the hospital. If not this year, there's always the next intake."

"What about school fees?" I'd no money of my own after making my mother's debt payments, and as long as my stepfather refused to fund me, the door was closed.

"I believe there are scholarships. You'd need a personal recommendation, of course."

There was something in his eye, a sort of greedy loneliness that I recognized from all those long afternoons dancing with strangers.

"Here's my card." He handed me a sharp-edged rectangle of paper. "Give it to the medical director and say you're interested in nursing. Or you can fill out an application and I'll pass it on to Matron."

It read: *William Acton, General Surgeon*, followed by a row of letters that meant nothing to me but were apparently enough to carry weight with hospital officials.

Perhaps I'd misjudged him. I shouldn't be so distrustful; it closed doors and pushed people away. My last year in school my form mistress, distressed that I wasn't going on for my Higher Secondary Certificate, had offered to come home with me to persuade my parents. There were only a handful of girls sitting that examination, perhaps four or five in the entire country, and she was sure I could be one of them. I'd refused. I couldn't bear to bring her to my stepfather's house to witness his refusal and my humiliation. But maybe I should have fought harder.

So this time, I said "thank you" and really meant it. Tucking the card into my pocket, I felt the engraved name slide under my fingertips.

Perhaps my luck had changed. I'd heard people say that luck—good and bad—came in phases, like the story of Joseph in the Bible. My mother had sent me to a school founded by Methodist preachers, and the quiet chanting, the standing and sitting, and opening of hymnals had been a solace to me, even while I'd thought about dreadful, evil things, like poisoning my stepfather.

But the salesman, Chan Yew Cheung, had also talked about luck. In fact, he'd said that he was about to be very fortunate though he'd ended up dead in a ditch.

THERE WAS A RATTLE IN THE CORRIDOR, AND SHIN, CARRYING YET another box of files, barged in. He stopped short, surprised.

"Well, I'll be on my way," said the surgeon, suddenly brisk.

Shin circled warily into the room. He looked at William Acton, then at my flushed, excited face.

"Is there anything that you need, sir?" Shin asked.

"You're one of the summer orderlies. A medical student, is that right?"

"Yes, sir."

They were like two dogs sizing each other up, but I paid little heed. A door to a career that I'd thought was closed had cracked open, and perhaps I might squeeze through.

"Tell Rawlings I came by," and with a brief nod, the doctor was gone. Shin stood in the doorway watching him for a moment.

"Are you all right?" he asked.

Of course I was. A year ago I'd have been more shy, but working at the May Flower had inured me to strangers. And he hadn't really tried anything. Not like the various *buayas* whose wandering hands I slapped away. Though if, like Rose or Pearl, I had a hungry child waiting for me at home, I wouldn't have had the luxury of refusal. Sometimes I wondered whether my mother's decision to remarry was my fault. Had she, staring at my too-short clothes and the empty sack of rice in the corner, decided that marriage was her best option? But no, she'd liked my stepfather as well. There was something about him that appealed to her, I couldn't deny it.

"Let's take a break for lunch," said Shin. "The canteen's still open."

He locked up and we crossed the grass to another building. The red earth broke apart in coarse warm crumbs, and large black ants, each the length of the top joint of my finger, scattered frantically underfoot. Shin was very quiet; his earlier good mood seemed to have evaporated.

"He said they have at least a dozen fingers in the pathology collection," I said, pleased to have something to report. "We ought to cross-check the records to see if any of them are missing."

It was a relief to reach the shaded walkway, out of the burning glare. An orderly in a white uniform wheeling an old man in a wheelchair gave Shin a friendly thumbs-up as they passed.

Shin nodded glumly. "Is that all you talked about?"

"Why?"

"There are rumors about that doctor."

"What's wrong with him?"

"He's a good surgeon, very competent. But they say he has an eye for local girls."

"That's not surprising—they're all like that."

He shot me a swift glance. "You've changed."

Of course I had. Things like love affairs and call-outs and mistresses no longer shocked me; I'd learned more about them in a week from the other girls at the May Flower than I ever had in my school days, even if Hui said I was still hopelessly naïve.

"How do you know about him anyway?" I asked.

"My roommate told me."

The card William Acton had given me lay in my pocket, like a train ticket to a long-awaited destination. I wanted to tell Shin about the possibility of nurse-training but he didn't seem particularly encouraging. We weren't equals anymore, I thought resentfully. I didn't have a scholarship to medical school, or the luxury of choosing summer jobs.

At the canteen, I wanted to try the exotic Western food—sardine sandwiches, chicken chops, and mulligatawny soup—listed on the blackboard. Shin said patronizingly, "You should see the mess hall at our college. There's a much better selection." Then he stopped, remembering, I supposed, how much I'd wanted to go to university. I fixed a stiff smile on my face to hide my irritation.

It was now two in the afternoon, and the tables were mostly deserted. When we were almost done, we were joined by the orderly who'd been wheeling the old man earlier. He had a jowly face, like a cheerful piglet. Drops of perspiration trembled on his upper lip.

"How come you're here on your day off?" he asked Shin, plonking down a steaming bowl of fishball noodles. "*Wah!* You even brought your girlfriend. What kind of cheap date is this?"

I couldn't help smiling; his small eyes were so humorous. "I'm Shin's sister. He's making me work for him today."

"I didn't know you had such a beautiful sister. Why didn't you introduce us earlier? I'm Koh Beng and I'm single." We shook hands across the table. His palm, as I feared, was sweaty. "What kind of work are you doing?"

"Cleaning out the pathology storeroom," said Shin.

"Nobody wanted that job. Don't you find pickled organs frightening?"

"Sorting the files might be worse," I said.

"Have you seen the preserved head? Apparently if you hold it up at midnight, it talks."

I gave him a skeptical look, and he winked. "There are other strange things locked up in that room: a sorcerer's *pelesit* that looks like a grasshopper in a glass bottle and has to be fed blood every month, and a finger from a weretiger—one of the *harimau jadian* who can put on a human skin and walk around in daylight." Turning to Shin, he said, "How about I help your sister clean up?"

Shin looked exasperated. I said quickly, "We're almost done," though it wasn't true at all. "What time is the last train to Ipoh?"

"I'll take you back," said the irrepressible Koh Beng. "I'm heading there this evening. I'm single, by the way."

"So you mentioned."

"Just making sure." Koh Beng might look like a piglet but I couldn't help finding him amusing. What's more, he clearly knew it.

"I'll take her back myself," said Shin coldly. "Or you can stay over if you want. My friend said you could bunk with her for tonight."

"Who's this friend?" asked Koh Beng, taking the words out of my mouth.

"A nurse."

"Your brother's only been here a week but he's already caused so much drama among the nurses."

"That doesn't surprise me." Still smiling, I felt vaguely irritated. But it was true, there was nothing surprising about Shin acquiring yet another girlfriend.

SHIN'S FIRST GIRLFRIEND WAS TWO YEARS OLDER THAN US, THE cousin of one of my school friends. To be honest, I hadn't expected him to pick her, though she was nice enough. What I'd liked about her, however, was that she seemed so mature and even-keeled, though I didn't realize he was dating her until almost a month had passed.

"Shin's out a lot, isn't he?" I'd remarked to my mother one evening.

We were sitting at the kitchen table in companionable silence. The oil lamp shone on her sewing and my library book. I'd given up on poisoning and was now reading Sherlock Holmes purely for entertainment. All was calm and ordinary. You could scarcely believe that Shin and my stepfather had traded blows here, wrecking the old table, and then smashing out into the back courtyard, or whatever finally happened that terrible evening. But that's the way people are, I think. We forget all the bad things in favor of what's normal, what feels safe.

My mother bit off her sewing thread. "He's probably seeing Fong Lan home." Fong Lan was the daughter of the carpenter who'd built my mother's new kitchen table—my stepfather's way of apologizing to her after the fight with Shin.

"That's nice of him."

My mother gave me an odd look. "He's going steady with her, you know."

I was taken aback, but perhaps I shouldn't have been. Eventually Shin was bound to find a girl he liked.

Fong Lan had a round face and gently slanted eyebrows, and she adored Shin. People were surprised that he'd chosen her out of all the girls who mooned after him. There were disparaging remarks, like "her calves look like lo bak," the giant white radishes, but if Fong Lan heard, she didn't seem to care. That was part of her appeal, that mature sincerity of hers. Sometimes she was so good that it made me want to scream. Yet I, too, was drawn to her. When she talked to me in her soft, serious voice, I felt that I wanted an older sister like her to comfort me. To cherish me and love me.

Once, coming home unexpectedly early, I'd caught her with Shin. It was a quiet, empty afternoon, so still I'd thought no one was home. I could whistle loudly, meddle with all the things that my stepfather didn't like us to disturb. Stupid restrictions like tearing the next page off the daily calendar, or changing the radio dial to a different station. I could do all of them, but instead, I walked decorously upstairs.

At the top of the stairs, I cast my schoolbag aside and slid noiselessly down the corridor in my socks. And then I stopped at an unfamiliar sound—a gasp and a soft moan. A girl's voice, coming from Shin's room. I froze. There was a tingling sensation, as though my skin was seizing up, shrinking too small for me. And through the open door, I saw them.

They were on the floor of Shin's room, that space I was no longer permitted to enter. Fong Lan was leaning against his bed. The front of her blouse was open revealing the pale, heavy swell of her bare breasts as she bent over him, her hair parted like a shining curtain. Shin's head was cradled in her lap. One of her hands splayed possessively on his chest. His face was turned away, but I could see hers. She looked entranced, as though she'd never seen anything so beautiful as Shin. And he was beautiful. It was obvious even to me at that moment, the lean careless length of his body, the sharp tilt of his chin.

In that instant, I understood a great deal. About Shin, and about me. And how there were some things that you could never have. In all the years I'd lived in that house, I'd never seen Shin so relaxed, without the watchful tension that wound his body like a spring. When I'd held him in the darkness behind the chicken coop, I'd felt it: the rigidity and anger that wouldn't go away. But here, in the soft hazy afternoon light, was a different Shin, one that I'd never seen before. And I felt horribly, sickeningly inadequate. No matter how close we were or what secrets we shared, I could never give him this peace.

A choked gasp forced its way out of my throat. Fong Lan lifted her head but I was already gone, running down the long corridor. When I think about that shophouse in my memories, it's always a dark, endless tunnel both upstairs and downstairs. Not knowing what to do, I ended up wandering around in a daze, and only returned when I was sure my mother and stepfather were back. Shin had acted as though nothing had happened. He showed no reaction when I came home, so late that the lamps were already lit and my mother was scolding me in fear and relief. But Fong Lan talked to me a few days later.

"I know you saw us the other day," she said. "It must have been awkward for you."

Her very softness and meekness felt like a stab to the heart.

I tried to shrug it off. "Don't worry about it."

But she said seriously, "I really do love him, you know. We haven't done it yet. I don't want to tie him down if I got pregnant. But I will if he wants to."

I wanted to shake her. What kind of thinking was this? My mother had warned me, stamped it into my head. Chastity was one of the few bargaining chips women had. No matter how good-looking Shin was, Fong Lan was a fool. And yet, part of me couldn't help admiring her. She really did love him, I thought.

Haltingly, I tried to give her advice even though she was two years older than me. She listened patiently, then shook her head. "I know what it's like in your family," she said. *So he's really told her everything,* I thought in amazed resentment. "But I want to make Shin happy. And if it means giving myself to him, that's all right with me."

Was that love or stupidity? But maybe that was just the hardheaded part of me, calculating my chances of survival. I wouldn't give myself away to some man, become one of his possessions. Not without the economic assurance of a wedding ring. Even then, from what I could see of my mother's choice, perhaps the price was too high.

I NEVER DID FIND OUT WHAT HAPPENED WITH FONG LAN BECAUSE not long after, Shin broke up with her. And strangely enough, when it was all over I found myself defending her.

"You're supposed to be loyal and faithful," I'd said, six months before Shin left for Singapore. We were sitting at the round marble-topped table studying. At least Shin was. I had nothing to prepare for, no university to go on to. "You're not like your name at all."

He'd barely looked up from his textbook. "What are you talking about?"

"Why did you break up with Fong Lan? She cried buckets afterwards. I know she did."

"Are you telling me to date her again?" He looked annoyed.

"She seems a lot more serious than whoever it is you're with now," I'd said defensively.

"And what about you? You think that being serious will change Ming's mind?"

That was a low blow. Shin narrowed his eyes and turned a page. "Did Fong Lan ask you to talk to me?"

"No."

"Then don't meddle with what you don't understand." His face flamed, as though someone had pressed a burning brand across his cheekbones. "And stop talking about names! I have been faithful. As much as I can!"

Furious, he slammed his textbook shut and left.

AFTER LUNCH AT THE CANTEEN, WE WENT BACK TO THE STOREROOM and started on the files. It wasn't as bad as I'd feared; most of them were quite straightforward. But sorting out the pathology samples was a head-ache since they were in no semblance of order at all.

The collection was highly eccentric; I supposed that in this far-flung corner of the Empire, whoever was running the pathology department prob-ably felt like God. We didn't find the preserved head or blood-drinking grasshopper that Koh Beng had mentioned, but there was a two-headed rat, its naked tail a drifting worm in amber liquid. Dr. Rawlings's pre-decessor, a Dr. Merton, had apparently promised a number of patients that they could have their body parts back after he'd studied them. These were denoted by a little red X in the corner of his crabbed records.

"Who'd want to come back for a gallbladder?" I said.

"Some people want to be buried whole," Shin said seriously.

I shivered, remembering what the salesman, Chan Yew Cheung, had said when I'd danced with him—about witchcraft, and how a body must be buried in its original form to rest in peace.

"Here we go," said Shin, reading from a file. "Finger, left ring, Indian male laborer infected with parasite. Preserved in formaldehyde."

I combed through the shelves of specimens. Almost everything had been unpacked, and I still hadn't seen any actual jars of severed fingers.

"Another one—right forefinger from a double-jointed female contor-tionist."

"Not here, either," I announced.

In fact, despite records indicating at least twelve amputated digits in the hospital collection, we could not locate a single one.

"How's that possible?" I pored over the ledger again. People made jokes about doctors' handwriting but in this case it was no laughing matter. Dr. Merton's scrawl was a conga line of ants, the hasty loops of someone who didn't care if it never got transcribed.

"Anything else missing besides fingers?"

"I checked. So far nothing else is missing." I waved the ledger triumphantly at him from where I perched on a cardboard box, amid a sea of papers.

"Still so competitive," he complained. "I thought of it first."

"No, you didn't." I turned back to the file.

"Spider. On your hair."

I froze, eyes closed while Shin removed it. In the past, he'd have flicked it off, stinging my forehead smartly. Now, he handled it delicately and impersonally, like a stranger.

"It's really disappointing how you don't scream about things like this," he murmured.

"Why should I?" I opened my eyes.

Shin's face, that familiar set of planes that made up his nose and cheekbones, was so close that I could reach out and touch it. What made someone good-looking? Was it the symmetry of features, or the sharp shadows of his brows and lashes, the mobile curl of his mouth? In the very center of his eyes, so much darker than mine, I could see a tiny light, a gleam that sparked. Then it winked out and I was falling, drawn into a tunnel. Images flickered. Railway tracks submerged underwater. A ticket to nowhere. Fish swimming in a mirror. Somewhere, a midnight shape stirred, shadow rising from the depths of a river. The air thickened, a clot in my lungs. I gasped. Toppled forward.

"What's wrong?"

Shin caught me as I fell, my thoughts tangled like riverweed, slippery and coiling. Dizzy, I steadied myself, pushing back. Sliding my hands along the width of his shoulders, the hard muscles that were those of a man and not a boy. My heart was racing like a horse on treacherous ground. If I weren't careful, I'd make a fatal stumble.

He watched me with concern, dark brows frowning. Whatever it was I'd seen in his eyes—reflected shadows, a looking glass linked to another realm—was gone. There was only Shin and even then he was half a stranger to me.

"Do you often have spells like this?"

Spells. That was the right word. Dizzy spells, magic spells. The crooked twitch of a severed finger that had led us somewhere strange. I couldn't speak, could only nod.

Shin's hands gripped my shoulders. The pressure made me feel better. Then he was loosening my collar, working the top buttons quickly and deftly. Dazed, I wondered how many women he'd undressed. But he was careful, touching only the material of the dress. Careful not to touch me.

"Have you been tested for anemia? Lots of girls your age have it."

Practical as always. I inhaled. Sunlight flooded back into the room, and the spell, whatever it was, lifted.

"Shin, have you ever dreamed about a little boy and a railway station?"

"No." He sat down with a sigh, ignoring the dust.

"Well, I do. And it's very odd because he talks to me. I feel as though I've met him before."

"A little boy—is that me?"

I swatted him with a file. "Stop being so egotistical."

He laughed and dodged. The file flew out of my hand and papers exploded everywhere, thin loose sheets covered with crabbed handwriting. It was Dr. Merton's writing—lists and more lists of things mixed in with supplies that he'd ordered. Formaldehyde, spirits of tincture, scalpels. Fixatives for glass slides. And then I saw it: *Finger donated by European patient. Dry preservation in salt.*

I waved it under Shin's nose. "This is it—the only finger so far that isn't preserved in fluid!"

He read aloud as I peered over his shoulder. "Apparently this was a one-off, do-it-yourself preservation. Someone, a fellow doctor named—can't quite read this—MacFarlane or MacGarland, who had a finger amputated on a jungle trip. Blood poisoning after an animal bite. I hope he didn't do it himself."

"No, it says W. Acton. William Acton—that surgeon who was just here. He told me he'd donated his friend's finger." The coincidence unsettled me, like a dark undertow.

"That's a nice friendship," said Shin drily.

I ignored him. "Packed in salt, which was probably all they had on them at the time. I wonder what they were doing."

Discovering an actual record of the finger was a relief, I told myself. It had been removed by a proper doctor for medical reasons. The rest of it, the salesman's obsession with luck, was just superstition.

"And here it is." Shin took the now-familiar glass bottle out of his pocket and set it next to the other specimens we had already checked off.

"Put it behind, on the upper shelf," I said with a shudder.

The sun sank lower, the light so golden that you could almost take a bite out of it, like the layered butter cake, *kuih lapis,* a cousin from Batavia in Dutch Indonesia had once brought to our house. Each moist slice had smelled like all the spices of the East Indies. The storeroom was almost done, the wooden racks wiped down and filled with rows of specimens. All the files had been put into filing cabinets and relabeled. Looking at the list of cross-tagged specimens, I felt a warm glow of achievement.

"Do you think Dr. Rawlings will pay extra for such a good job?" I asked Shin.

He was reading another file with a frown. "Doubt it. He agreed to one day's overtime. That includes you, by the way."

"We'll split then?"

"Yes." Shin said suddenly, "Are you having money problems?"

"There's something I want to buy." Changing the subject, I said, "What are you doing with your money?"

He glanced over his shoulder at me. An opaque, don't-ask-me-questions look. "Saving up."

Not for the first time, I wondered why Shin was working so hard. He had a scholarship, and my stepfather had also given him a generous living stipend. Whatever truce they'd come to after that terrible night when Shin's arm was broken, it had worked itself out into an agreement that I wasn't privy to. My stepfather was a hard man but he kept his word.

But Shin had continued working during the university term. His sparse correspondence mentioned a part-time job, and last summer and Christmas, work had kept him from coming home. What was he doing with all that money? At the May Flower, you could easily run up a tab. It wasn't just the dancing of course. Ordering drinks or asking girls privately for call-outs, which meant buying them dinners and who knew what else, could easily spiral out of hand. I'd seen it happen and hoped Shin wasn't doing that for some girl down in Singapore. Should I say anything to him?

No, it wasn't my business anyway.

17

AFTER LEAVING THE HOSPITAL, WILLIAM TAKES REN TO A CAFÉ downtown where foreigners like to congregate. Ren, hesitating over the choices, whispers that he'd like a ham sandwich, please. Ham is a Western delicacy, brought in tins from Cold Storage, but William seems to think nothing of it.

Ren takes his sandwich outside where Harun, the driver, is waiting patiently by the car, an Austin that William purchased from his predecessor, Dr. Merton. The same physician who'd passed along the tenancy of the white bungalow, Ah Long, and Harun. Harun takes pride in its gleaming bonnet, the gentle curves of its chassis. It's not large but it suits a bachelor like William, who drives himself on weekends.

"The other doctor never drove," Harun said, explaining that Europeans come and go. Some leave after two years while others become lifers, so comfortable in their lush tropical lifestyle with servants that they can no longer cope with returning to England.

Ah Long told Ren that Dr. Merton hadn't been a real doctor anyway. He spent his time dissecting diseased organs and cutting up dead bodies: neither of which Ah Long approved of. All parts of the body should rest together, he'd muttered. None of this scattering here and there. That only led to trouble, like the hungry ghosts whose remains were dispersed among strangers. Bones should be claimed by some filial son, not left in that dreadful room at the hospital filled with body parts in jars, all collected by Dr. Merton.

That must be the pathology storeroom, Ren thinks urgently. The one that made his invisible cat whiskers flicker. He's sure that's where the finger is. But who was the shadowy figure in the door this morning? Perhaps it was Dr. Rawlings, the pathologist who replaced Dr. Merton.

Dr. Rawlings is a family man, which is why he didn't take over Dr. Merton's bachelor quarters. Instead, he'd requested a larger bungalow for his wife and children. But they didn't stay. One year—a year of monsoons and biting heat and scorpions found in shoes—was enough for them and they went back to England. Ah Long said that many of the foreigners here are a bit peculiar. Why else would they live like this in exile, with their families half a world away, he said darkly.

"Even the ladies?" asked Ren.

"Of course!" said Ah Long with a snort. "Like that daughter of the Thomsons. Lydia, they call her. There was a big scandal about her in England." What it was exactly, Ah Long wouldn't say. Now, Ren thinks about Miss Lydia helping out at the hospital earlier, and wonders what she's run away from.

REN WATCHES A KNOT OF BOYS PLAYING *SEPAK TAKRAW* WITH A woven rattan ball. The ball flies out, almost striking the car. Ren grabs it in time. The boys come running, glancing guiltily at the gleaming car and Ren's white houseboy's uniform.

"Here you go." He tosses it back. They're younger than him, about eight or nine, the same age as Yi was when he died. One of them offers him a peppermint, dug from the depths of his pocket. It has bits of fluff on it, but Ren accepts it with grave ceremony.

"Do you work for the *gwai lo*?" the boy asks in Cantonese.

"My master's a doctor." Ren rubs the peppermint surreptitiously on his sleeve before popping it into his mouth. It tastes cold and furry.

"You work at the hospital?" Ren shakes his head, but the boy continues. "Have you seen the ghost there?"

"Lots of people have died in that hospital," says another boy.

"I've never seen a ghost." Except Yi, thinks Ren, but only in dreams so it doesn't count.

"Did you hear that a woman was killed by a tiger just last week?"

"But that wasn't in the hospital," says the other boy. "That was in a rubber estate."

"It's a ghost tiger, a white one you know?"

"No, it's a weretiger—it turns into an old man."

Ren's stomach clenches in alarm; this account of an old man who turns into a tiger is all his fears come true. "Who said it turns into an old man?"

The smallest boy pipes up, "Someone saw an old man walking in the rubber estate in the dark. But when they went to look, there were only tiger prints."

Ren can't help asking, "Did he have a missing finger?"

The boys look at each other. Ren can see their minds busily working, no doubt adding that detail to the story.

Unbidden, a memory wells up in Ren. The crooked shadows of a plantation at dusk, the figure of an old man, dressed in white. It's too far to see his face but he walks with that familiar stiff gait. The gloom deepens, the trees closing in like silent figures, the only light the whiteness of the old man's clothes. Ren runs after his master, calling Dr. MacFarlane to come back to the house. It's one of his master's fits, when he shivers with cold, sweats feverishly, and doesn't seem right in his mind.

It's so dark that Ren can barely see his own feet. There's the familiar suffocating panic, the fear that the old doctor will fall down or get lost or turn to show him a snarling, unrecognizable face, and Ren will be all alone again in the dark.

Now Ren shivers despite the blazing sun. The boys are just repeating a local story, he tells himself. Still, how long has it been since Dr. MacFarlane died? He counts anxiously. There are now only fifteen days left. He must get the finger back this evening. Then he'll bury it in Dr. MacFarlane's grave and make things right.

The little boys drift away. After buying the items on Ah Long's shopping list, Ren and Harun wait in the shade. To pass the time, Ren learns to roll cigarettes, though the thin paper is fiddly and the tobacco falls out. Harun is patient, not complaining when Ren makes ugly, stumpy cigarettes that look like carrots, rolling and rerolling the same piece of paper so as not to waste.

"You mustn't smoke though," says Harun, taking it away. "How old are you again?"

Ren swallows. "Thirteen."

Harun studies him carefully. "I started working when I was twelve years old. There were nine children in our family and I was the oldest. It's not easy."

Ren keeps his head down. First he must complete his task. "Do you think the tiger killed the woman in the rubber estate?"

Harun rubs his chin. "No matter what the magistrate says, it's strange. Tigers become man-eaters when they're old or sick and can't hunt, but who ever heard of a tiger that stopped partway and refused to eat its kill? There must have been something wrong with the body."

"Do you think a man can become a tiger?" It's the same question that Ren has asked Ah Long and William in turn.

Harun takes a long drag on his cigarette. The end of it glows bright red. "My grandmother told me about a tiger village, near Gunung Ledang in Malacca. The posts of the houses are made of *jelatang*, the stinging tree nettle, the walls of men's skin, the rafters of bones, and the roofs are thatched with human hair. That's where the weretigers live, the *harimau jadian* who change their shapes. Some people say that they're beasts possessed by the souls of dead people."

Ren doesn't like this story. It's too much like the ramblings of Dr. Mac-Farlane in his last days, when the old man would rouse himself from his fits, giving fragmented accounts of where he'd been and what he'd done.

"I went far this time," he said to Ren once, his pale eyes wandering. "I killed a tapir six miles away."

"Yes," Ren said soothingly. "Yes, I know."

"I'm afraid," he muttered, clutching Ren's small square hand. "One of these days, I won't return to my body."

Ren doesn't like to remember Dr. MacFarlane like that, all rheumy-eyed and shaking, his pink scalp visible through the strands of grey hair. He wants to remember him cradling a sick baby, taking apart a wireless to explain how the batteries work. It was malarial fever, that was all. Soon Dr. MacFarlane would recover, take large doses of quinine, and all would be back to normal. But two days later, a local hunter stopped by to show off the tufted ears and tail of a tapir. He said it was a tiger's kill, partly eaten, that he'd found six miles away and Ren had stiffened at the news, glancing at Dr. MacFarlane, who was silently writing in his notebook.

"Is that so?" the old man had said, his eyes placid and hooded. But Ren, remembering his remarks, had wondered.

Now, Ren regards Harun with a worried expression. "Is that a real story?" he asks, "About the tigers with human souls?"

Harun exhales; a thin stream of smoke drifts out of his nostrils. "My grandmother would never say if it was true or not. She used it to frighten us into going to bed." He stubs the cigarette out. "I think *Tuan* will go to the Club next for dinner. If you want to go home, I'll give you a lift. Better not walk until after the hunt."

"Will there be a tiger hunt?"

"Tonight. There's a goat tied up in the rubber plantation and a local hunter, Pak Ibrahim, will lie in wait for it with *Tuan* Price and *Tuan* Reynolds. The others will sit up late at the Club, waiting for news."

Spotting William's lanky figure, they both scramble to attention. He's deep in conversation with another foreigner, a man with a toothbrush mustache. Ren listens covertly as they mention tigers.

"Apparently Rawlings had a bee up his bonnet at the inquest. Wanted to make it a suspicious death," says the man.

"Yes, I heard," William says. "The magistrate overruled him."

"What else could it have been except a tiger? Farrell hasn't any patience for tall tales."

Ren's heart sinks. They've decided it was a tiger after all.

Harun opens the car door as William folds his legs into the back of the Austin, and just as Harun predicted, tells him to drive to the Kinta Club at the top of the hill in Changkat.

"Harun can send you back after he's dropped me at the Club," he says to Ren as an afterthought. "Or do you want to stay to hear if they catch a tiger tonight?"

Ren explains that he forgot something at the hospital, but yes, he'd like to wait. In the mirror, he sees William and Harun exchange an amused glance. It's the indulgent look that grown-ups give to children's whims, and it makes Ren feel hot and embarrassed, though he tells himself he has a task to complete.

////

REN FINDS HIMSELF BACK AT THE BATU GAJAH DISTRICT HOSPITAL at that odd hour when late afternoon is turning into evening. The sky beyond the covered walkway is powdery pink, the sun burning low between spectacular clouds that float like cream cakes. But Ren has no time to admire them; the fizzing tingle he sensed this morning at the hospital is still there, running like a live wire. Who or what can be sending him a signal, if it isn't Yi?

First, he must check the pathology storeroom. Near the outbuilding, now striped with the long shadows of trees, he hesitates. The door that was ajar this morning is closed. Ren tries the handle softly; it gives way under his hand.

Inside is a large, high-ceilinged space with windows that open onto the other side of the building. From William's offhand remark about storerooms and moving boxes, Ren imagined a warehouse piled with relics, but this room is very orderly. Late shafts of sun slant in, although there's a growing dimness in the corners, as though tiny unseen creatures are gathering in the shadows.

Ignoring the faint buzzing in his ears, Ren steps farther in. This is the room he imagined, when the task of finding Dr. MacFarlane's missing finger fell upon him. This room, with its rows and rows of specimens in every conceivable kind of glass container. Next to the tall windows is an empty box and a step stool, as though someone has just left it. The impression is so strong that Ren can almost see a slim figure unpacking the last box. No, the way the stool is positioned makes him think that it was used to place something high up on a shelf.

The finger is definitely here; he only has to close his eyes to feel the tingle. High on that shelf. He pushes the stool closer and climbs up. Past the bigger containers with their hideous, floating contents, past a jar with a two-headed rat in it. It's hard to feel with his cat sense now, there's too much static. He never imagined there'd be so many specimens. Straining precariously on tiptoe, Ren's eyes are barely level with the shelf he wants.

He moves a few of the bottles, peering behind them. The light is fading fast now, lavender and grey. Ren has the feeling that he isn't alone. "Yi," he says aloud. The sound of his voice hangs in the air and there's an expectant hush, as though fine pale grains of silence are trickling through a giant hourglass.

Fighting anxiety, Ren patiently shifts the glass specimen jars to peer behind them. They clink softly; it's on this shelf, or maybe the next one. He can't quite tell. He slides his hand in and scrabbles around. His cat whiskers twitch hopefully. Pulling his fist out, Ren opens it to find a glass vial. Inside is a finger, dried to a blackish color like a twig.

Heart pounding with mingled relief and horror, Ren climbs down and examines his prize. It's almost exactly the way that Dr. MacFarlane described. "Preserved in salt," he'd said. "It will likely be the only one of its kind—the other specimens should be in alcohol or formaldehyde."

Ren stuffs it in his pocket. It's the first act of theft he's ever committed and he mumbles a guilty apology under his breath, though he's not sure whether it's to God, or Yi, or Dr. MacFarlane for taking so long to find the finger.

The shadows are darker now, heavy as though a veil has dropped on the room. The stolen finger is a dead weight in his pocket. He's outstayed his welcome. Furtively, Ren shuts the door behind him, skin prickling, the short hairs standing up on the back of his neck. Once outside, he walks, then trots, and finally, when no one stops him, breaks into a run all the way back, down the covered walkways and long corridors, as though he's fleeing for his life.

18

"SO, OUT OF ALL THE SPECIMENS IN THAT ROOM, ONLY THE FINGERS are missing," I said.

After returning the bucket and cleaning rags borrowed from the janitor's closet, Shin and I cut back between some *angsana* trees with their falling gold petals.

Shin frowned. "How many fingers were on the original list?"

"Fourteen."

I didn't want to say it was a bad number. Shin had no patience for things like that, but I could see from the brief twitch of his jaw that it had, of course, registered. For Cantonese speakers, thirteen was a good number. *Sup sam* sounded a lot like the words *sut sang*, which meant "always survive." Fourteen, on the other hand, was terrible because it sounded like "certain death."

"I should inform Dr. Rawlings," said Shin. "It's bizarre to have so many missing fingers."

An orderly in a white uniform emerged from a distant building, carrying a tiffin container. Turning, he shielded his face against the low-setting sun. Something familiar about his gait and angular figure made my throat constrict. Nearer and nearer the white figure came. When he was about forty feet away, he lifted the hand that was shielding his face to squint at us. My heart sank as I recognized the slant-jawed man from the dance hall last night: Mr. Y. K. Wong himself.

Maybe he really was a demon, doubling himself so that everywhere I went, he followed me. But no—it was coincidence, a stroke of bad luck. Besides, there was no hint of recognition on his face, eyes screwed tight against the setting sun.

"Shin!" I choked back panic. "Who is that?"

He glanced over his shoulder. "That's my roommate, Wong Yun Kiong. The one I told you about. We call him Y. K."

"I thought Koh Beng was your roommate." The cheerful, porky one.

"No, Koh Beng's just a friend."

We were out in the open, on the grass beneath the giant trees and there was nowhere to hide. If I made a run for it he'd surely recognize me. Or perhaps he already had.

"Please don't let him see me!"

"Why?"

"I'll explain later. Please!" Squeezing my eyes tight, I buried my face in Shin's chest. It was the only thing I could think of. For an instant, he stiffened. Then his arms slid reluctantly around me. Warm breath on my neck, the heat of his skin. It gave me a strange sensation, a light-headedness that I put down to anxiety. I'd danced with scores of strangers; this was nothing to get flustered about.

Footsteps crunching on dry leaves drew nearer. Then I heard a voice. I recognized it right away, though I'd only heard it once.

"Hey, Lee Shin! You brought your girlfriend here?"

I clutched Shin, feeling his shirt slide between my fingers.

"I'm off duty," said Shin. "Come on, can't you see I'm busy?"

The tread of feet, circling closer. Shin's chest was broader than I remembered, harder to span with my arms. His heart was beating rapidly, or was it my own?

Y. K. Wong's voice again. "I'll let you off if you introduce me to your girlfriend."

"She's very shy and you're embarrassing her—go away!"

A laugh, then the footsteps retreating. "Don't forget to introduce me!"

I froze, counting the seconds. When I reached ten, I jerked my head up to see if he'd really gone, but Shin gripped me warningly. "Not yet!" he hissed. Then, "You'd better have a good explanation for this."

The heat from Shin's hand on the small of my back seeped feverishly up my spine. Releasing me abruptly, he said, "What was all that about?"

Red-faced, I gave a vague account of how Y. K. Wong had come looking for the finger. Shin's jaw tightened. "How did you really meet all these
men—first that salesman with the finger, and now my roommate? If you
won't tell me, I'll ask him myself."

I'd have to come up with something better. "I went to a dance hall with
friends," I said at last. "That's how I met them both—the salesman and
your roommate."

"Why are you going to places like that? It's all right for men, but not
for you, especially since—"

"Since what?" I said. "Since I'm a girl? So you can go tomcatting all
over town, but I should wait at home to get married?"

It was easier to pick a fight than admit the shameful truth: that the
best-paying job I could get at short notice involved smiling and letting
strangers put their hands on me. I was furious at Shin's superiority, telling
me what to do, yet ashamed of my own stupid, shortsighted choices. For if
I feared Shin finding out, how much worse would it be if my stepfather
did? And what about nurse-training, that I'd been so excited about earlier?
Moral-character recommendations mattered, particularly for unmarried
women; I hadn't thought so far ahead when I'd blindly followed Hui to
the May Flower.

A pause. "Has anyone asked you to marry him?"

"There's no one to marry," I said bitterly. Ming's name hung in the air
between us, unspoken yet so clear that I almost expected it to ring like a
bell.

Shin said coldly, "Well, don't get married without consulting me."

"Why?"

He looked irritated. "Because you'd probably make a stupid decision."

"What makes you think I'm stupid? I said no to the pawnbroker's
cousin!"

As soon as the words left my mouth, I wanted to kick myself. That
was an embarrassing interlude Shin didn't know about. After he'd gone
off to medical school, I'd in fact had a proposal. Hearing that I wasn't going
to study anymore, the local pawnbroker had approached my stepfather on
his cousin's behalf. I'd said no, and surprisingly, my stepfather hadn't pressed
the issue.

"The pawnbroker—you mean my father's friend? That old goat." Shin spoke quietly, but his face had turned pale.

"Not him, his cousin," I faltered.

Shin didn't resemble my stepfather—at least, not much. Everyone said he favored his long-dead mother. But when his face blanched, it was exactly the same way that my stepfather's turned white with rage.

I hated to see that look on his face. It made me want to curl up, cover my eyes, run away. For deep in the darkest, most cowardly recess of my heart, I was afraid that one day I'd turn around to discover that Shin, in some monstrous, nightmarish twist, had transformed into his father.

"Don't look at me like that," he said bitterly. "I won't do anything. I never have."

He walked off. I knew those squared shoulders, that dropped head, and I was filled with unbearable pity and misery.

After a bit, I caught up behind him and tugged his hand. "Friends?"

He nodded. It was getting dark, the buildings fading into grey nothingness. We walked in silence for a while, hand in hand as though we were children again. Like Hansel and Gretel lost in the woods, I thought hazily. My face felt dull and increasingly hot. Whether we were following a trail of breadcrumbs or headed to a witch's den, I'd no idea.

At last I said, "I'd better get to the station."

"It's too late," he said. "The evening train's gone."

"What shall I do then?" I sank down on the coarse grass, too tired to care about stains on my dress. There was no one about anyway, although the electric lights in the hospital had winked on.

"Stay over. I told you I fixed it up. Don't worry about Y. K.—he's off tonight to visit his parents."

My head drooped. It was heavy, as though an invisible dwarf was standing on it and stamping its feet triumphantly. Shin felt my forehead. "You have a fever! Why didn't you say anything?"

SHIN'S NURSE FRIEND WAS OUT, BUT HE FOUND ME A SPARE BED IN the staff hostel for visiting relatives. As he was signing the register, Koh Beng came around the corner.

"Not going back to Ipoh tonight?" He wore a fresh shirt and cotton trousers with a comb tucked in the back pocket, his hair plastered wetly to one side. It was Saturday after all, and the night was just beginning.

"My sister's tired," said Shin.

Koh Beng gave me a sly glance. "I heard from Y. K. earlier that she's not really your sister at all. You dog!"

I looked at Shin. *What are we going to do?*

"That's right, she's my girl," he said coolly.

"Why didn't you just say so?"

"Because I'm signing her in as a relative." Fortunately there was no one at reception to hear this, though a few nurses had passed through, dressed fashionably to go out. It might have been my imagination, but at least a couple of them gave me unfriendly stares.

Koh Beng looked disappointed. "Well, Ji Lin, if you ever get tired of him, don't forget about me."

I smiled weakly. My head throbbed as though the invisible dwarves were now pounding it gleefully with mallets; I wondered if I was going to have another strange dream. "I'm going to bed."

Shin pressed a bottle of aspirin into my hand. "If you need anything, send me a message."

I nodded and followed the housekeeper into the women's side of the staff hostel. The housekeeper, an older auntie-type lady, didn't say anything either. Her back was stiff with disapproval, and I wondered if she'd over-heard Koh Beng's loud remarks. She unlocked a room, a narrow cell-like space with just enough room for a single bed, and handed me the key along with two thin cotton towels.

In the doorway, she turned back, her mouth a thin line. "The guest-rooms are really only for family members, not 'friends.'"

"But we are family," I said. "By marriage, that is." I'd meant to say by *our parents'* marriage, but my tongue was thick and dry, as though it was too large for my mouth.

She looked relieved. "Oh, so you're getting married, then? Did you register already?" Lots of young couples registered early at the courthouse so they could apply for housing together. Not having the energy to dis-abuse her, I smiled feebly.

"So how long have you known each other?" she asked.

"Since we were ten years old."

"Childhood sweethearts, then!" The housekeeper looked pleased. "And such a pretty, well-dressed girl like you."

Here was my cue to advertise Mrs. Tham's dressmaking shop but I felt so ill that I could barely speak. After she'd left, I washed up. I'd have loved to ask the nurses about what it was like to work here, but instead I swallowed two aspirin tablets and lay down. My last thought before I fell asleep was to wonder whether or not we'd locked the pathology storeroom door.

I WAS FLOATING. WEIGHTLESS IN WATER. ABOVE ME WAS A CIRCLE OF light. With a few lazy kicks, I swam towards it. My head broke through, and gasping, I found myself gazing at a familiar scene. The same sunlit riverbank, overgrown with thickets of bamboo and *lalang,* the same clear river.

In real life, I couldn't swim this well but now I delightedly did a few flips. Peering down through the crystalline water, I saw the bleached sand of the riverbed, shadowed with ripples, then the shallow bottom dropping off into blackness. What was it, this nothingness on the bottom of the river? Uneasy, I paddled away from it. The shadow was still there, half a body's length behind, as though the bottom of the river had fallen away or been eaten by darkness. And it was moving.

The faster I swam, the faster it closed on me. Lungs burning, my thrashing arms and legs propelled me desperately forward. Ahead on the riverbank, a figure burst into view. It was the little boy from the train station.

"Over here!" he shouted.

In a burst of terror, I exploded out of the water and flung myself on the riverbank, wheezing. The little boy bent urgently over me.

"What was that?" I gasped. "That shadow under the water?"

He blinked. "I'm not really sure myself. I can't go in the water, you see." Yet his averted gaze made me think that he was lying, or at least, avoiding the topic. "You shouldn't go in, either. Come on!"

He turned and started walking fast, his head barely higher than the tall grass. I knew where we were heading already: the railway station. I could see its peaked *attap* roof. Besides, there was nowhere else to go. All around us was green, half-cultivated wilderness, the remains of abandoned farms with tapioca plants and papaya trees. Farther back, the thick blue ridge of hills and jungle pressed in.

When we reached the platform, the little boy turned with a sigh of relief. "I was frightened when I saw you in the water."

"Has that shadow always been there?"

He nodded. "It's to keep people on this side from going back over. The last time you came in the water, it didn't notice you. But this time it did. That's a bad sign."

"Why's that?"

He studied my pajamas carefully. To my surprise, they were dry and clean as though I hadn't just swum a river and dragged myself through muddy undergrowth. "You don't belong here."

"What's your name?" I asked.

He looked unhappy again. I'd become accustomed to that look; it meant that he didn't want to lie but was unwilling to tell me for some reason. It struck me then: this quiet land, the empty station with a train that was always idle, could only be a waiting room.

"Are you one of my mother's children?" I asked. Was this why he had called me older sister? "One of the Confucian Virtues?"

He looked astonished. "You're very clever," he said admiringly. "Because that's your name, isn't it? Wisdom."

"Are you Ren, Yi, or Li?"

The troubled look again. "I'm not your mother's child, though I'm part of the set. But I don't understand why you're the one who keeps coming here when I'm trying to reach my brother."

"Do you mean Shin? He's my brother, too."

"No." He hesitated, chewing his lip. "I'm worried that my brother is going the wrong way. Following the wrong master."

"Do I know him?"

"No, but you'll recognize him." The little boy's eyes were shadowed with unease.

Although the coal-black locomotive with its empty carriages stood idle at the station, its position had changed. The first time it had been close to where the tracks rose from beneath the river. The second time it had been half out of the station, as though pulling away. Today it was lined up exactly with the platform. Staring at the train tracks, I had the disconcerting realization that there was only one line. No double tracks for a returning train, no platform on the other side, either.

The little boy followed my glance. "Don't worry. You've never arrived by train, so you can go back on your own. At least, this time."

I shuddered at the memory of the blackness in the depths of the river. "So you want me to tell your brother to stop whatever he's doing?"

The little boy looked sad. "Yes. And tell him to beware the fifth of our set. There's something a bit wrong with each of us, but the fifth one is especially bad. You should be careful, too."

"I'll do my best. If I meet your brother, I'll pass him the message."

"You mustn't say you've met me." He looked so serious that I nodded solemnly as well. "I won't forget your kindness. If you ever learn my name, then you can call me."

Call you? I'd no intention of coming here again. And of course, it was a dream, I told myself. Only a dream. With that thought, my consciousness dropped off a shelf into somewhere grey and soft and empty.

19

IN THE END, THEY DON'T KILL THE TIGER.

Ren stays up, sitting with Harun and the other drivers on a long bench behind the Kinta Club, as they talk and smoke and wait for their masters, until his eyelids droop. He has no memory of Harun bringing him, stumbling with sleep, to the car. It's long past midnight by the time they drive William home, bumping over the gravel drive. Ren goes straight to bed and isn't aware of anything until the sun is shining in his face.

"It's past eight o'clock already," Ah Long growls, looking in on him.

Ren jumps up, remembering the hunt last night. "Did they get it?"

"No. Though they waited all night."

The hunters had concealed themselves in a makeshift hide positioned downwind from a tethered goat. It was a place carefully chosen to appeal to tigers, under shade and close to water since tigers drink copiously after feeding. The hours had dragged on and on, punctuated only by the occasional terrified bleating of the goat. But the end result was the same. Not even a glimpse of a tiger. Afterwards there were dozens of theories. It was the wrong spot; they should have used a spring-gun trap; they should never have embarked on this without a *pawang*, or medicine man, to charm the tiger.

"Are there really such people?" asks Ren.

To his surprise, Ah Long nods. "They can call leopards and wild boar, too. Even monkeys. It depends on how powerful they are." He rubs his upper lip gruffly. "Well, that's what they say. Now make sure you lay the breakfast table before he gets up."

/////

"*TUAN*, ARE YOU GOING TO CHURCH?" ASKS REN. WHILE WILLIAM ate breakfast, he polished his master's shoes with brown Kiwi shoe polish, purchased yesterday in town, till they were bright. William inspects them and says they remind him of ripe chestnuts, though Ren has no idea what he's referring to. Some kind of fruit, he thinks, though he can't imagine a fruit that looks like shoes.

"Yes, I'm going this morning." He'll drive himself as Harun has Sunday off.

"Is it true that the tiger has left this area?"

William nods. It's as if the tiger has vanished utterly, leading to lurid speculation that it's not a normal beast. Word has already gone round that Ambika was a loose woman and that's why she was taken. Rumors like this make William noticeably uneasy. Ren can only conclude, as he stands on the gravel drive to see the car off, that William must be a kindhearted and sympathetic person.

When the housework is done, Ren hurries back to his quarters to examine the finger that he took—no, stole—from the hospital yesterday, though it fills him with a nameless dread. The trousers he wore last night are still hanging on their hook. Ren takes out the bottle, setting it on the window ledge. Outside, the thick bamboo hedge is wet and soft with dew. A mynah bird picks its way across the grass, head cocked in a yellow-eyed stare. In the morning sunlight, the finger looks just as sad and grisly as it did yesterday in the pathology storeroom.

Ren stares until he gets dizzy but his cat sense is strangely quiet. Yesterday, his head was filled with its quivering hum, but today there's only stillness. A hushed expectancy.

Squeezing his eyes shut, Ren wills his cat sense to return. He's missed it desperately in the three years since Yi died. It was gone when he needed it most: those last few months with Dr. MacFarlane, when he said those strange things that confused and alarmed Ren. The old doctor's eyes would open wide as he whispered, in a glassy trance. Long, detailed descriptions of killing deer and wild boar, creeping silently from behind them. The sudden rush, choking the throat by biting. Wrenching the head to break the neck.

/////

THE FIRST DEATH OCCURRED DURING THE RAINY SEASON, WHEN THE monsoon hung like a grey curtain over the wet red earth. Ren can't forget that time; it plays back like a reel of film that he doesn't understand, no matter how often he watches it. If he closes his eyes, he can still see the figure of the old doctor, writing in one of his notebooks. He's been ill, vomiting in the bathroom downstairs though when Ren goes to check on him, there's nothing to clean.

"I cleaned up myself," Dr. MacFarlane says. His eyes are bloodshot and when Ren serves him a simple supper of leftover curry, he grimaces. "Take it away. I can't eat meat."

Later, Ren finds him staring at the endless rain streaming off the veranda roof. "Ren," he says without turning around, "what do you think of me?"

No one has ever asked Ren that question before. At least, no grown-up. Auntie Kwan was always busy telling him what to do, not asking for his opinion, and for an instant, he misses her desperately. Tongue-tied, he gazes at Dr. MacFarlane's nose, a trick that the old man taught him for when he feels too shy to meet someone in the eyes.

"You are a good person," Ren says at last. He wonders whether Dr. Mac-Farlane is concerned about the rumors that he's losing his mind, or if he's even aware of them.

His master studies him for so long that Ren wants to look away, at his own small bare feet, or out of the window, but that's impolite. Instead, he forces his gaze higher until he looks Dr. MacFarlane in the eye. And to his surprise, the old man looks sad.

"Let me show you something," he says, walking with his stiff, familiar gait to the rolltop desk where he keeps all his papers. The keys are kept on a ring in Dr. MacFarlane's pocket. After his death, the lawyer will go through every drawer but not before asking Ren, suspiciously, if he has touched anything.

Dr. MacFarlane takes out a photograph. There are two Malay men in the picture, bare-chested and squatting against a wall. The expressions on their faces are friendly, yet wary. The one on the right has what looks like a cord or a string tied around his upper arm.

"Which one of them is like me?" says the old man.

Ren wrinkles his brow in concentration. Is his master having another fit? But no, he's calm and lucid. Then Ren sees it.

"The groove on his upper lip." He points at the man on the right. "He doesn't have one and neither do you."

Dr. MacFarlane looks pleased, as proud as when Ren put the wireless radio back together after taking it apart.

"Yes," he says. "That's called a philtrum." The troubled expression returns to his face.

"Who is this man?" asks Ren.

"I took this photograph five years ago, when I was traveling with a friend. We were in a little hamlet called Ulu Aring, and this chap," he taps the man on the right, "was the local *pawang*." Dr. MacFarlane speaks quickly, fluently in a way that he hasn't in many days.

"Was that when you lost your finger?" As long as Ren has known Dr. MacFarlane, he's been missing the last finger on his left hand.

"Yes, the same trip. When he saw me he was very excited." The old doctor places one finger above his upper lip. "He put his hand right here, and called me *abang*."

Older brother.

"Why?"

"He said this missing upper lip groove is the sign of a weretiger."

Ren is silent, wondering if the old man is joking but there's no hint of it in his pale eyes. There are stories about tiger-men, who come from the jungle to snatch children and gobble up chickens. He studies the black-and-white picture.

"Did you see him change into a tiger?"

"No, though other people said they had. When the mood struck, he'd say, 'I'm going to walk,' and enter the jungle, burning incense and blowing it through his fist until his skin changed and his fur and tail appeared. Then he'd hunt for days until he'd eaten his fill.

"When he was done, he'd squat down and say, 'I'm going home,' and turn back into a man. In his man-shape, he'd vomit up the undigested bones, feathers, and hair of everything he had eaten."

Ren suddenly recalls Dr. MacFarlane's vomiting fit and the retching, gagging sounds that came from behind the closed door.

"The other sign of a weretiger," Dr. MacFarlane continues, "is a deformed paw. Whether it's a front or hind leg, there's always one that's defective. When I lost my finger on that trip, the *pawang* told me to bury it with me so I could be made whole again—a man. I didn't believe him at the time." He falls silent.

Ren shifts uneasily, studying the old man's profile. There's an expression on his face he hasn't seen before; a sly flicker, or is it a shadow that passes, like an eel, behind his eyes? "Do I look like a murderer to you?" Dr. MacFarlane asks.

Suddenly, Ren is frightened. He takes a step back, then another. Dr. MacFarlane, still staring out of the window, doesn't notice when he leaves.

Ren can't help but hear the words *Do I look like a murderer to you?* echo in his head over the next few days whenever he looks at Dr. MacFarlane. It's a bewildering, frightening question. And so, when the foreign ladies in their light, fluttering dresses come trooping up the long gravel driveway a few days later to check on the doctor, Ren is glad of their interruption, though he rushes to tidy up.

When the ladies enter, they're relieved to find the bungalow neat and clean, and Dr. MacFarlane seated in a rattan armchair, a book on his lap. They're accomplices, the old man and the boy, though as Ren scurries back and forth, keeping other doors closed so they won't see the rest of the house, he feels like a traitor. He suspects that it might be better if these women took charge, but how is he to explain that?

One of the ladies, stiff-bosomed like the prow of a ship, announces, "You can't possibly stay here alone, especially with a man-eater loose." Her high, sharp voice cuts through the room as Ren enters, balancing a tray with teacups. There are no biscuits; they ran out weeks ago.

Dr MacFarlane's voice is heartier than he's heard it in a long time, though the hand that grips the armchair trembles slightly. "Rubbish! I'm not alone anyway."

"A young woman was taken from a coffee plantation." The lady glimpses Ren and nods for him to set the tray on the table. She's waiting for him to leave the room. Exiting, he lingers near the door. He can't make out much because she's dropped her voice.

"—stalked from behind. Neck broken—"

Listening, Ren finds the description frighteningly familiar. When they take their leave, Dr. MacFarlane's face is grey and tight. All his earlier spirit has deserted him.

Later, when Ren sweeps the downstairs bathroom he finds a strand of dark hair in the corner. Longer than his arm, it's hair from a woman's head. Staring at it, Ren doesn't know whether he missed it last time, or whether one of the ladies used the facility during the visit.

That night, he dreams that Dr. MacFarlane is bent over and vomiting in the downstairs bathroom again. It's very dark in his dream; what little light there is blue and wavering as though a lightning storm is raging outside. Transfixed, Ren watches from the open door as Dr. MacFarlane lifts his head, slavering, his eyes like a wild animal. Thrusting his left hand into his mouth, the one with the missing finger, he pulls out a long, coiling black strand of woman's hair.

THE MEMORY ENDS, LIKE A STRIP OF FILM THAT FLICKERS TO A HALT. Ren has an uneasy feeling that at some point he's made a misstep, although he has no idea what it was. If only he'd had his cat sense to help him at the time.

Now, he turns his attention back to the glass bottle. There's no hiding place in his bare little room, but he's saved an empty tin and slips the vial into it. Tucking it under his shirt, he walks out to the very end of the garden, right where the green lawn gives way to jungle near the rubbish dump. There, he digs a hole in the soft earth and buries the tin, placing a large stone to mark the spot.

When he takes leave to return to Kamunting, he'll dig it up and rebury the finger in Dr. MacFarlane's grave and be done with his responsibility.

WILLIAM LISTENS TO THE CHURCH SERVICE WITH ONLY HALF AN ear, his eye busy scanning the pews. Holy Trinity is built of dark wood, shady and cool, but though it's still morning, it's so humid that sweat trickles down his collar. The church is quite full as there are now more locals than Europeans who attend. The Tamil woman standing next to him shifts over, and William wonders suddenly whether he smells like blood.

The scent of the operating room often clings to him with its sharp top note of disinfectant and murky undertones of bone dust and blood. It never quite leaves his nostrils, even though he's scrupulous about washing his hands and bathing frequently. But he hasn't been in the operating room since Friday, so it must be the ghost of a scent.

On Friday, there was an explosion on a mining dredge. One man lost both hands above the wrists, and William had resorted to Krukenberg's procedure, popular since the Great War. He seldom performs it, preferring to save every inch of wrist that he can, but in cases like this it's the best he can offer. By dividing the two bones of the forearm, the stump can be used like chopsticks. It's an ugly solution that amplifies the mutilation. There will be no discreet hook, no wooden hand to deceive at first glance; only two raw-looking prongs like lobster claws instead of forearms. But they work far better than prostheses. The man will be able to grip items with full sensation, open doors, even handle implements. Thinking it over, William is sure he did the right thing, though he can't imagine that any woman would like to be touched by those sad claws. What is a hand without fingers? The loss of even one throws everything off balance.

Now the congregation is kneeling, reciting together:

> "We have left undone those things which we ought to have done,
> and we have done those things which we ought not to have done.
> But thou, O Lord, have mercy upon us . . ."

William doesn't kneel as he's standing in the back, though he has the urge to do so. *Those things which we ought not to have done*—the words perch on him like soft heavy birds.

He considers the question of Ren. William didn't instruct him to shine his shoes, but they were done this morning, placed neatly at the entrance. For the first time, he truly understands his mother's sighs about the worth of a good servant. But Ren is only a child. He's so obviously bright that it's selfish, almost monstrous, to keep him for himself. *I should send him to school.*

Down in one of the front pews, he spots Lydia's profile and is struck again by how her coloring resembles Iris's, his fiancée, with her fine freckled skin and bright hair. Iris smiling at him: that familiar feeling of infatuation, when he thought he'd do anything to please her. Iris, cold and distant, accusing him of canoodling with other women when it was ridiculous, he never did, not once when he was with her. The irony of it. And then Iris, furious the last time he saw her, her small pink mouth open in a silent scream. *Murderer.* He shudders at the memory.

WHEN THE SERVICE IS OVER, LAST NIGHT'S UNSUCCESSFUL TIGER hunt is the talk of the congregation.

"What did I say?" It's Leslie, his young colleague from the hospital. He grins. "They were bound to make a hash of it with Price on board."

Leslie dislikes Price for some reason. In a small community like theirs, every minor offence counts, which is why William has to be careful that nobody ever connects him with poor Ambika's dismembered torso. So he must stay friendly with Leslie, who talks too much, with too many people.

"About our get-together," says Leslie, referring to the monthly dinner party that William hosts next. "Is it all right if I fix up some entertainment?"

William isn't particularly keen, but he says genially, "Whatever you like."

"It's a surprise!" says Leslie, looking pleased as he heads off. Too late, William realizes he forgot to mention that he's promised Lydia she could come to their next gathering, but it doesn't matter. Lydia fits in well with that crowd. Far better than Ambika ever could have.

The rumors that Ambika was singled out by witchcraft or angry spirits in the form of a tiger are troubling, mostly because they accuse her of being a loose woman. Which she was, he supposes. Suddenly and acutely, he misses her. A fog of misery and loneliness descends on him, but Ambika's little hut remains empty. She will never return to it.

William tells himself that from now on, he'll be a better person. Put in a good word for that Chinese girl in the pathology storeroom yesterday, the one who'd asked about nursing. The girl was charming with her cropped hair; it went well with her straight brows and dark eyes, tilted like a doe's, as she stared him down. She was like a pretty boy, all slim limbs and narrow waist, so that he felt like seizing her, hard, to hear her gasp. He wonders what it would be like to trace a finger along that slender nape, down the hollow between her small pointed breasts. She's not his type, but when he thinks about her, he wants to touch her.

His type is more like Nandani, the girl whose leg Ren saved. Even as he considers this, he sees her face in the crowd. It startles him—is it really her, or do all local girls with long braided curls look similar? But she's smiling shyly, her heart-shaped face dimpling. William has a sudden rush of confidence.

Sometimes—unexpectedly—what he wishes for comes true. Doors open, obstacles are removed. Like Rawlings's suspicions of foul play, brushed aside by an impatient magistrate. Or the fortuitous timing of that salesman's obituary in the newspaper. Call it coincidence or just plain luck, it's happened a little too often in his life.

Smiling back, he makes his way over to Nandani. She leans on wooden crutches.

"How's the leg?" Her English, as he recalls, isn't so good, not like the other girl, the Chinese one. They speak a patois of Malay and English, but that's all right.

"Better," she says shyly.

"I'll give you a ride," he says. She lives on a nearby rubber estate, after all.

But Lydia has found him. "Are you going back, William?"

His first reaction is annoyance, but then he realizes that it is in fact a good thing. What was he thinking, to give a local girl a lift home in front of everyone at church? He's slipping up. It's better to have Lydia around. Perfect, in fact, as he can drop her off first, and then Nandani. "Would you like a lift?"

Lydia is delighted. "Well, if it's not too much trouble."

"No trouble at all—I'm dropping off a patient." He deliberately charms her.

Lydia stops to tell her parents she won't be going back with them. From their glances, they're pleased he's making a move on their daughter. It's a misunderstanding he'll have to eventually clear up, though it's understandable. He's the right age and from a good family. There's talk around

Lydia that nags at him, though he can't recall what it's about. William has a feeling that he ought to investigate. But in the meantime, the sun is shining, everyone is smiling, and the tiger hunt promises more excitement in the future.

Lydia sits in front, of course. William helps Nandani into the back with her crutches. She looks intimidated, so he gives her hand an extra squeeze. She drops her eyes, and William is sure that she likes him. Today may be lucky after all.

20

MY EYES OPENED TO AN UNFAMILIAR CEILING. THE FLOOR CREAKED, a voice echoed in the corridor, and I remembered that I'd stayed over at the nurses' hostel. Grey light seeped in through the single window. It was Sunday morning.

Last night's headache had vanished, though I wondered whether there was something wrong with me, some brain disease that gave me vivid delusions. Every dream I'd had of that deserted railway station had been preceded by a bad headache. The little boy's words about how there ought to be five of us lingered. I sat on the edge of the narrow bed, counting us off. There was Shin, and me, and the little boy. He'd also mentioned his brother and a fifth person, someone he seemed quite nervous about. The memory was beginning to fade, the way that dreams do.

I had the odd fancy that the five of us were yoked by some mysterious fate. Drawn together, yet unable to break free, the tension made a twisted pattern. We must either separate ourselves, or come together. I could certainly see that about Shin and myself. He was my paper twin, my friend, my confidante. And yet I envied and resented him.

I washed up quickly in the white-tiled, institutional common bathroom. It was deserted, the voices in the corridor having long gone elsewhere. Yesterday's frock was too grimy to be worn again, but Mrs. Tham had insisted on packing a modern cream and green geometric print *cheongsam*, fitted like a sheath. I'd thought I was done with *cheongsam* after making the grey one that I'd worn to the salesman's funeral, but Mrs. Tham had other ideas, declaring that such a tricky dress should be the backbone of every dress-maker's arsenal. Unfortunately, I'd underestimated the seam allowances. Once I put it on, I was sure I wouldn't be able to eat a thing. Why, why had I let her pack for me yesterday? It struck me that both Mrs. Tham and Shin possessed the uncanny ability to drag me into situations that I didn't plan for. If yesterday was any indication of what might happen, I'd be lucky if Shin didn't make me clean the hospital toilets today.

THE RECEPTION AREA WAS EMPTY. EVERYONE WHO'D BEEN OUT ON Saturday night was probably still sleeping it off. I wondered where Shin was and what he'd done last night, as I headed over to the cafeteria for breakfast. A faint, foggy mist clung to the wet grass as I crossed, looking for a shortcut. Approaching a corner, I heard the low hiss of angry voices.

"Don't deny it! You've been crying your eyes out over him—a married man!"

"—none of your business anyway."

I hesitated. The next instant, someone rushed around the corner and cannoned into me. It was a young nurse, her face puffy, her eyes watering suspiciously.

"Are you all right?" I asked.

She burst into tears. There was nothing to do but offer her my hand-kerchief; I couldn't very well leave her crying on the grass. From what I'd overheard, it sounded like the same sad story I'd observed at the May Flower. Married men were trouble.

"Did you hear everything?" My face must have given me away, for she said, "It's not like I was having an affair with him. They're just picking on me. Can you please not tell anyone? I might get suspended if Matron finds out."

"Don't worry, I'm just a visitor."

She looked relieved. "It's just that, of course, you'd be sad if somebody died, right?" Tears welled up again in her eyes.

People crying always made me feel guilty, especially my mother, the few times I'd found her silently weeping in her darkened bedroom, her eyes wide open and the tears running down her face as though she was sleep-walking. This nurse looked so utterly miserable, with her crooked knees and crumpled uniform, that I patted her back while she blew her nose loudly.

"I couldn't even go to his funeral last weekend in Papan, because I had to work."

My ears pricked. How many funerals could there have been in that town last weekend?

"What did he do?"

"He was a salesman, one of my patients. We were friends," she said too quickly.

So I'd found her—the nurse who'd given the salesman the finger. Was it fate, or some dark link, like a cold strand of riverweed entangling us? Too many peculiar events were connected to this hospital. I couldn't help thinking that if you believed the souls of the dead lingered for forty-nine days after death, then this hospital must be full of them.

"Were you going somewhere?" she asked, with a guilty start.

"To the cafeteria, but I got lost."

"I'll take you. I was on my way there myself." She pursed her lips. "Let me wash my face first."

The little nurse—she was almost a head shorter than me, though I was considered tall for a girl—hurried off. I waited, wondering whether she'd change her mind and abandon me. But my experience at the May Flower had taught me that people confided all sorts of things to strangers, and she'd been practically bursting to tell someone.

Presently, she returned looking better. She still had a rabbity air about her, but it suited her pale complexion and small front teeth. "I'm Pei Ling, by the way."

"My name's Ji Lin. I stayed at the hostel last night, to visit my brother—I mean, my fiancé." I stumbled over the words.

She gave me a complicit look. "You mean your boyfriend? They're awfully strict at the hostel. Don't worry, I won't tell. What's his name?"

"Lee Shin. He's an orderly."

"I don't think I know him." She frowned intensely, as though she was calculating something, then stopped, twisting her hands. "You've been kind to me," she said, cutting short my protests. "No, you have. Lots of people don't notice me—I'm that kind of person. But will you do me a favor?"

"What is it?"

"You said your boyfriend was an orderly at the men's hostel. I don't know anyone there. At least, not anyone I trust. Do you think you could ask him to fetch a parcel for me? I'm not asking you to steal. It was mine in the first place." Face red, voice shaking, she must have been desperate to ask a stranger. Or perhaps a stranger was the best method if she didn't want to involve anyone she knew. "Yew Cheung had a friend in the men's hostel who used to keep things for him. He said he'd give it back to me, but he died so suddenly."

"Why don't you ask his friend for it?" That must be Y. K. Wong, I thought. He'd said at the May Flower that he was the salesman's friend.

"Because I don't like him. And he'd probably use it against me." Eyes averted, lips trembling.

This sounded suspicious but I might learn something more about Y. K. Wong, if I had to deal with him again. "All right, I'll ask Shin."

Relieved, she said, "It's in the common room of the men's hostel. Yew Cheung said he hid it in a vase the last time he came because his friend was out. It was only supposed to be a temporary hiding place, and I'm worried that someone will eventually find it."

AT THIS EARLY HOUR ON A SUNDAY MORNING, THERE WERE HARDLY any people in the cafeteria. Those spooning food into their mouths looked bleary-eyed. They'd probably worked the night shift like Pei Ling.

"Do you like being a nurse?" I asked as we loaded our trays with tea and toast and soft-boiled eggs.

"It's all right."

Eagerly, I asked about the qualifications required, and how to apply.

"But why would you want to be a nurse?" Pei Ling assessed my fashionable *cheongsam*. "You look like your family's well-off."

"No, I'm just a dressmaker's assistant. This was made at our shop."

She sipped her *teh O*, sweet black tea, glumly. "Being a nurse isn't easy—if you make a mistake, Matron chews you out."

"But it's interesting, isn't it?" I said. "And you can be financially independent."

I never heard her answer, because Shin slid into the seat opposite.

"Where were you? I was waiting for you at the women's hostel until someone said your room was empty."

There were shadows under his eyes, and his dark hair was sleek and wet, as though he'd stuck his head under the tap. Despite that, he still had a handsome, wolfish look. You could tie Shin up in a sack and roll him around a field, and he'd still come out attractively tousled. Some people were just lucky, I thought enviously.

I glanced at Pei Ling to see if she had the usual slack-jawed reaction to my flashy stepbrother. That always happened to my friends, but Pei Ling had fallen silent, staring at Shin. It was almost as though she was frightened of him.

"Shin, this is Pei Ling. She's a nurse here."

He put on his polite smile, the one used to charm old ladies. "I'm Shin," he said. "Thanks for looking out for . . ." He paused and I could tell he was having the same confusion about how to refer to our relationship. "Her," he said finally, jerking his head at me.

Very smooth, Lee Shin, I thought, exasperated, though I hadn't managed any better myself. "Pei Ling was wondering if you'd do her a favor. Can you fetch something from the men's hostel for her?"

"No!" she blurted out. "Just forget it."

"Are you sure?" I'd never seen anyone have that reaction to Shin before.

"Yes. I have to go now." Standing abruptly, she shoved her chair back as she fled the cafeteria. Stunned, I followed her as best I could in my stupidly tight dress.

"What's wrong?" I asked breathlessly. She'd sounded so desperate this morning, as though she'd had no one else to ask. "Don't you want Shin to get your package back for you? I'm sure he'll do it."

"How well do you know him?"

"Since we were children," I said, puzzled.

She bit her lip, looking away. "I've seen him around with Yew Cheung's friend. The one I don't like." Not knowing what to say, I recalled Y. K. Wong was Shin's roommate here at the hospital.

"Forget it. I'll get it back myself." Pei Ling walked off stiffly, her back radiating a clear *do not follow* sign.

Returning to the cafeteria, I found Shin eating the remains of my *kaya* toast. "You're losing your touch with women," I said gloomily. "And give me back my breakfast."

"Too late." He stretched his long legs out under the table. I felt like kicking him, except the *cheongsam* I was wearing was too narrow to allow it. "What was that all about?"

I told him about Pei Ling and her connection with both the salesman and Y. K. Wong—though when I mentioned that his roommate had tried to follow me home on Friday night, Shin's face darkened.

"Why didn't you say anything to me yesterday?"

"Just pretend you don't know. I don't want to get involved with him." Thankfully, Y. K. Wong didn't seem to have glimpsed my face yesterday. "Though I wonder what Pei Ling wanted you to get for her in the men's hostel."

Everything connected to the severed finger, including Pei Ling and her odd request, cast an uneasy shadow. Half of me was rabidly curious, while the other half warned it was best to forget about it. In any case, we were almost done cleaning up the storeroom—a couple of hours more and I'd be heading back to Ipoh.

Shin had finished what remained of my breakfast and now gazed speculatively at Pei Ling's untouched plate.

"You can have hers as well."

"Don't want it."

"Hers is better—she didn't even take a bite," I pointed out.

"I only want your food," he said languidly.

I rolled my eyes, relieved we were on friendly terms again. Though I ought to be careful with Shin. He might blow hot and cold again. So I said nothing and ate Pei Ling's toast instead. It bothered me, that she'd seemed so frightened.

A shadow fell across us, and I looked up to see Koh Beng, the porky-jowled orderly. Although it was only morning, his face was covered with a thin sheen of sweat. "Are you all right?" he asked. "You didn't look well last night."

It was kind of him to remember. Koh Beng sat down and started eating. Noodles again, with thin succulent slices of pork liver ladled on top of the steaming hot soup. I wished I'd ordered that as well. "Want some?" he asked.

"We were just leaving," said Shin, standing. I got up as well, discreetly tugging my dress down. Koh Beng's gaze lingered on my legs.

"Eyes on the table!" I said, rapping the wooden tabletop.

He grinned. "I like a girl who speaks her mind."

He was interrupted by a commotion outside. People were running back and forth and shouting.

"What is it?" I asked.

Koh Beng kept eating his noodles. "Probably a monitor lizard," he said dismissively.

Monitor lizards could grow up to five feet long and preyed on stray chickens, rodents, and whatever else they could find. The thought of one roaming the hospital gave me goose bumps. I glanced at Shin but he was frowning, head cocked as though he'd heard something.

"Come on," he said.

Away from the main hospital buildings, the hill sloped downward, connected by little walkways and stairs. Shin was much faster than me, and by the time I came out onto the walkway where he'd stopped, a group of people had gathered at the bottom.

"Step aside, please!" Two men with an empty stretcher brushed past.

Shin turned and made his way back towards me. "Don't look."

"What happened?"

In answer, he seized my elbow and led me swiftly away. Craning my neck, I caught a glimpse of the men loading someone onto the stretcher; I could just make out a small bare foot.

"How did you meet that nurse again?" Shin asked in an undertone.

"I ran into her on my way to the cafeteria. Why?"

"Because she just fell down those steps. It's quite bad. No, don't go back. There's nothing you can do right now."

"Is she dead?"

"Looks like a head injury. Someone found her just now."

Shocked, I felt like crying. What a horrible thing to happen to Pei Ling, and barely half an hour since she'd left the cafeteria.

"Was she running when she left you?"

"No, she was walking. Shin, what should we do?"

"She's already being seen by doctors. A hospital is a good place to have an accident. If it was one," he added under his breath.

I stopped. "What makes you think so?"

"She landed quite a distance from the bottom of the stairs. If you tripped, you normally wouldn't fall so far because you'd catch yourself. There were railings, too. If you were pushed, on the other hand—" He sighed. "When she told you about her parcel in the men's hostel, was there anyone around?"

"Not the first time. But when we were outside the cafeteria, there were people passing."

Anxiously, I scanned the scene below. The stretcher with its sad burden, the pathetic small feet sticking out, one bare and one still shod in a sensible nurse's shoe, had made its way behind another building. The people dispersed, though a lone figure continued to watch from a distance. I recognized the crooked profile as Y. K. Wong's.

"I thought you said he was gone last night!" I hissed, pointing him out to Shin.

"He must have come back this morning. You're not suspecting him, are you?"

I wasn't sure what to think. Pei Ling's calamity unnerved me; it seemed too coincidental that she should have such a terrible accident right after confiding in me. Once again, I thought of the black shape moving deep in the river of my dreams.

"Shin, can you look for Pei Ling's parcel in the men's hostel common room? She was worried that someone else would find it. We ought to keep it safe for her." I gave him a pleading glance.

He didn't say anything, just raised his eyebrows and walked off. I knew he'd do it though. We'd had pet ducklings when we were younger, two sweet yellow balls of peeping fluff. Mine disappeared one afternoon. Cats' dinner, people had teased, but Shin had silently and doggedly searched the neighborhood for days, long after all hope for the poor duck was gone. Recalling this, I felt a rush of gratitude. Though Pei Ling's words lingered in my head: *how well do you know him?* It was a good question. We were no longer children. Even now, I wasn't sure why Shin hadn't come home for almost a year. Besides, how long could I rely on him? The only real family I had was my mother, and she was the one who required looking after.

At the sound of approaching footsteps, I straightened up, suddenly fearful that it might be Y. K. Wong. There was something uncanny about that man, the way he appeared in unexpected places. But it was only Koh Beng.

"Hello!" he said cheerfully. "Waiting for Shin?"

"Yes, he's gone to fetch something." I hesitated, wondering whether to mention Pei Ling's accident to him.

"Want me to show you around?"

I agreed quickly. It wasn't wise to wait near the men's hostel, where Y. K. Wong might well run into me if he returned. Hopefully, Shin would have the good sense to come looking for me.

Koh Beng was an interesting guide, full of gossip and colorful stories. This was where the first blood transfusion in the hospital had taken place. That office was where the previous director's wife had caught him trying on a nurse's uniform. Size XL. I couldn't help laughing, even though most of the tales were dreadful.

"Are you really Shin's girlfriend?" he asked suddenly.

"Why?"

Koh Beng hesitated. "Because he has another girl. Down in Singapore."

"How do you know?"

"He talks about her all the time. Said he met her in Singapore."

How was I supposed to react to this news of supposed infidelity? Perhaps just a brave, upset face would be good enough. "Oh," I stared at my shoes. There was an odd, squeezing sensation in my chest.

"I'm sorry." Koh Beng drew a little closer. "If there's anything I can do—" He put a hand on my shoulder.

"Ji Lin!" It was Shin, coming down the hallway. "Why'd you go off like that?"

Koh Beng dropped his hand.

"He was giving me a tour."

Shin slid his arm around my waist, and I stiffened. Noticing my reaction, Koh Beng smiled awkwardly as he turned to go. "Let me know if you ever need any help."

"WHAT SORT OF HELP WAS HE OFFERING YOU?" ASKED SHIN.

"Nothing," I shouldn't have been annoyed. Koh Beng's well-meaning advice had nothing to do with my situation. I slipped out from under Shin's arm. "We don't have to pretend right now. There's no one else around."

Shin gave me a searching look. Sometimes, I wondered just what was going on behind those quick dark eyes. When he smiled, they crinkled up at the corners, and he smiled a great deal more nowadays than he ever had when he was younger. I wasn't sure whether I liked that. He'd learned to use his face to his advantage.

"I've something strange to show you," he said after a pause.

"Did you find it?" But there were loud voices, the clatter of footsteps. It sounded like a crowd was coming through the corridor; certainly it wasn't a good place to examine mysterious stolen packages. Besides, I didn't want to risk running into Y. K. Wong again.

Shin tried a door. It was locked. The next door opened into a storage closet, with a small window that let in faint grey light. We ducked inside while the voices chattered:

"Such a horrible thing to happen! Who was she again?"

"That small nurse. The one involved with a married patient."

"I'd have thought she'd have more sense."

"Perhaps the wife put a curse on her."

The voices moved farther down the corridor. I discovered that I'd been holding my breath and let it out in a rush.

Shin said quietly, "It was inside the vase in the common room."

The storeroom was cramped and dim, but felt safer than the hallway, especially if Shin really had taken something. He started to unbutton his shirt.

"What are you doing?" I hissed.

"I hid it in my shirt," said Shin, surprised. Then he grinned, "Oh, were you hoping I was going to strip?"

"Who wants to see you take your shirt off?"

"You should talk. You used to go swimming with almost nothing on."

"I did not! I barely went in the water. I can't swim well—you know that!"

"I'll teach you if you want." He leaned closer, warm breath against my ear. For a wild instant, I wondered if he was going to kiss me.

////

I'D BEEN KISSED BEFORE. BY A BOY I DIDN'T REALLY CARE FOR. It was the year before Shin left for medical school, when I was still pining hopelessly after Ming. Ming had a friend named Robert Chiu, a boy from a wealthy family who lived close to Ipoh, and as I always wanted to be near Ming, I couldn't help running into Robert a fair amount as well.

It was Robert who kissed me, on a bench outside the watch repair shop. Shin was off somewhere with yet another new girlfriend and Ming had been called away. I didn't understand why Robert was always around. If I had a grand house with a long driveway and a shiny black car parked in it, I wouldn't spend my afternoons down in a backwater like Falim, but he turned to me. Abruptly, as though he'd made up his mind, he seized my shoulders. His mouth was wet and hot and insistent; I couldn't breathe. There was nothing heart-pounding about it other than the sheer panic I felt in getting him off me.

"I've liked you for a long time," he said. "I thought you knew."

I shook my head. My face was scarlet, my hands trembling. The last thing I wanted was a heart-to-heart talk with Robert but he'd clasped my hand in both of his and I couldn't see any means of escape without shoving him off the bench. It was flattering yet horrific, like a slow-moving accident.

Fortunately, Ming emerged at that point. I felt vaguely ashamed, yet hopeful. Now was the time for him to burn with jealousy, since Robert was still holding my hand, but he only looked at us in his mild, reasonable way, and said to Robert, "Oh, did you talk to her already?"

I jumped up, snatching my hand away. "I'm sorry," I said to Robert. "Thank you very much, but no thank you."

He looked astonished. "You mean it's no good?"

"No. Not at all." And then I fled.

Irrationally, all I could think of was if I married Robert, then I'd be mistress of a large house in Ipoh with a Victrola, on which I could play as many popular songs as I liked. Tempting as that might be, it also meant fending off his sticky embraces. I recalled the girlish bloom on my mother's face soon after she remarried, when I'd caught her sitting on my stepfather's lap. There'd been something about that man that she liked, even now. But whatever it was, I wouldn't find it with Robert. I was quite sure about that, though when Ming came to talk to me in his quiet, concerned way, I unexpectedly burst into tears.

"What's wrong?" he asked worriedly. "Did he frighten you?"

I shook my head, pierced with sorrow. Ming didn't care for me in that tight, aching, can't-live-without-you sort of way. He was just being kind, like an older brother.

"I'm sorry," he said. "He's not a bad person though." *And he's a good catch.* Though Ming had too much delicacy to voice that. Unlike Shin, I thought bitterly, who'd probably urge me to hurry up and marry into money. I said as much to Ming, but he seemed surprised.

"No, Shin doesn't know about this. And don't mention it to him, will you?"

So we hadn't. But whenever I thought about my first kiss, all the painful squeezing feelings of heartbreak and disappointment churned up. Not for poor Robert but for myself, because that was the day I truly understood that Ming would never love me.

LATER ON AT THE MAY FLOWER, THERE WERE SO MANY TIMES THAT men tried to get fresh that I'd learned to twist away at that telltale lunge. So when Shin got too close in the broom closet, after teasing about taking his shirt off, I panicked and shoved him back so hard that he hit the door with a thud.

"Ouch! What did you do that for?"

How could I possibly say that I'd thought my stepbrother was going to kiss me? It was ridiculous; besides, Koh Beng had just confirmed my suspicions that Shin had a girl in Singapore. And yet, there'd been an odd flutter in the pit of my stomach when he'd leaned in. As though a thousand moths were gathering around a candle that had silently and mysteriously been set aflame.

It was only because Shin was so good-looking, I decided. I was tired of dancing with paunchy old men and underage schoolboys, and now I was finally appreciating what I'd taken for granted across the dinner table all those years. This was such an outrageous thought that I started giggling hysterically. Working as a dance hostess had clearly ruined my morals.

The door opened abruptly. We both froze, blinking in the sudden light.

"What's going on in here?" A sharp, spiky voice with the flattened intonations of a foreigner.

Shin turned swiftly, all laughter gone. "I'm sorry, Matron."

So this was Matron. I felt sick. All my hopes of applying to the nursing program, with its requirements of good moral character, would be shattered if she happened to remember later that she'd caught me with a man in a broom closet.

"I hope that isn't one of my nurses behind you," she said, clearly not amused as we stumbled sheepishly into the corridor.

Shin said, "No, ma'am." There was an awkward pause. Then he blurted out, "She's my fiancée."

"Your fiancée?" Her disbelief was palpable.

"I just proposed to her."

"In the closet?"

I could almost see the little cogs turning in Shin's head. It was hopeless, I thought. A made-up tale with nothing to validate it. But to my amazement, he put his hand into his trouser pocket and produced a small velvet-covered box. The ring inside was a simple twist of gold with five tiny garnets set like a flower. Slipping it onto my finger, he grinned triumphantly at Matron.

She was so taken aback that she could only smile weakly. "Well, Mr. . . . Lee, is it? Please refrain from such behavior on hospital grounds. But congratulations!"

Shin ducked his head, looking as pleased as though he'd performed a magic trick. For it was indeed magic. All suspicion and censure evaporated as Matron softened up. She shook hands with both of us, wishing us the best. Shin was deliberately charming, which was good because I was dumbstruck.

I walked a little behind the two of them, trying to compose myself. The ring on my left hand was too loose—I had to curl my fingers so that it wouldn't slip off—but that was to be expected since it had been sized for another girl. How would she feel about Shin using her ring to get out of trouble in this manner?

This pretty, slender gold ring had been chosen with great care. I couldn't imagine that any girl would refuse it, and for a moment, I was overcome by an unexpected tide of desolation. A choking loneliness that made my teeth ache.

21

REN IS EXCITED ABOUT THE UPCOMING DINNER PARTY AT WILLIAM'S house. It's a monthly affair that rotates among a set of younger doctors. Some have wives, but even the married ones often live as bachelors because their families are back in England. So it will be mostly men, says Ah Long. The few wives that stay face the boredom of languid days, stretching into emptiness. With plenty of servants and no housework to do, they volunteer at charities, play tennis, and, if gossip is to be believed, swap husbands.

"Why?" asks Ren. Switching people and houses seems troublesome to him, but Ah Long shakes his head and says that he's too young to understand.

But Ren does understand. Sort of. It's to do with not being happy although he thinks that William is a good master and some woman is bound to want him. The lady at the hospital comes to mind, the one with the soft hair like a steamed sponge cake. Lydia, that's her name. She followed William home on Sunday after church.

From his master's overly polite face, Ren could tell that he wasn't pleased. Apparently he'd planned to drop Lydia off first before sending a patient home, but Lydia managed to insist on a visit. Ren only paid attention because the patient was Nandani. His patient, he thinks, with a small welling of pride.

When William and Lydia stand together in the front room of the bungalow, Ren is struck again by how similar they look. Tall and pale, with large high noses and long hands. He can't tell whether Lydia is attractive or not, but she seems used to attention from the toss of her hair, and the confidence with which she crosses her long legs in their white leather sandals.

"How is the patient? Nandani, I mean?" Ren asks shyly, but William's face brightens.

"Doing well. Do you want to see her?"

"Yes."

"It'll be educational for you to check her progress," says William. "I'll bring her over to the house one day."

Ren glances at Lydia, but she's studiously examining the bookshelf and gives no indication of hearing their plans. She walks through the house with William, giving suggestions about arranging the furniture for the upcoming party. Some of it, Ren thinks, is actually quite good advice.

"There won't be many women on Saturday," says William solicitously. "Are you sure you want to come? It might be awfully boring for you."

She slips her arm through his. "Oh no, I'd love to. Would you like me to arrange the flowers?"

From the alarmed look in William's eye, Ren knows that flowers are the last thing on his mind. It's almost comical, except his master is suffering.

"No need. Ah Long here will manage everything." And with that, William takes her out to the car to send her home.

REMEMBERING THIS, REN ASKS AH LONG LATER WHETHER THEY should get flowers for the house. Ah Long frowns. "Yes. We'll need a centerpiece for the table and something near the front." Despite his air of long suffering, he's enjoying the party preparations.

On Tuesday, Ah Long decides to bleach and starch the table linen again, though it was put away clean last time, because it has yellowed. On Wednesday, Ren dusts and wipes, turning the spines of the books out and aligning them neatly. Ren recognizes some of the titles, the same as in Dr. MacFarlane's house. *Gray's Anatomy*, issues of *The Lancet* and *Annals of Tropical Medicine and Parasitology*. The long words had first been pronounced by Dr. MacFarlane and later Ren learned to copy them out, sitting at the kitchen table. He nods at them, old friends, as he mops the floor.

Three plump chickens are in the wooden coop at the back. They'll be made into chicken cutlets and *Inchi Kabin,* crispy twice-fried chicken served with sweet-and-spicy sauce. Local beef is tough and lean, and comes from water buffalo, so Ah Long will make beef *rendang,* slow-cooked dry curry with coconut, to round out the main dishes. In the meantime, on Thursday they move all the furniture in the living room and wax the floor.

"In case they want to dance," explains Ah Long. "Though there are only two ladies coming." Still, he hauls out the gramophone while Ren sharpens the needles. There'll be another Chinese waiter hired for that evening to serve drinks. William takes little interest in this flurry of prep-arations. When Ren asks about him, Ah Long shrugs. "He's got a new hobby."

Now that he's mentioned it, Ren realizes that his master has taken to disappearing after dinner. "Didn't he use to go for walks in the mornings?"

"Morning, evening, what does it matter? As long as she's willing," Ah Long mutters under his breath.

On Friday morning, the gardener delivers cut flowers to the kitchen door, and Ren carries a heaping armful to the dining room to sort out. If there were a lady in the house, she'd arrange the flowers on the day of the party, but tomorrow will be devoted to cooking. Food spoils quickly in this heat, so everything must be freshly prepared. As Ren trots back to the kitchen for a second load of greenery, he finds the gardener deep in discus-sion with Ah Long.

"You, boy!" says the gardener. He's Tamil, his wiry squat body burned dark by the merciless sun. He's the friendly one who speaks Malay; the other gardener speaks only Tamil. *"Mau lihat?* Want to see something inter-esting?"

Excited, Ren follows the gardener into the garden. Ah Long stumps moodily after them as they go around the back, right up to where the man-icured lawn peters out into undergrowth. This is the frontline of the gar-deners' endless struggle against the surrounding jungle. Walking around the perimeter of the garden, they approach the patch of uneven ground where Ren buries the household garbage—and where the finger that he stole from the hospital is interred, the glass vial safe within its empty bis-cuit tin.

Ren's pulse quickens. His eyes fix on the stone that he placed as a marker.

It looks suspicious on a patch of newly turned ground. He didn't expect anyone to come to the garbage dump. Nobody does, only Ren.

"*Sini*," says the gardener. "Here and here. Can you see?"

He points out traces: bent and broken branches and a print pressed into the soft wet earth. It is a tiger's pugmark.

At least, that's what the gardener says although Ren can't really tell from the blurred half impression. But something has definitely passed that way. Something large and heavy. Deeper in, under the trees, the dry leaves form a thick carpet. It's only where the bare earth is exposed that there's a print. The men squat near the pugmark, wider than the palm of a man's hand.

"Left front paw," the gardener says.

"How do you know?" asks Ren.

The gardener explains that the front paws tend to be larger than the back. There are four toes and a dewclaw, corresponding to a thumb, on the front paws of a tiger. It looks as though the animal was standing under the trees at the edge of the garden. That one foot, the front paw, is the only mark on the edge of the lawn.

"Tigers are cunning," says the gardener. "It was checking the house."

Ren's heart races. What does it mean that the print is right next to the stone that marks the buried finger? He wishes there was some grown-up he could ask for advice, but if he tells William, he'll have to admit to the theft of the finger. Unconsciously, he squeezes his own small hands, wringing them anxiously. There are nine days left of Dr. MacFarlane's forty-nine days of the soul. Surely that's enough time to return the finger?

Ah Long peers at the blurred print. "This tiger is missing a toe," he says. "The small toe on the left front paw."

Ren closes his eyes, inhaling. His ears are sharpened; the hairs on his head prickle. He listens hard, but there's nothing. Not a flicker from his cat sense. Only a silence so profound that it fills the green hollow of clipped lawn that the white bungalow sits in, like a fishbowl in the middle of the jungle.

"Should we put out an offering?" the gardener says diffidently. He's Hindu and Ah Long is nominally Buddhist; between the two of them lies a tradition of little offerings and sacrifices, but Ah Long scowls.

"What are we going to offer—a chicken? I only have three and they're needed tomorrow. Besides, we don't want it to come back."

If it were wild boar or deer then they might scatter blood or human hair to keep them away, but such things don't deter a tiger. The gardener makes a little bow to the silent jungle and says something in Tamil.

"I asked him, Sir Tiger, please do not come back," he says with a slight smile. Ren gazes at his dark, wrinkled face. He has no idea whether the gardener is really worried or if this is just one of those things that happens from time to time, like monsoons or floods. In his time with Dr. Mac-Farlane, they never had a tiger roam so close to the house despite all the old man's ravings. Or perhaps, there were no marks outside because the tiger lived within. The image of Dr. MacFarlane's white face, his left hand with its missing finger curled on the thin cotton blanket, swims before Ren's eyes, and he blanches.

Ah Long catches his arm. "No need to be so frightened! Tigers range for miles, and it's long gone by now."

THAT EVENING, AH LONG INFORMS WILLIAM ABOUT THEIR DISCOV-ery in the halting English that he uses with his employer. It's the second tiger pugmark discovered near the bungalow; the first one occurred around the time that poor woman died.

"So *Tuan*, you no go out alone at night," Ah Long concludes.

A flicker passes over William's face. "You too. And Ren, don't wander around by yourself."

Ren fetches a dish of fried *ikan bilis*, tiny little fish in spicy chili *sambal*. Serve from the left, remove plates from the right—that's what Auntie Kwan taught him. The room is stuffy despite the open windows. The flowers that the gardener brought in—bird of paradises, canna lilies, thin woody branches of hibiscus—are stiff and look like funeral offerings. Ren's skin is tight and shivery; his throat hurts. The pawprint in the garden is a gnawing worry.

"Not well?" William beckons Ren over and places the back of his hand against his forehead. It's a large hand, professionally impersonal. "Hmm. Fever. Go and ask Ah Long for an aspirin and lie down."

Ren hasn't finished the dinner service or the washing up, but William has given him an order. He walks to the kitchen, and the old man, examining his pale face with concern, hands him an aspirin and tells him to go to bed.

Ren walks unsteadily out of the kitchen door, down the covered walkway to the servants' quarters in the back. His face is burning, his legs rubbery. Growing up, Yi was always the sickly one; if there was flu or food poisoning, he was bound to get it before Ren. "I'm the warning system," Yi had said, scrunching his face up in a smile. "I'll go before you." And in the end, he had.

Ren, shivering now in his narrow cot, pulls the thin cotton blanket over himself. Despite the warmth of the room, he's freezing. His bones ache. Yet there's a sense of peace, that lightheadedness that comes with being sick. He can't think coherently about the tiger anymore.

And then he begins to dream.

It is the old dream, the one where Ren stands on a railway platform, only this time the train is stopped at the station. And Ren isn't there. He's on a little island—more like a sandbar—in the middle of a river, gazing at the train from across the water. Sunlight shines through the train's empty windows. Where is Yi?

Ren walks from one end of the sandbar to the other, shading his eyes as he squints across the water. Then he sees him, scrambling and waving wildly on the opposite bank. He jigs from one foot to the other in a familiar manner. How could Ren have forgotten that jig?

"Yi!" he yells. The small figure on the other bank puts his hands around his mouth and calls back, but there's no sound.

Why is there no sound? And then Ren realizes something else. Yi is so small. Not only due to the distance, but because he's still eight years old, the age he died. It's Ren who's changed. But Yi looks so delighted to see him that there's a lump of happiness in Ren's throat.

Now Yi is pantomiming, *How are you?*

He points at himself and gives a thumbs-up. "YOU?"

Yi also gives a thumbs-up. *Don't worry.*

About what? He must mean about the tiger and Dr. MacFarlane and all the deaths before and the ones to come. Of course Yi would know. He always knew everything that troubled Ren.

Ren calls back that he's fine, he has a job and has also found the finger and is keeping it in a safe place. It's difficult to mime all of this, but Yi seems to understand. Perhaps the sound works only one way, but Ren doesn't want to waste his time with Yi figuring it out.

Time is running out.

Even as he thinks this, water laps his bare feet. Jumping back, Ren realizes that the sandbank is getting smaller, or perhaps it's the water that's rising.

"There's a tiger in the garden," he shouts across the water. "But don't worry, I know what to do."

Yi looks concerned.

"I'm going back to Kamunting after the party."

Yi shakes his head.

"It's all right, I have permission. Then I'll do what Dr. MacFarlane told me to."

Yi's arms explode, pantomiming something complicated. The small face is tight with worry.

"I'm not frightened," Ren says.

Ask the girl.

What girl? Ren can't think of any girls or women except Auntie Kwan and she's gone down south to Kuala Lumpur.

The water is rising, rippling translucently over the muddy sand. There's something odd about it. It's viscous, a little too thick, but clear enough that he can see every pebble and floating leaf. There are no tiny fish in the shallows. No crystalline shrimp, no water skaters. Nothing living.

"I'll swim over to where you are," calls Ren. "Just wait!"

He puts one foot in the water. It's surprisingly cold and a swirling current tugs at his ankle. But the other bank isn't too far.

No! Yi doesn't want him to get in the water. Now he's urgently signing him to stop.

Ren isn't a fast swimmer, but he's confident he can dog-paddle far enough. He stands ankle-deep in the shallows. It's freezing. He's never felt cold like this. Dr. MacFarlane once borrowed a large, expensive-looking book of fairy tales when he was teaching Ren to read, and Ren had pored over the beautiful illustrations of snow and ice and the kind of gloomy weather that Dr. MacFarlane said was so common in Scotland. *Dreich,* he'd called it. There was a story about a little girl who sold matches, and the last picture showed her lying in the snow. Her eyes were closed, but she was smiling and the artist had drawn faint blue shadows at the corners of her mouth. Was this chill what she'd experienced?

He grits his teeth. Beyond the shallows of the sandbank, the water is murky. Something stirs in it, and he hesitates. On the opposite bank, Yi is signing frantically. *No no no!* But Ren is bigger and stronger now than when they were parted. He looks at the river with the confidence of an eleven-year-old and is sure he can make it.

Now the water is up to his waist, swirling and eddying darkly. It tugs hard. The chill is almost unbearable, eating through his spine and sucking all the heat out of his body.

Yi is kneeling on the other bank. His face is contorted, tears stream down as he gesticulates wildly. *STOP!*

Ren wants to tell him not to cry; he'll be there soon. But his teeth are chattering so much that he can't form the words. With a final rush of courage, Ren plunges his head under the icy black water.

22

MORNING. I STARED AT THE CEILING AGAIN—THIS TIME THE familiar one at Mrs. Tham's house. Sitting up, I fumbled for the ring Shin had given me, still knotted in a handkerchief. I wondered what she looked like, this girl whose finger was a different size from mine. The soft metal and rich color indicated it was twenty-four-karat gold. My mother always told me to make sure to get twenty-four-karat jewelry, not eighteen or some other inferior number.

"Because you can pawn it," she'd said matter-of-factly. "You get a better deal."

Of course, she must have had some experience with pawnshops after my father died. In my brief time working at the May Flower, men had given me gifts: silver pendants, thin bracelets. I'd been reluctant to accept anything, but the other girls said I was foolish to turn down one of the few perks of the job. My mother had been right, however. None of those trinkets was worth anything at the pawnshop, though I'd tried a couple of times, thinking to reduce her debt faster. I wondered how much money Shin had spent. He was always the one who ended things with girls, not wanting to commit. As far as I knew, he'd never given anyone a gift like this.

YESTERDAY AFTER MATRON HAD LEFT US, I'D TRIED TO RETURN IT to Shin with a smile, saying, "You should keep this safe for your girlfriend." That was nice and friendly and just what I might have said to him a few years ago.

"Hang on to it," he said. "It'll look suspicious if you give it back after telling everyone we're engaged."

That was when I ought to have followed up and asked what his girl-friend was like and when he was bringing her back home, but somehow, I couldn't. If you'd told me a month ago that I'd feel so awkward and sad about my stepbrother getting married, I'd have laughed it off, but now there was only a strange loneliness. It was like losing him all over again, like when he'd decided to shut me out. But there was a difference: it wasn't simply that Shin was being friendly, as though whatever had troubled him before was now resolved. He'd become more reliable, more grown-up. More at-tractive.

There. I'd said it.

Well, Shin had always been attractive, just not to me. Or perhaps I'd willfully looked the other way. I tried my best to conjure up Ming's long, gentle face, the stubborn cowlick on the back of his head, but it was useless. The infatuation that had sustained me for so many years had faded, leaving a vague sense of confusion and guilt.

So instead, I made up some excuse about getting back to Ipoh right away. I still hadn't seen Pei Ling's parcel, but by then we were standing in front of the hospital where Matron had left us, in full view of passersby. Best for Shin to keep it safe and unopened at the hospital and return it to Pei Ling when she recovered from her fall.

When I got on the train, I took off the ring and wrapped it in my handkerchief. It didn't seem right to wear it since it wasn't mine. I tucked the handkerchief into my rattan basket and felt the sharp edges of the card that I'd received from the foreign doctor. *William Acton, General Surgeon.* Curling my fingers around it, I'd thought perhaps I would contact him after all.

ON TUESDAY AFTERNOON I WENT TO SEE HUI, ESCAPING DINNER with Mrs. Tham's family. She'd hinted that I ought to be there that eve-ning because there was a young man she wanted me to meet: her husband's nephew, who'd been jilted by some minx and was now determined to get married before the end of the year. Just to show that he could, apparently. I didn't think this boded well for anybody.

I took Shin's ring with me, as Mrs. Tham was bound to snoop while I was out. The garnets sparkled like pomegranate seeds. Garnets were the bloodstone, meant for protection. When I was a little girl, an Indian peddler had come by selling necklaces of round garnet beads strung on cotton thread.

"Keep your daughter safe from harm. From evil, nightmares, and wounds. Also good for love," he'd said to my mother, and surprisingly, she'd bought me one.

I'd kept that string of garnets for years, until one day I'd gone wading in the river with Ming and the frayed cotton string had finally snapped. The tiny beads slipped into the running water, and were never found. Remembering this, I tucked the ring back in my pocket. It wasn't mine to lose.

Hᴜɪ ᴡᴀs sᴛᴀɴᴅɪɴɢ ɪɴ ꜰʀᴏɴᴛ ᴏꜰ ʜᴇʀ ᴍɪʀʀᴏʀ, ᴘᴏᴡᴅᴇʀɪɴɢ ʜᴇʀ ꜰᴀᴄᴇ with a look of determination. A good powdering was supposed to take at least ten minutes to apply, the powder puff not rubbed but slapped against the face, mouth, ears, eyelids, and neck. Slap, slap, slap, with lots of vigor. A really good application of powder should last for hours, so that your skin emerged "tinted, smooth, and lovely"—according to the magazines. I wouldn't know, as I'd never managed to devote more than thirty seconds to my powder puff.

"Ji Lin! What are you doing here?" Hui looked pleased.

I sat on her bed. "Are you working tonight?" I'd hoped that she was free to have dinner at one of the roadside stalls that grilled stingray wrapped in banana leaves, but she was clearly getting ready for an evening out.

"No. It's a call-out."

Call-outs paid well, much better than dancing, and Hui had no day job like my dressmaking apprenticeship. She couldn't bear it, she'd said. Snipping and measuring all day, though I'd pointed out that call-outs seemed worse.

"Not to me," she'd said. She was always vague about what happened on call-outs; there was dinner and some form of physical contact though she said it was mostly kissing and being felt up. "It's at a restaurant—there's a limit to what they can do in public."

I'd once asked her if she'd ever done anything else. She'd looked amused and closed her eyes in a long blink. "Of course not." We'd both laughed uncomfortably. Sometimes I worried about her.

"You're looking gloomy today," said Hui.

Not wanting to explain all the details of the weekend, I simply said we'd returned the finger to the hospital. I thought she'd be glad to hear that, but she lifted her eyebrows.

"And who is 'we'?"

"My brother and I." I remembered Shin's breath against the nape of my neck when he'd held me, reluctantly, under the *angsana* trees. The blood rose in my face, and the more I tried to will it away, the worse it got.

Hui examined me carefully. "This is your stepbrother, correct?"

"Yes. He's getting married. Or at least, he's serious about someone. I'm glad for him."

I was afraid Hui would make fun of me, but instead she put her arm around me. "Oh, darling. Men are beasts, aren't they?"

"It makes me feel lonely, that's all. We've known each other since we were ten years old. I'm . . . I'm very fond of him." Such inadequate words. They couldn't even begin to explain how restless and disturbed I felt. And perhaps I was confusing simple affection with something else. "It's ridiculous, anyway."

Hui got up and walked over to her dressing table. "But you're not related." Her eyes watched me in the mirror. She was playing with the rouge pot, opening and closing the lid absently. "I'd like to meet him, this stepbrother of yours."

"Why?"

"Because men are liars." There was a sharpness in her tone I'd never heard before. I knew Hui had left some village to come to Ipoh and that she rarely went home, but other than that I'd tried not to pry, accepting whatever she wanted to share. She'd done the same for me, after all.

Hui glanced up. "Don't look so worried about me, Ji Lin. You really are sweet."

Touched, I tried to laugh it off, changing the subject. "Can you tell the Mama that I won't be in this week?"

"Why not?"

I explained about Y. K. Wong following me after work last Friday and then almost running into him twice at the hospital this weekend. It was too many coincidences for comfort.

"Tell her my mother's ill or something." And I really needed to find another job, though it didn't seem like a good time to bring that up.

"What about the private party in Batu Gajah this Saturday?"

"I'll do that." It would pay well.

We talked about the arrangements for the party, though my heart wasn't really in it. It might be the last time I worked with Hui and Rose and Pearl. *Perhaps it's for the best.* Especially if I wanted to become a nurse. Still, melancholy settled over me, like a personal rain cloud. Goodbyes were always like that.

Hui said, "Let's practice drawing your mouth." A cupid's bow was tricky, and I never had the patience to do it properly.

"Don't bother with me—won't you be late?" I said, as Hui, pleased with her handiwork, brushed cake mascara on my eyelashes.

"Let him wait."

"Who is it?"

"That bank manager who comes in on Wednesdays."

He was in his late fifties, liver-spotted like a toad with a habit of licking his lips. "Don't you mind?"

"Old is better," she said carelessly. "Young men expect you to fall for them and do all sorts of things for free."

"Hui!" I said, laughing. "You're terrible."

"Don't trust men, Ji Lin," she said sadly. "Not even that charming brother of yours."

Hui told me not to wait for her. She wasn't done with her toilette, though I'd hoped to walk out with her to her date, but she shook her head, "It's getting late," and so I went downstairs.

It wasn't actually late at all. In fact, it was still early enough that I'd be just in time to sit down for dinner with Mrs. Tham and her husband's nephew. Not wanting to go home, I turned up Belfield Street instead. Trishaws and bicycles rushed by, squeezing past bullock carts and the occasional motorcar. At the corner of Brewster Road and the wide green space of the Ipoh *padang*, a cricket field built by the local Chinese community to commemorate Queen Victoria's Diamond Jubilee, I stopped in front of the FMS Bar and Restaurant. FMS stood for "Federated Malayan States," and both locals and expatriates came to drink at the long bar and order Western dishes prepared by a Hainanese chef: sizzling steaks and chicken chops, washed down with icy beer. I'd never been inside, though I'd passed its gracious, colonial façade many times.

One day, I decided, I'd go in and buy myself a steak. Though I wasn't sure if they allowed single women. As I turned to go, the wooden doors of the FMS Bar swung open. My heart jumped as someone caught me by the arm.

"Ji Lin?" It was a young man with a fashionably skinny mustache. Because of this, I almost didn't recognize him.

"It's me, Robert! Ming's friend, Robert Chiu."

Robert was the one who'd given me that unwanted sticky kiss on the bench outside the watchmaker's shop. He was very much the young man now, and knowing what I now did about the price of things, expensively turned out. But he gave me the same eager, half-excited look he had then, which surprised me. If I'd been turned down by some skinny girl from Falim, I probably wouldn't have been so happy to see her again, but Robert evidently had a more forgiving disposition.

"What are you doing here?" His eyes traveled up and down. I knew that look; at work I was very careful with men who stared like that, but it was just Robert, I told myself. And besides, he'd no idea about my part-time job.

"I was just passing by," I said.

Evening had fallen, that magical blue twilight hour, and the yellow radiance from the FMS Bar shone through the door and window transoms.

"I haven't seen you in so long," he said. "How have you been?"

We chatted about inconsequential things. Robert was reading law in England and was back for the holidays. He talked hurriedly, the words tumbling out as though he was afraid I'd walk away. Stories about university and people I didn't know that I listened to with only half an ear.

He'd stopped talking and was staring at me again.

"I'm sorry," I said guiltily. Poor Robert, all that money and still so dull. "You were saying?"

"Nothing. Just that, you look nice."

It was probably the light that spilled out from the bar, warm and flattering, bathing everything with a golden glow. Even Robert looked rather distinguished with his expensive clothes and neatly slicked hair. I dropped my eyes but Robert misunderstood.

Encouraged, he said, "I heard from Ming that you're not married yet."

I said cheerfully, "No, I'm apprenticed to a dressmaker." Best to be brisk at times like these.

"Do you like it?"

"Yes," I said, lying through my teeth.

"I'm surprised that you didn't go on for higher studies. Like teacher training or nursing."

"No money, I'm afraid."

He gave me a quick, embarrassed glance. "Have you thought about scholarships? My family sometimes awards them to bright students—the Chiu family foundation, you know."

"I'm not in school anymore."

"It doesn't matter. I can give you a personal recommendation."

I looked at the ground, not knowing what to say. This was a great chance and any other girl would be jumping at it—and at Robert. Yet I couldn't help thinking that everything came at a price. So I thanked him, saying it was very kind and I'd think about it. "And now I'm afraid I really ought to go."

Robert wouldn't hear of me walking home. "It's not far," I said, laughing.

He insisted though, and I soon discovered why. He led me around the corner to a gleaming new motorcar. It was cream-colored, with sweeping curves and a grille that shone silver in the last of the evening light.

"Get in," he said, opening the door. It was lovely. The seats were camel-colored leather, soft as a baby's cheek, and the whole thing smelled rich: of leather and lemon wax and a faint whiff of gasoline. I sat down, crossing my feet to hide the scuffed toes of my shoes, and inhaled deeply. It would be easy to get used to traveling like this. Or maybe not. Because Robert, unfortunately, was a terrible driver.

I gripped the door handle, my knuckles turning white as Robert launched the car into the street with a queasy lurch. There was a grinding sound as he pressed various levers with his foot and yanked on others with his hands. We shot through an intersection (Robert waving in a friendly way at a furious trishaw man) and barely missed a fire hydrant. The worst part was that he kept talking.

"So, Ji Lin," he shouted, over the din of someone honking at us, "will you be around all summer?"

As if I had anywhere else to go. I said politely, "I'll be here," through gritted teeth. And then finally, in a cloud of exhaust fumes, we were at Mrs. Tham's shophouse.

"Oh, this place," said Robert. "I had to pick up my sister's dress here once."

My legs were weak and rubbery, and I was forced to take Robert's hand as he helped me out. Perhaps this was his routine with women, terrorizing them in his car so that they fell—literally—into his arms.

Mrs. Tham was out of her shophouse in a flash. It was clear she'd been watching for me.

"Ji Lin, I'm so glad you're back." She glanced at Robert. "Who's this?"

"I'm an old friend of her brother's," said Robert, though he and Shin had never particularly got along.

"Oh!" Mrs. Tham's curiosity struggled with her desire to impart news. The latter won. "Ji Lin, we just got a message that your mother's ill."

This was the news that I'd been dreading, ever since my mother had remarried. That she was "ill" could have meant anything, despite the fact that so far, her injuries had been confined to a twisted elbow or finger-marks on her wrist. The image of Shin's broken, dangling arm was always in the back of my mind.

"She had a miscarriage."

A miscarriage? By Chinese counting, which added a year, my mother was forty-two and approaching the most dangerous age in life, since the homophone for forty-two sounded like "you die." My heart plummeted.

"Will you go home tomorrow morning?" said Mrs. Tham.

"Yes, I'll take the bus." It occurred to me that just this afternoon I'd asked Hui to tell the Mama I wouldn't be in for the rest of the week because my mother was sick. How flippant I'd been! And now, like a curse, my words had come home to roost. I thought about the blackness in the river of my dreams, that ominous shape that stirred underwater.

"I'll take you. Right now if you want," said Robert. I'd completely forgotten about him. "It's not far by car."

"Would you really?" Mrs. Tham said. "That would be so kind."

Sick with dread, I ran upstairs to pack, leaving her to ply him with questions. Once in the car, we sat silent. The one consolation was that Robert's driving improved when he wasn't talking.

After a while, he said, "If it's very bad, we can send her to hospital. The district hospital in Batu Gajah is a bit farther than the Ipoh General Hospital, but she might get better treatment."

"Why?"

"Because my father's on the board of the Batu Gajah District Hospital."

I hadn't known that. Rich people lived in a different world, one where jobs and recommendations came easily. If I were cleverer about things I might be able to get better care for my mother, but I could hardly think. In the past few weeks, the people around me had been struck by a death, a horrible accident, and now a miscarriage.

Shin would say it was ridiculous and besides, who knew how many other incidents had occurred in this area in the same time frame? That poor woman I'd read about in the newspaper who'd been killed by a tiger, for example. Not everything could be attributed to fate, though there were others who would surely tell me to buy a charm against evil spirits. I sat in Robert's big car, twisting my hands in my lap and trying not to cry as we rushed on into the darkness.

23

IT'S COLD. SO TERRIBLY COLD THAT REN THINKS HIS HEART WILL stop. The bones of his skull ache. The water feels thick, like runny gelatin or clotted blood. Shaking his head like a dog, Ren peers at the far shore. Yi is running up and down frantically, pure terror on his face as he mouths: *Get out of the water!*

He starts paddling in earnest. It's not so cold if he swims, or perhaps his arms and legs are simply becoming numb. The farther he goes, the more the pain recedes and Ren has the funny feeling that he's shedding his body. Something scrapes his leg. Gulping water, Ren looks down to see a row of gaping teeth and a glazed eye that floats past under his foot. A dead crocodile. It rolls, drifting deep in the river current, white belly showing for an instant, then drops away into the darkness. There are other things, too, deep in the river. Dead fish, dead worms, dead leaves. Ren gives a cry of disgust.

Panicking now, arms and legs flailing. The current drags at him. His head goes under again and he sees more shapes. A Chinese man drifts by, neck hanging at an awkward angle as though it's been broken. A young Tamil woman, mouth open but eyes mercifully closed. No body, only her serene, decapitated head. Ren is crying, struggling. Bursting with terror, water searing his lungs.

A chunk of wood hits him. Gasping, Ren surfaces and makes an empty grab at it. As it floats out of reach he sees that Yi has launched it. Another log drifts towards Ren. This one is bigger and as it smashes into him, he sees Yi's despairing face. *Go back!*

AND HE DOES. HE DOES.

Ren is lying facedown on the floor of his room. His hands flatten out like a gecko on a ceiling only there's nowhere to fall, he's already at the bottom. After a while, he starts to cry.

The door opens. It's Ah Long, his face creased with worry.

"*Aiya!* Are you hurt?"

Dizzy, Ren sits up. Ah Long feels his forehead. "I checked on you earlier—you had a high fever."

"What time is it?" Ren's voice is a dry croak. Ah Long wipes his face with a warm towel.

"About five in the morning."

"It was so cold." The memory of the freezing water makes the hairs on his arms stand up.

"That was the fever."

Ren realizes that he feels fine. No chills, no burning weakness. He swings his legs experimentally. The dream recedes, like water flowing backwards, and most wonderful of all, his cat sense, that invisible, electric pulse which tells him about the world, is back, humming quietly in the background.

Ah Long wrinkles his brow, studying him. He looks like a grizzled old monkey. "You were shouting a lot. Who were you talking to?"

"My brother. My twin brother who died."

Ah Long squats on his haunches so that his face is almost level with Ren's.

"Do you often dream about him?"

"Not often. But it feels so real." Ren explains about the train and the river, and how if he'd tried just a little harder he might have made it over to the other side.

"Has your brother ever asked you to come to him?"

"Why?"

Ah Long sighs and looks up at the ceiling. It's quiet. So quiet in that dark and empty hour before dawn, when not even the birds are stirring. Malaya is situated near the equator; the sun doesn't rise until seven in the morning, and the days are almost exactly twelve hours long.

"Do you believe in ghosts?" asks Ah Long.

Ren is surprised. Ah Long treats religion with the same suspicious necessity with which he regards electricity, radios, and motorcars.

"I don't know," says Ren. But the dreams aren't the same as those stories he's heard of pale apparitions that haunt banana trees, or women with long black hair and backward-pointing feet.

"I had an uncle who could see them," says Ah Long. "He was a cook in a household in Malacca. A lot of peculiar things happened in that house, he said. They had a beautiful daughter who was supposed to marry a dead man."

"Did she really?" Ren is so interested that he sits up straight.

"No, though he was from a very wealthy family. They wanted her to become a ghost bride."

"What happened to her?"

"She ran away with someone else. But years later when my uncle was a very old man, he said she came back to visit him. And strangely enough, she looked exactly the same as when she left home at eighteen. Though that's another story.

"My uncle saw ghosts all the time. It was very disturbing. Unlike the living, they were always in the same place. For example, there was one particular rickshaw that he said always had a passenger in it: a little boy who'd try to sit on people's laps. And another time a woman sat next to his bed all night, combing her hair and crying. But he gave me some advice that I'm going to tell you right now, because I think you need it."

"And what's that?"

"Don't talk to the dead."

Ren is silent for a moment. Nobody has ever given him any advice on this. "Why not?"

Ah Long scratches his head. He looks tired and old. "Because the dead don't belong in this world. Their story has ended—they have to move on. You can't be obeying them from beyond the grave."

Ren's thoughts fly instantly to Dr. MacFarlane. "Won't honoring their wishes make them happy?"

"*Cheh*, happy or not, that's their business, not yours." Ah Long gets up creakily. "If you're feeling better, go back to bed."

"But today is the party," Ren suddenly remembers.

"I've been cooking for more years than you've been alive. As if I couldn't manage without you!"

Ah Long sets a tin mug of warm Horlicks next to Ren and turns to go. He puts one hand briefly on Ren's head. "Remember what I said," he says gruffly.

After drinking the hot malted-milk drink, Ren lies down, pulling the thin cotton blanket over himself. Ah Long doesn't understand, he thinks. There's just a little more to be done, and then it will all be over.

24

BY THE TIME ROBERT'S CAR STOPPED WITH A SCREECH OF BRAKES outside my stepfather's shop, it was almost eight in the evening and quite dark. Robert jumped out but I was already at the front door, fumbling for my keys. All was dim behind the shutters; were things so bad that they'd taken my mother away? Wind stirred in the shadowy overhang, the ghosts of siblings waiting to be born. Or maybe they were already wandering this world somewhere.

The door opened with its familiar creak. My stepfather's face peered out. Deep fissures between his mouth and nose underscored his resemblance to a stone carving. To my surprise, he looked relieved, even pleased to see me.

"Where's my mother?" I asked, my heart in my mouth.

"Resting. She's all right."

He stared at Robert, then at the car that was beached on the curb like a gleaming whale. Robert offered his hand, introducing himself, as I ducked past anxiously. A shadow appeared behind my stepfather. Shin.

I'd always told myself that Shin didn't look like his father, but from certain angles, there was an eerie similarity. The flickering oil lamp my stepfather carried made their features swim, so that for a nightmarish instant, they looked like the past and future of the same person. I mumbled something about wanting to see my mother, but couldn't disguise my brief recoil.

Shin must have noticed because he turned away. "She's resting in the downstairs office—it's best if she doesn't climb stairs right now."

My stepfather's office was a narrow, gloomy room halfway through the long shophouse. He kept his accounts there along with a metal filing cabinet and a large black abacus. As we hurried through the dark shophouse, I said, "Why didn't you light more lamps?"

"After the doctor and Auntie Wong left, my father put the lights out. You know how he is."

I did know. My stepfather had a propensity for sitting in the dark, especially when he was troubled. I remembered again that terrible night when he'd broken Shin's arm. Then, too, the house had been dark and silent.

"What did Auntie Wong say?"

Auntie Wong wasn't related to any of us but had lived next door since before my mother and I had moved in. She was the neighborhood busybody, but she was fond of my mother.

"Apparently there was a lot of bleeding. She called the doctor. He was gone before I arrived, but it sounded like an early-term miscarriage." Shin spoke deliberately, in a tone that reminded me that he was partway through his medical training. But this was my mother, not some stranger, and I ran the last few yards to the room and opened the door.

A single lamp burned on the desk, illuminating a makeshift pallet on the floor. My mother's face looked paler than usual, her forehead high and bare, as though her skull was pushing its way through the thin veil of flesh.

Her hand was dry and cold, but she forced a weak smile. "Ji Lin, I told them not to worry you. I just felt a bit faint so Auntie Wong called the doctor."

I squeezed her hand. "Did you know that you were pregnant?"

She glanced at Shin, embarrassed. Taking his cue, he quietly left.

"I didn't think so. I've always been irregular, you know. Besides, I'm too old to have a baby." She was forty-two. It was still possible; some of my friends had siblings who were decades younger.

"You need to keep him away from you." Why couldn't my stepfather leave her alone? I could barely speak, I was so angry. My mouth was filled with bitterness.

"Don't say that. It's his right. I'm the one who's failed, not giving him more children."

I bit my lip hard. There was no point berating her in this frail state. I'd have to find another way, and I thought again about how I'd wanted to poison my stepfather.

LATER THAT EVENING, WHEN MY MOTHER WAS RESTING AND MY stepfather had gone up to his room, Shin and I went out to eat. It was suffocatingly hot. Most places were closed already, but Shin took me to a roadside stall that served *hor fun*, wide flat rice noodles, in soup. We sat down at a rickety folding table, one corner of which was propped up on a brick, next to three men who were taking a break from an all-night mahjong party.

As Shin went to order, I listened with half an ear to the men discussing their mahjong debts. My mother, too, must have joined such parties to run up a debt of forty Malayan dollars. Thinking of the money made my stomach turn, and when Shin set a bowl of steaming *sar hor fun* in front of me, I could only stir it listlessly with my chopsticks.

He sat down opposite and began to wolf his noodles. Under the hissing carbide lamp, with its fluttering circle of moths, he looked nothing like my stepfather and I felt a surge of relief. I pushed my untouched bowl across to him.

"I need you to talk to your father."

"About what?"

It didn't seem right to discuss our parents like this, but I had to say it. "He has to leave my mother alone. She can't get pregnant again."

Shin's face was pale under the bright white carbide lamp. "I already told him so when I got in this evening."

"Will he listen to you?"

He shrugged. This conversation was just as awkward for him as for me. "I did tell him there were other options."

"Like what? Visiting prostitutes or becoming a monk?" I stabbed a fish ball viciously out of Shin's bowl. I didn't care what my stepfather did as long as it kept him away from my mother.

"Like contraception." He scowled to hide his embarrassment. "Anyway, you needn't worry about things like that."

"Even I know about French letters." Or what they called the "male shield"—as though it were something valiant. "I'm sure he won't do it, the old bastard."

That was usually Shin's line, not mine. Generally I avoided calling his father names. By doing so now, I'd crossed an invisible boundary.

I was never quite sure how Shin felt about his father. After all, my mother often made foolish decisions that made me feel like shaking her, but I still loved her. I suspected it might be the same way for Shin, no matter what his father did. Perhaps that was what it meant to be family—you were shackled together by obligations that you could never escape.

But instead of getting annoyed, he gave me that thoughtful stare again. "How do you know so much about things like this?"

All I really knew came from listening to the girls at work. They said that the best thing was French letters, or condoms, widely distributed since the Great War. But I couldn't explain how I'd learned that to him.

"It comes from not having any feminine delicacy," I said crossly.

Shin said, "If I can get him to agree, he'll probably keep his promise."

Yes, that stiff-necked, cold man would keep a promise. Just as he would never forgive a debt. Shin's words set off a faint click in my head. Suddenly, I understood.

"You made a deal with him."

"No, I didn't."

"I'm not talking about today. I meant two years ago. When he broke your arm."

I'd caught Shin by surprise; I could see it in his frown and how he dropped his head, staring at the soup.

"You did, didn't you? What was it about?"

But Shin's mouth tightened. He never would explain to me what had happened that night.

"Well, I can make a deal with him, too."

"Don't." Shin caught my wrist, a swift hard movement. I flinched. Realizing himself, he slowly unpeeled his fingers. "You must never make a deal with my father. Promise me, Ji Lin."

I didn't say anything. There was a way to get what I wanted from my stepfather. The question was, what would he want in return?

////

It was very dark on the way home. The shapes of the houses as they leaned against each other, windows shuttered against the night, looked all wrong to me. When Shin returned to Singapore, I'd have no one to confide in about family troubles. It was different for him. He had someone else.

"The ring," I said, remembering. "I need to give it back to you."

"Keep it for now," said Shin. He'd been very quiet since dinner; a dangerous sign because it meant he was thinking about something. "What were you doing with Robert earlier?"

"We happened to run into each other. By the way, what did you do with Pei Ling's package?"

Shin frowned. "It was silly of you to get involved with her. I think it's going to be troublesome."

"I just wanted to help," I said, dismayed. "Did you open it?"

"Of course I did! You should never keep unknown packages for people. Didn't you think it was odd that she should seize on you, a stranger, to retrieve something for her?" He said coldly, "Your name means 'wisdom.' Sometimes I think you're incredibly stupid for someone who's supposed to be clever."

I was furious. It wasn't through lack of brains that I wasn't progressing in life. "Well, your name means 'faithfulness,' yet you switch women all the time!"

That was a low blow, and Shin set his shoulders and walked faster, leaving me behind. I followed, fuming, though I knew that his name meant more than faithfulness. *Xin* also stood for integrity and loyalty, just as all the Virtues had deeper and wider meanings, and I couldn't really complain that Shin failed in those areas. In the darkness, I thought again about what the little boy had said in my dream. *There's something a bit wrong with each of us.*

I'd been walking slowly, not wanting to give Shin the satisfaction of chasing after him, but when I turned the corner, he was waiting for me. Once, annoyed that I always tagged along, another boy had locked me into a disused shed. He'd run off laughing and I'd been reduced to panicked tears until Shin had come searching for me later. Recalling this, I mumbled, "I'm sorry." He started walking again, two steps ahead. Soon he'd return to Singapore. The next time I saw him, he'd be bringing his fiancée back. I felt that painful pressure in my throat again, as though I'd swallowed a chopstick.

"I said, I'm sorry!"

Shin turned. "That's not an apology. That's just shouting."

I should have known better than to accuse him of unfaithfulness. For some reason that was a sore spot with him. "Don't be cross, Shin. I was just feeling jealous."

"About what?" He stopped beneath the shadow of a tree, its leaves trembling in the moonlight. The darkness made it easy to say things I never would have otherwise.

"I've been hateful and envious about you going to medical school. And for being a boy. And getting to choose what you want."

Shin was silent for a long moment. "Is that all?"

There was a sharp edge to his voice. I had the uneasy feeling that I'd failed some kind of test. What more should I have said? After all, he'd had one girl after another and I'd never objected before. It was too humiliating to start now.

We arrived home without exchanging another word. I felt miserable, the way I always did when Shin and I were fighting, though this time I wasn't entirely sure what the argument was about. Within, all was dark and silent. My stepfather had gone to bed, and after checking on my sleeping mother, we made our way to the kitchen. I lit the lamp and the room filled with its warm glow. Shin still looked irritated with me, but he said, "Wait here," and disappeared upstairs.

I had a bad feeling about this; an intuition that I might regret seeing whatever was in Pei Ling's package. Restless, I prowled around the kitchen. As I put away the dishes, I felt the sharp prickle of being watched. Had Y. K. Wong somehow materialized inside the shophouse? Ridiculous, of course. I froze, listening to the dull thump of my pulse, the ringing silence of the house. Seizing the heavy meat cleaver, I turned to face the open doorway.

There was indeed someone standing there in the shadows. But it was only Shin. Or was it? The flickering lamplight gave him a hungry, angry look I'd never seen before. That wolflike stare, like an animal at the very edge of a campfire. For an instant, I didn't recognize him and I was afraid.

Shin glanced at the cleaver in my hand and his mouth made a bitter twist.

"Did you think I was my father?"

It wasn't his fault that they shared the same flesh and blood. "No . . . I was just startled."

Shin walked slowly in, watching me intently.

"Has he laid a hand on you?"

"Who? Your father?" That man had barely acknowledged my existence for the past ten years.

He sat down at the kitchen table and put his head in his hands. "I was worried about you. When I was gone."

"He couldn't be bothered with me," I said bitterly. My stepfather had better ways to control me. Ones that involved the foolish fondness that still lingered in my mother's eyes, the bruises on her arms. "And anyway, if you were so concerned, you should have answered my letters."

Shin's eyes turned dangerously blank. "You seem to have done quite well without me."

"What do you mean?"

"I'm talking about Robert. You never said anything about being on such good terms with him."

This was so unfair that it took my breath away. "I told you we only met by chance tonight!"

Shin's eyes traveled up my pretty dress, taking in the lip rouge and cake mascara that Hui had added when we'd been laughing and joking in her room only a few hours ago. It was an appraising, angry stare, and it made me burn hot and cold at the same time. It was useless to explain things to him, and in any case, why did I have to?

"Robert has been very kind to me," I snapped.

"Yes," said Shin. "With his father's money."

"Why should you care? After all, you ran away from here as soon as you could."

"I didn't run away."

"You never even came back for holidays. You just left me. In this house." To my horror, tears welled up in my eyes. Tears of anger, I told myself, gritting my teeth. Shin started to say something but I cut him off. "Do you really think I want to be a dressmaker? I hate it. But it's not like they'd waste any money letting me study further."

"Ji Lin—"

"So don't come back now and say you were worried about me. As far as I can guess, you made some kind of deal with *him*. So you wouldn't have to work for him, and you could go and do whatever it was you wanted. You coward!"

If I wanted to, I could really hurt Shin. Hurt him in a way that was nasty and bloody, like hooking the soft guts out of prey. My heart was hammering, my breathing ragged. I almost expected to see blood all over the kitchen table.

"Is that what you think I did?" Shin's face had gone dead white, a handsome death mask.

I braced myself for what would surely be a withering counterattack, but to my surprise, he said nothing. Just gave me that stricken look, the one that he never showed anyone else, not even when he was being beaten within an inch of his life.

I didn't want to see Shin like this. And yet, at that moment, I hated him. I remembered how he'd looked, lying in Fong Lan's lap, her hand sliding possessively down his bare chest. The way she'd gazed into his eyes, smiling.

Shin put a slim brown paper package on the table. "You can look at it, or not," he said. "I'll let you decide."

He turned and walked out of the kitchen. Frozen, I stood waiting to hear his footsteps go upstairs again, but instead I heard him walk all the way to the front of the shophouse and pull open the front door, with its telltale creak. Then the spell broke. I ran down the hallway, that long, narrow passageway through the dark bowels of the shophouse.

"Shin!" I said, "Where are you going?"

"Back to the hospital."

"I thought you were staying over tonight."

"I have to work tomorrow." The way he said this, with weary patience, broke my heart.

"There aren't any trains or buses right now."

"I know. I borrowed Ming's bicycle."

"But it's so far." It would take him more than an hour on dark, unpaved roads, and towards Batu Gajah, the road climbed steeply.

"Then I'd better get started." He gave me the ghost of a smile. "Don't worry, I'll be fine."

Shin wheeled the heavy black bicycle, which had been standing in the front of the shop, out into the street. I followed after him, helplessly.

"Go back inside," he said softly, glancing up at the darkened windows of my stepfather's room. "Please."

"Shin—I'm sorry." I put my arms around him from behind, burying my face in his lean back. I could feel his chest rise and fall

"Don't cry," he said. "Not in the street. Or Auntie Wong will come out and there'll be even more strange rumors about our family."

This attempt at humor only made me sob harder, though I tried to muffle the noise. Crying silently was a skill that both of us had learned in this house. Shin sighed and propped up the bicycle. After a long moment, he turned around. Even then, I wouldn't let go. I had the feeling that something terrible would happen if I did. It was a silly thought, but it made me feel so dreadfully lonely that I hugged him tighter.

"I can't breathe," he said.

"Sorry." We were talking in whispers, mindful of standing in the street though all the neighbors must have gone to bed by now. The moon shone down, sharp shadows in silver and black. Shin looked exhausted.

"Let me go with you. I'm worried about you riding on such dark roads."

"And how?" he asked, stroking my hair. He'd never done this before and to hide my confusion, I buried my face in his shoulder. Tomorrow he would be someone else's again, but tonight he was mine.

"I'll ride on the back. We'll take turns to pedal."

"You're too heavy. I'd fall over."

"Idiot," I said, jabbing him. He grabbed my wrists, pulling me closer. Breathless, I raised my face. I was almost certain he'd kiss me now, but he paused. Lowered his hands. In the moonlight, I couldn't read the expression in his eyes.

"You should take care of your mother," Shin said.

He was right, of course. Mortified, I tugged my wrists free. What had I been thinking, hoping that my stepbrother would actually kiss me?

"Be careful," I said, stepping back. I watched as he struck a match and lit the kerosene bicycle lamp. Shin swung on, an easy fluid movement, and rode off into the night.

25

Falim
Tuesday, June 16th

OF COURSE, THE FIRST THING I DID WAS TO GO STRAIGHT BACK INTO the kitchen and open Pei Ling's brown paper package. Shin had mentioned that she still hadn't regained consciousness from her fall. A shudder traveled through me. I was almost certain she'd been pushed and that Y. K. Wong had something to do with it. Never mind that I didn't have any proof. It was just a feeling, a twitch in the air.

As I unwrapped the double layer of butcher's paper, there was a rattling clink. I held my breath as a glass specimen bottle and a packet of papers slid out onto the kitchen table. I knew the shape and size of that bottle well by now. It contained a thumb. Not dried and withered, like the finger I'd taken from the salesman's pocket, but preserved in a yellowish fluid like most of the other specimens from the storeroom. I stood the bottle upright next to the lamp. Strangely, it didn't frighten me as much as the salt-cured finger with its blackened crook. Perhaps because it had an unreal air, like a scientific wax model. I was sure it came from that missing list of specimens we'd compiled.

The packet also contained some papers. Pei Ling's girlish handwriting had addressed the envelopes to Mr. Chan Yew Cheung, the salesman. It didn't seem right to read other people's correspondence, but Shin's warning about doing favors for strangers rang in my ears. A quick glance confirmed my suspicions. They were love letters—pages and pages of infatuated yearning. My eyes skipped over them, though not before picking up fragments like *when will you tell your wife*, and even more embarrassingly, *your lips on my skin.* In any case, the letters were genuine. And extremely indiscreet. No wonder she'd wanted them back. If they'd been sent anonymously to Matron, Pei Ling would have been dismissed.

At the bottom of the pile was a sheet of paper, torn from a notebook. The handwriting was different from Pei Ling's—a more masculine hand. On the left side was a list of thirteen names, all locals. Chan Yew Cheung was the second-to-last one. There was a check mark next to it, a bold slash as though someone had marked it off. On the right side of the paper was another, shorter list. This one had only three names on it: J. MacFarlane, W. Acton, L. Rawlings.

I stared at the two lists. There was a pattern that I could almost see. Next to the name "J. MacFarlane" was a question mark and the words *Taiping/Kamunting.* I remembered that name, written-up in the pathology storeroom ledger as a specimen donated by W. Acton. I'd met William Acton myself when I was cleaning the room out. And surely L. Rawlings must be the same Dr. Rawlings who ran the pathology department. So the second list was British doctors associated with the Batu Gajah District Hospital.

The back of the paper contained numbers: running totals of what looked like initialed payments. Taking a fresh sheet of paper, I carefully copied the lists and wrapped the package back up, wondering if Shin had mentioned any of this to Dr. Rawlings.

It was past midnight. The roads were deserted at this hour and Shin had only the dim halo of the kerosene bicycle lamp. When I thought about him riding for miles in the dark, past silent mining dredges and lonely plantations, I felt a surge of anxiety. I could imagine, all too clearly, Shin getting run over by a lorry or dragged off by a tiger. A water buffalo had been killed recently, its half-eaten carcass recovered in a nearby plantation. Something was hunting, out there in the shadows. Hadn't Chan Yew Cheung died on such a night, coming home late?

I checked my sleeping mother. Brushing the hair gently from her thin face, I was thankful she was all right, though a treacherous part of me thought that if she died, there'd be nothing holding me hostage to this house.

/////

My mother recovered slowly, more so than from her miscarriages in the past. My stepfather said no more than usual, but he spent a surprising amount of time sitting with her. I wondered if, for the first time, he'd realized just how frail she'd become. She was very pale and her lips had no color, which alarmed me.

"Has the bleeding stopped?" Auntie Wong asked when she stopped by.

"Mostly," my mother said.

Auntie Wong looked at me. "If she has a fever, you must take her to hospital. It could be an infection."

I wanted to take her to the hospital right away, but it would have been exhausting for her to move. Astonishingly, my stepfather voiced the same concerns. He sat next to her and took her hand. "Let me know if you don't feel well."

I'd never heard him speak so intimately to her before, but she didn't seem surprised, and I wondered whether this was the way he occasionally treated her in the privacy of their bedroom, when the doors were closed. Maybe that was enough to keep her foolishly hopeful. But I still hated him, I decided. Nothing would change my mind about that.

Later, Ah Kum came and sat in the kitchen as I boiled pork bone soup, to which I'd added dried red dates to build up my mother's *yang* energy.

Ah Kum said, "Your father's really worried about her. That's so sweet."

I nodded. Ah Kum had only moved to Falim this past year and was perhaps unaware that we weren't related at all.

"Did your brother go back already?"

"Yes, last night."

Ah Kum sighed and I remembered how she'd been all over Shin last time he was home. At the time I hadn't cared much: strange how only ten days had made such a difference.

"Does he have a girlfriend?" she asked.

Shin hadn't announced anything to our parents but that wasn't surprising, either. "I think so," I said, recalling Koh Beng's well-meaning warning to me in the hospital. "Down in Singapore."

"Oh, Singapore is far away! Perhaps he'll change his mind and pick me."

"Perhaps." I admired her single-minded determination.

"We'll have six children," Ah Kum said jokingly. "And they'll all be beautiful."

I forced myself to smile. "What makes you think so?"

"Just look at you and your brother—such a handsome family!"

Embarrassed, I hung my head. There'd be trouble if anyone knew how my feelings had changed towards Shin. I could imagine my stepfather's rage, my mother's shame. The whispers from the neighbors that there must have been something improper going on in our house.

"You'll cheer me on with your brother, won't you?" said Ah Kum. "Especially since you've got a rich boyfriend. I heard he sent you home last night in a big car."

I'd completely forgotten about Robert, but I ought to thank him. Write him a note, though I wasn't sure how to get in touch with him. My problem was solved, however, when Robert stopped by that afternoon, and then again the next morning. The first time he brought dried Chinese herbs. The second time, he brought chicken soup in a blue-and-white porcelain tureen. It had been made, he explained, by his family cook, using the silky-feathered, black-skinned chicken that was especially good for invalids.

It was all very thoughtful of him, and I felt guilty, especially after seeing how the soup had sloshed onto the soft leather of his car seat. Robert's atrocious driving must have contributed to it, but I didn't mention that as I rushed to blot the stain. He spent some time chatting with my stepfather. I'd no idea what they talked about, but my mother, who had recovered enough to sit up in the family room and greet him, was pleased.

"Such a nice young man!" she said as I reheated the chicken soup for her. I kept quiet. I hadn't been able to remove the soup stains from Robert's car seat. It gave me an uneasy feeling. One more thing that I owed him.

IT WAS NOW FRIDAY, AND I'D BEEN BACK IN FALIM FOR THREE DAYS. Three days in which the color had returned to my mother's face and she'd moved back upstairs to the bedroom she shared with my stepfather. I wouldn't let her do any housework, despite her insistence she was fine.

"What's the point of my being here?" I said, reminding her that Mrs. Tham had given me the week off. I'd have to return to Ipoh tomorrow, however, because of the private party on Saturday.

In these three days, I'd had no word from Shin. If he'd been run over by a lorry or eaten by a tiger, the police would surely have contacted us by now. Still, I couldn't help glancing at the clock as the long, hot Friday afternoon advanced, expecting him to return for the weekend.

I'd hidden the brown paper packet with its severed thumb in Shin's empty room. I knew where he used to keep his treasures, under a loosened floorboard in the corner, and I pried it up and slid the paper packet in. Standing in Shin's room, the smooth wooden floorboards under my bare feet, I found it hard to believe that he'd occupied it for so many years. It was completely empty.

When he'd left for medical school, he'd sorted his belongings in a frenzy of activity. I'd watched silently from the doorway as he'd systematically cleared everything out, even the cheaply printed kungfu novels that we'd both collected.

"Can I have these?" I'd asked.

He'd nodded, barely turning his head. And I'd known then that Shin never meant to come home again.

Traitor, I thought. *Deserter.*

I threw myself on the neatly stripped bed, wondering if Fong Lan had lain here with Shin, and what they had done together. Whether he had unbuttoned her blouse slowly, and bent to kiss her, his hand sliding up to cup her breast. Had he smiled lazily at her the way he had at me, looking down through his lashes? Lying there in the darkness, I squeezed my eyes shut. I must kill it quickly: this raw, newborn emotion that fluttered in my chest.

So when Friday afternoon came round and I heard my step-father's voice raised in greeting in the front of the shophouse, I told myself that I mustn't run out to greet Shin like a loyal dog. Still, my pulse quickened as footsteps made their way down the long passageway, all the way to the back kitchen where I was chopping up a steamed chicken. It was best to look cheerful, I decided. Not as though I'd stayed up half the night catching up on ten years' worth of jealousy in one fell swoop. Cheerful and brisk, that was the way to go.

"Back again?" I said. "I was afraid you got squashed by a lorry."

Turning, I was mortified to discover that it wasn't Shin, but Robert who stood behind me.

"Is my driving really that bad?" he asked in surprise.

"I'm sorry—I thought you were Shin."

Robert's eye brightened at my flustered expression. "I don't mind," he said. "I like it when you talk to me like that, Ji Lin." This wasn't good. The way he said my name, shyly yet with pleasure, had all the hallmarks of infatuation. I'd seen it before at the dance hall, though it was easier to shrug off while being smoky-eyed Louise.

"I always envied Shin and Ming," said Robert. "And how the three of you were so close growing up."

I tried to laugh it off. "You have sisters, don't you?"

"It's not the same." He drew closer, and I glanced at him in alarm. If he tried to go in for a kiss again, I might end up flinging the chicken at him. I wondered why I was so resistant to him. After all, he was a good catch. Not knowing what else to do, I served him some steamed sweet rice cakes, the kind that were puffy like clouds.

"Did you say that your father is on the board of the Batu Gajah District Hospital?" I asked casually.

He nodded through a mouthful of cake.

I took out the copy I'd made of the lists in Pei Ling's package. It was worth a try, if he had any information that could shed light on them. "Do you recognize any of these names?"

Robert studied it for a long moment. "Lytton Rawlings—he's the pathologist. And this one, William Acton, is a general surgeon."

"What about J. MacFarlane?"

"I don't think he's on staff." Robert frowned. "But I've heard that name before. There was an odd story going around, something to do with a woman's death up in Kamunting. Where did you get these lists from—the hospital?"

A chill shadow swam below me. I regretted asking Robert, with his blundering, well-meaning ways.

"It's nothing," I said.

"You look so sad, Ji Lin," said Robert. "Are you worried about anything? Because if you are, you should tell me."

His face with its silly, fashionably thin mustache peered anxiously at me. Of course I had worries. Worries about mahjong debts, loan sharks, and losing my part-time job. Plus the small matter of severed fingers and falling in love with my stepbrother, but I couldn't possibly tell Robert any of this. At that moment, Ah Kum walked in. Finding us gazing at each other over the kitchen table, she backtracked with a congratulatory smirk.

My mother pressed Robert to stay for dinner, but he had a previous engagement. I was relieved. Shin still hadn't arrived, and it was better if they didn't meet. He had a bristling antagonism towards Robert that was part envy and part I didn't know what—natural dislike, I supposed.

To my surprise, my stepfather came out to see Robert off with me. After his sleek, cream-colored behemoth had taken off with a squeal of brakes, leaving a skid mark on the edge of the curb, the two of us were left standing on the street. My stepfather, chewing on a toothpick, was expressionless as ever, but I felt his mood soften, which gave me the courage to say, "Robert's father is on the board at the Batu Gajah Hospital."

He grunted.

"He said that if I'd like to apply for a scholarship to study nursing, he'd put in a word for me."

This was an old, sore argument that we'd had. My stepfather didn't consider nursing a suitable job for a young woman, what with having to bathe and perform intimate acts for all manner of strangers, including men.

He turned to look at me. "It's not a job for a single girl. But if you're married, you can do as you please."

I could hardly believe my ears. "Why does it matter whether I'm married or not? The job's the same."

"You'll be your husband's responsibility then."

"Does it matter to whom?"

My stepfather removed the toothpick from his mouth and regarded it. "As long as he makes a living, I don't care who you marry or what you do afterwards."

I took a deep breath. "Do you promise?"

He looked me in the eye. It was impossible to know what my stepfather was thinking at times like this.

"Yes," he said. "Once you're married, you're not my responsibility anymore. Nor your mother's." He nodded at the black scrape that Robert's car had left on the curb. "But learn how to drive properly."

26

IT'S SATURDAY, THE DAY OF THE PARTY. AH LONG LET REN SLEEP IN, and it's almost nine o'clock in the morning when he wakes with a start. The fever has gone and the mysterious sensation of well-being still remains.

Hurrying, he scrambles into his white houseboy's uniform. Ah Long is already busy in the kitchen, stirring a large pot of beef *rendang*, slow cooked with coconut milk, and aromatic with kaffir lime leaves, lemon grass, and cardamom.

"Fever gone?" he asks.

Ren nods, bright-eyed.

"It's nice to be young," Ah Long grumbles, but he seems pleased, and after Ren has eaten breakfast, he sets him to work on the hundred-and-one last-minute preparations for the party.

William is around. Ever since the tiger print was discovered at the edge of the garden, he hasn't gone out in the evenings but has, instead, locked himself up in his study and written more letters.

Ren often wonders where those letters go. The postman comes by and picks a few of them up, but never the letters with the thick, cream-colored envelopes addressed to a woman named Iris. Ren puzzles over this and can only conclude that William takes them to the Club and drops them in the postbox there. Or perhaps he hands them directly to her at some sprawling colonial bungalow. As much as he tries, Ren can't picture what this Iris lady looks like. The only foreign woman who comes to mind is Lydia.

She's the one that he imagines opening the letters, drinking tea on the veranda. Going to the hospital with William. The funny thing is that they almost get along. It's just that the master always pulls back, as though Lydia reminds him of something he wants to avoid. It must be very disappointing for her; there's no one else around so well suited, according to servants' gossip.

Ren sets the long table with plates and silverware and starched napkins cunningly folded into peacocks. The cutlery is real silver, from William's family in England with a crest and a curling, ornate "A" engraved on each piece. Ren spent all of Wednesday morning polishing it. Each spoon and fork is weighty. Ah Long says it's a measure of the master's quality. The last doctor he worked for had stainless knives and forks, not good silver like this. When Ren timidly asks William if his family is famous, William only laughs shortly and says something about black sheep, though what sheep have to do with silverware isn't clear to Ren.

William is on edge today. He smokes cigarette after cigarette, leaning on the wooden railing of the veranda and gazing at the lush green leaves of the canna lilies that surround the bungalow. It must be because of the note he got this morning, delivered by a Sinhalese youth of thirteen or fourteen with a sullen look.

Ren is shaking out a dustcloth at the front door when the boy comes by on a bicycle.

"*Tolong kasi surat ni pada awak punya Tuan.*" Give this letter to your master, he says in Malay.

It's a folded handwritten note. The writing has a childish, unformed air as though the writer isn't very confident about the letters. *Mr. William*, it says.

"Do you need something from my master?" asks Ren with curiosity.

The youth looks scornful. "Not me. My cousin. Tell him she wants to see him soon. Her leg is acting up."

Ren has a flash of understanding. "Your cousin is Nandani? How is she?" Ren remembers the warmth of Nandani's smile, the curling strands of her pretty black hair.

"She wants to see *him*." He purses his mouth. "I guess you wouldn't know, a little kid like you. How old are you?"

"I'm almost thirteen."

The other boy laughs. "Don't lie. You're ten. Maybe eleven."

He's the first person to guess, and Ren falls silent. At this victory, the other boy says in a friendlier manner, "Give him the note, all right? You know, her father found out."

"About what?"

"Never you mind." He scowls and cycles off, leaving Ren holding the note. Not knowing what to do, Ren goes into the house and hands it to William. To his surprise, William doesn't open it but puts it into his pocket.

"Do you need to send a reply?" Ren wonders why William won't open the note.

"No. It's just a misunderstanding." William turns and walks back out onto the veranda.

At seven o'clock in the evening the first guests arrive, the men in light tropical dinner jackets made of cotton drill, the two women in pretty frocks. Lydia towers over the other lady, a mousy little brunette who's the wife of one of the young doctors.

They mill around the front room, sipping drinks mixed by the waiter hired for the evening. He's a friend of Ah Long's, a young fellow Hainanese who works at the Kinta Club. His deft hands squeeze limes and shake ice into submission. Ren would like to watch, but Ah Long has him scurrying about so he only catches snatches of conversation amid the clink of glasses and laughter.

There's Leslie, the red-haired doctor who's on good terms with William, saying anxiously to the mousy wife, "I hope you don't mind, Mrs. Banks. I didn't realize there'd be ladies tonight and I arranged for entertainment. Dancing, you know. Girls, but a very decent sort."

"Oh, I don't mind at all," she says, although she looks worried.

Ren ducks past them with a tray, wondering which of the men is Dr. Rawlings. Guiltily, his thoughts fly to the buried finger in the garden. Has the doctor noticed that the specimen is missing from the shelf? Ren recalls that tingling electricity, like a burst of static before a message comes through, that he sensed near the pathology room. He tilts his head from side to side, wondering if his cat sense will tell him if the source was indeed Dr. Rawlings.

But there's no time to look. The long side buffet in the dining room is laden with tureens of *rendang* and fragrant, steaming rice. Sour green mangoes are shredded in a *kerabu*: a salad tossed with mint, shallots, and dried shrimp drizzled with lime and spicy *sambal* sauce. William likes local food and it's fashionable to serve a curry dinner, though as a nod to the less adventurous, Ah Long has turned the breasts of the three chickens into cutlets, smothered with onion gravy and tinned peas. The dark meat has been twice-fried as *Inchi Kabin*, and there are little glass dishes of pickles and condiments.

And now they're sitting down, William escorting little Mrs. Banks in on his arm, since married women take precedence over spinsters. Ren, standing at the sideboard to assist, scans the long table and the animated faces of the men, as they unfold starched linen napkins and sip from glasses. Real crystal glasses, as Ah Long informed him.

Lydia is at the other end of the table from William. She laughs often, easily outshining timid Mrs. Banks. Leslie leans over, murmuring something to William, who looks exasperated.

"Dance-hall girls? What on earth were you thinking?"

"—didn't realize there'd be ladies tonight." Abashed, Leslie drops his voice as William shakes his head.

"You ought to have told me."

"I thought it would be more fun to surprise everyone."

William beckons Ren over. "Tell Ah Long that there'll be some girls coming. How many?"

"Five," says Leslie. "And a chaperone. From a respectable establishment."

"Very well. Five young ladies. When they arrive, show them into my study. I hope," he says glancing at Leslie, "this is not a disaster."

"It's just dancing. Nothing more than you'd get at the Celestial on a weekend afternoon." Leslie's hair is such a surprising color, the sort of gingery orange that Ren has only seen on cats. With a start, he realizes he's been staring and the two men are watching him in amusement.

"The dance hall will send a chaperone," Ah Long says when Ren scampers off to inform him of this exciting development. "They're quite strict about these things, otherwise they can't do business."

"Why's that?" Ren wipes a dish.

"They don't want any trouble, at least the decent places don't."

"What about the not-decent places?" asks Ren.

"Those places you shouldn't go to. Not even when you're older."

Ren would like to hear more about dance halls, but he has duties to perform. The furniture must be rearranged and the floor powdered for dancing. As he drags the furniture to the sides, there's laughter and the clink of glasses from the dining room. Ren wonders whether there'll be leftovers, but even as he considers this, his sharp ears catch a discordant note from the kitchen.

"*Nanti, nanti!* You cannot go in there!" That's Ah Long's voice. Then, more urgently, "Ren!"

Dropping the tin of talcum powder, Ren sprints back. Is it the dance-hall girls? If so, why are they in the kitchen? But there's only one young woman—Nandani. She looks completely out of place as she tries to explain something to Ah Long. Furious, he's barred the door with one arm, still clutching a *wok chan,* the steel spatula he uses for stir-frying.

"You cannot bother him now. Go home!"

Nandani's eyes light up when she sees Ren. "I want to see your master."

"Does your leg hurt?" Glancing down, Ren sees her leg is still bandaged.

"No, it's better."

Ren takes Nandani out through the kitchen door to the covered area outside.

"How did you get here?"

"My cousin gave me a ride on his bicycle. I need to talk to your master."

She looks so sad and desperate that Ren is worried. Maybe she's sick and needs medical help.

"My father is sending me away," she says. "To my uncle in Seremban."

Ren still doesn't understand what this has to do with William but he sees the distress in her eyes. "I'll tell him. Wait here."

When Ah Long's back is turned, Ren slips through to the dining room and quietly approaches William.

"*Tuan,* Nandani is here to see you."

William doesn't turn his head, but his face turns pale beneath his tan. "Where is she?"

"Outside. Behind the kitchen."

William is silent for a moment. Then he pushes his chair back. "I'll just be a moment," he says cheerily to the gentleman on his left. To Ren, he murmurs, "Bring her round the veranda on the other side."

As soon as William stands up, Ren feels a sharp tingle, a warning that an invisible clock has started to tick, running down the seconds and minutes that William is away from his guests. It's rude to leave in the middle of dinner like this, and William doesn't like loose ends and untidiness. So he hurries off to lead Nandani around the back of the house to the veranda.

She limps and stumbles on the uneven ground. "You can lean on me," Ren says. They keep their voices low, although Ren doesn't know why. The lights from the dining room cast warm shadows onto the grass; there's a swell in the conversation and a burst of laughter.

"Who are they?" Nandani asks.

"Some doctors from the hospital. Are you hungry?"

She shakes her head, but Ren thinks that he'll get her and her cousin a plate of food before they go. On the other side, William is already waiting, a dark shape on the veranda. Seeing him, Nandani hurries eagerly over.

Ren can't hear what they're saying at this distance, but William must be telling her something, because she nods from time to time. Then he puts an arm around her, or is it both arms? Ren is fascinated. Craning his neck, he can't make out much in the gloom. Is Nandani crying? Ren takes a step sideways and bumps into someone. It's Ah Long. He's come padding around the corner in the darkness like an old, moth-eaten cat.

"Why did you tell him she was here?" he says sourly. "Best to let her go away."

"I thought she might be ill."

"*Tch!* It's just lovesickness. But she's the wrong kind of girl to be playing around with."

"Why?"

"Because she's the naïve type who'll swallow all his sweet talk. How long has he been gone from dinner?"

The minutes are trickling away and the empty spot that William has created by disappearing from his own dinner party is beginning to collapse on itself. Ren can feel it yawing and vibrating: the faint alarm of dinner guests who wonder why their host is absent for so long.

A figure comes up to the dining-room window. It's Lydia; she says something over her shoulder about fresh air and disappears again. Ren has no idea whether she's seen anything. Probably not, since it's dark.

When he turns around, William has gone in, and Nandani stumbles back to Ren. To steady herself, she puts her hand on his shoulder. It's cold and Ren suddenly has a bad feeling, as though it isn't really Nandani, but some other chill and bony creature following him in from the dark.

WILLIAM SLIDES BACK INTO HIS SEAT JUST AS DESSERT COMES OUT. *Sago gula Malacca*, pearls of tapioca drizzled with coconut milk and dark brown coconut-sugar syrup, and *kuih bingka ubi*, that fragrant golden cake made from grated tapioca root. Ah Long has really outdone himself, but William has no appetite. He forces it down anyway, nodding as he pretends to listen to the conversation.

When dessert is over, the guests drift back to the front room, now rearranged for dancing. William overhears Mrs. Banks saying nervously to her husband, "Perhaps we should go home early."

He wishes they would all go home right now. It's rattled him, Nandani showing up at this dinner party. She's become a dangerously unpredictable factor, but mostly he's angry with himself. *Stupid, stupid*, he thinks, as the familiar feeling of self-loathing washes over him. William should have realized early on that Nandani's willingness was actually a naïve infatuation. Bad. Very bad. If a few stolen embraces are enough to give her delusions, then it's best that their connection end.

Of course, he hasn't said anything like that to her, only kind words and noble expressions of regret. He hopes that will satisfy her, though if she goes to her employer—the plantation manager who's Lydia's father—and makes a fuss, it will be damaging. How ironic, considering that he was far guiltier of being involved with Ambika. William decides then and there that he must limit himself to paid women. That's better than being accused of seducing young virgins. He's a fool, despite all his resolutions. And yet he can't help himself.

The tall, stooped figure of Rawlings, the pathologist, drifts over and William hesitates. He's not afraid of Rawlings anymore, not since the magistrate ruled Ambika's death an unfortunate accident, but he's still wary around him.

Tonight, Rawlings looks more like a stork than ever. "Too bad about the tiger hunt, eh?"

William nods. "I'm sure they'll try again."

Rawlings rubs his jaw. His hands are large and white, and William tries not to imagine them slicing through skin with dissecting scissors. It's silly, since he himself is a surgeon. *But I only cut open the living.* Not like Rawlings, whose patients are all dead.

"You know I wasn't happy with the inquest."

William keeps his face neutral.

Rawlings says, "There's always cases like this, when something's fishy but nobody believes you. Had one when I was stationed in Burma: they said it was witchcraft, people dying one after the other, but that was rubbish. It turned out to be arsenic poisoning from a private well."

"And your point is?"

"This case," says Rawlings, scraping at the floor absently with his shoe. "That woman, Ambika. It gives me the same feeling."

"Surely you're not suggesting that someone's keeping a pet tiger!" William laughs uncomfortably.

"Not the tiger. The vomit. Remember how I said when we found the head, there were traces of vomit in the mouth?"

Unbidden, the image of Ambika's broken body flashes in William's mind, the way he found it half lying under a bush. A headless torso with grey, rubbery skin.

"If she ingested something poisonous, that would account for the kill being untouched. Animals have surprisingly good instinct: if it went for the stomach and intestines first, as most of the big cats do, it might have decided there was something in the body it didn't like. But Farrell didn't believe me, of course. Probably we'll never prove it unless a proper investigation is done—who were her associates, whether there'd been any lovers or scandals. All this local talk about witchcraft and tigers is just a smokescreen."

This is becoming a terrible evening for William. He swallows, reminding himself that he hasn't committed a crime. Though given the force of public opinion, being associated with both Ambika and Nandani would be enough to sink him in this small social circle. People will follow him with their eyes, drop their voices when he enters a room. William has already had a taste of this back home.

Steady, he tells himself. It's only Rawlings grumbling. His luck will save him. "So have you ever come across any true cases of witchcraft?" he says, hoping to distract him.

"No. Though I've seen some amazing runs of luck."

"What sort?"

"You know, gambling, or things like not getting on a boat before it capsizes and so forth."

For an instant, William is tempted to tell Rawlings about his own peculiar fortune: how time and again he has narrowly avoided trouble by the merest twist of fate. Like stumbling upon the obituary of that salesman, the only witness to his affair with Ambika. But it's best not to say too much to Rawlings, who's still pedantically listing different types of luck. "The Chinese say it's your fate. You were in China, weren't you?"

"I was born in Tientsin. My father was Vice Consul," William says, relieved that the topic has shifted.

Rawlings looks at William with interest. "Were you now? So do you speak Chinese?"

"No, we came back when I was seven. I had an amah who taught me to speak Mandarin but I've forgotten it."

He hasn't, however, forgotten the gracious streets, the European buildings on wide roads in the foreign concessions, and behind them the jumble of alleys and *hutongs.* In his memories, it's always winter in Tientsin, that city in the far north of China. A cold dry winter with the tang of burning donkey dung and a bone-chilling wind blowing in from the steppes.

"I'm surprised you didn't enter the Service as well."

There are reasons why he hasn't followed his father's footsteps, but he doesn't discuss them. Instead, he says, "I can still write my Chinese name, though I can't pronounce it properly."

He pulls out his shining black fountain pen, and writes three characters awkwardly on a sheet of paper.

"Is that Chinese?" asks Leslie, peering over his shoulder. The guests crowd around curiously.

Lydia squeezes his arm, saying she's impressed. "I've got a Chinese name, too. A fortune-teller wrote it for me in Hong Kong."

"I used mine as my secret mark in boarding school," says William lightly. "For years and years. Which is probably why I can still write it. Ren—how do you pronounce this?"

Shyly, Ren shakes his head. Although he can speak Cantonese, he can't read many characters. Ah Long might be able to, though. Chattering and laughing, the group pours into the kitchen, despite William's protests that it would be easier to call his cook out.

To his horror, the first thing he sees is Nandani sitting quietly at the kitchen table with a plate of food. He glances sharply at Ren, who lowers his head guiltily. The boy must have given her something to eat. Well, he can't fault him for that. *He's a better man than me*, thinks William, wishing desperately that Nandani would disappear and not look at him with her sad eyes.

Ah Long is disgusted that so many people have invaded his kitchen, but he wipes his hands on his grubby white apron and peers at the piece of paper.

"*Wei Li An.*"

"There you go." William smiles awkwardly, wanting to get away from the kitchen and Nandani as soon as possible. "It's my name—'William.'"

"But what does it mean?" asks Lydia, staring at Nandani, who shrinks further into her seat.

Ah Long says something in Chinese to Ren, who nods.

"He says most Chinese names for foreigners just copy the sound of their name, but this one has a meaning." Ren points at the middle character, the one that looks most complicated. "This word is *Li.* It means doing things in the proper order, like a ritual. And this one, *An*, means peace. If you put them together with *Wei*, it means 'for the sake of order and peace.'"

The kitchen has fallen silent. Ren, raising his eyes from the paper, discovers that everyone is staring at him and looks frightened.

"Is this your houseboy?" Rawlings breaks the stillness.

William nods. Despite itching to get away from Nandani, who sits frozen, like a mouse, he's proud of Ren's soft-spoken, clear explanation.

"Where on earth did you find him?"

William ushers everyone out of the crowded kitchen. "It's a long story," he says, "best told over a *stengah*."

Someone puts a record on the gramophone, and outside there's the ebb and swell of conversation. Two guests linger in the kitchen: Lydia, who has gone over to chat with Nandani, and Rawlings. Making an excuse to the others, William returns. He has to stop Lydia from talking to Nandani, in case she sniffs out their relationship. Lydia's good at things like that.

But when he edges into the kitchen, Lydia is already turning to go. Catching his eye, she smiles, assuming that he's come back for her. He manages a weak grin as she passes through to the drawing room, feeling a wave of guilt wash over him.

Rawlings is still talking to Ren, and not wanting to follow Lydia or speak to Nandani, who watches him with miserable eyes, William leans against the doorway and listens to them.

"The *Li* in your master's name—isn't that one of the five Confucian Virtues?" Rawlings says.

"Yes," Ren replies. "Actually my name is one of them, too."

"Is that right?" says William. "Which one are you?"

"I'm Ren." He fidgets with the cuff of his white houseboy's uniform.

"*Ren* is benevolence isn't it? *Yi* is righteousness, *Li* is ritual or order. *Zhi* is wisdom and *Xin* is faithfulness." Rawling counts them off on his fingers as he recites, "*Without* Li, *what is there to distinguish men from beasts?*"

Ren looks impressed. "How do you know them all?"

"I studied a little." Rawlings regards him thoughtfully. He has a surprisingly easy manner with children, unlike himself, thinks William. Of course, Rawlings has children of his own.

William sneaks a quick glance down the hallway. Lydia is still standing there, ostensibly chatting with someone. If he goes out now, she's bound to catch him and ask all sorts of questions about why Nandani is sitting in his kitchen right now.

"Ren, Dr. Rawlings here is our chief pathologist," says William. To his surprise, the boy gives a little twitch, like a start of recognition.

"Do you take care of the pathology storeroom? The one at the hospital?" Ren asks hesitantly. It's not his place to question guests.

"Why, do you want to see it?" Rawlings looks amused.

Ren shakes his head. A baffled expression appears on his face, as though he's unaccountably disappointed.

There's a commotion at the front door.

"Ah, our visitors," says William in relief. "Did you hear about Leslie's surprise?"

"What is it?" asks Rawlings.

"Some dance-hall girls from Ipoh. Ren—get the door."

But Ren is transfixed. Eyes wide, his thin, childish shoulders almost quivering. He looks like a bird dog, William thinks. Exactly like a dog that, though disappointed at first by a false lead, has now locked onto the correct scent. Then, like a small sleepwalker, Ren walks straight out of the kitchen, down the long narrow passage, and opens the front door.

27

THERE WERE FIVE OF US GIRLS ON SATURDAY NIGHT: HUI, ROSE, Pearl, myself, and another girl called Anna. She usually worked Thursdays and Saturdays, so I'd never met her before. Anna was very tall—taller than me—and plump in a voluptuous way. The Mama said that she'd chosen Anna for this private party because foreigners didn't like to stoop when they were dancing.

"Is that why you picked me as well?" I asked as we waited for the hired car. She gave me a hard stare, as though she thought I was being cheeky, though I was quite serious.

"Of course not!" said Hui, squeezing my arm. "She picked you because you're popular."

The car that the Mama had hired was large, though not as long and graceful as Robert's. Anna sat in the front seat because she was the biggest, and the rest of us squeezed into the back. One of the bouncers, the one with a mole on his chin called Kiong, would be our driver and chaperone.

"No loose behavior," said the Mama, raking us over with a razor glare. "It'll be three hours of dancing, from nine to midnight. Kiong will handle the money. If there's any trouble, let him know at once."

Kiong, his wide face impassive, nodded. There were rumors that he was either the Mama's nephew or one of her lovers, but I was glad it was Kiong. He'd always struck me as reliable, and he never bothered to flirt with us girls. Rose and Hui were giggling over the car. Pearl said she'd never been in one before. If I married Robert, I thought, I'd get to ride in his cream-colored beauty with its soft leather seats every day. But I'd also have to do things like sit on Robert's lap and kiss him.

The idea made my teeth ache. I didn't want to think about Robert, though if I imagined it was Shin instead, I felt a strange, stirring excitement. But it was no use thinking about Shin—that only plunged me into greater gloom.

IN THE END, SHIN HADN'T COME BACK TO FALIM UNTIL SATURDAY. He pushed open the front door just as we were sitting down for an early lunch.

"Thought you'd be back last night," said my stepfather.

"I had to work."

Shin didn't look at me, although I'd jumped up to fetch him a plate of fried noodles. I had a sinking feeling. Perhaps he'd thought over all the nasty accusations I'd made on Tuesday night and decided that he hated me after all.

"You'll stay for the weekend?" my mother asked. Shin nodded.

Except for the papery skin beneath her eyes and the way she took the stairs more slowly, she was almost back to normal, which made me feel less guilty about leaving her.

"I'm going back to Ipoh after lunch," I reminded her.

"Can't Mrs. Tham spare you until Sunday?"

Mrs. Tham had in fact said that there was no need to rush back, but I couldn't possibly tell my mother that I was getting paid to dance with foreigners at a private party. It was the first and last time I'd do anything like this, I decided, because I was going to ask Robert for a loan. Far better to owe him money than the loan shark my mother had gone to for her mahjong debts. The next installment was due in less than a week. I gritted my teeth. If my stepfather found out, there'd be none of this quiet sitting around the dining table. His rage was sudden and unpredictable; he might be icily practical about it—or not. Glancing at my mother's lowered head, I only knew it wasn't worth the risk.

"*Sambal,*" grunted my stepfather, holding out the dish without looking at me.

As I spooned the aromatic chili paste out, I listened to the three of them talking. Shin asked my mother how she was feeling and discussed tin-ore prices with his father—a normal, polite conversation, though it rankled. Perhaps because they were treating Shin as an equal now. Leastways, more of an equal than me. I sat quietly, eating my noodles. Shin didn't speak to me at all.

And now my mother was going on about Robert and how often he'd been coming by. I shot a swift glance at Shin, but he merely looked bored.

"It would be nice to have Robert over for dinner. To thank him for everything, you know," my mother said hopefully.

"Ask him to come next Friday," said my stepfather. This surprised me. He'd never taken any interest in my friends. "You'll be home, too, Shin."

"Of course." Shin's face was expressionless.

"Ji Lin and I had a talk the other night," my stepfather went on. Alarmed, I stared at him. What was going on with my stepfather today?

"About what?" My mother glanced anxiously at me.

"I told her that if she gets married, she can go ahead and do whatever she wants. Whether it's nursing or becoming a teacher or running away to join the circus." He put a spoonful of *sambal* on his plate and squeezed lime juice on it.

I lifted my eyes. "You promised, didn't you?"

"Yes. When you're married, you won't be my responsibility, or your mother's, either." To my surprise, my stepfather wasn't looking at me. Instead, he was watching Shin. Very carefully, like a cat observing a lizard.

Shin continued eating with bored indifference. Just last weekend at the hospital, he'd told me angrily to tell him before I got married because I was bound to make a foolish decision, but there was no trace of that concern right now. His eyes were cold, and they never once met mine. Pushing back my chair, I murmured something about packing and went upstairs. Perhaps I shouldn't have been surprised. I knew how little my stepfather thought of me, how useless I was as a girl, and not even his own daughter. But for Shin to freeze me out again was more painful than expected. I wondered, not for the first time, whether I loved him or hated him.

As I folded the thin cotton blanket, my mother came into my room. Glancing timidly at me, she sat on the bed. "Is Robert picking you up?"

"No."

"You know, I'd be very happy if it worked out with him."

"He hasn't proposed to me," I said tersely.

"But if he does, will you think about it?"

"All right."

I raised my eyes to see Shin's head poke in. As usual, he didn't take a single step into my room. It was an old habit, though what did it matter now since neither of us lived here anymore?

"Father wants to know where the receipts are," he said to my mother.

"Oh, I'll get them." She got up and so did I. I didn't want to be left alone with Shin. Remembering how I'd lifted my face expectantly in the moonlight, and how he'd paused and released me instead, filled me with hot humiliation.

"Ji Lin," he said in a low voice as I brushed past in the narrow hallway. Even though it was noon, only a little light filtered into the corridor that ran alongside our two small rooms. It was so gloomy in this shophouse, so long and narrow, like living in the belly of a snake.

"What?"

"I need to talk to you." Shin bent his dark head towards me.

"Not when you were so rude to me downstairs."

For an instant, he frowned. Then the corner of his mouth twitched.

"You really are blunt," he said. "Don't you know how to act like a girl?"

Indignant, I opened my mouth to inform him that I was in fact the number two girl at the May Flower on Wednesdays and Fridays, but closed it without saying anything.

"But that's what I like about you."

A knife twist. Yes, he was fond of me. So fond that he didn't even see me as female.

Shin said more seriously, "Did my father really promise that he wouldn't interfere with you if you got married?"

"He said he didn't care who it was as long as he had a decent job."

"I see. That's good, isn't it?"

Why was Shin so pleased about that?

"Are you all right?" He peered closely at me, and I forced myself to look cheerful.

"I opened the package you got from Pei Ling," I said, changing the subject.

He raised an eyebrow. "And?"

"I think you should tell Dr. Rawlings about the missing fingers. They're hospital property after all."

"I was going to," said Shin, "Except when I went back to the storeroom to look for the original finger—the one you put away—it had disappeared."

"What do you mean, *disappeared*?"

Shin put a hand over my mouth. "Not so loud."

"I put it on the shelf, behind the two-headed rat," I said softly, not wanting my mother to overhear us.

"Well, it's not there anymore."

"Are you sure?"

He gave me an exasperated look. "If I inform Dr. Rawlings that I managed to locate one of the missing fingers but now it's disappeared again, he'll think I'm mad. Or that I stole them myself. Best not to say anything."

"But if someone checks the catalog, they'll find that specimens are missing. And the last person who tidied the room was you."

I never heard his answer because at that moment, a heavy tread on the stairs warned us of my stepfather's approach. Hastily, we sprang apart. Shin disappeared into his room, and I made my way downstairs, coolly passing my stepfather as though I hadn't just been standing in the hallway discussing stolen body parts with his son.

BUT I COULDN'T STOP THINKING ABOUT IT, EVEN AS I SAT IN THE hired car that Saturday night, listening to Hui and Rose chatter with only half an ear. And then the car was pulling up a long curving driveway. It was very quiet and dark, just as most of the journey had been, down empty roads fringed with jungle trees and the rustling leaves of rubber and coffee estates.

When the car stopped behind a row of vehicles, there was a moment of silence. Then Rose and Pearl spilled out, adjusting their dresses and smoothing their hair. I'd never been to such a large private bungalow before. Lights blazed from the front windows so that the surrounding trees and long expanse of black lawn pressed in on the house. Faint sounds of laughter and the tinny music of a gramophone wafted out through the open windows. I glanced at Hui, but she was looking at the door. There was a hard expression on her face, and I realized that she was nerving herself up to go in. We were used to locals, but foreigners were a different matter. Frankly, I was terrified.

"Front door or back?" she asked Kiong.

He consulted a piece of paper. It was so dark that he had to hold it up and squint. "Front," he grunted.

Kiong knocked on the door and handled the introductions. I stood behind Anna, the only girl who was taller than me, and blindly followed the others in. There was a rush of noise. I hardly knew where to look, but it was all right since we were being ushered through to the side.

"Ren, show the ladies into the study."

The hair on the back of my neck turned to needles. I had a good memory for voices, their pitch and timbre, and there was no use telling myself that all Englishmen sounded the same. I should have considered the possibility that William Acton, surgeon at the Batu Gajah District Hospital, might be at this private party. And now I was stuck.

We waited in another room until they were ready to have us, which was quite normal, said Pearl. Besides, we were a little early. Kiong was always a stickler for punctuality. The room was somebody's study: a very neat person, judging from the desk with its exact angles of ink jar and blotting paper. There was a tiger skin—a real one—on the floor. Rose said it gave her the shivers, but I thought it looked rather sad with its green glass eyes fixed in a petrified stare. That would be me, I thought, after William Acton recognized me. Goodbye to any chance of a nursing career, at least at this particular hospital.

"Did you see that little houseboy?" said Rose. "The one who opened the door for us? I thought his eyes would fall out of his head, he was staring so."

I hadn't noticed, but Hui had. "He's a bit young to be chasing women," she said wickedly. She was simmering with nervous energy: the same high spirits that had drawn me to her from the start.

Kiong knocked on the door. "Time to go."

After that, it was business as usual. Kiong brought us out, rather like a string of show ponies, while a young red-haired doctor introduced us. That was Rose's regular, she whispered.

"Very nice dance instructors from a respectable establishment," he said loudly. There was some ribbing going on, but not too much. William Acton was talking to a guest in the back and didn't seem to be paying attention, thank goodness. I'd noticed a couple of ladies—it was always better to have mixed company, though I wasn't sure whether, for their parts, the ladies were that pleased to see us. One of them looked like a mouse, but the other was very tall and fair.

She laid a proprietary hand on Acton's arm and started the dancing. There were five of us girls, and at least a dozen guests, all men except for the two ladies who were already gamely dancing. I'd have thought they would hang back at first, but most of the guests were young and apparently up for a good time. They were, by and large, polite though. No shouting out or calling dibs on girls as though we were cattle, which I'd been secretly afraid of without the strict dance-hall ticketing system. It was easy to see how an affair like this could go horribly wrong.

I danced with a short man with sandy hair, then another with sweaty hands. The music was very fast, faster than the live band at the May Flower played, and it was popular dances from five or six years ago like the Charleston and the Black Bottom. I realized that was to see whether we were any good at all. Which was ridiculous, because of course we could dance.

When the music stopped, we were panting from all that high-spirited leaping about and waving our arms. If they kept up this pace, I'd collapse before the evening was over, but thankfully the next piece was a waltz.

This time, I danced with a quiet young man who held my waist a little too tightly. You had to watch out for the silent ones; they could be troublesome in a sneaky way. As we spun sedately around the room, I kept an eye out for William Acton. If I were lucky, he might never dance with me at all, and perhaps with all the extra kohl and face powder, he wouldn't recognize me anyway. We made a tight turn near the dining room, and I glimpsed a small figure in white.

It's astonishing how much detail you can see in an instant. The flash of a face before it's gone, like a lightning strike. For a moment, I couldn't believe my eyes. I wanted to turn back, but my dance partner was steering us in the opposite direction.

"What is it?" he said. "You look as if you've seen a ghost."

That was exactly how I felt. The small square face, serious eyes and closely clipped hair. It was the little boy from my dreams. I stumbled and almost fell.

"It's nothing," I said.

He swung us around, but the doorway was empty now. I must have been hallucinating.

"You Chinese girls are so slim," my partner said, smiling. He slid his hand farther down my back. "Has anyone ever told you that you look exactly like Louise Brooks?"

His breath smelled of beef *rendang*. Twisting sharply, I realigned the gap between us. Another glance at the dining-room doorway. Still empty. My little ghost was gone.

"She does, doesn't she?" It was William Acton. "May I cut in? Host's prerogative, you know."

My partner looked irritated but relinquished me. I wasn't sure whether to be happy about this or not. Overall, I thought it was a change for the worse, even though I was thankful Acton had saved me from an awkward embrace.

We danced in silence, my shoulders tight and my neck stiff with alarm. He was a good dancer, as most foreigners tended to be. They must have all had training.

Just when I was beginning to think that William Acton hadn't recognized me, he said, "So how have you been, Louise?"

28

REN IS RUNNING IN AND OUT OF THE KITCHEN, CLEARING THE PLATES from the dining table. It's agony because the signal that he first sensed at the hospital is now here. Calling him, ever since he opened the front door. His ears ring, his skin tingles. It's been so long since Yi died. Three years of being alone, the only beacon in a wilderness, and now the signal is coming again.

Someone like me, he thinks. He wants to drop everything and search, but Ah Long gives him one task after another.

When Ren opened the door earlier, the girls entered in a rustle of skirts, soft voices, and suppressed laughter. They passed in a blur, and Ren, dazed and staring, was unable to pinpoint exactly where the signal came from.

And now they're dancing in the front room where the gramophone is playing. The air is electric with nerves and the animal curiosity of the guests. Ren can feel a fog of excitement that colors everything tonight with unease.

He peers into the front room every moment he can steal away, much to Ah Long's annoyance. The other Chinese waiter looks over Ren's shoulder.

"Which one are you looking at?" he asks, his eyes fixed on the girls.

Ren frowns, trying to feel his way with his cat sense, the invisible filaments floating like jellyfish tendrils. "I'm not sure. I can't tell."

There are five girls, all Chinese, wearing fashionable Western frocks. The music twitches infectiously, and the dance is very fast. They scissor their legs and touch their knees, reaching up with their arms. The men, panting in the heat, remove their jackets one by one.

"I like that one," says the waiter with a grin. He points out a girl in a pink dress, with arched, knowing eyebrows. "Though she's good, too." The tallest girl, with a chest that jiggles as she dances. It makes the back of Ren's neck hot, yet he's also obscurely embarrassed for her. But neither of them is right.

The room is crowded with people taller than Ren. Those who aren't dancing stand around laughing and clapping as the gramophone record is changed.

"Ohhh . . . the one with the short hair. Nice legs." The waiter, enjoying himself, cranes his head at a slim girl in a pale blue dress, her hair bobbed to reveal the nape of her long neck.

Ren's heart thumps wildly. Straight brows, large eyes, black hair cut in bangs that fly as she swings past on someone's arm. The buzz in his head is so loud that he staggers, steadying himself against the wall. She looks right at him, and her eyes go wide in recognition.

Ren tenses, ready to run out and grab her wrist, but Ah Long's scowling face appears. Hissing like an old goose, he herds Ren and the waiter back to their duties, though Ren hardly hears his instructions.

"What's wrong with both of you?" says Ah Long sourly.

"It's just a bit of fun," says the waiter, but Ren is silent.

How does she know him? Is it the same electric signal that he feels? No, it was something else, a visual recognition. It bothers him, the shocked expression on her face.

"No falling in love," Ah Long says. "We've had enough of it tonight." He jerks his head at the empty seat at the kitchen table where Nandani sat half an hour ago.

"Did she go home?" asks Ren. It's dark outside, the new moon barely a sliver in the sky. He goes to the screened kitchen door and opens it into the face of the Sinhalese youth who delivered the letter.

"Where's Nandani?" he says without ceremony. "She asked me to come back to get her, so here I am." He pushes his way into the kitchen. "Nandani!"

"She's not here," says Ah Long. "She went home."

"She can't walk far. How could she go home?"

He's right. Nandani was limping, leaning on Ren's shoulder even as he took her round the house to meet William earlier.

"Well, she went out about twenty minutes ago." Ah Long frowns.

Without a word, the cousin goes out again. Ren stares at the swinging door, wondering if he should help him look.

"She's probably waiting outside," says Ah Long. "Now hurry up and collect the empty glasses."

The other waiter goes to tend bar. Ren follows him, unease in the pit of his stomach. The night is so dark. Is Nandani outside, peering longingly in from the open windows? But he forgets about her as he goes into the front room again, because the girl in the pale blue dress is dancing with William right in front of him.

The couples twirl like flowers floating down a stream, and Ren sees his master laugh. But she's not smiling. Her expression is serious, and she says very little although she dances well. All the professional girls do. Even Ren can tell that.

William catches his eye and to his amazement, points at Ren with his chin. The girl glances up and stares at Ren. There it is again, that unbearable electric charge that makes him want to grab her hand. Every time they whirl past, her head turns, as though she's checking that Ren is still there.

William says something to her. Her mouth moves but what is she saying? And why is his master's head bent, as though he's considering something? Ren thinks about Nandani, waiting somewhere in the night and a feeling of protest rises in his chest. It isn't right for William to do this, not with the girl in blue, her straight dark brows frowning.

He tries to read her, to read William in the same way that he could sense the trails of energy at the hospital, but no matter how much he stares at them there's nothing, only a curious blank spot. Ren is dimly aware of noises, a disruption coming from the kitchen. He wavers, not wanting to leave his spot by the door, then scampers off.

In the kitchen, Nandani's cousin is angrily telling Ah Long that he can't find her though he has searched the grounds.

"What's that got to do with us?" Ah Long balls his fists into his dirty white apron.

"She was here. If she's gone missing, then it's your master's fault."

Ren says, "I'll find her. She might be round the other veranda."

222 //// Yangsze Choo

"Not you." Ah Long gives Ren an irritated look. "You're too small. Ah Seng!" He calls the part-time waiter over. "Go and help him look again. Take this lamp."

Ah Long's bushy eyebrows draw sharply down, and Ren suddenly understands his concern. Somewhere, out in the ferny rustling darkness, a predator has left deep paw prints in the soft earth.

"What about Nandani?" he cries out anxiously.

"I don't want you out there," says Ah Long. "She's probably halfway home already."

It's a reasonable assumption, and besides, there are now two people searching for her. Ren goes back to the front room to collect his tray of dirty glasses. The air is thick with cigarettes and sweat. William is dancing with someone else now, the girl with the arched eyebrows in pink. Ren hesitates, wondering whether to tell him that Nandani has disappeared, but thinks better of it. He'll only be bothered by the interruption. As he turns away, he hears the girl in pink loudly repeating her name for William. "Hui. It's *Hui*," she says coquettishly.

William seems to be paying just as much attention to her as he did to Ren's girl, the one in blue, and for some reason that's a relief.

A guest asks for a fresh drink, but the waiter who should be tending bar is still outside looking for Nandani. Ren only knows how to make one drink, a whisky *stengah*, and he does it the way that William likes, with so much Johnnie Walker that the frosted glass is the color of Chinese tea. Amused, his patron calls a friend over, and Ren finds himself surrounded by laughing faces as he mixes drink after drink.

"Sorry, no more ice," says Ren, gathering up the ice bucket and tongs in relief. Dodging between people, he makes a beeline to the kitchen. Perhaps the waiter and Nandani are back by now. But there's only Ah Long's stooped, skinny figure peering anxiously out of the back door.

"Did they find Nandani?" Ren's stomach gives an uneasy flip.

"Not yet."

"Let me look." Ren is sure he can find her. His cat sense twitches once, twice.

Ah Long frowns, his wrinkled neck angled like a tortoise. "Check the house. Just in case she came back through the side doors."

Ren races off on silent feet. He knows how to nip around without going into any of the public spaces where the guests spill into, mingling and talking. The back hallway, the corridor between the study and the dining room. At every window, he pauses and peeks out just in case Nandani happens to be waiting on the other side, in the dark. There are too many stories about vengeful women who come in the night, tales of the *pontianak*, a woman who dies in childbirth or pregnancy and who drinks men's blood. She looks like a beautiful lady with long hair, and can only be tamed by stopping up the hole at the nape of her neck with an iron nail. Or is it by cutting off her own long nails and stuffing them into the hole in her neck? Ren isn't sure, except that she's very angry with men. There are other creatures, too, child spirits like the *toyol*, used as a sorceror's servant to steal and run errands. It reminds him uneasily of his own disturbing task. Ren shakes his head with a sharp, doglike movement. There's something about tonight—a restless unease, the laughing dancers, Nandani's pained face—that sends a long shiver up his spine.

His cat sense has gone quiet, the invisible tendrils curled back as though they're afraid to penetrate the silent outer reaches of the house. All is hushed, quivering in expectancy. It would be faster to run but running is worse, as though he's giving in to his fears.

When he gets to William's study, he freezes, hand on the door. The tiger skin on the floor, its mouth open in a rictus, is not what he wants to see right now. Not in the darkness, with the faint new moon gilding the dead eyes.

Ren lets out a whimper. *Yi*, he thinks. *I don't want to be alone.* He gazes from the passageway into a brightly lit slice of drawing room, and there she is, his girl in blue, leaning against the wall. She looks straight at him. Glances around, then slips into the corridor beside Ren.

"I'm Ji Lin." Her voice is low and friendly. "Who are you?"

"I'm Ren." His chest clenches. One, two. *Breathe.*

"Ren . . . meaning 'benevolence'?"

"Yes."

"But you've grown bigger!" Wide-eyed, she studies him with surprise. Then she catches herself. "I mean, you look like someone I've met. Do you know me?"

Ren doesn't know how to reply to that. Technically, he's never seen her before but he believes with all his heart that they belong together. The sensation is so strong that his throat squeezes tight. "No," he says at last, though it feels like admitting defeat.

"How old are you?"

"Eleven." It's the first time since leaving the orphanage that he's told anyone his real age. Seen up close, she's shockingly pretty. Or at least, she is to him, though some might say her cropped hair and slender frame are too boyish.

"Do you have a brother?"

"Yes. No." Ren stumbles over this question. Auntie Kwan said he must stop telling everyone he had a brother since it confused people. But Yi still exists for him. "Yes," he says at last.

"What's his name?" She watches him closely, as though this is some kind of test. Ren desperately wants to pass it.

"Yi."

A long exhale. "Ren and Yi. Well, the 'Ji' in my name is *zhi* for wisdom. Does that mean anything to you?"

"*Ah Jie*," he blurts out. Older Sister. That's the right way to call her though he understands exactly what she's saying. They're part of a set, she and him; he's known it all along. A wave of giddy exultation washes over him, and she laughs, her eyes sparkling.

"And your brother Yi," she says excitedly. "Let me guess, is he younger than you? About seven or eight years old?"

"Yes." Ren is about to tell her that Yi is younger than him because death has increased the distance between them, but he pauses, not knowing how to mention it. Not here, in the gloomy shadow of the windows. "Do you know my brother?"

Now it's her turn to hesitate, as though she's said too much. "I'm not sure. But I have a brother, too. His name is Shin, for *xin*. So that makes four of us out of five."

"There're five actually. If you count my master."

"What do you mean?"

"He has a Chinese name, too—he said so tonight. It's got the *Li* in it, for ritual."

"Are you sure?" She looks disturbed for some reason.

"Yes, but maybe it doesn't count, since he's a foreigner."

"Ren!" Ah Long appears in the corridor.

Guiltily, Ren spins round. He's supposed to be searching for Nandani, not talking to strange young women. "Coming!" he says, but Ah Long has seized his shoulder.

"Did you find her?"

"No." Ren doesn't understand why Ah Long is so worried.

"Don't go out right now."

"Why?"

"*Aiya!* Because the tiger is in the garden. Ah Seng and that boy, Nandani's cousin, swear they saw it just now."

"Where?"

"At the bottom of the garden where you bury the garbage—remember the paw print? Stay inside for now!"

"Did you tell the master?"

"He's gone for his shotgun."

"To kill it?" asks Ji Lin.

Ah Long glances at her as though he's just registered her presence for the first time. "To frighten it off, so the guests can leave. You can't kill a tiger with that kind of shot."

He turns on his heel and disappears. And now Ren realizes that the mood in the house has changed. There's a rising buzz, cries of alarm and pleasurable excitement. *A tiger! The same one the fellows at the Club were waiting up for the other night?* Mrs. Banks is wailing to her husband, *I knew we should have left earlier,* but the men are enthusiastic. This is what they have come East for: adventures like tigers in the garden, Oriental dancing girls, and cobras in their beds. Rawlings says loudly, "It's probably gone already," though nobody wants to believe him.

But Ren has a terrible, sinking feeling. There have been too many co-incidences tonight, too many warning signs. He should have paid attention to them, but he's been distracted. Now Nandani is gone, and the tiger is waiting, right where its pugmarks were found yesterday. What kind of beast returns so soon when there is no kill?

Ren knows that spot is where he buried the finger. If he returns the finger, perhaps the tiger will give back Nandani. With a strangled cry, he darts towards the veranda.

"What are you doing?" Ji Lin catches him by the sleeve.

"I have to get it back." He has the peculiar sensation that she'll understand him. "It wants the finger."

"What finger?" In the dim light, her face has a greenish pallor.

"Dr. MacFarlane's finger! I must put it back!"

With a sharp tug, Ren frees himself and runs out of the veranda doors. Now is the time to get it, before William comes out with a shotgun. He's not afraid of the tiger, he tells himself. This kind of spirit tiger, that only hunts women with long hair.

It's a lie though, because he's terrified. His head is pounding, his lungs burning. But Ren is certain, down to the marrow in his bones, that there's very little time left for Nandani. Perhaps she's already dead. But no, the tiger has come back as a sign to him. A last chance.

I'm sorry, he gasps. He should have obeyed Dr. MacFarlane's wishes from the beginning. He promised, didn't he? This is what happens when promises are broken.

Outside, the darkness has a wet green scent, as though the earth itself is exhaling. Ren runs blindly over the lawn, heading for the rubbish dump. Breath wheezing as he trips, scrambles, gets up. Behind him, distant shouts. Doors slamming, windows opening.

And now he's scrabbling in the soft earth, heaving aside the stone that he used as a marker. No spade, nothing but bare hands and broken fingernails.

Hurry, hurry!

Then he hears it, a rumbling snarl. It's pitched so low that the air trembles; he can feel the reverberations in his bones. Every muscle in his body freezes, the hairs on his head stand on end. At this moment, Ren is no longer a boy or even human. He's nothing but a hairless monkey caught on the ground.

The growl goes on and on, a steady rolling that fills the air. Dazed, he can't tell which direction it comes from. Then there's a coughing bark, a harsh rattle that cuts off abruptly and silence.

From the house he can hear faint shouts. A girl's voice screaming *stop* or *no*.

But Ren is digging like a madman. So close, he can feel the edge of the biscuit tin. Thumbnail tearing. Sliding up the lid. It's open and the little glass bottle clinks into his grimy hand. Ren heaves a sigh. Crouching, he turns towards the house. And then there's a flash and a deafening roar.

Eyes wide, Ren hits the ground. He's so surprised, he feels nothing but numbness. Lifts his left hand. It's wet and slippery and looks like raw meat. Then the pain hits him in the side. Ren folds over, crumpling like old newspaper. The last thing he sees is his girl in blue. She's holding him in her lap; there's blood all over her pretty dress. It's all right if it's her, he thinks as he presses the glass vial from his good right hand into hers.

29

KIONG WAS THE ONE WHO GOT US ALL OUT THAT NIGHT. AS SOON AS he realized there was trouble, from all the shouting and carrying on, and then of course, that gunshot, the sound that cracked open the night. It was he who, searching for me as the last straggler, ran out with the crowd spilling onto that dark lawn and grabbed me. I had no memories of that. If I closed my eyes, I was still there. The white muzzle flash, the high sharp scream of a young animal.

My dress was covered in blood, dark blotches staining the pale blue silky material. None of the other girls wanted to sit too close to me. They huddled up towards the other side of the car, talking in hushed tones. Pearl was crying. She had a little boy of her own, I remembered.

I should have stopped him. When the boy took off, rocketing out of the veranda doors, I should have gone back to the house to warn them that he'd gone out, but like a fool, I ran after him, stumbling around in the dark in that unknown garden, tripping and falling and circling back to the house. If only I hadn't wasted all that time! And then the black shape of the man, coming out of the house with a gun. I knew it right away— one of my stepfather's friends used to hunt wild boar—that sticklike shadow and the way he was carrying it, tucked under his arm.

"Stop!" I screamed as he lifted it. "No!"

But it was too late.

Shouts behind us: *Acton, did you get it?* But I already knew what he'd shot. I raced past him, sobbing. The old cook pushing his way through with a lantern, his face grey. And in the circle of lamplight, the boy crumpled on the ground.

So small. That was the first thing I thought when I saw that pathetic little body, the shadows of the trees and bushes looming above him. He must have been digging, because his arms were stained up to the elbows with earth. There was a look of utter astonishment on his face. I couldn't look at his left side and arm, soaked in blood that looked black in the light. That arm—was there even a hand left? I was on my knees beside him, on the rough grass and upturned earth. He looked at me and his mouth moved.

"Put it back," he said faintly. "In my master's grave. I promised." He pressed something into my palm with his good right hand. Men shoved past, barked orders.

"Move aside! Move, please!"

A hand grabbed my elbow. It was Kiong. "Time to go."

"Wait!" I wanted to hear what the men were saying as they lifted him up, his limp body just like Pei Ling's dangling foot. There were doctors here tonight; they'd know what his injuries were like and if he would live or die.

Kiong dragged me away. I couldn't break his iron grip on my arm. "We're leaving now."

And so we had. The other girls were already waiting in the car. There was a flurry of questions when they saw me, but I'd no words to answer them.

"But what were you *doing* out there?" said Hui. She seemed agitated, more so than me in fact. Numbness paralyzed my hands and feet; my tongue was thick and dry.

"I saw him run out," I said at last. "So I tried to stop him."

"You might have been shot!" Hui squeezed me hard.

"Don't," I said. "My dress has blood on it."

THE WAY BACK SEEMED SHORTER THAN OUR JOURNEY OUT, ON MILE after mile of pale, ribbonlike road. After a while, the other girls started talking again, speculating about what had happened.

"What an idiot, shooting his own houseboy," said Rose.

"Well, it seems he's an orphan, so there's no family to complain on his behalf if he dies," said Anna.

I said nothing, only stared out of the window. My fingers were still clutched tight around the object that the boy Ren had given me. I had a stomach-clenching feeling that I knew exactly what it was from the shape of the slippery glass cylinder. I didn't have to look. Didn't want to look.

There were no pockets in my dress, and the little bag I'd brought with me had been left behind in the rush of leaving. There wasn't much in it anyway, just my house keys and lip rouge. Hui had taught me not to leave telltale information like my name or address in my bag if I ever had to go out for work. But in the meantime, I had nowhere to put my burden, this unwanted gift that Ren had slipped me.

Why did he have the finger? It was like a curse, one of those dark tales when you try to discard something but it always returns to you. The image of the little boy from my dreams and Ren's face blurred together. The same, yet not the same.

Now we were passing streets that I knew, the village of Menglembu, and very soon, Falim, where my stepfather's shophouse was. Kiong planned to drop us off at our homes since it was so late. But how could I possibly slip into Mrs. Tham's dress shop in a bloodstained dress with no keys?

"Stay over with me," Hui whispered, as though she'd been reading my mind. "I'll lend you clothes."

I hesitated, and she must have sensed it, because she said, "You've had a shock. Come on, I'll take care of you."

She said it so kindly that my throat closed up. I would really like that, I thought. For someone to pry open my tightly clenched fingers and take away the little glass bottle with a dead man's finger in it. As we passed my stepfather's store on Lahat Road, I bit back the urge to jump out, run home. I wanted my mother. Wanted to bury my face in her lap, feel her soft hand on my hair, and forget about everything but the two of us.

I didn't want to think of Shin—of that pleased look on his face when he'd discussed my stepfather's promise about my marriage. *Isn't it a good thing?*

"All right," I said to Hui. "I'll go with you."

////

In Hui's rented room, I washed up and borrowed some paja-mas. While I was cleaning my face off with cold cream, Hui came and sat on the dressing table.

"You all right?"

I nodded numbly.

"Go to sleep," she said.

Hui's bed was a narrow single, and as soon as my head hit the pillow next to her, I felt a heavy current dragging me away. A chilly paralysis seeped into my arms and legs. I tried to keep my eyes open, but I was falling. Dimly, I heard Hui saying something, but I couldn't understand her. The current was far too strong. And so I fell down, down, deeper than the deepest lake, until I reached that place I was beginning to know so well.

This time, I stood by the sunny shore, my bare feet ankle-deep in the clear water. It wasn't cold at all, just the same, dreamy after-noon heat that made the trees in the distance shimmer. And like before, I was lulled by the calm, though I was quick to step out of the water. That limpid, deceptively clear water that harbored a rising black shadow.

There was no one around, not even the little boy. Since I was here any-way, I set out to look for him through the waving grass, but when I got to the deserted railway station, there was no one to be seen. Nor was there a train, as there had been each time before.

Time stretched on—I'd no way of knowing how long. Anxiety gnawed at me as the sunlight remained fixed at an angle. I didn't want to be stuck here. What had the little boy said? If I discovered his name, I could summon him.

"Yi!" I called softly.

The silence was unnerving me. I turned towards the other side of the platform, and there he was, standing right behind me. So close that he could have stretched out a small hand to touch my back. I gave a little shriek.

"You called." He was looking very serious. No smile, no cheerful wave. Now that I examined him carefully, there were differences between them. Ren was taller, his face longer and more grown-up looking. A distance of perhaps two or three years separated them.

"I met your brother."

He nodded warily.

"He got shot tonight." Remembering the darkness and the swinging lantern light, blood blossoming over that broken body, my eyes filled with tears.

"I know. That's why the train's gone."

The train that traveled on a single line, only in one direction.

The little boy climbed onto a wooden bench, and I sat down beside him. It was easier to talk this way. "You're dead, aren't you?" I said. "They said that Ren was an orphan—that his whole family had died."

He turned his head away, that small round head that was now so familiar. Although he and Ren were disconcertingly similar, they were also different. Their mannerisms, their voices. I remembered the delighted look that Ren had given me just a few hours ago. How happy he'd been to see me, as though he'd been waiting for me all his life, and I felt like weeping again. "That's right. I'm dead." Yi's face swung back to mine. It looked smooth and guileless, but I had the feeling that he was concentrating very hard. It unsettled me, how much younger he seemed than Ren, yet older. Perhaps it was the way he talked sometimes, like an adult.

"Why didn't you tell me?"

He swung a small sandaled foot, frowning. "Nobody else has ever shown up the way you do. They all come by train. But you just . . . appear. That's good, I think."

"Why?"

"Because if you came by the train, you'd be like all the others. Like me."

I was bursting with questions, but he glanced at me, shaking his head slightly.

"Is Ren going to die?"

"I don't know." That pensive look on his face. "The train's gone. That means another one will be coming soon, but I don't know who'll be on it."

"Is that what you did? You got off at this station by yourself?"

"Yes. A long time ago. We were twins, Ren and I."

Twins. "Like Shin and me. We're not really twins but we were born on the same day."

"I don't know Shin," he said frowning. "He doesn't dream like you."

"No, he doesn't," I said slowly, remembering the paper amulet Shin's mother had given him. A charm against nightmares to call the *mo*, that black and white beast of a dream-eater, to gobble them up. Though if you called the *mo* too often, it would also devour your hopes and desires.

Yi said, "So that makes four of us. Did you find the fifth one?"

"I think so." I thought back to William Acton, and how Ren had said the *Li* in his name stood for ritual. Order. Something bothered me about it. Perhaps it was because he was a foreigner, and I couldn't understand how he had a Chinese name.

"I told you, there's something wrong with each of us. Things won't go the right way."

"What am I supposed to do? And what about the finger that Ren gave me?" I'd hidden it, rolled up in my bloodstained dancing frock when Hui was in the bathroom.

Yi sighed and swung his short legs. "That's his master's business. Do what you think is right."

Alarm was rising in me, like a distant thin bell that was starting to ring. No, had been ringing for some time now, except I hadn't been paying attention. "Look at me, Yi. Why aren't you more worried about Ren?"

He hunched over, twisting his body away as though he couldn't bear to look me in the eyes. All of a sudden, he was a child again.

"You've been waiting for him to die, haven't you?"

That guilty, guilty look. The scrunched-up, miserable face, about to cry. I wanted to shake him, but I'd never touched him before. Not even that time when I'd been chased out of the water by the black shape in its depths.

"How could you?" I said bitterly. "Your own brother."

He was bawling now. Shoulders shaking, fists curled into his eyes.

"I didn't mean to. At least, not in the beginning." Hiccupping. Smearing the tears across his face. "I love Ren. He's everything to me."

"Why did you stay then?"

He shook his head. "We'd never been apart before. And I knew he was miserable without me. How was he going to manage alone? So when the train crossed the river, I got out. This is the very first stop on this side. I'm sure there are better places farther in, but I didn't want to go without Ren."

"And so you stayed." I looked hard at him.

"I wasn't the only one. There are always a few of us who get off. You saw them before."

I remembered the distant figures of people wandering this shore the first time I had drifted down the river.

"In the end, however, they all give up and go on. There's no point, you see. From this side, you can't call anyone over or talk to them."

I watched him carefully. "But you could."

He nodded. "We've always had this twin thing. When I got off the train, I found that I could still feel it. Very faint, like a radio signal. So I didn't go on. Not as long as I could still sense Ren at the other end."

He looked so small and pitiful: a child who'd been waiting for his brother for three years. Waiting alone, on a deserted shore. My heart went out to him, but at the same time, I knew that what he'd done was horribly wrong.

"I found that as long as I'm here, I can call him to this side of the river and then things happen to him. Accidents and stuff. Sometimes, I think I'll get on the train and go away. But I always chicken out. I don't want Ren to forget me."

"I don't think he's forgotten you."

But he wasn't listening to me. "At first I thought I'd just watch and wait. Sometimes I can see bits of what he's doing. Then I realized I'd have to wait a long, long time if it was going to be the rest of his life. And Ren is always changing. He's growing up. One day, he'll forget all about me."

"So you tried to lure him over?"

Yi turned to look at me. There was such misery in his eyes I couldn't be angry with him. "I thought we'd be happier together. But I've never managed to get him over. Not really. Though just the other night he had a high fever and he showed up on that sandbar." He pointed to a thin sliver of white in the river.

"He wanted to cross over. He did! He even jumped in by himself. I was terrified because of the water. There's something in it, that's made so that people can't swim back to the other side."

I shuddered at the memory of that black shape, rising from the depths of the water.

"But I made him go back. There's no use coming that way. He would have just separated from his body and it would be even worse."

"Like a coma, you mean?"

Yi blinked. "I don't know what that word means."

"When your body's alive but the mind is gone."

"Yes. Then we'd both be stuck here waiting for his body to die."

"Well," I said wearily, "you've got your wish. Your brother is dying right now."

Yi dropped his head. Stared miserably at his feet.

"So what are you going to do?"

He burst into tears again. "*Yi* means righteousness. I'm supposed to be able to choose the right thing, but I can't!"

"Don't cry," I said, resisting the urge to hug him. Now that I knew exactly where I was, I had a tingling sensation of danger. "You meant well."

"But that's not good enough!" he shouted, rubbing his red, anguished face. "Meaning well isn't the same as doing the right thing. Maybe we're all cursed. We should have all been born together in the same family, or even as the same person, not separated like this by time and place."

The five of us should have made a kind of harmony. After all, weren't the Confucian Virtues supposed to describe the perfect man? A man who abandoned virtue lost his humanity and became no better than a beast. Dazed, I wondered whether that was happening to all of us.

"It's all a problem with the order—the way things are being bent and rearranged. The further each of us strays, the more everything warps," said Yi miserably. "And the fifth one is the worst."

"What are you saying?"

But he was fading. The world was fading back to grey, and struggle as I might, I could only gasp and thrash as my mouth and face were covered with a choking softness.

"Yi!" I screamed. "Leave Ren alone!"

30

REN'S EYES FLUTTER OPEN. CLOSE. OPEN AGAIN. THERE'S A DRYNESS in his mouth, a thick feeling in his head, as though someone has stuffed it with cotton wool. An unfamiliar face swims into view. A foreign woman, her hair pinned severely back with a white cap.

"He's awake."

Another face. It's William. Mouth tight and strained. Two lines are etched deeply under his eyes. "Ren, can you hear me? We're at the hospital."

The hospital. That explains the feeling of empty air around him, the hollow length of a hospital ward. The bed is bigger, too, longer than the cot Ren sleeps on. There's a heaviness on his left side, and he can't feel his arm at all.

"Does it hurt?"

Under the layers of numbness, there's pain in Ren's body. A deep ache that's buried by some artificial means. The light is bright; it's daytime already.

"Mr. Acton, you'd better go home now." It's the nurse. "You've been here all night."

"Just a moment, Sister." William turns back to him.

How strange. Ren can see all these threads coming from William now. Gossamer threads that spew out, like the unraveling of a silkworm. He's never been able to see them before, only felt their spark of energy. But now his cat sense is stronger than ever, or perhaps it's just that his body is so broken. He knows it without even looking at William's haunted face.

"Ren, I'm so terribly sorry. I shot you last night."

So that's what it was, the flash and the roar that tore him apart. Ren looks at William with wide, unblinking eyes.

"But you'll be all right. Well, almost. You've lost a lot of blood but we managed to take out most of the shot. It was the wadding around the shot that really worried me—infection in the soft tissues, you know." William's jaw is moving like a clockwork toy that's been wound too far.

"Mr. Acton!" It's the nurse again. "That's quite enough!"

William stops. Passes a tongue over dry lips. "Yes, of course. If you need anything, let me know."

It's hard to speak; Ren's throat is so parched. "Nandani," he says. His eyes signal a question.

William stares at him blankly. "Ah. Nandani. I don't know where she is. Don't worry—she's bound to turn up."

No, you have to find her! Ren's anguished expression cuts like a knife. William makes a tight grimace. "Of course we'll find her. All right? Just . . . rest now. It's very important that you get some rest."

REN SINKS BACK INTO HALF SLEEP. DIMLY, HE'S AWARE OF DOORS opening and shutting. The sun climbs higher then starts to wane, though Ren doesn't know what day it is. Somewhere, his body is getting weaker and colder, or is it feverishly hot? His painful side is examined, the bulky dressing on his arm unwrapped.

"—bleeding again. Looks bad."

"—risk of infection."

REN CLOSES HIS EYES. BEHIND THEM, ANOTHER LANDSCAPE UNFURLS, bright and burning like a fever dream. And there it is, the tiger that he's feared for so long. It stands before him, unbelievably large. Lean muscular bulk tapering into a twitching tail. This isn't the moth-eaten, forlorn tiger skin that's stretched out on the floor of William's study, or the wraithlike white creature Ren has imagined, wandering in the jungle with

Dr. MacFarlane's face. It's simply a huge, bright beast. An animal that he cannot comprehend. Surprisingly, Ren feels no fear, just an overwhelming sensation of relief.

So that's what you are, he thinks, though it seems undignified to address it.

The stripes on its brilliant coat ripple; the yellow eyes glare like lanterns. Ren can only drop his gaze. The tiger makes a deep *hrff* sound. Then it turns and walks away, with a deliberate tread that's heavy and delicate at the same time. Where is it going?

In the shimmering landscape, Ren sees a familiar shedlike outline—a railway station, just like the one he boarded at Taiping when he took his first and only train ride after Dr. MacFarlane's death. It seems quite natural to follow. He takes a step forward. Then he remembers something.

"Nandani—where is she?" he calls after the tiger.

There is no answer, only the white tip of its tail swaying hypnotically. Then he sees them: the uneven tracks of a woman's feet. Slender, pretty footprints, the left leg dragging in a limp.

"Is Nandani here?" If she is, she must be heading towards the station. Ren takes another step. The tiger turns its head and snarls. Is that a warning? Ren doesn't know, but his side hurts, a fiery pain that spreads through his body, up his useless left arm and hand. Gritting his teeth, Ren forces himself to walk on, following the footprints towards the train station.

31

A CRASH. THE BREATH WAS KNOCKED OUT OF MY BODY, MY FACE pressed against a hard, cool surface. For a moment I lay there, motionless.

"Ji Lin—are you all right?" Hui stood over me; I was lying on the floor of her room, tangled up in the thin cotton blanket. The sun streaming into her room was high and hot.

"You fell out of bed, having a nightmare," she said. "Thrashing and crying about someone named Yi. I was afraid to wake you."

Chinese people have an aversion to suddenly waking people from sleep, in case the soul separates from the body. I hadn't thought that Hui would be so superstitious, though I was grateful for it. Who knew where I'd been wandering?

I sat up groggily, my thoughts a nest of ants. I had the feeling that I'd almost managed to grasp something slippery, the tail end of an idea that had vanished with a flick, just as Yi's crying face had.

"What's wrong?" said Hui.

I glanced at the blue dress I'd worn last night. Still neatly rolled up on a chair, just as I'd left it. I didn't want to tell Hui about the finger in its glass bottle. It would only upset her. There were other, more pressing worries. Like whether Ren had survived the night, and what to do with the slim glass vial wrapped in my bloodstained dress.

////

AND SO, THE FINGER HAD RETURNED TO ME. I EXAMINED IT WITH A feeling of inevitability and horror when Hui had gone off on an errand, after lending me a frock. It was the same, down to the number on the lid and the slight dent on the metal screw top.

Dr. MacFarlane's finger, Ren had said before he ran out into the night. How had it found its way from the pathology storeroom, where I'd left it, to last night's party? I felt sick. If only I'd stopped Ren from rushing out. Or if I'd shouted louder as William Acton walked purposefully out of the house with his shotgun tucked under his right arm. The trail went round and round, the finger appearing and reappearing—yet I had the dim sensation that there was a pattern to all of it. When I'd asked Yi what to do with it in my dream, he'd seemed strangely uninterested. *Do what you think is right,* he'd said. But perhaps it was just because all he really cared about was Ren. And Ren, as we both knew, was dying.

RESTLESS AND AGITATED, I HEADED OVER TO THE MAY FLOWER. Perhaps Kiong had further news of what had happened to Ren. It was nearly noon; the dance hall wasn't open yet, so I let myself in through the back door and waited in the corridor outside the Mama's cramped office. It was a squirrel's nest with a desk piled high with papers, but I knew better than to underestimate her. She was an excellent businesswoman.

Kiong wasn't around, said the Mama, but she was well aware of last night's fiasco.

"Is the boy all right?" I asked, unable to hide my concern.

"No idea. But likely he's still alive since no one's come to look us up yet. We didn't get paid, either. Well, that's why I don't like doing private parties. I heard you saw the boy who got shot. Was it bad?"

I nodded, not wanting to talk about it.

"Poor child."

"I don't think I can work here anymore."

Now seemed as good a moment as any to quit. I was unlikely to find another part-time job that paid as well, but it wasn't worth the risk. I'd ask Robert to lend me the money.

She didn't look surprised. "Thought you might feel like that. Well, I won't say I'm not sorry—you're one of my best girls on the afternoon shift. If you change your mind, let me know. Can you pitch in once more next Saturday, though? I'll be short a couple of girls."

I nodded. As I left, it occurred to me that this was one of the last times I'd walk down the grubby mint-green corridor. All the laughter and comradeship, the sore feet, and the slapping away of wandering hands would come to an end. Though perhaps it was better this way.

32

EVERYTHING IS FALLING APART, THINKS WILLIAM.

It's Monday morning now, and he's headed back to the hospital to check on his small victim. For victim is the right word. Over and over, William has replayed the scene from that night: Ah Long taking him aside with the news of the tiger in the garden, the feverish excitement that descended on the whole party, and himself, unlocking the gun closet to get his shotgun. Why, why did he think of that?

It's not as though William hunts much; the Purdey is another expensive Acton relic, like the good silver and crystal glasses that he's lugged halfway round the world. Why bother, when his family has as good as disowned him anyway? It's because titles and breeding open doors everywhere, even if he pretends to scorn them. Perhaps that's what drove him to get the gun out: thinking it would be a grand gesture to fire a few rounds into the darkness and scare off a tiger. What a fool he is!

All his mistakes have been made when he's been overly emotional. In fact, he had misgivings earlier that evening, but he'd thought it was about Nandani and how he must disentangle himself from her. When he walked out of the house, the gun under his right arm in the field carry that his father had taught him so long ago, he had another moment of doubt, but it was too late, even though the girl had screamed for him to stop.

How had she known, that girl Louise, that the rustling in the bushes was Ren, and not an animal? If he closes his eyes, he can still see her, running out of the darkness into the pool of light spilled by Ah Long's lantern.

Pale blue dress, face tight with terror. And even then, the dark part of himself that he's always tried to suppress found her panic alluring, with those slender legs and long-lashed eyes—like a frightened doe.

Thank God he'd loaded it with number-six shot. If it had been buckshot, even at that distance and with the inevitable scatter, Ren would certainly have died. Rawlings said it was one of the messiest injuries he'd seen on a child. One of the fingers on his left hand had been shot raggedly off. The fourth finger, the ring finger. William finds himself wondering illogically whether that means Ren will never get married because there's nowhere to put a ring. But such thoughts are useless because Ren, inexplicably and despite all the care that he's had, is dying.

HE CAN'T UNDERSTAND IT. NOBODY CAN. THE WOUNDS WERE cleaned and stitched up. No vital organs were hit. Perhaps it's the shock. William has heard of men on battlefields who drop dead, their hearts stopped like clocks. Still, it doesn't explain Ren's precipitous decline. The fear is sepsis, especially in the tropics where injuries rapidly turn putrid.

"How old is this boy?" Rawlings had asked that night, as they worked on, searching in the bloodied mess for the shot wadding. It was vital to remove as much of it as possible, there being little to combat infection other than rinses of carbolic acid.

"Thirteen, he said."

"Nonsense! He can't be more than ten or eleven at the most."

William felt himself shrink in shame. Of course he should have known. If Ren dies, nobody will really care. William will be made out to be the fool who shot his own houseboy, but it will all blow over because Ren is an orphan with no one to speak for him. *Except for me*, thinks William.

WHEN WILLIAM GOES OUT TO THE CAR, HE FINDS AH LONG STANDING next to it. He's holding a steel tiffin carrier, the kind they use for packed lunches. The lines on his face look deeper than ever.

"*Tuan*, let me go to hospital."

"You want to see Ren?"

A nod.

"All right." William feels a stab of guilt. Of course the old man must be fond of Ren.

At the hospital, William reviews Ren's chart. Not good. He's continued to run a low fever. Worse still, the boy's face has begun to take on the sunken look that William dreads. Ah Long puts the tiffin carrier on a table and sits by Ren's bed, speaking to him quietly in Cantonese. Ren doesn't respond; his eyes are closed and there are blue shadows under them. There's nothing more that William can do. Irresolute, he stands there wondering what Ah Long is saying.

"Sleeping, is he?" he asks.

"Or wandering."

William frowns. That makes no sense at all. Ah Long fumbles in his pocket and produces something in a small slim glass jar, the kind that anchovies come in. William looks at it in disbelief. It's the shattered end of a child's finger, floating in tea-colored liquid.

"Is this Ren's?" he says, trying to swallow the bile in his throat.

"Yes. I look for it."

God. It's so terribly sad. It reminds him of MacFarlane's finger, the one he had to amputate because of blood poisoning on that trip they took, but it's worse because it's child-sized and preserved in this horrible fashion.

"You do know that we can't reattach it," says William, thinking that Ah Long must have spent hours combing the bushes and grass for this one small finger. It's a wonder that he found it before the crows did.

Ah Long nods. He's about to set it on the table by Ren's bed when William stops him. If Ren wakes up, he might be frightened by it. What is Ah Long up to, with his barbaric superstitions? William pockets the glass jar.

"I'll keep it, just in case." He turns on his heel, about to resume his duties. "By the way, what's the fluid?"

Ah Long looks blank.

"What did you preserve it in?" asks William patiently. He needs to know as he'll have to change the fixative.

"Johnnie Walker, *Tuan*."

/////

WHEN WILLIAM RETURNS TO HIS OFFICE, THERE'S A VISITOR WAIT-ing for him. With a sinking sensation, he recognizes the tall spare figure of the local police inspector, Captain Jagjit Singh. He hasn't seen him since the discovery of Ambika's body in the rubber plantation; there's been no reason to since Ambika's death has been ruled a misadventure. But now he's standing in William's office as though he belongs there. The same Malay constable is with him.

"What can I do for you, Captain?" says William cordially. "Is this about the shooting? I called it in yesterday, and they said I could just come down to the station and give a statement."

"I'd actually like to take a statement about something else."

"A statement about what?" William's alarm is growing. Is this still about Ambika?

Captain Singh studies William's face. "So you haven't heard? About one of your patients—Nandani Wijedasa."

"Has something happened to her?"

"I'm afraid she's dead."

William sinks down. "Dead? How's that possible?"

"Mr. Acton, when was the last time you saw her?"

William thinks rapidly, his mind scattering and reforming itself. "Saturday night. She came to my house."

"What for?"

William considers lying, but instinct tells him not to bother. "She wanted to see me before she went away. What happened to her?"

Captain Singh watches William with sharp amber eyes. "Was she upset?"

"Somewhat." William takes his glasses off and polishes them. "Her father had found out we'd been friendly and he was sending her away. To an uncle, I believe."

"And what kind of relationship did you have with her?"

This is the question that William has been dreading. "I flirted with her. I thought she was attractive, and I came by a few times to where she lived and we went on a couple of walks."

"You didn't know her long?"

"She had the accident with her leg quite recently."

Captain Singh nods. "Yes, there wasn't much time for a relationship to develop."

"May I ask where this line of questioning is going?" William's voice is sharp and cold.

Captain Singh spreads his hands. "According to her family, the only unusual change in her routine this weekend was that she went to see you. Her cousin said that she was quite upset when she left your house."

"Yes, I told you that already. She didn't want to go to her uncle's, but I thought she should do what her father wanted. And that she was reading too much into our friendship. Now, please tell me what's happened to her."

The captain suddenly becomes brisk. "On Saturday night she went missing from your house for a short while, but was later discovered walking on the road by her cousin, who gave her a ride home on his bicycle. She went to bed as usual. At half past eight on Sunday morning, her body was discovered lying in the bushes a little way from her home."

"Was it a tiger?" William's mind instantly leaps to Ambika's poor sad corpse.

"No, though it seems there was a tiger in your garden on Saturday night."

"Yes," says William distractedly.

"I'm afraid in Miss Wijedasa's case, she was violently ill. We're investigating the possibility that there was some kind of accident. Or suicide." His eyes rest thoughtfully on William.

"Suicide? She was upset, but she wasn't suicidal!"

"Her family doesn't think she was, either. This morning, the body was brought in for an autopsy."

"Who did it—Rawlings?"

"Yes. According to his first impressions, she ingested something early in the morning, before breakfast. Perhaps some folk remedy—her mother said she'd complained of stomach pains."

"So why did you need a statement from me?" William's head is foggy now, his knees weak with tension.

"We just wanted to confirm her movements this weekend. Though it appears you spent most of Saturday night at the hospital attending to your houseboy," Captain Singh says smoothly. Is it William's imagination, or has the man been stringing him along? "When I looked up recent deaths in this area, I noticed that another patient of yours died not too long ago. A salesman—Mr. Chan Yew Cheung of Papan—who apparently dropped dead on the road."

"I read about it in the newspapers. Poor chap."

"According to his wife, you were the last doctor to see him."

"That was for appendicitis, half a year ago."

"Nothing to do with his subsequent heart failure or broken neck, of course."

"Is that what happened to him?" It's the first William has heard about the details behind the salesman's death. The obituary had only said "suddenly," but cardiac failure and a broken neck sounds literally like overkill.

"Apparently he'd been drinking and fell into a storm drain, breaking his neck. Though one eyewitness said he'd complained of chest pains shortly before that. There was no autopsy though."

William supposes not, since there were more than enough plausible causes of death.

Captain Singh thanks him for his time and turns to leave. "You've had quite an affinity for deaths and accidents recently."

AFTER HE'S GONE, WILLIAM SINKS INTO A CHAIR. SO NANDANI IS dead. There's a hollowness in his gut, a tight misery. Did she die for him? No, that doesn't seem right. Still, the overwhelming emotion he feels is guilt, because didn't he wish, fervently and irritably, on Saturday night that Nandani would just disappear?

What would cause an otherwise healthy young woman to drop dead? William puts his hands over his eyes. A terrible suspicion is growing in him that there's a shadowy power that rearranges events to suit himself. That whole business with Iris, and Ambika, once she started asking for more money. Then the salesman, conveniently dying after stumbling upon his affair with Ambika. And finally Nandani. It's the fickleness of events that frightens him, as though he only has to say, "I wish it weren't so!" and the pattern reorders to suit him. Like a dark fairy tale, where all your wishes, however evil and stupid, are granted.

And perhaps, like fairy tales, there's a price to be paid in blood.

33

ALL WEEK, I SCANNED THE NEWSPAPERS FEVERISHLY TO SEE IF THERE was any mention of a death in Batu Gajah, but there was nothing. Though perhaps an orphaned houseboy didn't warrant a mention. When I looked at the little glass vial, I couldn't help recalling Ren's faint hoarse voice. "Put it back. In his grave," he'd said.

Chinese sometimes exhumed a grave. Bone-picking, it was called, when remains were disinterred seven years after death to be sent back to an ancestral village. If you had no family and died in a foreign land, you'd become a hungry ghost, wandering and starving forever. To prevent that, the bones were carefully washed with wine and laid out on a yellow cloth, before being packed in a jar. If even the smallest bone was missing, a substitute must be made.

Incomplete sets and broken promises. Dark thoughts, like an eel twisting in my head. I was so preoccupied that on Friday, Mrs. Tham told me to take the rest of the day off.

"Worried about your mother, are you?" she said.

I thanked her guiltily, though I was less anxious about my mother's health—which was improving—than her debts. Things had been a little too calm in the shophouse, no doubt because my stepfather had suddenly realized he could be widowed again. But all that goodwill might fly out of the window if a debt collector showed up. Clenching my hands, I tried to quell my rising apprehension. If Shin were around, it would have been some comfort. He was the one I most wanted to talk to about Ren getting shot and how the finger had returned to me, though I shuddered to think of Shin's reaction if he discovered I'd been working as paid entertainment. A shadow lay between us; I couldn't go running to confide in him. But the most pressing worry was Ren—whether he was alive or dead, and if my last-minute plea to Yi had made any difference. So when Mrs. Tham shooed me out of the dress shop, I headed straight down to Batu Gajah. I'd asked Kiong, after I'd given my notice to the Mama, for the address of the house that we'd gone to. He'd been reluctant.

"If the boy died," I said, "I'd like to make a soul offering. He was an orphan, wasn't he?"

Kiong grunted, then scribbled the address on a slip of paper. "First place I'd try, however, would be the district hospital. That's probably where they took him if he survived."

WHEN I ARRIVED AT BATU GAJAH STATION, IT WAS MIDAFTERNOON and just as hot as the day we'd cleaned the pathology storeroom. The hospital had seemed busy enough that I could probably risk a quick visit without running into Shin or narrow-faced Y. K. Wong.

As I got off the train, I noticed two men approaching, heads bent together. One was very tall and stoop-shouldered, with a great beak of a nose. He looked familiar, and I realized that I'd seen him at that ill-fated party. The other was William Acton. I darted behind a pillar, hoping they'd pass by, but they stopped right on the other side.

"Thanks for the ride." That was the tall one.

"Glad to save you the walk. You really think it was murder, Rawlings?"

Who had died? My thoughts leaped to Ren. But Rawlings was speaking again. "That, or suicide. There's no doubt in my mind that she either took it herself or someone poisoned her."

"God. I can't believe it."

"Wasn't she at your house on Saturday night—the local girl sitting in the kitchen?"

"Yes. She was a patient of mine, and she was friendly with Ren." He sounded oddly defensive.

"No need to blame yourself. Time of death was early Sunday morning, so who knows what happened." This was a bit too hearty, as though the other man had also seen through Acton's denial. "It was likely a vegetable toxin, though we may not be able to test for it. I'll ask the lab in Ipoh. Budget won't run to sending this all the way to KL if it's just a local girl committing suicide or taking some fool remedy. Farrell will have my head for it."

There was a sigh. "All right. Thanks for letting me know."

The quick clip of footsteps. I stayed where I was, thinking furiously. If William Acton really was the fifth Virtue, then he must be *Li*, order and ritual. He'd been with Dr. MacFarlane when his finger was amputated, and his name was also on Pei Ling's mysterious list. And now, someone else had died.

I waited a few minutes until I was sure they'd gone. The finger in its glass vial was in my pocket, since I couldn't leave it where Mrs. Tham might find it. I considered replacing it in the pathology storeroom, but I had a bad feeling. Somehow it had wormed its way out of there and buried itself in the dark earth outside William Acton's bungalow, as though it had an agenda. The idea made me shudder.

Deep in thought, I stepped off the curb without looking and was honked at. Startled, I raised my eyes to find that the car was an Austin, and William Acton was driving. I felt like kicking myself—what was the point of hiding only to be run over by him five minutes later?

"Louise," he said, leaning out of the window. "Want a lift?"

Since he'd already spotted me and it was a long, uphill walk to the hospital, I climbed in. Acton didn't seem surprised to see me, just distracted, as though he was mulling something over.

"How is Ren—your houseboy?" I said. "Is he all right?"

"He's still in the hospital. Are you working there today?"

He probably assumed I had a job there since I'd been cleaning up the pathology storeroom. But relief was flooding me. Glorious, heartfelt relief. Ren had survived!

"My brother's an orderly. I was just helping out."

"Your brother—you mean the chap who was with you the other day?"

"Yes."

Acton shot me a swift glance. "I didn't realize that."

"We don't look alike." I wondered why I always apologized for that.

"That wasn't what I was thinking." He grinned. "Anyway, do you want to see Ren? I'm going back myself."

William Acton was a much better driver than Robert was. At least, he changed gears without gut-wrenching swerves. Spared the terror of death by motorcar, I studied him surreptitiously, struck once again by his disarming manner. I suspected the reason he could be so casual was because he didn't really see me as a person, just another interchangeable local girl.

As the car began to climb the hill, he said, "Look here, Louise—on Saturday night at the party, did you happen to see a Sinhalese girl? Her name was Nandani."

That must be the girl they'd been discussing at the train station. The one who'd died. "Was she there to see you?"

He glanced quickly up and out of the window. *Guilty.* "She came by the kitchen and Ren gave her some supper." He was hiding something. A memory stirred in me: Ren's frightened face, white in the darkness of a corridor, and then the old Chinese cook coming out to tell him something.

"I think Ren was searching for her in the house."

A twitch. "Did he say anything to you? About why she was there?"

I shook my head. What he was concerned about? We were passing sprawling white colonial buildings now, beautifully set in manicured green lawns. The view from a car was very different from trudging along on foot. It was like a dream, the way the scenery slid by so smoothly, and I said as much to him. It was just small talk, but he seemed struck by it, and also eager to change the subject from Nandani.

"What sort of dreams do you have, Louise?" Acton gave off the same sticky sense of loneliness as some of the customers at the May Flower, the ones who stayed too long, paying for dance after dance. But now was my chance to find out if he really was the fifth one of us.

Yi had said we'd all gone a little wrong, perhaps in the way we'd failed to live up to our Virtues. My own choices—working at a dance hall, getting mixed up with a dead man's finger, and telling lie after lie—could hardly be called wise, despite my supposed cleverness at school. I imagined the five of us making a pattern. A set that fit together naturally like the fingers on a hand. The further we strayed, the more the balance in our worlds distorted. Less human, more monstrous. Like the claw of a beast.

And what about the unknown fifth? *The worst one of all,* according to Yi. Of course, *Li* stood for order. Ritual. Doing things in their proper way, not shortcutting for selfish desires.

"Sometimes I dream about a river," I said slowly. "There's a train and a small boy who's waiting for me."

"That's funny, I dream about a river, too."

"Is it always the same? Mine is—night after night, like a dream that continues; a story that unfolds."

"A story that unfolds." He seemed struck by this. "What a poetic way of putting it."

"What happens in your dream?" I was treading carefully here, feeling my way. I'd done this dozens of times at the May Flower. They said they wanted to dance but they really just wanted to talk about themselves.

"In my dream, I see someone standing in the river. She's always there. And she always says the same thing."

I shivered, recalling Yi's red, impassioned face, his guilty confession of luring Ren over. "Does she ask you to come to her?"

"No. She's very angry with me." A ghost of a smile. "And that's why," he added under his breath, "I write letters instead."

"Who is she?"

But the spell had broken. Acton laughed uneasily. "I must be boring you."

"Not at all," I said hastily. "It's very interesting."

He gave me a sharp look. "You don't talk like most local girls."

No, I talk like a dance hostess. But of course I didn't say so. The whole point of spinning out conversations like this was to run up a tab. Or, in this case, find out more information.

A spark was burning in Acton's eye now, a little flame that made me nervous. "You're a very interesting girl, Louise. Seems like fate, doesn't it, how we keep running into each other?"

We'd arrived at the hospital now and he'd parked the car, but he made no move to get out. Abruptly, I remembered Hui's warning: *don't get into cars with men.*

"Thanks for the ride," I said, tugging at the door. The handle was different from Robert's car, and for an instant, it stuck. I had a panicky moment when Acton leaned across me, but he was only helping to open it. Or was he? His hand brushed my knee. There were no bouncers here, no Kiong with his watchful eye, and I felt a spasm of fear. If he pinned me down, I wouldn't be able to get away. I yanked hard on the door and almost fell out.

"Are you all right?" he said. And then it was sunny again, a bright innocuous day, and I looked ridiculous, half falling out of the car. I told myself I must have imagined that sudden predatory feeling as I stared at his hands. Clever, surgeon's hands. They would have a viselike grip.

"William?" It was a woman's voice. The tall, fair lady from Saturday's party. She was standing under the eaves of the hospital as though she was waiting to be picked up, and now came over, her quick steps shod in patent leather sandals. White ones, in a style I'd never seen locally. I struggled up, red-faced and smoothing down my dress, hoping she didn't remember me from the party, but her sharp glance told me that she did.

Acton turned a blandly affable face to her. "Hello, Lydia. Didn't know you were in today."

Gone was the guilty distraction he'd betrayed earlier, and I realized it was because a local girl like me didn't matter. Lydia, however, was different. She was one of his own.

"Thanks for the ride," I said, preparing to slip off. I nodded politely at Lydia—it didn't seem right to ignore her although she was doing her best to pretend I didn't exist—but Acton said, "Hold up. I'll take you into the ward."

It was no use protesting I could find my own way. He was too quick, explaining to Lydia, "She's here to visit Ren. My houseboy, you know."

"Is that so?" Her expression softened. "Poor boy. How is he?"

"Not well. He's in an adult ward. Ran out of beds in the children's ward."

"Oh, that's why I didn't see him earlier when I went around with the lending library." She turned stiffly to me. "Are you related to him?"

I nodded. It was too difficult to explain the fierce protectiveness I felt towards Ren.

"William, we must talk," Lydia said in an undertone.

He glanced at his watch, suddenly busy. "Now's not really a good time. I'm due on the wards."

"I'll go with you," she said. "I'd like to visit your houseboy as well."

I trailed after them as he shot me a conspiratorial look over her shoulder. Yi had said to be careful, that the fifth one was the worst of us all. What did Acton want from me?

34

IT'S FRIDAY, BUT REN HAS NO SENSE OF WHERE THE TIME HAS GONE. He's been ill, though ill isn't the right word for the way he feels. More like damaged or broken. Some of the bandages have come off, including the bulky one on his left hand. The one that's now missing a finger. The nurses didn't want to tell him that, hemming and hawing and eventually roping a local doctor in to say those simple words to him. As if it makes any difference.

Ren longs, suddenly and inexplicably, for Dr. MacFarlane. His shaggy eyebrows, the raspy voice. He would have explained it, clearly and unsentimentally. *Better to lose a finger than the whole hand.* Or your life. What is it that he needs to remember about Dr. MacFarlane? An invisible counter in his brain hisses there are only two days left to keep his promise, but Ren is tired, so terribly weary that he can barely keep his eyes open. The nurses take his temperature and talk over him in hushed voices. William has been coming by twice a day.

"You've had a shock," he says jovially, though his eyes are grim. "Sometimes the body needs a bit of time."

"Did they find her?" That gnawing unease again.

"You mean Nandani? Don't worry, she made it home that night."

Ren shakes his head feebly. "No, she's still wandering. Somewhere out there."

A strained expression appears on William's face. Abruptly, he takes the nurse aside to discuss something, warning her with a shake of his head before he leaves the ward. A low fever runs through Ren's veins. There's another place he urgently needs to go to, though he can never remember where it is until he's actually asleep. He has the feeling that he's in the middle of a journey; everything else is an interruption.

Waking, a painful sensation. The nurse takes his temperature and looks unhappy. With an effort, Ren flexes his left arm, still encased in dressings, and wonders whether he'll still be able to work: shine shoes and iron shirts and make omelets. What if William doesn't want him anymore? There are so many other boys who need jobs—older, stronger boys with ten fingers. Ren wishes there was someone to talk to, but the ward is empty, the other beds like white cocoons.

One of the nurses said that Ah Long came by yesterday when Ren was asleep and left a tiffin carrier of sweet red-bean soup that Ren likes so much. Did Ah Long manage to clean the whole house by himself after the party? Ren's eyes are dry. His bones ache. *Time to go*, he thinks. But where?

Voices in the corridor. It's William again, making his second visit of the day. And behind him, someone else. That buzzing thrill that he can't forget. Ren struggles up. She's here! The girl from the party. Down the long, whitewashed corridor, he senses her approach. His cat sense flickers, the dullness around him burns away. But she's slowing, falling back. Why?

William enters the ward. Smiling, pleased to see Ren sitting up for once. "I've brought you a visitor."

But the person who peeks out from behind William isn't Ren's girl in blue, but Lydia. "Hello!" she says, in that overenthusiastic tone that people who aren't comfortable with children adopt. "I've brought you some books."

She wheels in a lending trolley of books and magazines, and Ren immediately feels guilty for misjudging her. "I went by the children's ward this morning, but I'd no idea that you were all the way over here."

William looks at Ren's chart and examines his dressings. Ren's eyes stray to the book cart. Lydia picks out an alphabet book with a Ladybird logo on it. "How's this?" she says.

Ren opens it to *A stands for Ambulance Train*. "Thank you," he whispers, trying to hide his disappointment.

"Give him a different one, Lydia," says William quietly. "He can read quite well."

"Oh!" Lydia colors. "Well, we're a bit low today."

Ren feels sorry for her, being chided like this. Yet the hopeful shine in her eyes says she doesn't mind. She hands over a book with a girl's name, Jane Eye or something like that. *Who's Jane and what's wrong with her eye?* Ren thinks. There's another one, a slim volume that slips out. *Heart of Darkness.* But Lydia seizes it swiftly, "Oh no, dear. Not that one."

But Ren catches that electric tingle. It's moving again, coming to the doorway. His girl from the party, her gaze serious, searching for Ren. And when she sees him, her face lights up.

REN IS HAPPY. VERY HAPPY. SHE SITS NEXT TO HIM, NOT WEARING blue today, but a crisp white cotton dress. "I'm glad you're all right," she says, pouring a glass of water for him. William and Lydia are down at the other end of the empty ward, Lydia ostensibly recataloging the books in her cart. Ren catches brief snatches of their conversation. But it doesn't concern him, because Ji Lin is sitting on the chair next to his bed, smiling at him.

"Does it hurt a lot?"

Ren wants to reassure her that he is much, much better, but a numbing weakness grips him. He gasps, soundlessly. Ji Lin stares at his ashen face in consternation.

"You don't look well. Shall I get the nurse?"

No, he doesn't want her to leave, but he can feel it dropping, that blurry grey veil that paralyzes and drifts him away. Back to that other place where he hasn't finished his task. Alarmed, Ji Lin glances at William and Lydia, deep in conversation at the other end of the ward. The tension in William's shoulders forbids interruption.

"I'll get the Sister," Ji Lin says, jumping up in her quick, boyish way. In the far corner of the ward, William's head jerks, surprised at her sudden exit.

Lydia tilts her face closer to his. They look nice together, standing by the window. Her mouth moves. What is she saying, that makes William's expression go hard, his mouth a thin line?

"—know about Iris," she says.

That's the name of the lady that William is always writing letters to. Those cream-colored letters on thick, soft paper that dents when you press a fingernail into it. William doesn't look happy.

"Let's not talk about this now," he says, turning away.

"Then when?" She's following him, careless about being overheard now since it's only Ren left in the ward. "We're the same, you and I," she says. Her eyes glisten, though whether it's with tears or some other emotion, Ren can't say. "I want to help. Please, let me help."

William gives her a forced smile. "I need to go."

Lydia stares after his retreating back. A breeze through the open windows makes the white curtains flutter; it's so quiet that you can hear the clock in the corridor ticking. Awkwardly, Lydia wheels her book trolley back between the empty beds. She pauses at Ren's bed as if she wants to question him, but at that moment Ji Lin returns. She looks troubled, her eyes downcast.

Lydia gives her a long, sideways glance. "You're Louise, aren't you?" she says.

A brief pause. "Yes."

"I was wondering how you knew Mr. Acton."

"I don't know him. He just happened to be passing the station this morning and gave me a ride."

Lydia doesn't seem quite satisfied with this answer and asks several more questions. Where she works, what her family does, how old she is. Ji Lin is polite but guarded.

"May I ask why you want to know?"

Dazed, Ren stares weakly at their two profiles. One with fair, curling hair, the other with cropped dark bangs.

"I was just curious about your . . . job. Whether you had any troubles or needed help." At the word *troubles,* Lydia's eyes sharpen with concern. But Ji Lin is careful, saying only that she works part-time at a dance hall, and it's all right.

Lydia studies her for a moment. "Well, let me know if you ever need a friendly ear. I'm interested in helping local girls find jobs, so they can better themselves. There are so many jobs that girls can do nowadays, if men would only let them."

"Thank you." Her words touch a chord, for Ji Lin's dark eyes go soft and she looks genuinely touched. "That's very kind of you."

"We women must stick together—in fact, I teach health classes to the girls on the rubber estates."

"What sort of classes?" Ji Lin looks interested.

"Well, mostly basic healthcare, feminine needs." An understanding look passes between them. "If you need any supplies, let me know. It's one of the ways I can do some good stuck out here. By the way," Lydia lowers her voice, "be careful around Mr. Acton."

"Why?"

"He's—well, odd things happen around him. Have you noticed?"

A curious expression appears on Ji Lin's face. "What sort of things?"

"Those who get involved with him tend to be unlucky. Especially young women."

WILLIAM INHALES SHARPLY. HIS STOMACH HURTS, LEANING OVER the white porcelain sink in the washroom, both hands gripping its slippery surface. A burning, twisting sensation. He lifts his pale, sweaty face, staring at the mirror.

So, Lydia knows about Iris. He should have seen it coming. Had, in fact, been struck by their resemblance. It doesn't matter whether they're second or third cousins once removed, or whatever Lydia said. He'd been too taken aback to pay attention.

And now, what should he do? What does Lydia want? It will be trouble. Lydia, with her bossy, well-meaning attitude. She's exactly what he hates. William wipes his mouth. Before they meet again, he must uncover every bit of information that he can about her: whatever secret from her past that's exiled her in Malaya for more than a year with no husband, no job, and nothing to do besides play tennis at the Club and volunteer. *Know thy enemy*, he thinks.

And then, in a spasm of furious anguish, he wishes Lydia would just disappear.

35

IN A FEW SHORT DAYS, REN HAD LOST A SHOCKING AMOUNT OF weight. Hollow cheeks, blue veins showing through papery skin. A faint, hoarse voice, as though every word was a struggle. But he looked happy to see me.

"About the finger you gave me," I said hesitantly, when Lydia had gone. I didn't want to bring it up but was afraid he'd be worried about it. "I kept it for you."

A spasm passed over his face. A look of alarm, or was it urgency? "Two days left," he whispered. "Put it back. In his grave."

I bent over, trying to catch his words. There was a grey, glazed look on his face.

"What do you mean?" I asked, but he didn't hear me. Ren's eyes had closed. There was nothing but his frail light body, the husk of a grass-hopper, left behind in the bed. For an instant, I was terrified that he'd died. I touched his hand. Cold, yet the narrow chest rose and fell unevenly. The nurse had said that Ren wasn't doing well, though they couldn't find a cause and I'd best not tire him. She was right; there was something very wrong with him.

"Are you a relative?" she'd asked.

"No. Why?" I said anxiously.

Her eyes darted past me uncomfortably. "Well, if you know any of his relatives, tell them to come and visit. Soon."

////

I LEFT THE WARD WITH A SINKING FEELING. THERE WERE STILL SO many questions that I had for Ren: how the finger had ended up buried in the garden and why he'd wanted me to put it into a grave. Unsettling thoughts, moving like shapes underwater. I'd asked the nurse whether Pei Ling had recovered from her fall yet, and she'd shaken her head. She hadn't regained consciousness. The nurse gave me an odd look, as if wondering why I was connected to all these unfortunate people.

Afternoon was waning, and people were beginning to leave. I couldn't shake Lydia's strained warning out of my head. What had she meant by telling me to stay away from William Acton? The way she'd lowered her voice as though afraid of being overheard made me wonder what she was worried about. She'd mentioned luck as well, which reminded me of the salesman. When people talked about being lucky, perhaps they simply wanted to feel powerful, as though they could manipulate fate. Like the gamblers who were obsessed with lucky numbers, or bought lottery tickets according to the number of colored scales on fish. It all seemed like a bad idea to me.

Turning a corner, I recognized the spot outside the cafeteria where I'd last spoken to Pei Ling. If I kept following this walkway down the hill, I'd pass the place where she'd had that disastrous fall. Here. She'd fallen from the stairs and landed quite a distance from the bottom. The sturdy handrail on each side of the narrow stairway reminded me of Shin's observation. If she'd stumbled, it was odd that she hadn't managed to break her fall. She might well have been pushed.

I glanced up, alerted by a sudden movement. A dark head had poked over the top of the stairs, but the late afternoon sun was in my eyes. There was a flash of white uniform, and for an instant, I thought it might be Shin, come to find me with his long stride. But whoever it was disappeared. Time to get going. The shaded walkways were empty as I cut round the side of the hospital. Passing the familiar door to the pathology storeroom, I paused. What if the finger from the salesman was still there, and the one that Ren had handed me was a doppelgänger, born like a worm, from the dark earth he'd dug it out of? It was such a disturbing thought that I felt I must see for myself. I tried the handle. Unexpectedly, it turned.

Inside, all was much as Shin and I had left it. I dragged the step stool over to the specimen shelf. Reaching up, past a kidney, then the jar with the two-headed rat. I peered behind. Nothing. The space where the small bottle had stood, containing a dried and blackened finger, was empty. So it hadn't multiplied itself like a nightmare. *Thank goodness.* I was about to step down when the door opened.

It was Y. K. Wong. I should have known it would be him. He was like a bad dream, appearing everywhere I went. Pulse thudding, I held my breath as he shut the door behind him, very deliberately.

"Looking for something?" he asked. "Like a finger?"

"There aren't any fingers on this shelf," I said defiantly.

"I know. I had a look the other day." He circled closer and I eyed him nervously from my perch. "Does Shin know about your job at the May Flower?"

So he'd recognized me at the hospital the other day, despite my attempts to hide my face. I felt absurdly vulnerable standing on the step stool, like a victim for a hanging.

"Let's start again," he said. Forced smile. The glimpse of a sharp canine tooth. "You lied to me about that finger. Were you one of Chan Yew Cheung's girls from the dance hall?"

"No—I picked it up by accident."

He gave me a disbelieving look. Another step, closing in. "Then what about Pei Ling? I heard you asking about her. Did she give you anything?"

What had Pei Ling said? That the salesman had a friend she didn't like at the hospital; who she was afraid would get his hands on her package. The lists, I thought. Those lists of doctors and patients and sums of money written in another hand. I was still standing on that ridiculous step stool and it occurred to me that if he shoved me backward, I'd crack my head open. Like Pei Ling falling off the stairs.

Half turning, I reached behind. My hand scrabbled over the glass jars. I hurled the jar with the two-headed rat at Y. K. Wong. It smashed open against his arm in a spray of foul liquid. A cry of disgust as he doubled over. Then I was leaping, the biggest jump of my life, trying to get past him, but he caught me by the wrist. No breath to scream, I could only grit my teeth and yank hard. Slipping on the wet floor, he slammed past me into the door. For an instant he stood there, face tight as though he was making up his mind. Then with a twist of the handle, he was out and had locked the door on me.

"Let me out!" I shouted, banging on it.

He put his mouth against the door. "Think about what I asked you," he said. "I'll be back for an answer."

I YELLED UNTIL I WAS HOARSE, THOUGH BY THAT TIME, Y. K. WONG was long gone. It was Friday evening; there'd be only a skeleton staff for warded patients over the weekend. Panicked, I tried the windows. They were very tall and most of them had been painted shut. The only open window was a transom that flipped open horizontally across the top. The type that needed a long hook to unfasten. But it was so high up.

Dragging the table over to the window, I climbed up. Not quite high enough. I set the step stool on top. The fumes from the spilled formaldehyde made my eyes water, even as I averted them from the two-headed rat splayed on the floor. I was going to have nightmares about that. Up I went, feeling the double wobble of the step stool and the table, afraid to look down. I stuck my head out through the transom. Eventually someone would find me, though I feared Y. K. Wong might return first if I screamed. Taking a deep breath, I dropped my basket through the opening and heaved myself up. It was tight, even as I wedged myself sideways. Too tight. I was stuck, eight feet off the ground. *Please*, I thought, *I'll never eat another steamed bun again*. A ripping sound as my skirt caught in the hinge. The top of the window scraped my back, then I was through, scrabbling madly at the sill, legs dangling.

I lost my grip in a slithering crash. Sharp pain in my ankle as I landed, palms stinging from scraping against the wall. Running footsteps round the corner. I froze, terrified that it was Y. K. Wong returning, but it was only Koh Beng. I was glad to see his friendly, porky face.

"I heard a scream," he said. "Are you all right?"

"I twisted my ankle."

Fortunately Koh Beng seemed more interested in looking up my skirt, which I yanked down with a glare, than asking questions about how I'd managed to fall over behind a building.

"Did you see Y. K. Wong on your way over?"

"No." Koh Beng gave me a shrewd glance. "Did he want something?"

All I wanted was to sit down quietly somewhere until my hands stopped trembling. Should I report Y. K. Wong? He might claim it was a prank, or that I'd lured him into the storeroom to seduce him. In fact, broadcasting that I worked at a dance hall was enough to discount my testimony. If Shin found out, there'd be trouble; for all his cool quietness, he had an explosive temper. Distracted, I said, "He was looking for a package."

"Was it Pei Ling's? I saw the two of you talking right before her accident."

"She wanted some help." Not that it had done much good. "What sort of person is Y. K. Wong?"

"He's an awkward fellow. Tight with Dr. Rawlings, the pathologist. He's done a lot of work for him."

Rawlings was another name on that list—was that why Y. K. Wong had the storeroom key? I frowned, thinking hard.

"So what was in that package?"

How much could I trust Koh Beng? He seemed to know a lot about the goings-on in this hospital. I said slowly, "Lists of names and numbers. But please don't tell Shin about today. It's a private matter."

Koh Beng said sympathetically, "Don't worry, you can count on me."

He seemed pleased that we shared a secret, and recalling his talk of skulls and weretigers, I asked, "Do you know any superstitions about fingers?"

"Well, the Malays say that each finger has a personality: the thumb is the mother finger, or *ibu jari*. Then you have the index finger, *jari telunjuk*, which points the way. The third finger, *jari hantu*, is the ghost finger, because it's longer than the others. The fourth one is the ring finger; in some dialects they call it the nameless one. The little finger is the clever one."

The idea of fingers having personalities troubled me, as though they were five little people. Koh Beng gave me a sideways glance; I was sure he knew that I was hiding something. But he only said, in his friendly porcine way, "Pei Ling was a good friend of mine. I'd like to help. Those lists of names—can you bring them in to show me?"

I nodded. If he could make sense of them, I might have some bargaining power to deal with Y. K. Wong.

36

IN THE HOT, STIFLING AFTERNOON, REN CONTINUES TO SLEEP. Pushing past the veil of fog that drifts and numbs him. He has to get through, to the other place. That bright, feverish place where everything is clear as glass and sharp as stone. It takes every bit of his strength but suddenly, there he is. The long bleached grass, the low tangled bushes. There was a tiger here before, he remembers, but it's nowhere to be seen now. He casts around the muddy ground. What was he doing that was so important? Yes. Nandani. He has to find her.

William said that she made it home safely that night after the party, but Ren doesn't believe him. She's not in Batu Gajah. She's here. He's sure of it.

In that burning, dreamlike landscape, Ren follows the footprints in the soft earth. They lead onward, the left foot dragging, through the waist-high grass towards the train station that he glimpses in the distance. They must belong to Nandani, he thinks anxiously. Ever since he saved her leg that day, he's felt responsible for her, even though she's older than him. For some reason, Dr. MacFarlane's words come back to him, that affectionate reprimand. *Kindness will be the death of you, Ren.* But that's not true, is it?

Doggedly, he follows the footsteps. The trail wavers, as though whoever made it has become weaker along the way. His cat sense prickles, trembling in a single direction, only to be met by a high blank wall as vast as the sky. Beyond that, lies Yi.

Ren plods on, the brilliant light burning the landscape into his squinting eyes. The railway station draws steadily closer. It's the same direction as the wall that separates him from Yi. For some reason, a girl in blue comes to mind. What was her name again—Ji Lin? His thoughts flicker in and out. William dancing with her. Her eyes opening wide as she sees Ren. Running around the house in the dark, checking the windows for Nandani, or is it some other pale chill creature who might be peering in from the windows? The vengeful long-haired women, cheated in love. And at last, the roaring flash that breaks the night—but he can't recall any further. This is reality now, this bright sunny land that quivers with unknown expectation.

The footprints lure him onward, around a shrub with waxy dark green leaves. Oleander, he thinks, looking at the frothy blossoms, though he can't recall who dislikes it so much. An old Chinese man, wiping his hands on an apron and saying disapprovingly that the master should cut it down. Ren blinks and the memory is gone.

As Ren goes around the bush, he almost stumbles on her. She's sitting on the ground, nursing her left ankle. Her long dark hair is tangled, and when she raises her face to him, Ren has a terrible shock. It isn't Nandani at all. In fact, he's never seen this woman before.

They stare at each other in silence. She's Chinese, with a pale, rabbit-like look. Her eyes are pink at the corners, as though she's been crying, and when she stands up awkwardly, she's not much bigger than Ren. "Who are you?"

"I'm Ren."

She stares at him. "Are you a real person?"

"Yes."

Unexpectedly, she grabs him by the elbow. Her touch is icy cold, and Ren gives a cry of surprise.

"You're warm," she says. Bending over, she clutches her ankle. "I can't walk well. I must have sprained it." With a grimace, she straightens, and now Ren can see there's something wrong with her. One arm is bent, her shoulder set at a strange angle, as she shuffles forward. She looks broken, a puppet whose strings have been cut.

"Does it hurt?" he asks.

"Not really. I'm a nurse," she says. "So I think I might have broken my arm or dislocated my shoulder."

"Can't you remember?"

"It was a fall." She frowns. "My head hurts. Anyway, it will all be better once we get on the train. Yours, too."

Ren glances down and realizes that he, too, is injured. His left arm and side are wrapped in bandages, and he has the uneasy feeling that he ought to remember why, although he doesn't. They walk around the oleander bushes, and from here, there's a clear view of the train station. Ren's companion seems to take heart at the sight.

"Where did you come from?" she says.

"I don't know." He looks behind him, but there's nothing but waving grass.

"Come on," says his companion. "We need to get going."

37

SHAKEN, I TOOK THE BUS TO FALIM. IF I CLOSED MY EYES, I COULD still see Y. K. Wong's crooked jaw, that instant, calculating look right before he'd locked me into the storeroom. I wondered what expression he'd have when he returned to find me gone. Certainly, I'd have to deal with him soon. *Courage, my girl,* I thought, squeezing my hands against the rising anxiety in my chest.

I spent a quiet evening in the shophouse helping my mother. Observing her frail figure, I thought of Ren. I had a terrible suspicion he was dying; the greyness in his face had frightened me, his eyes shut like a soul unmoored. What could I do for him?

"Don't worry," my mother's voice broke in. "It will be all right. He likes you."

My heart gave a startled leap. But she was referring to Robert, of course. I listened with half an ear as she chattered on about how kind he was.

"Yes," I said nodding, thinking that I'd have to rely on that kindness quite soon. Shame flooded me. Surely Robert wouldn't turn me away if I asked to borrow money? It was quite different from accepting a pot of chicken soup. So many things had gone wrong recently that I felt sick with worry. And what had Ren meant by *only two days left?*

////

THE NEXT MORNING, I LET MYSELF QUIETLY OUT AND RETURNED TO Ipoh, explaining to my mother that I was helping Mrs. Tham finish a dress. "A rush order," I said, though the real reason was that I'd promised the Mama I'd sub in for a last shift at the May Flower.

It was past lunchtime by the time I reached Mrs. Tham's. "So here you are!" she said, without any preamble. "I thought you were going to be in Falim all weekend."

"I'm helping a friend out," I said guiltily.

Luckily Mrs. Tham wasn't interested as she was bursting with news of her own. "Your brother came looking for you. Him and also that young man."

"What young man?"

"The one who drove you home the other night. Robert, you said his name was."

Why on earth were Robert and Shin looking for me? They were an unlikely pair; they didn't even get along.

"First your brother stopped by and then as he was leaving, that Robert came too. I told them you'd gone back home."

"Did they say what they wanted?"

"No, your brother said he had to meet someone." Mrs. Tham drew a little closer. "Are you going steady with that Robert?"

"We're just friends."

She gave me a disbelieving look; I could hardly blame her. Robert and his enormous boat of a car attracted attention. Most girls in my position would probably be over the moon.

"If I finish early, I might go back to Falim tonight," I said.

"All right." Mrs. Tham waved cheerfully as I left. That was the advantage of having two places to stay over—you could always claim you were somewhere else. I needed at least a day or so if I was going to do what I had planned.

IN THE DIM BACK CORRIDOR AT THE MAY FLOWER, THE MAMA stopped me and pressed an envelope into my hand. It made a lovely fat crinkling sound. "They paid up for the private party. Well, Kiong went to collect it from that red-haired doctor. It's your share, plus the back pay that you're owed. Cleaned out your things already?"

"Almost."

I kept a spare frock in the dressing room, which I planned to wear today. All of us girls did, just in case there was a rip or spill. Feeling pensive, I hurried down the corridor with its peeling mint-green paint. Hui was in the dressing room patting rouge on her cheeks. She did Saturdays from afternoon all the way through the evening shift.

"You on today?" She looked surprised.

"She asked me to help out," I said, struggling with my dress.

"Here, I'll help you." Hui deftly unhooked me. I must tell her soon that I'd quit, but it didn't seem like the right time now, not when we were rushing to get ready.

I'd never worked a Saturday afternoon before; it was crowded and the band played more local dances like *joget*. The music was cheerful, and forgetting my worries briefly, I quite enjoyed it, though I didn't see any of my regulars. I'd miss this: the waxed dance floor, the sweating faces of the band members whom I now knew well enough to nod and smile at as we went by. The smell of cigarettes and sweat, my aching calves, and Hui's bitingly funny remarks. As I slid into the cordoned-off dancers' pen after a turn with a plump government clerk, I felt a stab of regret. Perhaps I shouldn't quit after all.

I knew only a few of the other girls today since we were usually on different shifts, but Anna had come in. I hadn't seen her since the night of the private party.

"I saw something good just now." Anna always had a sleepy, heavy air about her and today it made her tall figure somehow more voluptuous.

"What?"

"A really handsome fellow. He was waiting outside for a friend. I made him promise to dance with me when he came in."

The other girls giggled. I listened with half an ear.

"What do you mean by *really* handsome? You're always saying that!"

"But he was! He might be an actor from Singapore or Hong Kong."

There was a lot of eye-rolling, but we were all rather curious, myself included. Many Chinese opera stars were bombarded with love letters, home-cooked meals, and money from frenzied female fans. The only person I knew who looked as though he ought to be in pictures was Shin. Then a dreadful thought occurred to me: perhaps it was Shin.

"He was tall, with nice shoulders. Narrow hips," said Anna, "And he had this northern Chinese look, with a high nose and cheekbones."

Alarm was spreading; a swarm of fire ants pouring down my back.

"Look, there he is!"

My stomach plummeted. It was indeed Shin—and with him were Robert and Y. K. Wong. The three of them threaded their way through the crowd, Y. K. Wong leading them. His narrow face with its elongated jaw was alert as he searched the faces of the girls. Our eyes met. I had nothing, not even a fan, to block his triumphant gaze from where I sat, a large rosette and number pinned to my breast, like merchandise for sale. Panicked, I willed my frozen legs to jump up. A dull roaring rose in my ears as they came closer. Even if Y. K. Wong had spotted me, it meant nothing as long as Robert and Shin didn't. *Run!*

With a gasp, I was out of my chair, stumbling past the other girls with their cries of surprise. Y. K. Wong grabbed my wrist. "I've been looking for you."

I stared past him at Robert's shocked face. I couldn't bear to look at Shin. Robert's eyes were wide, showing the whites around them. His mouth opened. Closed. Opened again. "Ji Lin—are you working here?"

I dropped my head wretchedly.

"You're really working here? Like a prostitute?"

His voice was incredulous. Too loud, like a slap in the face. Time slowed to a nightmarish crawl. I saw Shin's jaw tighten, the telltale shift of his shoulders. I knew the danger signs when my stepfather snapped. Could see the future unravel in a gritty, jumping newsreel: Shin would hit Robert in the mouth, break his teeth and nose, and go to prison all because of my stupid, stupid choices.

I flung myself in front of Robert. There was a glancing blow to the side of my head, hard enough that my ears rang, though Shin must have held back at the last instant. I fell over, a tangle of limbs with Robert. Screams, a mad scramble. Discordant trumpet notes as the musicians wavered, then manfully started playing again. Shin was holding my face in his hands. "You idiot," he said.

Hui was shrieking like a harpy, "What are you doing?"

"It's all right." Gasping, I struggled up. "He's my brother."

I tugged at him. Desperation numbed my stinging ear. The bouncers were heading over purposefully. In the corner, the Mama's face was like thunder.

"Ji Lin!" Robert called, but I was running, slipping through the crowd that parted, surprised faces, mouths gaping in *ohs* and *ahs*. Dragging Shin with me, his hand in mine. Behind us, Kiong barreled his way through the dancing couples, colliding and apologizing. Through the side door, down the mint-green corridor marked *private*. The dressing-room door banged open. I grabbed my bag—the finger!

Kiong's shout echoed as he burst into the corridor. Then we were out, through the back door into the dirt road behind the dance hall where we ran and ran as though the devil himself was chasing us.

38

It was the end of everything, I thought. I don't know what possessed us, but we ran like children, Shin and I. As though we were ten years old and had been caught stealing mangoes from the neighbor's tree. We raced down street after street until I didn't recognize where we were anymore and doubled over, gasping, against a wall.

"You know, there's nobody chasing us," said Shin.

Kiong had done no more than stick his head out of the back door and yell, "Louise! What's wrong?" And likely nothing would have happened if I'd stopped and talked to him. Kiong was quite reasonable; arguments between customers happened all the time, and the only person who'd been injured was myself.

"Does it hurt?" Shin examined me, looking for bruises. "I didn't mean to hit you."

"I'm fine," I said, shrugging off his hand.

"I'm sure you are," he said drily. "Anyone who can run half a mile is probably in good health. Why were you running anyway?"

Shame burned my cheeks. "I couldn't bear it. The look on Robert's face. And all of you showing up together." The words, *like a prostitute,* still rang in my ears.

Shin sank down against the roughly plastered wall. My mother had drummed it into us that only beggars, drunkards, and opium fiends sat in the street in broad daylight, but there was no one around right now, so I sat down, too.

"Why'd you jump in front of him like that?"

"Because you were going to hit him."

"He deserved it. Bastard."

I grimaced. "Are you angry with me, too?"

"What do you think?" He gave me a long look.

I stared hard at a crack in the pavement. It looked like a map of the Kinta River. "There weren't many options. Not ones that paid well. But I'm not a prostitute." It was a terrible conversation to be having with my stepbrother, whom I might be in love with, I thought. I ought to keep a diary of all the worst moments in my life. It might be amusing in fifty years' time, but not now. Definitely not now.

"I didn't think so. Places like that are pretty careful with their girls."

"How do you know?" I watched him from under my lashes, frowning.

"I've been to dance halls before. There are lots of them in Singapore."

Suddenly, I was so annoyed with Shin that I could barely look him in the eye. "I suppose I shouldn't have worried about telling you, then."

He tilted my face up. "You were worried about me?"

Too close, I thought. He was much too close, and that casual touch disarmed me. With a jerk, I pulled away. "Not just you," I said. "My mother, Mrs. Tham. And Robert, of course. From his point of view, I'm ruined."

Shin's voice was icy. "He's an ass if he can't tell you're obviously a virgin."

I was so humiliated that I didn't know where to look. Ears scorching, my face blazing. I supposed I ought to be pleased that Shin had never doubted my chastity, since chastity was so prized in a woman, but the way he was doing things was so high-handed, I wanted to slap him. "It's none of your business," I snapped, jumping up.

Shin grabbed me by the arm, pulling me down. "Of course it is," he said through gritted teeth. "I don't like it. I don't like you doing a job like that at all. It's stupid and dangerous and you're lucky that nothing's happened—so far."

"I didn't have a choice!" How dare Shin tell me off, when he'd nothing to worry about other than studying and having a good time in Singapore? I buried my face in my knees.

Shin put his hand lightly on my head, as though he was afraid I'd shrug it off. "Why didn't you write and tell me you needed money?"

"How could I, when you never wrote back?"

"That was because—" he bit his words off. Whatever it was—another girl, another world I didn't know—he clearly didn't want to say, and I didn't press him. "I had a feeling you were doing something like this."

"What do you mean?" My voice was muffled.

Shin shook his head. "Some sort of shady job. Mother told me about her mahjong debts, after the miscarriage. She said you were paying them for her by dressmaking, but there was no way you were making enough money."

"Is that why you came today?"

"No, I'd no idea where you were working. It was Y. K. Wong who took me there."

I straightened up. "Why?"

"Don't know. But he's been asking about you in a roundabout way. And also if I'd noticed any of the specimens in the pathology room were missing. I played dumb, of course. Told him that I hadn't finished counting them."

So Y. K. Wong hadn't said anything to Shin yet about locking me into the storeroom. Was bringing Shin to the dance hall a way of putting pressure on me? A housewife came out from a neighboring gate and gave us a sideways glare. It was Saturday afternoon and able-bodied young people shouldn't be sitting on the pavement like this, so we started walking again in a desultory way. If we hit a main street, we were bound to find a bus stop, and then, I supposed, Shin would go back to Batu Gajah. The thought filled me with desolation.

"He also asked whether I'd heard about a weretiger's finger."

"A what?"

"Apparently, the hospital is supposed to have the finger of a weretiger in its collection."

My mind leaped to the night of the party and Ren's peculiar reaction, how he'd bolted out into the darkness when he'd heard about the tiger. I frowned. "Koh Beng mentioned it when we were cleaning out the pathology storeroom."

"Well, Y. K. said that people always wanted to buy it."

We'd reached a bus stop. There were other people, so we had to stop talking about severed fingers and weretigers, but I wondered if Y. K. Wong was secretly selling off pathology specimens. I'd heard that the hard stone from a tiger's eye and the bezoars formed in the bellies of goats and monitor lizards fetched outrageous sums on the black market. They were said to bring good fortune, bewitch a lover, or charm an enemy to death. I thought about the withered, blackened finger that had mysteriously returned to me and was, even now, rattling in my handbag.

"Shin," I said, opening my bag so he could glimpse it.

His eyes widened. "Where'd you get that?"

At that moment, the bus arrived. We were lucky enough to find two seats and as it rattled onward, I told him everything that had happened. Everything, including the dreams and Ren and his lost twin, Yi, across the river. I had to lean over and speak softly in his ear so that no one else would hear. Sometimes I think I will never forget that journey across town. The baking heat of the afternoon sun, the dusty breeze blowing in on us, smelling like the crushed Kaffir lime leaves in the lap of the woman in front of us. Shin's sharp profile as he gazed out of the window, listening intently to my words. I would never get tired of looking at him, I thought.

As luck would have it, this bus went across town to the Ipoh Railway Station, a white and gold imperial folly in the afternoon sunlight.

"I'll see you off," I said, trying to look cheerful.

"And where are you going?"

I clutched my handbag tighter. "Back to Mrs. Tham's."

"Liar," he said, without rancor. "Where are you really going?"

There was no use dissembling. "I'm going to Taiping. There's an afternoon train." I couldn't bear to go back to Mrs. Tham's, lest Robert should turn up, all red-faced and indignant. Or worse, full of apologetic recriminations. Besides, there was something else I'd promised to do.

To my surprise, Shin just looked at me. "How much money do you have?"

A fair amount, as a matter of fact. The Mama had handed me not only the money from the party but also my back pay.

"I've got money, too. Let's go." He started walking swiftly, long legs eating up the tiled floor of the station. "Time to do some grave-robbing."

////

OF COURSE WE WEREN'T GOING TO BE DIGGING UP CORPSES, I SAID indignantly, after Shin had bought us tickets. We were going to put something back, so it was more like grave-restoring. Shin said it was pretty much the same thing. I didn't know how to explain it, this urgent conviction that if I did what Ren asked, perhaps he wouldn't die.

"Yi said that the order was all messed up, and that we should try to fix it."

"What order?"

"The way things have been done. Like a ritual." I frowned, trying to recall what I knew about Confucianism.

"Has it occurred to you that you might just be hallucinating all of this?"

We got on the northbound train this time. Another third-class carriage with hard wooden seats, but my spirits rose. I loved trains.

"But what else can I do? And how do you explain the dreams, and Yi?"

"He only tells you what you already know," said Shin maddeningly. "It's like a conversation with yourself."

"What about Ren, then? He looks exactly like Yi, only older. And he recognized me that night."

"Coincidence. All small Chinese boys look the same."

"Dr. MacFarlane and his finger? The five of us and our names, and how everything fits together—how do you explain all of that?"

He shrugged. "I can't."

"If Ren dies, at least I'll have done what he asked." I shivered. Yi's words, *his master's business,* echoed in my head. Darkness. Rustling leaves. I thought of the newspaper article about a headless female torso discovered in a plantation. Who, or what, was Ren's master?

"And the thumb from Pei Ling's parcel?"

"You should tell Dr. Rawlings about it. Say that you suspect someone, maybe Y. K. Wong, is stealing body parts."

Shin said, fierce and low, "I'm going to kill Y. K. when I see him again. Locking you in like that."

"Don't!" Alarmed, I glanced at him. "But you ought to report him. If he's been selling weretiger fingers and goodness knows what else as amulets, that explains why the salesman had a finger in his pocket. They were friends—Pei Ling said as much, that her lover had a friend at the hospital who she didn't much like."

"And what about the rest of Pei Ling's package?"

That was more complicated. Perhaps it was blackmail, or they'd had a falling out of sorts. Dimly, I was aware that the patterns were moving, shifting into a new configuration, like the image of fingers I'd had in my head. Five fingers, playing an unknown tune. I had the uneasy feeling that it was a dirge.

THE NOTE NEXT TO THE NAME J. MACFARLANE ON THE HAND-written list in Pei Ling's package had said *Taiping/Kamunting.* I was sure that he must be the person Ren had referred to when he'd run out into the darkness that night. And I was equally certain that he was dead, since Ren had mentioned a grave.

Taiping was a quiet little town, the state capital of Perak though there was talk that Ipoh would soon receive that honor. I wasn't quite sure where Kamunting was. Perhaps it was one of the satellite villages around Taiping, just as Falim was to Ipoh. If Dr. MacFarlane was a foreigner who'd died in that area, there was only one place he could be: the Anglican cemetery.

I explained this to Shin, and he nodded, which made me suspicious. He was being far too docile about this spur-of-the-moment trip.

"Do you have work tomorrow?" I asked. Taiping was more than forty miles from Ipoh by rail, but it would take a while to get there because of the winding track and all the stops at Chemor and Kuala Kangsar. At this rate, we wouldn't arrive until five o'clock in the afternoon. There was a late train starting back at eight, more than enough time to visit the cemetery, but I was worried about Shin.

"I don't start my shift until tomorrow afternoon," he said, closing his eyes. "Stop talking. I need to think."

I couldn't tell whether he was just using it as an excuse to go to sleep, but I left him alone. The train jolted along slowly, the trees passing in a

steady green blur. The breeze from the open window blew away the cobwebs in my brain.

Ren, I thought. *Are you still alive?* Yi had said he'd discovered that as long
as he lingered on that shore, he could draw Ren to the other world. The
world of the dead. Perhaps the finger, that dried blackened digit that
rattled in my bag, exerted the same weighty pull. Ren seemed driven to
obey whatever promise he'd made, to the point of running out into the
night when there was a tiger outside. Or perhaps he'd been lured out to be
shot and killed in the dark.

The best I could do was to complete the task for him and bury that
finger. Sever at least one lingering attachment that drew him towards the
dead. The other one, however, I feared was too strong. The train rattled
onward, the jungle passing like a dream, and I closed my eyes.

There was a grinding hiss. With a start, I discovered that the train had
shuddered to a stop.

"Sleep well?" Shin looked amused. I had, in fact, though I realized with
embarrassment that my head was pillowed on his shoulder. People were
lifting their luggage off the racks overhead. We were the only two without
belongings.

"You were knocked out, too," I said, as we clambered off the train. "Or
were you just 'thinking'?"

He seemed to be in a remarkably good mood. "No, I'm done with that.
By the way, who was that girl at the dance hall? The one who tried to pull
my hair out?"

"That was my friend Hui," I said.

Somehow, I felt uneasy about this interest. *Please, Shin*, I thought, *not Hui*.
So far, Shin had never dated any of my good friends, no matter how they
made eyes at him. It hadn't mattered to me before, wrapped up as I'd been
with Ming, but it did now.

THE TAIPING RAILWAY STATION WAS A LOW, PRETTY BUILDING, BUILT
along the same colonial lines as the station in Batu Gajah with deep shady
eaves and gables. Taiping, situated in a lush basin at the foot of limestone
hills, was famous for being one of the rainiest towns in Malaya, as well as

for its proximity to Maxwell Hill, a small hill resort popular with honey-mooning couples. Not that that would have anything to do with me, since it was highly unlikely that I'd become Mrs. Robert Chiu in the near future.

Shin said, "What are you grimacing about?"

"Robert," I said. "It's all over with him."

"Does it matter to you?"

"I was hoping he'd lend me some money. To pay off my mother's debts."

Shin stopped. "Don't ask him. If you need money, I've got some." Irritated, he started walking again.

"Why was he with you today anyway?" I asked, running to catch up.

"He came looking for you at Mrs Tham's, then kept following me. I couldn't get rid of him if I tried."

"I suppose he was bound to find out. Though I told him long ago that we weren't a good match."

"What do you mean, 'long ago'?"

Too late, I remembered how Ming had told me not to mention Robert's kiss. "Before you went to medical school."

"Why didn't you tell me?"

"I told Ming," I said defensively.

For some reason, this seemed to annoy Shin even more, but he didn't say anything. Why did he care anyway, when he'd told me last week that it would be good if I got married? We walked along in silence; I was sorry because we were arguing again.

ACCORDING TO THE TICKET SELLER, THE ANGLICAN CEMETERY WAS about a mile away, near the Botanical Gardens. Shin stopped at a couple of different shops near the station and emerged with a brown paper bag. I hadn't accompanied him in because I was still wearing my emergency spare frock that I'd changed into at the May Flower, a canary-yellow slip of a dress. It looked more suited to going to a party than traveling around on the Federated Malay States Railways.

"What did you buy?"

He opened the paper bag. Inside was a brand new spade. There were other things too—a toothbrush, sticking plasters, and another flat package—and I asked him why he'd bought all of it.

"Because it looks suspicious to buy just a spade. They'll be wondering what I'm planning to dig up."

"I always knew you had a criminal mind," I said.

Shin laughed and the unease between us dissipated. We had a quick bite at a nearby coffee shop, though I was itching to get to the cemetery. What if Dr. MacFarlane wasn't buried there at all? But Shin said he wouldn't go on without eating and neither should I.

"Later is better. Fewer people around," he said as he polished off a plate of *char kway teow*, fried rice noodles garnished with bean sprouts, eggs, and cockles.

"What if it rains?"

Shin shrugged. "Don't forget, this was all your idea."

His dark eyes held mine, and despite all my willpower, I flushed. It made me feel dizzy, being looked at like that. There was a light in Shin's eyes, a queer flicker that made my stomach knot as though I was falling down a hole. His gaze traveled slowly down my neck, the hollow of my throat. The canary-yellow dress I was wearing clung flatteringly, because it was cut on the bias. A new method, Mrs. Tham had explained, accentuating the natural figure. Involuntarily, I crossed my arms over my breasts.

"Do you always dress like this for work?" he asked.

"No." I started to explain that this was a spare frock that I didn't often wear. Shin listened as I stumbled over my words, and all the while he watched me with that unreadable gaze, so direct that it felt more like being touched than looked at. "Do you not like it?"

"I like it. I think a lot of men would." He turned his head away, so I couldn't see the expression on his face.

"I'm sure the girls in Singapore dress better than this," I said, trying my best to make a joke.

"None of them look like you."

I was suddenly keenly aware of how close we were sitting, and how his legs and mine were scissored beneath the small round marble-topped table. If I wanted to, I could reach my hand out under the table and place it on his thigh. Slide it up slowly, feel the hard muscles contract. But instead, I put both my hands on the table and stared fixedly at them.

"Shin—" I said.

"What is it?"

"I'm sorry I've put you through so much trouble. I wish I were a better sister to you." An unbearable sadness filled me.

"Are you really sorry?" His expression was sharp and fierce.

"Yes, I am."

"Don't be. I haven't been a good brother to you, either."

He got up abruptly and paid the bill.

39

WILLIAM HAS BEEN BUSY. BUSY IN A WAY THAT HE DISLIKES, MAKING small talk and ferreting out information, but he does it anyway, pressed by the memory of Lydia's hungry, needy insistence, her eyes shining with emotion. *We need to talk,* she'd said in the hospital ward. What is she planning? Better to prepare an ambush than be trapped, he thinks.

The first person on his list is Leslie. If anyone has gossip, it will be him.

"Lydia?" says Leslie, looking up from his slice of pineapple. They're on tea break at the hospital canteen. "Are you finally interested in her? I've always thought the two of you were a good match."

William hides a grimace. Apparently Lydia isn't the only one with this impression. "Why is she out here?"

"Isn't she looking for a husband?"

"I wouldn't think she'd have trouble on that front." Lydia is attractive and there's a bigger pool of men in London than in a small town in Malaya. It's not even like Delhi or Hong Kong, where she could meet the rising stars of the Civil Service.

Leslie rubs his nose. "Well, there's some talk about why she left. A broken engagement—apparently he died."

"What did he die of?"

"Drowning. A boating accident."

William thinks that he ought to be more sympathetic to Lydia, but the memory of her sharp eagerness, the way she said that the two of them were alike, still unnerves him. There has to be more. He can feel it.

Next is the wife of one of the plantation managers, a friend of Lydia's mother. It's easy enough to run into her in town when she's buying groceries on Saturday morning with her Chinese cook. William suspects her cook is cheating her; the bill sounds far too high.

"Poor Lydia's had a hard time," she says as she writes down figures in her housekeeping notebook. "Such a pity about her fiancé."

"I might have known him," says William, lying through his teeth. "Andrews, was that his name?"

"No, it was a Mr. Grafton. A gentle, scholarly man—her parents were so fond of him."

"Did he drown?"

"Oh no. It was heart failure, on a train of all places. Apparently he was quite sickly. Such a disappointment to the family." And there's nothing else she has to add, despite William enduring another half hour of chitchat.

The last person William speaks to is Rawlings.

"Lydia's been a bit nervy recently. Says she wants to talk to me, though I've no idea why." He dangles the bait, but Rawlings seems distracted. Perhaps it's the heat, rising like a wet, suffocating blanket around them.

"Well, she's always had an interest in you. When she first came out, she asked if you were the same Acton as someone she knew."

That would be the connection to Iris, William thinks. So she's known who he is for a while. Has she been investigating him? The thought makes the back of his neck burn. How dare she. He bites down on the thought, says genially, "I had no idea. Perhaps we've friends in common."

"Be kind to her," says Rawlings. "She's got a bit of a savior complex, but she means well. And she's good at what she does. I've said before that the hospital ought to be paying her for all that volunteering."

Yes, Lydia is trying hard, in her amateur way, to connect with him. The question is: how to parlay that into an advantage?

"Why is she in Malaya, anyway?"

"Ah, she was engaged to some rough fellow and came out to avoid him. My wife knows her people—they said it was a bad match."

William barely recalls that Rawlings has a wife, since she's back in England with the children. Still, none of the information that he's gathered about Lydia adds up. There's no doubt that she's lost a fiancé, but the facts all contradict each other.

He wants to ask Rawlings more, but Rawlings is preoccupied.

"Do you trust the local staff?" he says abruptly.

William laughs. "I don't trust anyone." Except Ah Long in some respects. And, of course, Ren. The boy still isn't recovering, but William mustn't think about that right now.

He steers the conversation back to Lydia. "You said she had a difficult relationship?"

"Apparently he tried to assault her during an argument. Poor girl. That's probably why she's so highly strung."

So Lydia has been a victim. Interesting how that term changes the way he views her. Why is she so interested in William? What does she know about him? He thinks rapidly: Lydia's father runs the rubber estate that Ambika worked on. Yes, he can imagine that in Lydia's busybody, do-gooding way she might have known Ambika, even counseled her about her alcoholic husband. But she also said she knew Iris. That's worse. Ambika and Nandani are just two local women he's been involved with, but the talk around Iris is something that's hounded him out of England already.

He takes a breath. Has Lydia heard the tale he's told of how he tried to save Iris? He's deeply ashamed of it, but it's too late to retract. Besides, most people seem to believe it. Even he does, most days. Except when those dreams come again, the dreams of Iris by the river, her skirts heavy and dripping with riverweed. Lank hair clinging to her bony white forehead.

What had that girl Louise said when he'd given her a lift? She'd said that she dreamed of a river: like a story that unfolded. William doesn't want that. He never wants to see what comes next in his dreams of Iris.

40

Taiping
Saturday, June 27th

WE TOOK A TRISHAW TO THE ANGLICAN GRAVEYARD AT ALL SAINTS'
Church. It was a pretty ride through the low and pleasant town, with its
white colonial buildings and shophouses, and great *angsana* trees in bloom,
their golden petals drifting like showers. The thick grey clouds that had
swallowed up the afternoon gave the grass on the *padang* in front of the bar-
racks an eerily vivid green cast. On impulse, I'd stopped to buy a bunch of
flowers, white and purple chrysanthemums. It was the second time this
month that I'd bought flowers for the dead.

At the graveyard, Shin paid the trishaw man, and I went in, looking
for Dr. MacFarlane's resting place. The church itself was a large wooden
building with a steeply pitched roof and carved Gothic arches. Some of
the graves were elaborate affairs with carved angels and stonework boxes,
while others were simple crosses. They seemed to be placed in a somewhat
haphazard order, and I looked about for a newer section.

Shin walked across the clipped grass. "Find it?"

"Not yet."

There was no one around. Not a bird stirred in the enormous hushed
silence, the grey sky a bowl, as though the whole world was waiting for the
rain to come.

"Actually, Robert had some information—he said you'd showed
him the lists," said Shin, after a pause. "That's why he was looking for
you."

"Why didn't you mention it earlier?"

"I thought you'd be heartbroken over him, but you must be fine since you managed to eat so much."

I rolled my eyes. "What did he find?"

"Apparently there was a Dr. John MacFarlane in the Taiping area. An old Malaya hand who'd been out here for twenty years; before that he was in Burma. He'd a loose connection to the Batu Gajah District Hospital—subbed in occasionally when needed. A bit of an eccentric with no wife or family. And as we saw from the pathology records, he donated one of his fingers about five years ago, after a trip upriver with Acton."

"So what was he doing here in Taiping?"

"Not Taiping, but somewhere farther out. One of the neighboring villages."

"Kamunting," I said at once. "That was the name on the paper."

"Out here, he lived a semiretired life with a private practice. Said he'd never go back to Scotland, which he'd fled forty years ago, leaving three assertive sisters behind. And that's all."

"What? There must be more."

Ren had said *my master*, though the way he had pronounced it, with unthinking fidelity, sent a shiver down my spine. Who was his real master—was it William Acton or this Dr. MacFarlane whose directive he had followed without questioning?

"That's all the hard information that Robert could find. He did say there was gossip, too, but it could have been slander, etcetera, etcetera. Very conscientious, our Robert."

"Robert is a decent person."

"So decent that he dropped you like a hot potato today," he said bitterly.

I didn't reply because I'd found it. A fresh grave with a thin fur of grass, the few words on the headstone sharply cut as though they had been chiseled yesterday:

John Alexander MacFarlane
b. July 15th, 1862 d. May 10th, 1931
Deliver us, O Lord.

I stiffened, calculating the dates. Yesterday, Ren had whispered there were only two days left; taking them into account, it added up to exactly forty-nine days since his death. My mother had told me that the soul wandered for those forty-nine days, restlessly weighing up its sins.

"What did he die of?" I asked.

"Malaria, apparently. He'd had it on and off for years."

I laid the bunch of flowers on the grave, since there was no vase or crevice. They looked naked and forlorn lying on the bare ground, the leggy stems stripped of leaves. There was something peculiar about the grave: a wooden stick had been driven into it at an angle. It was about six inches long and looked like part of a broom handle. I didn't dare touch it—it looked so deliberate—but I'd never seen anything like this before.

"Pass me the spade," I said. Shin shook his head warningly. "Why?" Then I saw the elderly Tamil lady, her thin hair knotted in a bun, wearing a deep brown sarong. She was making her way over to us and shouting something. "Does she want us to leave?"

We stepped back from the grave, but the woman kept advancing. It turned out that she was waving a welcome to us. Apparently there weren't many visitors to the cemetery, and she was pleased that we'd come.

"*Tinggal, ya, tinggal!*" she said in Malay. "Stay, stay. Do you want water for the flowers?" She was the caretaker's mother; her son was out at the moment. "Going to rain," she said, looking at the sky. "How come you came so late? You friends? Patients?"

I didn't know what to say, but Shin just smiled. "Did you know him?"

To my surprise, she gave a quick nod. "We know who all the *orang puteh* around here are, though he lived farther out on the Kamunting side. He treated my nephew for ringworm. Such a pity he died. He was younger than me."

She shuffled off to get some water for the flowers. It seemed to distress her that they were just lying on the grave, so I carefully gathered them up again. Returning with a jam jar, she said, "So where are you two from?"

"Ipoh," said Shin. "I'm a medical student. I'm sorry to hear that Dr. MacFarlane died."

"Oh, one of his students. Well, he was sick for a while. In fact, people said he lost his mind. His housekeeper left, you know, and then it was just the old man and that Chinese boy."

My ears pricked up. "Was his name Ren?"

"I don't know. A small houseboy, about ten or eleven years old. He was a good boy. Took care of everything in the house when the housekeeper left. Can't have been easy with the doctor like that. I saw him at the funeral. All shaken up and trying not to cry, poor thing. You know him?"

"Yes, he's a relative," I said slowly. Shin gave me a look.

"How was the old doctor at the end?" he asked.

The caretaker's mother fixed her eyes on the grave. I'd noticed she kept glancing at the stick that was buried in it, and finally she made a sharp *tch* sound and pulled it out. Now I could see that it was quite a bit longer than I'd thought, part of a broom handle about four feet long, with the end sharpened like a stake.

She tossed it aside contemptuously. "Well, he was always odd, but no more than the other *orang puteh*. He'd buy any rare animal that a hunter brought in. A kind man, though. He treated many people for free. But towards the end, he got so strange that people didn't want to go anymore." The caretaker's mother was clearly enjoying this conversation. "In fact, before he died, I heard that he went to the local police station and confessed to all sorts of crimes."

"What sort of crimes?"

"Let's see, I think it was cattle stealing, or killing livestock. Even dogs were taken in this area. Didn't matter if they were chained close to the house or not. He also said he'd killed those two women who went missing. Both of them rubber tappers who worked at the nearby estate."

Alarmed, I glanced at Shin; neither of us had expected anything like this.

"So did they arrest him?"

"They sent him home. There was something wrong with his head. He'd have these fits from time to time." She looked exasperated. "All those things that happened, those were done by a tiger. A man-eating tiger. There were many sightings. Didn't it come out in the newspapers?"

"That must have been terrible for you." Shin put on his most sympathetic look, and the old lady couldn't help simpering.

"They said it was an old male that could no longer hunt. Anyway, it's gone now."

"Did they get it?"

"No, although they set traps and even had a *pawang* come in to charm it. In the end, it just disappeared. Right around the time the old doctor died."

My thoughts flew to the tiger in the garden, in Batu Gajah last weekend. The man-killer that they said had already taken an estate worker a few weeks ago. Unreasonably, I also recalled the salesman's death from a broken neck and wondered if something had chased him that dark night until he fell into a ditch. But this was wild speculation. A distance of sixty miles or more separated Batu Gajah from Taiping. Could a tiger range so far?

"What's that stick for?" asked Shin, pointing at the broom handle that she'd pulled out of the grave.

The caretaker's mother looked embarrassed. "That's just stupidity. From time to time it happens. Local people, you know. My son always pulls it out. He says it's disrespectful to the dead."

"But why do they do it?"

"Two or three days after the old doctor died, someone or something tried to dig him up. My son found a hole near the grave, like a child or an animal had been working all night. It didn't get all the way down—we bury them deep. He sat up and kept watch for a few nights, but it never happened again. When the locals heard about it, they said the old man wanted to get out of his grave. Such rubbish, because if you'd seen the hole, it was clearly something trying to get in, not out! But from time to time, people put stakes in his grave to make sure he doesn't come out. I'm not worried myself; I'm Church of England," she said proudly.

The light was fading, the grey sky pressed down with almost palpable weight. I couldn't see how we could possibly bury the finger in the grave with the caretaker's mother hovering around like this. Would we have to come back at night? The thought filled me with unease.

Shin said, "Is there a public restroom?"

"The vestry's still open, though I was just about to close it up."

"Go ahead," I said quickly. "I'd like to read the inscriptions."

As soon as they were out of sight, I was on my knees, digging the loose earth up with the spade. Thank goodness Shin had thought to buy one! The earth on the grave was red clay from the tin ore that had made this region's name. I chose the spot where she'd removed the stake from, since the soil was already disturbed there. *Hurry!* Pulse racing, I hastily scooped the earth aside, all the while keeping an eye out for the old lady's return. It had to be deep enough that it wouldn't be easily found, especially if people kept poking sticks into the grave.

When I'd dug about an arm's depth in, I took out the glass bottle. It seemed colder and heavier than before. Today was the forty-eighth day since Dr. MacFarlane's death. Had I made it in time for whatever Ren had wanted? A shadow moved at the corner of my eye. The branch of a tree, whipping in the breeze, but it spurred me into action. Lifting the finger that I'd taken from the salesman's pocket, I dropped it deep into the hole.

41

Batu Gajah
Saturday, June 27th

REN IS WALKING, FOLLOWING THE FAINT TRAIL THAT WAVERS LIKE A tiger's stripe through the high grass. He has a vague memory of a hospital bed, but it fades. What's real is this world of sunlight and wind, with the small pale woman, the one he found sitting in the grass. She's the one who urges him on every time he pauses to look around.

"We mustn't miss the train," she says.

Ren wrinkles his brow. "Is there another one?"

She gives him a sideways look. "I don't know. Come on!"

He doesn't like the way she moves, her broken body inching forward, one shoulder bent and a leg dragging. No one should be able to walk with injuries like that, but he doesn't ask about it. He's afraid that she'll grab his elbow again, the way she did earlier in that icy, bony clutch. But he's sorry for her, and he can't let her go alone. Besides, there's a tiger in the tangle of grass and bushes. From time to time, he glimpses a lean striped shape, though whether it's leading him on or warning him away, he can't say. Ren has the sudden memory of an old man, a foreigner, wandering among the trees. It floods him with dread and pity and love, that dark loneliness, and he puts his head down and keeps walking.

They head towards the train station in the distance. How long have they been walking—months, days, or minutes? But at last they arrive. The train station is remarkably similar to the Batu Gajah Station. Long and low, with deep eaves to keep the rain and sun off, it has wooden benches and a large round clock. A train is waiting, the big steam locomotive gently hissing. People mill around the station, though when Ren looks at them directly, they flicker and fade away. It's only out of the corner of his eye that he sees their blurred figures. A shadow child runs across the platform, clutching the hand of its mother who enfolds it as they climb into a carriage. For an instant, Ren envies that warm gesture.

"Hurry!" says his companion.

"Where are we going?"

She looks impatient and distracted. "Just get in!"

"I don't even know your name." A moment of doubt strikes him. Why should he follow this strange lady onto a train—after all, wasn't he looking for someone else? He strains to remember. Yes, Nandani. "I can't go with you, I'm looking for someone."

"Don't be silly! My name is Pei Ling," she says. "I'm a nurse, so you ought to follow me." But even she frowns, as though she can't quite understand her own logic.

"No, thank you," says Ren politely.

"Heavens! What a silly boy you are! Do come—I don't want to go alone." She makes a pitiful face, as though she's the child and not him, and Ren wavers.

"All right," he says, putting one hand on the lintel of the train door. As soon as he touches it, he feels a deep quiver, a vibration that shakes his field of vision. In that instant, he can see everyone clearly—all the other passengers who are sitting or standing or getting onto the train. But nobody gets off, and none of them have luggage.

Ren climbs in and there is Nandani, her heart-shaped face looking pensively out of the window. Delighted, Ren slides into the seat next to her. "Hello!"

But to his surprise, she looks frightened. "What are you doing here?"

"I was looking for you."

"No, you mustn't! Don't follow me."

Ren stares at Nandani, her curling hair and plump, pretty figure. Why isn't she happy to see him?

"Come here, little boy," says the nurse, Pei Ling, patting the seat. "Sit next to me."

He shakes his head. He'd rather sit with Nandani than this pale lady with her crooked shoulder and dragging walk. In fact, the more he looks at Pei Ling, the more frightened he feels. He scoots next to Nandani, but she shakes her head anxiously. "Please get off. They'll close the doors soon."

Ren can feel a deep low humming, as though the entire track is a live wire. Yi lies that way, somewhere at the end of that track. He's sure of it. The two young women are arguing now in harsh whispers. Nandani wants him to leave, but Pei Ling is stubborn and says he should stay if he wants to. She reaches out to grab his hand and Nandani gives a gasp of outrage.

"Don't touch him!" she snaps.

"Why not? I already did." And it's true, the elbow that Pei Ling grabbed earlier is cold and numb now.

Ren feels worse and worse as they squabble. "I want to stay," he says to Nandani. Her expression softens.

"All right," she says. "We'll go together."

Ren closes his eyes, telling himself that it's all right. He's going to Yi.

There's a twitch. An electric tingle. The quiet loneliness with its undertones of sadness and blood—the one that's been drawing him onward, reminding him of the old man wandering in the darkness—winks out abruptly. His cat sense blazes up. The hair on his head rises, his skin constricts. He hasn't felt a signal this strong, not since the hospital. Pictures flood him. A girl digging with a spade. A glass bottle, dropping into a hole. And the hole widens, becoming a grave. What—no, who is it? Ren's heart is thudding wildly, the first time that he's taken note of it since he's come to this strange land. And all of a sudden, Ren realizes that he doesn't want to ride this train anymore, not with Nandani and especially not with small, crooked Pei Ling with her icy hands.

But the doors are closing. He can hear them farther down the train as they slam shut, the sound getting nearer. *Bang. Bang.* The faint buzz, that promise of Yi farther down the line, weighs against him, pulling him down even as he struggles to rise, every nerve in his body twitching.

"What's the matter?" cries Nandani.

Bang. The door in the next carriage crashes shut, as though slammed by an invisible attendant. Ren sees the door on their own carriage quiver as though it's about to go as well. Desperate, he makes a mad dive. Feels the air cut his ears, the force of the door brush his skin. And it's bright, so very bright now that he can only grimace and squint as tears leak out from behind his eyes.

////

SOMEONE IS MOPPING THE FLOOR. THERE'S THE SWISH OF WATER BEING wrung out, the clatter of a bucket. Ren is lying on a bed—a hospital bed, as he now recalls. His chest heaves, his heart races, because didn't he just dive through a train door? He's here yet still there, the fragments of the two places overlapping. If he closes his eyes he can still see Nandani's shocked expression, the faint smirk on Pei Ling's blanched face. No, he doesn't want to think of her.

"Awake, are you?" A wiry little man is looking down at him. In one hand he holds a mop. Ren blinks painfully and struggles to sit up. His mouth is parched, and the custodian pours him a cup of lukewarm water. "Shall I call the nurse?" he says in Cantonese.

Ren shakes his head. "What day is it?"

"Saturday."

There's a bustle, some noise in the corridor, and one of the nurses sticks her head in. Gravely, she beckons to the custodian. "Can you lend a hand?"

He follows her out. Ren can hear their voices from the next ward.

"—move to the morgue?"

"Yes, her family's been contacted."

After a few minutes, the custodian returns for his mop, a troubled look on his face. Through the open door behind him, Ren glimpses a gurney being wheeled out. Someone is lying on it, covered in a white sheet. "Who is that?"

"Another patient."

Two pale feet stick out. Slim enough that they can only belong to a woman. There's something about their stillness that makes Ren's stomach lurch.

"Why is her face covered?" Ren says. "Is she dead?"

The custodian hesitates, mumbling, "Sometimes it's time for people to go."

Time to go. It gives Ren a mixed-up sensation. "Did you know her?"

"She was a nurse here."

A sick feeling in Ren's gut. Those narrow feet, the left one hanging at an odd angle. He tries to scramble out of bed; he must see her face! But the pain in his side twists. He gives a cry of anguish. Alarmed, the custodian makes a grab at him. "What are you doing?"

"I think I know her. Please, let me see her!"

Drawn by the commotion, the nurse looks back in. "What's happening?"

"The boy says he knows her."

She purses her lips and shakes her head. "Out of the question!" and gives Ren an annoyed, disapproving glance, as though he's done something wicked.

The gurney is being wheeled away and Ren wants to cry. Instead, he digs his fingers weakly into his pillow. "What was her name?"

"Pei Ling."

And now Ren is really sobbing. Not for that little nurse Pei Ling, but for Nandani, because he finally understands where she has gone.

42

No sooner had I dropped the glass bottle with its withered finger into the hole I'd dug in Dr. MacFarlane's grave than I heard Shin's voice, deliberately loud to warn me of their approach. Frantically, I shoveled earth back into the hole and stepped away. As Shin and the caretaker's mother came around the corner, I waved and joined them, tucking the spade back in the bag.

"Seen all you wanted?" asked the old lady.

Shin seized my hand in his. "Yes, we must get going." We thanked her for her time, and let ourselves out of the churchyard as quickly as possible.

"What's the matter?" I asked him under my breath, as he set a brisk pace. "Why are you holding my hand?"

In answer, he turned it over. It was streaked with red clay.

"Do you think she noticed?"

"Hope not. There's some on your knees, too."

I glanced down. All my excursions lately had ended in dirt and grime. From the cobwebs and dust in the pathology storeroom, to Ren's bloodstains, and finally this. Earth from someone's grave.

"Did you bury it?"

"All done," I said softly.

Glowering clouds had hidden the sunset and gave the sky a hazy, bluish quality. A trembling dusk descended. I could taste the humidity in the back of my throat with every breath that I took.

"What time is it?" Absorbed as we'd been in the old lady's tale, I'd forgotten to check the clock at the church.

Shin glanced at his wristwatch. "Twenty to eight."

The late train to Ipoh left at eight o'clock, and we were still a mile away from the station. I glanced around anxiously, but the street was deserted with not a trishaw in sight.

Shin looked at the sky. "I think it's going to—"

The heavens opened and the first fat raindrops splattered, like flattened tadpoles, on the dusty road.

"Run!"

I never could understand those English books in which people go on long damp walks over the heath (whatever that was) in the rain with only a deerstalker hat and an Inverness cape to protect them. Rain in the tropics is like a bathtub upended in the sky. The rain falls so hard and fast that in a few minutes you're soaked to the skin. There's no time to think, only the overwhelming need to run under shelter. And run we did.

The nearest cover was a distant stand of shophouses, and we raced to the covered five-foot walkway in front, gasping. Water poured in hissing sheets from the eaves, turning the dirt road into mud.

"What shall we do?" I said, after we'd waited a good five minutes. There was little chance of this downpour stopping, and meanwhile, the minutes were ticking off towards eight o'clock. How would we catch the train?

"We can run for it," said Shin.

And so began our mad dash, zigzagging from one shelter to another like beetles scurrying out from under a flowerpot. There were intermittent blocks of shops and large rain trees, but it was no use. I knew it even as I fought down the panicky feeling of being late. That train would leave without us. My shoes were slick with water and twice I almost turned my ankle.

"You all right?" asked Shin.

I put my hand on the trunk of a tree to steady myself. "Yes," I said, gritting my teeth. I'd never complained about things like this before and

I wasn't going to start now. If being a good sport was the best way for us to be together, then I'd keep playing along.

Shin kept his eyes firmly fixed on my forehead. "Just a little farther," he said. "Over there."

We still weren't anywhere near the train station, and when I glanced at his wristwatch, the hands pointed at five to eight. It was impossible.

"Do you still have the ring I gave you the other day?"

I stared at him, wondering why he was suddenly bothered about it. I should have returned it to him earlier, and embarrassed, I unwrapped the handkerchief.

"Put it on," he said.

"Why?"

He looked exasperated. "Just put it on and follow me."

A few doors down, Shin stopped and glanced up at a signboard. Then he went in. It was a small hotel. I'd never stayed in a hotel before. When my mother and I had visited Taiping long ago, we'd stayed with one of her aunts, a fierce-looking woman who seemed to have inherited all the backbone that my mother lacked. I wondered if she still lived in this town and what she'd think if she saw me going into a hotel with a man. Even if he was my stepbrother.

The other girls at work had taught me to be wary of hotels. *Never meet a man there.* Not even in the reception area. It was a test, they said, to weed out those girls who would, and those who wouldn't. And now here I was, about to step into one. A rather rundown one from what I could tell. But today's circumstances were different, and besides, I was with Shin. That was all right, wasn't it?

The interior of the hotel was gloomy and dank. A single electric lamp lighted the front desk, where Shin was signing a book. The clerk was an older woman, and she gave me a piercing glance. "No luggage?"

"We missed the train back," said Shin easily. "So we'll just need one night."

She looked at him, and then at me again. I did my best to appear unruffled, as though I missed trains every day. Speaking of which, why was Shin so familiar with this process? How many women had he taken to hotels? I stared at his back and the older woman met my eyes knowingly.

"Mr. and Mrs. Lee," she said, reading the register. "Newlyweds?"

"No," he said, "We've been together for a long time." He put his arm around me, careful to show off the ring on my finger.

"Do you want a meal?"

Shin looked at me. "Just tea and toast."

"We'll send it up," said the clerk. She squeezed her bulk around the desk and led us up a worn flight of stairs. "You're lucky tonight, this is the only room left with a private bathroom."

The room was small and sparsely furnished, with stained-glass window shutters in a flower pattern that overlooked the rainy street in front. But I was staring at the bed, not the view. Neatly made up with sheets and two stiff high pillows, a thin cotton blanket stretched tightly over it. A double bed. What had I been expecting, two twins?

"Shin," I said as soon as the clerk had left us. "Why didn't you just say we were siblings?"

"We don't have enough money for two singles. Besides, claiming you're my sister sounds more suspicious since we don't look alike." He spoke reasonably, but there was something about his averted face that made me think that he was nervous. I'd never seen Shin like this before, and felt even more skittish. It was best to be hearty, I decided.

"I've never been in a hotel before," I said cheerfully.

Silence. I couldn't really ask him if he'd ever been in one, because clearly he had, though I'd no idea under what circumstances. Perhaps it was all my imagination, but I couldn't help thinking of Shin meeting women in hotels. Eager young women, sophisticated older women. What did it matter since it wasn't my business?

"I'll go and wash up," I said.

To my surprise, Shin opened the brown paper bag he'd bought earlier and, after rummaging around, produced a brand-new men's shirt. It was plain white cotton, packed flat and tight with the collar still bound in cardboard and pinned into place.

"Here," he took out the pins and passed it to me. "You can have this."

"Don't you need it?"

His clothes were wet, too, but he shook his head. "Go ahead."

When I went into the adjoining bathroom, a small tiled boxlike space, I understood why. One glance in the narrow mirror, and I was mortified to discover that my wet dress clung to me. No wonder Shin had kept his eyes glued to my forehead. Shivering, I stripped off and washed up with the thin, hard cotton towels. Then I put on the men's shirt. Somehow, though less revealing than what I'd been wearing earlier, it looked far more provocative. Not knowing what to do, I stood in the bathroom for a good long while, trying to gather enough courage to go back out. But when I pushed the door open softly, Shin was gone.

A tea tray sat on the bed. I drank the tea, ate most of the toast, and even brushed my teeth with the toothbrush he'd bought at the pharmacy. Then I climbed into bed and turned the lights out. Unreasonably, tears of disappointment threatened to squeeze their way out of my eyes. What had I been thinking, that Shin would finally make a move? That was clearly never going to happen. The things he liked about me—blunt, straightforward, a good sport—weren't descriptions anybody used for heroines in novels. They were only good for sidekicks like Dr. Watson. I buried my head beneath the hard pillows and sobbed silently.

The door opened, and I froze. Shin stood silhouetted against the corridor light. Then he shut the door with a quiet click, went into the bathroom and started washing up. It was best to pretend I was asleep. Gritting my teeth, I vowed I'd never let him know I'd cried. No sooner had I decided this than he came back in again and slid into bed beside me.

The sound of the rain had lessened, but it was still drizzling steadily. I could hear water running off the roof, the creak of the bed as Shin lay down. I held my breath, heart pounding so fiercely that I was afraid he could hear it.

"Are you asleep?" The way he said it, so softly, made my heart break. It wasn't fair for Shin to use that tone of voice with me. I exhaled, but it came out as a strangled sob.

"What's the matter? Are you crying?" He sat up suddenly.

It was useless to hide it, not when Shin pulled the pillow off my face. The street lamp shone in through the rain-flecked windows and he could see my disheveled hair, the tearstains on my face.

"Is it Robert?"

Shin, you idiot, I thought, rubbing my face. Robert was the least of my worries, but Shin leaned over me. He wasn't wearing a shirt and I had that feeling again. That breathless, churning sensation whenever he got too close to me. I squeezed my eyes shut.

"Do you really like him that much? He's not worth it."

"I'm not crying about Robert."

"Then what is it? Are you in pain?"

This was so ludicrous that I didn't know whether to laugh or start crying again, while in the meantime, Shin was sitting half naked next to me. I could only say, "Why did you go away just now?"

"I was thinking." He was watching me, eyes dark and unreadable. My stomach twisted, hard. I couldn't lie on my back and have him lean over me like that; it was a disadvantage for me. When had the muscles of his arms and chest become so lean, so beautifully cut in the half-light from the window?

I struggled to sit up. "Again? About what?"

"I've been waiting for years. I don't think I can wait anymore." He put his hand on my waist, beneath the shirt. I could see the pulse throbbing in the hollow of Shin's throat, the half-anxious, half-questioning look in his eyes. I couldn't breathe.

"Has Robert kissed you?"

I nodded, wordlessly.

A flash of anger. "Well, I'm better."

I was sure he was going to say something else rude but instead he put the other hand behind my neck and kissed me.

There was a weak feeling in my legs, spreading up slowly towards the center of my body. A hot, melting sensation. His lips were soft and fierce. They trailed over my skin, forced my mouth open. I could feel the beating of his heart, the grip of his hand as it slid dangerously up my waist. "Shin!" I drew my breath in sharply, but he kissed me harder, on my mouth, my neck, pulling impatiently at the shirt I wore. This was everything I'd hoped for, yet so much faster and more urgent that it almost frightened me. "Wait!" I said, breathlessly, as we slid back onto the bed.

"Why?" He was tugging at the buttons now.

"Because we can't. We shouldn't." My thoughts were jumbled, falling apart even as I wrapped my arms around him.

"Yes, we should. Otherwise you won't be mine." Shin buried his face in my neck again, his hands cupping my breasts. An electric current shot through me; I gasped and smacked them away.

"I've always been yours. So please stop."

"No, you haven't." He sat up, running his hand through the dark hair that fell across his face. "This past month is the first time you've ever looked at me like this—it's always been Ming with you!"

Cheeks blazing, I couldn't think of what to say.

"Though if it were Ming, I'd be willing to give up. But not for someone like Robert," he said bitterly.

"Shin," I touched his face. "I thought you didn't like me."

"Of course I do. It's always been you."

"Then what about all those other girls?" I said indignantly. "What were you doing with them?"

"Trying to forget you, you idiot."

His mouth lit a slow, fevered trail between my breasts. To my shame, a moan escaped my lips and I bit them hard. Shin went on kissing me deliberately, taking his time. Touching me expertly, filling me with a yearning, slippery ache. There was a buzzing in my ears; my skin burned. I had that strange feeling again, that twisting mixture of curiosity, fear, and unbearable excitement. I didn't know this Shin, this stranger with the lean, hard body of a man, not a boy. I didn't know myself, either. That part of me that wanted to bite him, suck the tips of his fingers, consume him. He groaned softly as I dug my fingers into his back, feeling dizzy with triumph and pleasure. Then I felt his knees nudging my legs apart, that urgent heat pressed against my thigh, and I realized he was serious.

"I said, wait!" With an effort, I shoved him off.

"I told you," his eyes were hot and soft, "I'd make you mine."

"There isn't any 'mine' about it!" I sat up and buttoned up the shirt, right up to the neck, although my heart was racing. My head felt foggy. Shin flopped over and put an arm over his face.

"Robert won't want you if you're not a virgin." His voice was muffled.

"Is that what this is all about?" Enraged, I said, "He doesn't want me anyway. I'm not that popular!"

"Are you blind? You've no idea how much trouble I've had, getting rid of your admirers over the years."

"You did what?"

"Ah Hing from the dry-goods store. Seng Huat from my school. Oh, and the math tutor next door." He counted them off on his fingers.

Furious, I hit him with a pillow. "You mean to say I had a chance with the math tutor?" I'd had a crush on him one summer because he wore glasses and parted his hair the same way that Ming did. "You beast, Shin! You selfish, selfish beast!"

He grabbed my arm and pulled me down on top of him.

"What was I supposed to do? You never looked at me. And anyway, if they didn't have the guts to stick around they weren't worth it."

We were so close, our faces not six inches from each other. My heart was hammering, my breath coming in faint gasps. Despite my best efforts to glare at him, a dizzy happiness was seeping through me.

"Do you hate me?" That half-anxious look again. I'd never seen Shin like this—between the two of us, he was always the cool one—and I flushed. He must have noticed, because he said, "If you don't hate me, then let me do it," and started kissing me again.

It would be easy to give in, let this slow ache consume me. My arms slid around him, feeling the muscles of his back flex as he rolled over, so that he was on top of me now. An alarm went off in my head; every warning my mother had given me. What was I doing?

"No!" This time I shoved him so hard that he fell off the bed.

"Are you worried about getting pregnant?" Shin was kneeling, looking up at me. In the rainy half-light that poured in through the shutters, he was impossibly handsome. "Because you needn't be. I bought something from the pharmacy."

"So you were planning this right from the start?"

"Of course," he said. "I told you I was doing some thinking."

"Is that why you came along with me today?"

"Yes."

I wanted to hit him. "And all of that helping out with burying the finger, that was a lie?"

"I don't really care about the finger. I just wanted to be with you."

"You could have been with me anytime," I said. "You didn't have to lie about it."

"No, I promised my father." He stopped, as though he'd said too much.

"What did you promise him?" A feeling of dread descended on me. I remembered crooked blue shadows, the darkness of a chicken coop, and the way Shin's broken arm had dangled grotesquely. "Tell me or I'll never forgive you! What happened that night?"

In a flat low voice that was suddenly tired, Shin said, "He said he'd seen the way I looked at you; it set him off so we got into a fight. That's when he broke my arm. I promised I wouldn't lay a hand on you. Not in that house. In return, he was to leave you alone." He sighed. "And that's all."

I put my hand on his hair, the way I'd always wanted to. "What are we going to do now?" I said softly.

Shin buried his face in my lap, his arms wrapped around my waist. "You can let me sleep with you. Tonight."

I thought about it. "All right. But just sleeping. Nothing else."

He lifted an eyebrow, but he didn't say anything, just climbed back into bed and put his arms around me. My chest was filled with a sweet painful turmoil, like a bird beating its wings. Turning over the scenes of our childhood, our many arguments and rivalries. Had I managed to catch up to Shin, or had he, by playing a cool and patient game, ensnared me instead? I lay on my side, listening to the rain and Shin's breathing, feeling ridiculously happy.

43

THE CALL COMES ON SUNDAY EVENING, INTERRUPTING THE COOL hush of the veranda, where William is sitting in a cotton shirt and a sarong. The air feels heavy and sticky, prelude to a monsoon. He lies in a woven rattan chair, the ice in his glass tinkling as he tilts it. William remembers walking by a frozen lake and hearing the loose chunks of floating ice ringing against the shore. Like bells chiming, Iris had said, her charming face pink with cold. That was right before she accused him of infidelity, of kissing another woman. Of all the things he's done, he was never untrue to her. It must have been a mistake, he'd told her. "I know what I saw," she'd said coldly. "At the Piersons' party." The only person he'd kissed that night in the darkness of the hallway, no witness save the grave ticking of a grandfather clock, was Iris herself. And ironically, it was because he'd been filled with sudden affection for her after a day spent, enjoyably, with friends. Recalling this injustice, a surge of resentment rises in William. So much for Iris's neuroses, her uncanny ability to ruin good moments. But it's a memory from another time, another life, and William presses the icy whisky glass against his forehead, listening as the telephone rings and rings through the empty bungalow.

On the eighth ring, Ah Long picks up the receiver. He's not as fast as Ren was, scampering to pick up the telephone. Then he's at the veranda door.

"Lady, *Tuan*."

Right on time, William thinks. After all, he didn't go to church this morning; Lydia would have missed her chance to speak to him then. He takes a deep breath. "Hello?"

Her voice is faint and uncertain, even if you discount the crackling of the telephone line. "William? It's Lydia. Will you be in early tomorrow morning?"

"How early?" This is both annoying and alarming. "Surely it can wait?"

More crackles on the line. "—talk about Iris."

A strong wind is blowing, whipping the thin cotton of his sarong around his ankles. The smell of rain.

"What did you say?" he shouts.

"Meet me at seven. At the European wing."

There's a crooked flash of lightning and the phone goes dead. William stares at it. Tomorrow morning then. Despite the poor reception, there was a note of triumph in Lydia's voice that makes the bile rise in his throat. What else has she been up to, sleuthing around in her amateur way? Squeezing his eyes shut, he prays for the dark fortune that has followed him, to favor him again.

By six on Monday morning, William is up and dressed. The storm that raged all night is gone, leaving only swathes of flooded grass and a steady dripping from the eaves. Ah Long serves a tepid breakfast of toast with tinned baked beans in tomato sauce. No eggs. William can't stomach them this morning and besides, he misses Ren's delicate omelets. The whole house misses Ren. In the gloom, it's empty and full of shadows. Ah Long says gruffly, "When is the boy coming back?"

"I'll look in on him today."

Ren's condition has been so strange, his deterioration so precipitate, that William is filled with sick dread that he'll arrive at the hospital and find Ren dead. But he mustn't mention such thoughts to Ah Long, who's superstitious.

Darkness on the winding road before sunrise. The Austin's headlamps scatter shadows that melt into the bushes and trees. What does Lydia want from him? He has a bad feeling, one that only intensifies when he gets to the hospital. A milky blush seeps from the horizon, and though the buildings are quiet, there's the indefinable sensation that people are beginning to stir. It's 6:45 a.m. He's early.

The district hospital, built in a tropical half-timbered style, has a whimsical charm. Glancing up, William approaches the dark bulk of the administrative offices in the European wing. It's one of the few two-story buildings in the low, gardenlike hospital—surely Lydia must be somewhere around here. Instinct takes him round the corner. And there she is, her bright hair recognizable from a distance.

Lydia stands on the wet grass beside the building, head turned towards a young Chinese man with a crooked jaw. Judging from his white uniform, he's an orderly coming off the night shift, but the tension in the way they face each other alerts William. In the dim light, they don't notice his quiet approach.

"—nothing to do with me," says Lydia. "You can tell Dr. Rawlings all you like."

The man opens his mouth, but William never hears what he says because there's a crash. A flickering shadow that plummets, smashing into the young man's head. He drops, dead weight crumpling. William runs. Gets on his knees, but it's no good. He can see it right away. The skull has been smashed in, there are bits of nameless splatter on his hands, his shirt. The iron smell of blood and brains. Someone is screaming, a high hysterical sound. Whatever fell has shattered, but William recognizes the fragments. A heavy terra-cotta roof tile, the kind on the roofs in the hospital, the covered walkways, and wards. He stares upward. There's nothing to be seen, only the open windows on the second floor and above them, the unbroken ridge of the roofline.

THE WHOLE AFFAIR IS HORRIBLE, SHOCKING EVEN TO WILLIAM TO whom blood and open wounds are no strangers. He can't imagine what it's like for Lydia, who's led, crying and trembling, from the scene. The police arrive and take statements. They go up on the roof and note that a couple of tiles are missing, though whether that's due to last night's storm or whether they were gone months earlier, no one can say.

"Looks like the roof was being repaired," says the sergeant, pointing out some tiles stacked in a corner of the building. "It might have hit you, sir."

"Miss Thomson is the lucky one." Indeed, Lydia could have easily been killed. A mere two feet separated her from the unfortunate orderly whose head was split like a watermelon.

"Did you know him?" asks the sergeant. "Wong Yun Kiong, also known as Y. K. Wong. Aged twenty-three."

"He did a lot of work for Dr. Rawlings, I believe." Remembering Lydia's words, *you can tell Dr. Rawlings all you like,* he wonders at this.

"Will you take the day off?"

William shakes his head. "I've patients to see."

When he's finally released, he notes the tremor in his hands, the weakness in his knees. It's a tragic, freak accident, but he can't shake the feeling that there's something wrong. The instinct that told him, just as the shadow fell, that doom was coming. For after the shock of seeing the body, his first reaction was that the wrong person had died. *It should have been Lydia,* he thinks, even as he's filled with sickening guilt. That dark fortune that follows him, rearranging events to save him, has taken an inexplicable turn. Something's wrong with the pattern, he thinks, even as he walks, dazed and nauseated, back to his office. Or has he been seeing everything upside down?

He stops. There is indeed something wrong, something that registered as a flicker in his vision even in the dimness of the early morning. William turns back to the police officer.

44

I LAY IN THAT DOUBLE BED WITH ITS UNYIELDING PILLOWS, MY HEAD on Shin's chest and wished that time would stop, in this moment, forever. It was morning. The rain had ceased, and there was a clear, bright hush in the air. Shin was asleep.

The darkness was gone. As though the months and years that we'd lived in that long, narrow shophouse over the tin-ore dealership had turned into something else, though what it was exactly, I couldn't say. I only knew that I was happier than I'd ever been. Dangerously happy. I pressed my lips to Shin's collarbone. His skin was warm and tasted like salt.

Suddenly worried, I sat up, but the shirt I was wearing was still buttoned and my underwear was in place. In the bathroom, I examined myself seriously in the black-speckled mirror. Love hadn't done anything miraculous, though my cheeks went pink when I recalled how Shin had pinned me down last night. If he'd kept insisting, I might well have given in though I gave myself a stern talking-to. What were we going to do? I couldn't see any clear path for us.

When I went back into the room, Shin was still lying in bed. I bent over him, admiring his long lashes, and he grabbed me by the waist. Several breathless minutes ensued. "We have to catch a train." With an effort, I disentangled myself.

"Why do you always say no to me?"

"I just don't think this is right for us to do."

"You'll regret it," he said. "Do you know how hard it is to get away like this? To go to a different town, find a hotel where nobody knows us?"

I thought at first he was joking, but the look in his eyes was deadly serious. He unbuttoned the shirt I was wearing and began to kiss my throat. I couldn't breathe, couldn't resist as his hands roamed over my skin, touching me skillfully, making my legs weak, my stomach clench.

"Stop!" I gasped.

Shin's face was flushed. "Ji Lin, please," he said, in a husky voice I'd never heard before. "Please, please."

I knew what he was asking. My heart gave a treacherous lurch, but I was sure that if we did this, it would be the wrong way, the wrong order. Miserably, I said, "I'm sorry. We can't. Won't you wait?"

He got up abruptly and went to the bathroom. I could hear the water running as he stayed in there a good long time. I put my head down on the warm place where Shin had lain, feeling obscurely wretched. Perhaps he'd think that I didn't really love him. After all, Fong Lan had been so willing to give herself to him. Thinking of Shin's other girlfriends made my chest tighten painfully. How had he learned to kiss like that and what else had he done with them? But I wasn't going to be jealous, I thought. I wouldn't be like that, clinging and crying, even if he left me one day.

When Shin returned, he was back to normal. His dark hair was sleek with water and my yellow dress, which I'd hung to dry last night, was on his arm. "Trade your dress for that shirt," he said, jokingly.

"What about your shirt from last night? Isn't it dry?"

"I want the one you're wearing."

I turned red, and surprisingly, so did Shin. I went into the bathroom, changed, and gave him the new men's shirt I'd been wearing, now sadly crumpled since I'd slept in it. After that, not knowing what to say, we went down and checked out of the hotel. The same clerk was there and she gave us a look.

"There was some noise from your room last night."

"Yes," said Shin. "I fell off the bed."

She pursed her mouth, and I had to stifle the hysterical urge to giggle, squeezing Shin's hand instead. And so we left Taiping, that rainy, romantic little town between the limestone hills. One day, I thought, I'd like to come back with Shin. And do everything properly.

////

I WAS HEADED TO FALIM, SINCE I WANTED TO CHECK ON MY MOTHER. Shin would go on to Batu Gajah for his shift at the hospital. "Be careful when you go home," he said. We'd held hands secretly all the way on the train; it wasn't proper to display physical affection in public, but when no one was looking, Shin had sneaked a couple of kisses. I was so happy that I must have been grinning like an idiot, and Shin wasn't much better.

"I can keep a secret," I said.

In answer, Shin put his lips against my ear. "See?" he murmured. "You're all flustered now."

I hated to admit it, but he was right. Recalling how Shin had said, *I'll make you mine*, I wondered if all men had this power over women. Whether by laying hands on us, by caresses and sweet words, they could bend us to their will. I didn't like that idea. But no, Robert had kissed me before and the results had been disastrous.

"Shin," I said slowly. "Do you have another girl?"

"No."

"Then whose ring is this?"

"It's yours. Didn't I give it to you?"

I was dumbfounded. Certainly, he'd handed it to me in front of Matron, but I'd assumed he was just playing along. Shin looked sheepish. "I meant to do it in a better way—not like that."

"I thought you had a girlfriend in Singapore. Koh Beng said so."

"That's because when I'm in Singapore, I say I've a girl back in Ipoh, and vice versa. Otherwise it's troublesome. People ask if I'm available, or try to set me up. But it's always been you."

I felt giddy. "You bought a ring for me?"

In answer, he kissed the palm of my hand. "I thought I might as well go for it. Especially since Ming got engaged."

"But it doesn't fit."

"The way you eat, I thought you'd be fatter by now."

Shin twined his fingers through mine and I burst out laughing. It seemed wrong to be so happy. I thought of the look on Ren's face, the delight as though he'd been waiting all his life for me, and a shadow fell upon me.

"I'm worried about Ren. Will you look out for him, and also Pei Ling? Find out if she's recovered from her fall."

At Ipoh Station, I lingered, not wanting to leave him. Shin said, "You'd better go. Otherwise I'll end up getting out with you." Not caring if other people saw us, he kissed me hard against the doorway of the train. Then he went back to his seat. I put my hand against the glass of the window; he placed his on the other side. I stared at Shin's ring that glinted on my own middle finger. The ghost finger or *jari hantu,* as Koh Beng had called it. Shin tapped on the glass. Startled, I met his eyes. He shook his head. *Go!* And so, with a last glance, I went.

BY THE TIME I GOT TO FALIM, IT WAS NEARLY NOON AND THE SUN'S white glare made me squint. I walked the last bit home in a daze. The interior of the shophouse was dark and cool, and it took me a few seconds to realize that Robert was standing there. With my mother and stepfather.

I froze. I'd meant to slip quietly in, not walk into a committee meeting.

"Where have you been, Ji Lin?" My mother's anxious eyes took in my canary yellow frock, which unfortunately looked more like a party dress than ever.

"Why? What's the matter?" I forced myself to speak coolly, though the pulse was hammering in my neck. How much had Robert told them?

"Robert said he couldn't find you at Mrs. Tham's."

So. Not that much after all. I stole a look at him. He had a disheveled, agitated air, as though he, not I, was the one who'd spent the night away from home. My stepfather said nothing, but his long, silent stare gave me the most anxiety.

"I was out with my friend Hui. You remember her, don't you?"

My mother had never met Hui; I prayed desperately she'd pick up on my silent plea. Her eyes cut sideways to my stepfather and amazingly, she said, "Oh, that's right. I should have thought of that. Well, I'll go and start lunch then."

With this and other excuses, she managed to remove both herself and my stepfather, though not before he fixed me with a slit-eyed gaze.

As soon as they were gone, Robert said, "I want to talk to you."

I didn't like the insistence in his eyes, but there was nothing for it but to go on a little walk with him, away from the shophouse. We trudged along in silence, the noonday sun burning down on our heads. I felt dizzy and thirsty, my chest tight with dread.

"How long have you been working there?" he said at last.

"A few months."

"I asked around," he said awkwardly. "It's a fairly decent dance hall, but it's not a good job. You do know that, don't you?"

Of course I knew it, though Robert proceeded to give me a long-winded lecture. I wished desperately that he'd go away, back to his world of servants and cars and trips to Europe, but I couldn't afford to antagonize him, either.

"Look," I said at last. "What do you think I do at the May Flower?"

"You dance with men. For money." He wouldn't meet my eye, and I realized he was busy imagining all sorts of other, unspoken things.

"Yes. I'm a . . . dance instructor," I said. "And I'm there two afternoons a week. But I don't do call-outs, though I'd probably make more money that way."

Robert didn't bat an eye at this talk about call-outs, and I realized with a faint feeling of surprise that he was familiar with the term. Perhaps he'd even gone on a few himself.

"Do you need money?"

Shin's voice rang in my head—*don't ask him for anything*—so I said, "That's my business. Besides, I'm not working there anymore."

He chewed his lip. "Let me help you, Ji Lin. After all, you stopped Shin from hitting me yesterday."

"I didn't want him to get into trouble," I said, but Robert wouldn't take the hint.

"I was shocked he got violent. Are you all right?"

It was on the tip of my tongue to remind Robert that he'd practically called me a whore in front of Shin, but I bit down hard instead. "I'm fine. And now if you'll excuse me, I have to change."

As soon as the words left my mouth, I saw Robert's dawning recognition that I was still wearing the same dress as yesterday. I felt like kicking myself; I'd led him right into it.

"Were you with Shin last night? Where did the two of you go yesterday?"

Dangerous. "I already said I went to my friend's."

I turned back, but Robert had something over me now; if my stepfather found out where I'd been working, who knew what might happen? "I think it's best if we don't see each other," I said as politely as I could. "Thanks for your concern, but I can take care of myself."

"But I want to," he said, following closely. "You need help."

I walked faster, itching to get away. With despair, I realized that he saw himself as my savior. Someone who'd rescue me from my unfortunate choices, my violent brother. It would have been funny if it weren't so awful. Robert seized my elbow. I froze. We were standing in the street and there were bicycles and people passing. Surely he wouldn't try anything here. I must have looked alarmed, because he dropped his hand uncomfortably.

"I only have your best interests in mind," he said.

Finally, after delivering yet another stumbling lecture about the danger of poor choices and how I ought to be more careful as a young woman, he left. But my troubles weren't over.

WHEN I GOT BACK, I HEARD RAISED VOICES COMING FROM THE family room on the second floor. Anxious, I raced upstairs as my stepfather came down. He didn't look at me, just brushed past furiously. My mother was sitting in a rattan armchair in the family room, her eyes closed. Hands pressed against her temples.

"What happened?" I studied her worriedly for visible injuries but couldn't see anything amiss. "Was it something I did?"

"No, no." She gave me a weak smile. Then dropping her voice, "But really, where did you go last night, Ji Lin?"

For a brief moment, I considered coming clean about Shin and how we felt about each other, but something warned me not to. "I told you, I stayed with my friend Hui," I said. "Don't you remember, the fashionable one?"

I'd mentioned Hui to my mother before, thinking she'd be interested in her clothes and style, but my mother didn't take the bait. She simply nodded, eyes wary. If only Robert hadn't alerted them! The fact that I'd returned from some unknown destination dressed in this frivolous, clinging yellow dress had made everything even more suspicious. But this was the dress that Shin had kissed me in. That he'd said he liked. For that reason alone, it would be my favorite dress forever, although I couldn't look at it without guilt. I always felt guilty around my mother; it was her very meekness and soft reproach that undid me.

"Are you and Robert all right?"

"We won't be seeing much of each other anymore." The sooner I set that expectation, the better.

"Why? He's such a nice boy."

"We're not suited." Looking at her distressed face, I added, "Please don't say any more."

"Is it because of Shin?"

I froze. "What does he have to do with it?"

"It's just that Shin doesn't like Robert for some reason."

"Shin doesn't like anyone," I said lightly.

"No, he likes Ming. And you. I'm glad that you have a brother now, even if the two of you argue. Family is really important. You'll find out when you get older."

She fell silent, and I wondered if she was recalling her miscarriages, those children who had never come into being. And I shuddered, thinking of Yi. Was he still patiently sitting at that railway station in the land of the dead, waiting for his twin to die?

"Mother," I said slowly, wondering if I was making a terrible mistake, "I have something to tell you."

45

DISASTER BLOWS THROUGH THE WARDS LIKE AN ILL WIND, BRINGING news of yet another freak accident. Death is no stranger in this hospital; it walks the halls every day, picking off the old and infirm. But coming so hard on the heels of Pei Ling's death, it lends a nasty chill to the whispers of the staff.

There's a vengeful ghost in the hospital, they say. Pei Ling fell down the stairs because she saw it. And that orderly, Y. K. Wong, was killed by a falling tile this very morning, because he saw the ghost walking on the roof of the hospital.

"Why on the roof?" asks Ren. He'll be discharged today. It's amazing how quickly he's recovered, says the local doctor who examines him. Absolutely astonishing, the change from one day to the next, but that's the way of children.

"It's nothing for you to worry about." Dr. Chin, the same man who informed Ren so awkwardly about the loss of his finger, frowns at a white patch of skin on Ren's elbow. It's exactly where the pale nurse, Pei Ling, grasped his elbow in that burning, dreamlike world. When Ren puts the fingers of his right hand in the same spot, it tingles. His cat sense grows stronger, as though he's opened a door to a twilit road. And outside, there are many chill white creatures. Ren thinks of the *pontianak* and other tales of angry lost women who come in the night, shrouded with their long black hair. You mustn't let them in, not ever, even if they scratch at the door with their long nails and call to you with sweet plaintive voices, promising knowledge and secrets. Though what if you went outside, just for a little bit, to talk to them?

The doctor palpates the elbow, but Ren feels no pain, just numbness. The mark looks uncannily like the grasp of a ghostly hand. "I could have sworn this wasn't here before," he mutters. Ren is silent. He understands that this is the price he must pay for abandoning Pei Ling on that train.

"Anyway, you'll be discharged today."

Most likely William will take him back at the end of the day. At least, that's what Ren thinks.

Dr. Chin gives him a curious glance. "Better check that he didn't go home early. I heard he was first on the . . . scene this morning."

The nurse says, "No, he's working." A look passes between them.

"And Miss Lydia?"

At that moment, Lydia herself appears in the open ward doorway. There's no color in her lips and her hair is flattened on one side as though she's been resting in an office, which indeed she has.

"Did you want me?" she says, hearing her name. "Need any help?"

"Oh! I heard you were there when the accident happened," the nurse says to her. "It must have been horrible."

"Yes. My father's coming to pick me up soon. I'm not quite up to driving myself," she says with a grimace. There are sympathetic, half-admiring nods at her foreign fortitude. Someone has draped a light, cotton shawl over her shoulders, but it doesn't hide the thin splatter of red brown on her blouse. Ren stares at it, cat sense tingling. Death covers her blouse, speckles her skirt, and he feels dizzy with horror. Yet despite her pallid face, Lydia is full of nervous energy.

She comes and sits down next to Ren. "Goodness, you look so much better!"

"Yes." He drops his eyes. Does nobody else see the blood on her? But it is very little, just a few splashes. To Ren's invisible feelers, however, a sticky grey web clings to her. He doesn't know what it means, only that he shrinks from her awkward friendliness. Is it bravery or something else that narrows the pupils of her eyes—fear or excitement?

"I meant to pass this to you," says Lydia, taking something out of her purse. "Will you be seeing your friend Louise again?"

Ren is momentarily confused—who's Louise? Then he remembers it's the other name for his girl in blue. Not knowing what to say, he nods.

"Could you give this to her?"

Ren flinches. It's a small glass bottle. The same kind that the withered finger came in, except this one is filled with a tea-colored liquid. Of course, this is a hospital, and Lydia volunteers here. It isn't surprising that she'd have the same kind of container.

"What is it?"

"Stomach medicine I promised her last time," she says.

Ren recalls the conversation between Lydia and Ji Lin, something about women being troubled once a month and how unfair it is. Obediently, he pockets the bottle, then recalls Dr. MacFarlane's rules for medication. "Should I label it with a dosage?"

"Just tell her to take all of it if she has a stomachache. It's a mild tonic; I take it myself. But don't mention it to anyone else—it might embarrass her." Smiling, she gets up to go.

Ren stares after her, wondering how nobody else senses the pall that clings to Lydia's retreating back. It's like an invisible shroud or cocoon, those fine filaments spun out of nothing. Lydia has apparently cheated death this morning. But from the looks of it, she's not unscathed.

46

My mother's face, already haggard, turned even paler when I told her. She closed her eyes for a long moment.

"But I was only dancing. Really. I never did anything else."

I'd decided to confess my dance-hall work since Robert might spill the beans at any moment. There was nothing I could do about my stepfather's reaction, but it was better if she, at least, were prepared.

"So if you hear anything from other people, you mustn't be shocked. Though there's a good chance it will never come up." I spoke with false confidence. "And Mrs. Tham, of course, doesn't know."

I was afraid that she'd start berating me for making such a stupid decision, but she only looked sad. "Was it to help pay off my debt?"

I hesitated, but there was no point denying it. "I've quit already. So you don't have to worry."

Her face twisted. "It was wrong of me to involve you—you mustn't do things like this anymore. I'll tell your stepfather about the money."

"He'll be furious! Besides, Shin said he'd help."

"I don't want you to worry about it. It's not your burden." She bit her lip. "Is that why Robert won't be coming—because he found out?"

"No. I'm the one who doesn't want to see him."

"But why? He's a good man, Ji Lin, if in spite of all that—"

"It's not right, since I don't care for him."

"You could learn!" She stopped, realizing that she'd raised her voice.

Then low and insistent. "Don't miss this chance, Ji Lin. It will make a huge difference—you'll regret it the rest of your life if you let him go!"

I'd never heard my mother so assertive and, frankly, it shocked me. I shook my head. "It's not an option for me."

"Then make it an option. Don't be so proud!"

It wasn't pride that was holding me back, but I could never tell her.

"Is there someone else?" she said sharply.

A pause. "Yes."

"Who is it?"

"Ming." I studied her covertly. How much did she want Robert as a son-in-law?

"Oh. Ming." My mother gave a sigh of relief. "You know that's not going to happen. He's engaged." Still, she gave me a searching look. Did she suspect?

At dinner, my mother and I watched each other warily. The prospect of her confessing her debts to my stepfather filled me with dread, but she seemed far more concerned about my missing a chance with Robert. I read the suspicion on her face; she didn't quite believe I was still hung up on Ming, yet not a word passed our lips because my stepfather was there. He sat, oppressively silent, while we picked at our food. You could have cut the air with a knife. I glanced at Shin's empty seat at the table too many times and when I caught my mother's eye, dropped mine guiltily. This was no good. I'd give myself away at this rate. So I went to bed, praying that morning would come quickly.

BUT WHAT CAME INSTEAD WERE DREAMS. NOT THE SUNLIT PLACE where I always met Yi, but other strange visions. Perhaps I'd been worrying too much about the events of the last few days, because I was at a railway interchange with many platforms and corridors and stairs that connected below the tracks. It was like a reverse image of the Ipoh Railway Station. That was white and grand, but here all was dark, narrow, and grimy. Dusk was falling, a blue hush, and crowds of silent, wraithlike figures were rushing here and there. All I knew was that I must choose a train soon, or be left behind.

The people themselves were indistinct. If I stared hard, they dissolved like smoke, but as soon as I glanced away they were back, bustling around on some important business. Walking over to the edge of the platform, I peered at the railway tracks. They ran away like crooked ladders into the distance. A pair of opposing signs pointed to *Hulu* and *Hilir*, meaning upstream and downstream in Malay, though that made no sense in a railway station. The track labeled *Hilir* made me think that far away, at the other end, I might find Yi. It was a wink of a thought that I dismissed, though I had the feeling that if I called Yi right now, he'd appear in that same noiseless, frightening way.

Sooty smoke drifted over the platform as a train rattled in. People hurried to get on and I hesitated, wondering if I'd be trapped here forever if I didn't make a decision soon. A spare old man—a foreigner with light eyes and a grey, scrubby beard—made his way across the platform. The edges of the dark suit he wore seemed to fray and blur as though it was unraveling into the falling dusk. His mouth moved as he pointed at my traveling basket.

"I beg your pardon?" I said.

Still no sound, like a radio that had gone silent, but I could tell from the careful, exaggerated movements of his lips that he was trying to speak to me.

Put it back, he mouthed, nodding at my basket. And I knew, in that inexplicable way of dreams, that he meant the remaining finger—the thumb from Pei Ling's package.

"Where? The hospital?"

But he only smiled. *Thank you for everything.* Then he was passing me, climbing onto the train.

"Wait!" I cried, running after him.

He turned and looked at me genially. Courteously. I stared into his eyes, those light-colored eyes, and realized that they had slit, vertical pupils, like the eyes of a cat. Horrified, I took a step back.

The old man bowed his head. *I am going now.* He put his hands together in a gesture of apology and gratitude, and I saw then that his hands were intact with all ten fingers. Steam and gritty smoke billowed. There was only the scream of the train whistle, the deep vibration of the tracks, and a greyness that descended on everything.

////

THE TRAIN WHISTLE HAD BECOME A CAW, THE HARSH CROAK OF A crow walking up and down the ledge outside my window. Pressing my hands against my eyes, it occurred to me that besides meaning "upstream" and "downstream," the words *hulu hilir* also meant "beginning and end" in Malay. I sat up in the morning hush. It was a dream, nothing more. Or was it? One way or another, I'd never wanted to talk to the dead.

Put it back, he'd said. Shivering in the cool morning air, I picked my way over to my traveling basket. I'd packed the lists of names to show Koh Beng as well as the severed thumb, the one from Pei Ling's mysterious package. Today I'd go to Batu Gajah and replace it among all the other specimens in that pathology storeroom, and put an end, hopefully, to all this.

But that's not what I told my mother. "I'm heading back to Ipoh."

She'd nodded without comment, though her eyes were doubtful. She was still worried about Robert. But I wasn't planning to see Robert again—only Shin. I had to tell him about my dream. Remembering the old foreigner's left hand, with its five intact fingers, I was certain that we'd done right in burying the finger in Dr. MacFarlane's grave.

WHEN I ARRIVED AT THE HOSPITAL IN BATU GAJAH, IT WAS HALF past eight in the morning. A little early for the crowd that had gathered, milling around in front of the main entrance.

"What happened?" I asked a middle-aged woman in a yellow *samfoo.*

"Accident. Police won't let us in, even though I told them I had an appointment and the poor fellow's dead already."

Alarm shivered through me. "Who died?"

"A young man who worked here. A hospital orderly, they said."

Shin! Terrified, I ran forward. "Let me through, please!"

A Malay constable was on guard, and I struggled frantically through the crowd, their irritation changing to murmurs of interest and pity.

"My brother's an orderly here," I said breathlessly to him. "Do you know who died?"

"I don't know the name, but if you're family, I'll take you through. This way, to the European wing."

Dry-mouthed, I ran after him. We crossed over to a part of the hospital I'd never been to. Around the corner of a half-timbered two-story building, we approached a knot of people. They were looking up at the roof, then at the grassy area next to the building.

"That's where it happened." The constable nodded, eyes on a tall Sikh officer who was putting away a notebook. "Captain Singh, she wants to know if it's her brother."

"What's his name?" His eyes met mine in a penetrating, amber gaze.

"Lee Shin," I said, holding my breath. "He's an orderly here."

He glanced at his notebook. "No. It was a Mr. Wong Yun Kiong."

My knees sagged. Thank goodness! But the name was horribly familiar. "Do you mean Y. K. Wong?"

"Did you know him?"

What should I say? As I hesitated, someone brushed past me.

"Inspector. I need to talk to you." It was William Acton, haggard and red-eyed, as though he'd been awake for hours.

The inspector turned, both men ignoring me.

"What is it, Mr. Acton? I thought you'd gone home."

"I've patients to see. But I just remembered something."

"According to your statement, a tile falling from the roof crushed Mr. Wong's skull."

"That's right. But it wasn't from the roof."

We all glanced up instinctively.

"I didn't realize it till afterwards, because it happened so fast. But there wasn't enough height."

"What do you mean?"

"Well, it was like a shadow dropping. But I'm almost certain that the tile came from the second floor and not the roof."

There was a pause. "This is a very serious charge, Mr. Acton. Are you saying that someone dropped a tile from the second-story window?"

It was possible, I thought, studying the building. The windows were tall and gracious, open to allow air to flow through. Acton hesitated. "Perhaps."

"Could you swear to it? It was still dark."

"I'm not sure that I could," he rubbed his face, "but that's my feeling."

"Feelings matter less than facts." Animosity crackled between the two men. Had they met before?

"I'm merely passing what information I can to the police."

"Of course, we'll go up and check the second floor," said the inspector smoothly. "But apparently it was locked at the time. These are administrative offices, aren't they?"

"Yes, though a number of staff have keys."

"Thank you, Mr. Acton. I'll keep it in mind."

William Acton hesitated, then turned away. I hurried after him to ask what had happened, hoping that the inspector had forgotten about me. Why had Y. K. Wong died?

"Louise," Acton said as I caught up. "Why do you always show up when I least expect you?"

I began a halting explanation about my brother, but he wasn't really listening. "The first time I met you was in the pathology storeroom, before that little nurse fell down the stairs. Did you know she died this weekend?"

Horrified, I shook my head.

"You were there at the party, the night Nandani disappeared. And now this morning again. Are you the angel of death, Louise?"

"Of course not!"

"But you know about the river in my dreams. Tell me, have you seen any dead people lately?"

He couldn't possibly know about Shin and me going to dig up Dr. Mac-Farlane's grave. My heart was pounding unsteadily. Acton gave a humorless smile. "I'm sorry. I'm in a foul mood today. How about a drink some time—how much do you charge for call-outs?"

Taken aback, I could only fix an automatic smile on my face. The same blank professional look I used at work. To him, I was simply a bit of skirt to take his mind off things. But two could play at this game and there were questions I wanted to ask. "Did you really see something fall from the second floor?"

"You don't believe me?"

"No, I do," I said earnestly. "I think that instincts matter."

He sighed. "There might have been someone on the second floor. Though why on earth would they chuck a roof tile out of a window?"

Why indeed? Though Shin's words, *I'll kill him*, echoed uncomfortably in my head. Of course he'd been angry after hearing that Y. K. Wong had locked me in the pathology storeroom. But he'd never do such a thing— or would he? I thought of Shin's silent fury, the darkness in my stepfather that I'd always feared.

"Are you all right, Louise?" said Acton. We'd stopped walking and people passing were beginning to give us looks.

"Did you know Y. K. Wong, the man who was killed?" I asked. Should I tell the inspector about my suspicious run-ins with him, or would it invite trouble?

"Not really. I saw him around." He rubbed his jaw, his complexion grey and papery. "In some ways it would be better if it weren't a freakish accident; if there were a logical reason for him dying."

"What do you mean?"

Acton made a nervous grimace. "Just a thought. A peculiar fancy. Have you ever felt that things have rearranged themselves a little too conveniently?"

My stomach clenched. This was exactly what Yi had said to me in that deserted train station, that the fifth one of us was rearranging events. *Everything's out of order.*

"As if fate changes to suit you?"

It was a stab in the dark, but Acton looked astonished. Then he laughed grimly, "What an extraordinary girl you are, Louise. But you understand. Perhaps I knew you in another life."

Just then Koh Beng came up from behind me. Startled, I wondered how much of our conversation he'd overheard, but he simply said, "Matron wants to see you, sir."

"Right." Acton glanced around. "Don't leave," he said to me as he crossed over to the next building.

I'd no intention of obeying him, though I waited a few minutes for the coast to clear. Koh Beng lingered. "What are you doing here, talking to Mr. Acton?"

"I ran into him when I was talking to the police about the accident."

"The police? Did you tell them about the fingers going missing?"

"No, should I have?"

Koh Beng gave me a sideways glance. Today he was different, nervous and not cheerful at all, as if the death of his colleague had shaken him up. "Did you bring the lists that were in Pei Ling's package? Remember, I said I'd look at them for you." As I fumbled in my basket, he added, "And what did he mean earlier, about someone on the second floor?"

"He thinks he saw a figure there."

"Did he tell the police?"

"I'm not sure if they believed him." I pulled the lists out. Koh Beng glanced eagerly over my shoulder.

"Well, this proves that Y. K. Wong was selling fingers," he said. "They're all patients who came into contact with him."

"How do you know?"

Koh Beng shrugged. "I keep an eye on things. People in hospital are worried and vulnerable; they're all looking for some assurance. Look, this chap here was definitely a gambler." He pointed at the list in my hand. "Gamblers will buy anything; don't you remember the craze for *burung ontong* nests?"

Burung ontong was a small bird that built an inconspicuous nest in high and inaccessible places. If a nest was put in a rice bin, it was said to bring great fortune to its owner. There'd been a mania for them not too long ago, with prices reaching ten or even twenty-five Straits dollars for a good specimen. Compared to locating a tiny nest, I supposed selling off pathology specimens was far easier.

"But Y. K. Wong didn't seem like he'd be good at soft-soaping superstitious people and selling charms." He was too stiff, too awkward, I thought, frowning. "I'd better turn these in to Dr. Rawlings or Mr. Acton."

"What for? He's dead now."

"There are still specimens missing, and I don't want them to suspect Shin, since he was the last person in charge of the storeroom."

A flicker crossed Koh Beng's face. "I'll do it for you." He held out his hand for the papers.

I stared at him. And realized what a fool I'd been. I'd been looking for a pattern all this time, but I hadn't seen this one. Why hadn't I paid more attention?

"That's all right." I edged away. To my dismay, the walkway was deserted.

"Where are you going?" He was smiling at me, a tight, angry smile.

"Shin's expecting me," I lied.

"That's too bad." He seized my arm, pinning it behind my back. A stabbing pain in my side. "If you scream, I'll cut you again," he said in my ear. Panicked, I couldn't see what he held in his left hand, only felt that it was very sharp.

"Keep walking," he whispered, as we marched in a grotesque, loverlike embrace, his right arm locked around my shoulders. Frantically, I looked around.

"Is it the lists you want? I'll give them to you."

In answer, he jabbed me again, slicing through the side of my dress. Then we were outside, crossing the damp grass. Still nobody. In despair I found myself frog-marched towards one of the outbuildings.

"It's a pity you figured it out," said Koh Beng conversationally. "I was hoping I wouldn't have to do this. What made you suspect me?"

I shook my head, but he cut me again. Tears ran down my face. "Tell the truth now," he said.

"You said Pei Ling was a good friend of yours. But she told me she didn't have any male friends. Not anyone she could ask to get the package for her."

"That's all?" We were still walking, not into the outbuilding but behind it. I dragged my feet, but he yanked me along.

"She said the salesman had a friend whom she didn't like. I thought that was Y. K. Wong, but it was you all the time." I remembered how Pei Ling had blanched when she'd first met Shin, telling me that he was friends with someone she didn't like.

"Yes, Y. K. was troublesome, digging for evidence to tattle to Dr. Rawlings. Too bad he always rubbed people the wrong way."

"Was it worth it, selling body parts?" I looked around desperately. We were so far away from the main hospital now!

"It was good while it lasted. Though that idiot Chan Yew Cheung had to go and lose a finger in a dance hall, of all places. Still in a bottle that could be traced from the hospital. He kept it because the specimen number was a lucky 168."

The numbers, I thought in despair. It was all about numbers.

"I thought he'd bring in more business but he tried to blackmail me instead. And his girlfriend was no better."

"You pushed Pei Ling down the stairs."

"It's your fault, really. The two of you stood right outside the cafeteria, stupidly discussing a package that Yew Cheung had hidden. I was sure it was the evidence he'd kept against me."

Poor, miserable Pei Ling. She'd only been concerned about getting her love letters back.

"I realized then that she had to go."

In the uproar over the discovery of Pei Ling's horrific fall, I remembered how Koh Beng had been the only person who kept eating. So busy pretending to be normal that he forgot to look surprised. I felt sick.

"How much does Shin know?" Koh Beng asked.

"Not much," I said, desperately trying to hedge my bets, "But he's suspicious."

"Just when I thought everything was settled. Give me the lists. And that glass bottle—I saw it when you took the papers out."

I'd no choice but to hand over everything, including the preserved thumb. "Did you kill the salesman, too?"

"No. It was just luck that he fell into a ditch." He frowned, thinking. My head was pounding, my chest tight with panic. He was heavier than me, though not much taller. In a fight, the only advantage I'd have was surprise. Throwing open a door, Koh Beng forced me up a flight of disused stairs.

"What happened to Y. K. Wong this morning? Was that chance, too?" I said, trying to delay him.

I didn't think he'd go for it, but he said in that terrifyingly conversational way, "I'd overheard him arranging to meet that Englishwoman, Lydia Thomson. It was to do with the fingers, though I don't know what he thought she knew about them. Always a pigheaded idiot, Y. K. Wong. Anyway, he was getting dangerous, so while they were talking, I went up to the second floor, picked a roof tile from the stack in the corner, and dropped it on his head."

"What if it had struck her?"

"Didn't matter. Simple is best."

We'd reached the top of the stairs, and opened another door. Dazzling sunlight hit us. It led to a flat roof that you could walk on. "Used for drying things," said Koh Beng cheerfully. "There aren't many two-story buildings here."

In that instant, I knew exactly what he was going to do and why he'd had no qualms cutting me in the side. Wounds like that wouldn't matter if my body were splattered all over the ground.

He must have seen it in my eyes, because he said, "I wasn't lying, you know. You really are my type. But it would have been better if you were a little more stupid."

47

REN'S EYES SNAP OPEN. HE'S BEEN DOZING, WAITING TO BE DIS-charged later today, but there's a jolt. Something terrible is happening to Ji Lin. Ren sits up. Dull ache in his side. In fact, the only place that doesn't hurt is his elbow, which is pale and cold. The nurses have remarked on that unusual blanched patch on his skin. They talk about it when they think he's sleeping. *Doesn't it look like a hand?* says one with a shudder. But none of that matters now.

Frantic, he looks around for a nurse. Tells her, stumbling over the words, that she has to look for a girl.

"What girl?" she says, annoyed.

"The one who came to see me on Friday."

"Oh, a visitor, is it? I'm sure she'll come soon."

No, Ren tries to explain. She's somewhere in the hospital. Over there, beyond the other building. The nurse sighs.

"When she comes, we'll let you know. Now don't get out of bed!"

In despair, Ren's eyes squeeze tight, tight. If he grasps the white mark on his elbow, putting his fingers exactly where Pei Ling put hers in his dream, his cat sense grows stronger. He doesn't like this new feeling, a dull heavy buzz that makes his teeth chatter, the bones of his skull ache. His lips move as he concentrates. *Where are you?*

Maybe it won't work, she's not Yi, but he thinks it will. It must. His fingers dig into that ghostly handprint on his arm. Dizzy, he holds his breath, calling.

And then it comes.

Blood rushes in his ears, his heart thumps wildly. It's not Ji Lin; it's the other one. Drawing nearer and nearer with long strides. Shoulders tense, he watches the open ward door like a small animal. It's a young man in a white uniform. Ren has never seen him before. Definitely not, because he's someone that you'd remember. *Ah. It's you,* Ren wants to say. His cat sense blazes up, an electric burst of relief, but his throat is so dry that nothing comes out.

"*Ah Kor,*" he says. Older Brother.

The young man's eyebrows go up. Then he gives a rueful smile. "Awake, are you? She'll be happy about that."

Who is *she*? But Ren already knows. This is the other half of his girl in blue. The two of them a matched pair, like Yi and him. And Ren recalls that tall lean shape in the doorway of the pathology room, the one that he thought was Dr. Rawlings but wasn't.

"You must be *xin,*" he says, excited.

Surprise, or is it a flicker of discomfort? "Yes, I'm Shin. Did Ji Lin tell you?"

Ren shakes his head hurriedly, "I've met the other ones. There's you, and me, and her, and my brother, Yi. And my master, William Acton. That's five of us."

Shin looks as though he's about to say something, but merely tousles Ren's head. "I came by yesterday but you were sleeping. We'll talk more when you feel better."

Urgently, Ren says, "No, you must find her—she's in danger!"

"Who?" But Shin already knows, his sharp eyes searching Ren's face.

"She's in the hospital. Someone's hurting her!"

"Where is she?" On his feet now.

"Beyond that building. On the roof." Ren points from the window to the spot that draws him like a tightening line. Is it his imagination, or can he feel a thin, soundless shriek? "Hurry! It will be too late!"

48

KOH BENG MARCHED ME ACROSS THE FLAT ROOF, THE TIP OF A SCALPEL shoved into the soft spot under my jaw. I opened my mouth to scream, but even if I did, no one would see us all the way out here, facing the jungle trees. They'd just hear my shriek cut off as I fell off the roof. Instead I went limp as if I'd fainted.

Koh Beng bent over instinctively to grab me, and as he did so, I yanked viciously at his knees, pulling him off balance. He fell, cracking his shoulder on the cement. Slammed into me. Rolling. Elbow in my face as I struggled to get up. "Bitch!" he hissed, grabbing my hair, but I scratched and bit and then we were twisting, struggling. As he dragged me towards the edge, the roof door burst open behind us. Koh Beng's head swiveled in surprise, but he'd no time to react before someone hit him in a low tackle. The breath was knocked from my body.

"Shin!" I screamed, but no sound came out. He fell on me as Koh Beng slashed wildly. I felt Shin gasp, jerk back as we rolled into the sickening emptiness at the edge of the roof. There was a dizzying instant when I saw the ground far below. Then my head smacked the gutter as we went over.

I MUST HAVE HIT MY HEAD HARD ENOUGH TO BLACK OUT, FOR THIS time I fell into the world of the unconscious with a terrific bang. I knew exactly where I was, right down to the polished wood of the deserted ticket counter. The waiting room for the dead. There was a hushed expectation in the sunlight glinting off the train tracks.

"Yi," I said.

He stood up. He'd been kneeling behind the counter, a child playing hide-and-seek, but he didn't look happy to be found. In his sad stare, I could already find the answer to my question.

"Why didn't you run away?" he said.

I should have, even at the risk of being stabbed. It was my curiosity, that foolish thirst for knowledge that had delayed me, wanting to hear the answers from Koh Beng. And now it was too late. "Am I dead?"

"Not yet." Yi's eyes squinted past me, as though he was looking at something far away. "But any moment now—you're dangling off the roof."

"Is Koh Beng going to kill me?" That would be like Pei Ling, shoved down the stairs. Or Y. K. Wong, crushed by a falling tile. *Simple is best,* Koh Beng had said in his frighteningly efficient way. "What about Shin?"

"He's grabbed you, but the other one is trying to kick him over."

"Please, not Shin!" Bitterly, I sank to my knees, pressing my forehead against the cool wood of the ticket counter. *You'll regret it,* Shin had said that morning, lying in the hotel bed. And I did. A vast, furious ocean of regret. I should have given myself to him while I could. Tears ran down my face.

"Get up!" said Yi. "It's not over yet!"

"What do you mean?"

"Choose!" he said. "Who will it be, you or Shin?"

"You mean which one of us will die now?"

"Yes. I told you, from this side, I can shift things. Just a little bit." He screwed up his small face with effort. "Like the accidents that happened to Ren."

"But that's wrong!" If Yi had any kind of immortal soul, I was certain this was absolutely forbidden.

"It doesn't matter!" he shouted. "I've already been left here so long. Right now, you're going to die. But you can choose him instead."

"You mustn't do this!" I said desperately. "It's meddling—like the fifth one you said was rearranging things."

"*Li?*" he said. "*Li* has nothing to do with this!"

"Then who's the fifth one of us? Is it Koh Beng?"

"Why are you so blind?" Yi's face was red, as though he was about to cry. "Of course it isn't him; the other one is still dangerous. Hurry—time is running out! Choose or I'll do it myself!"

The station shook. There was a deep rumbling, a tremor that jolted me to the core, and I had the sudden, terrified sense that time was moving in this place again. A train was arriving, or was it departing? Whichever it was, the narrow gap of opportunity was closing.

"I'll stay with you, Yi!" I screamed. "Let Shin live!"

"Do you mean it?" Yi's face broke into a strange little smile. "You'd really stay with me?"

"Yes!"

"Don't forget me."

BRIGHT. IT WAS TOO BRIGHT AND MY HEAD ACHED. VOICES. PEOPLE talking. I struggled, thrashing my arms. Why was I still alive? Yi had tricked me.

Hands steadied me, examining my body. "She's lucky to have survived that fall. The other chap didn't make it."

"Shin," I said thickly. My throat was painfully dry, but that was nothing compared to the panic I felt. I forced myself to sit up.

"Don't move." They were checking my arms and legs, asking if I could move my neck, but I didn't care about myself. Terror filled me.

"Where's Shin?"

"He's right here."

And he was. I stumbled up, off the gurney, for that was what I'd been lying on, despite their cries of alarm. Shin lay on the other bed in the room. His face was pale, with a chalky shocked look, and there was blood on his arms and shirt. When I came over, he opened his eyes.

"Why can't you listen to what the doctor says?" he said, ruefully.

Sobbing and laughing, I held on to him.

////

IT TURNED OUT THAT ALL THREE OF US HAD FALLEN OFF THE ROOF. It was a miracle, they said, but I was uninjured except where Koh Beng had sliced me in the side and neck. Shin had a fractured arm and cuts on his forearms—defensive wounds, as the local doctor pointed out with interest. And Koh Beng had broken his neck.

Bystanders, drawn by the shouts, had seen us struggling. By all accounts, I should have fallen first, then Shin, for Koh Beng had clearly been in a better position. But he'd suddenly and strangely plummeted past us in a tangle of limbs, breaking our fall. There was no explanation for it, other than missed footing. Or perhaps he'd intended to kill himself, as some were already whispering.

A chill of wonder and unease seeped through me. From the other side of the river of death, had Yi swapped Koh Beng and me around like pawns in some game, bringing me back from the dead by stealing a life? If so, what had happened to Yi—and was this, then, his dark gift to me? I began to tremble uncontrollably.

49

IN THE AIRY BUNGALOW, WHERE THE SUNLIT LEAVES OUTSIDE DAPPLE the whitewashed rooms a pale and luminous green, Ren sits in the kitchen with Ah Long, stringing beans. Ah Long is pleased that he's back and has made clear chicken soup especially for Ren to drink, though he pretends gruffly that it's for William. It's been three days since Ren's sudden recovery and discharge from the hospital. Three days of stillness and rest, and wondering what happened to his girl in blue.

She's alive; he knows that. There's been much talk, even scandal, about what happened at the hospital on Monday. Rumors about ghostly curses and stolen body parts. The neighboring servants buzz with gossip, asking Ren if he heard anything while he was in hospital. He tells them truthfully that he didn't see anything, though that doesn't stop him from worrying. The person who knows the most is William, but he won't say much other than that Louise is perfectly fine and there's no need to worry.

"Louise" is what William calls Ji Lin, and when he says her name, Ren senses a gnawing guilt. It's something to do with what Dr. Rawlings said that tumultuous Monday, coming into the ward later as William was checking Ren out, and drawing him hastily aside. Ren overheard snatches of conversation: *missing body parts . . . scandal . . . say nothing until the Board sorts it out.* From which he gathers that there's a secret, like a white and yeasty maggot, which threatens to undermine the neat and orderly life of the hospital.

Whatever it is definitely bothers William. He spends his free time gloomily sitting on the veranda, as though he's waiting for something to happen. When Ren asks if he's feeling all right, he says he needs a drink to fortify his stomach.

"*Cheh!* What stomach?" says Ah Long contemptuously. "Ice is bad for his digestion. And not so much," he warns as Ren makes another whisky *stengah*. Johnnie Walker is running low again; there's only an inch left in the bottle. "Miss Lydia is coming today."

It's five o'clock in the afternoon, and William is home early from work. Instead of putting on a cotton sarong, he's remained in his stiff-collared shirt and trousers, and now Ren understands why. If Lydia is coming, of course his master can't lounge around in native dress. For teatime, Ah Long prepares bite-sized balls of *onde-onde*, a treat made from glutinous rice flour and chopped palm sugar rolled in fluffy grated coconut.

Guiltily, Ren remembers the vial of tea-colored liquid that he promised Lydia he'd give to Ji Lin. He hasn't had a chance to do so and is worried that she'll question him about it. Fetching the bottle from his room, he slips it into his pocket. If Lydia asks, he'll show it to her to prove he hasn't been careless or lost it.

The doorbell rings. Ren gets up slowly. His wounds are healing astonishingly fast, but he's still not used to the loss of his fourth finger. The stump aches and the grip of his left hand is less sure, though it hasn't stopped him from doing most things. Losing the thumb would have been far worse, as Ah Long dourly pointed out.

Voices in the hallway. Lydia sounds subdued, yet there's an underlying current of excitement that Ren picks up from her. He remembers the thin sticky filaments that clung to her in the hospital and peeks worriedly out. Is she still in danger? The slanting afternoon sunlight casts patterns of light and dark in the hall. Lydia takes off her sun hat and a trick of the shadows makes it look as though she has long dark hair. Ren stops, surprised. The open doorway, the woman standing in it. For a fearful instant, he's reminded of the *pontianak*, that vengeful female spirit that comes calling at the doors and windows. Instinctively he starts forward, although it's already too late. William has let her in. You're not supposed to let them in. But these are foolish thoughts that his master would be offended to hear. Perplexed, Ren blinks. The dimness in his head recedes; his cat sense is fading and maybe that's a relief as well.

Lydia hands Ren her hat and parasol and smiles benignly at him. William shows her into the sitting room with its bent rattan furniture moved back into place after the party. Normally he entertains male guests on the veranda, but with Lydia he's stiffly courteous.

"What can I do for you, Lydia?"

Ren admires how his master gets straight to the point, no beating around the bush. Lydia parries with small talk about the weather and the terrible tragedy at the hospital.

"I heard that you made a statement to the inspector," she says. "Did you really see someone on the second floor?"

"I can't discuss that right now," says William. "But the police have a suspect."

"Won't you tell me?"

"I'm sorry, it's out of my hands."

She seems dissatisfied at this. "What did you tell the police about me?"

"That you'd called and asked to meet me. And when I arrived, it looked like you had a prior meeting with that orderly, Y. K. Wong. Why did you want to see me that morning, anyway?" he says. "They wanted to know about that as well."

"I'm afraid I told a little untruth." Lydia shifts uneasily. "I said that you and I were in the habit of meeting because we were secretly engaged."

"What?"

"I'm sorry. It was all I could think of at the time."

William gets up and walks to the other end of the sofa. Ren, still standing quietly in the hallway, can tell that he's agitated, even furious.

"Why on earth would you do that?"

"Because it looks bad for me. You know, meeting men before dawn in a deserted place. And a Chinaman, too."

"Lydia," William presses his side as though it pains him, "you'd better tell me the truth."

Ren doesn't hear what she says because at that moment, Ah Long calls him into the kitchen. The tea tray is ready, steaming and fragrant, the sweetmeats delicately arranged on patterned porcelain plates.

"Can you manage?" says Ah Long.

"Yes," says Ren proudly. Still, Ah Long helps him bring the tray in, setting it on the sideboard.

Ren sneaks a glance at William and Lydia. Their heads are bent together. He can't see Lydia's face, but William looks upset. *Bad digestion, too much stress,* Ah Long had said, and Ren remembers the time, right when that poor lady's body was found half eaten by a tiger, when William could only eat omelets, not meat. But William never takes medicine, only Johnnie Walker.

Hesitantly, Ren takes out the vial of liquid that Lydia gave him. Stomach medicine, she'd said. *Very mild. I take it myself.* It's almost exactly the same color as the tea, and Ren pours it into William's cup. There. If Miss Lydia asks him if he's put her medicine to good use, he can answer her properly. She likes William anyway, so she'll be delighted if it cures him.

Carefully and proudly, Ren places the teacups on the table.

"WELL?" WILLIAM'S VOICE IS CALM BUT INSIDE HE'S SEETHING. "What exactly happened on Monday morning, that you couldn't tell the police?"

From the corner of his eye, he sees Ren pour the tea at the sideboard before placing it on the coffee table. This is the wrong procedure. Tea should be set on the low table for the host or hostess to pour, but that's something local servants never seem to understand. William forces his mind away from irrelevant thoughts like this. Lydia. He has to manage her.

Brushing back her hair, she glances up at him. She's looking very handsome today but it fills him with dread—that fine coloring, those brilliant eyes. So much like Iris.

Lydia says, "That Chinese orderly—he said his name was Wong—wanted to speak to me. About you."

"About me?" This is so surprising that William sits down again.

"Concerning one of your patients, a salesman who died recently."

The salesman! The one who caught William and Ambika together in the rubber plantation, so long ago now it seems. The one who died so fortuitously. William's pulse races, even as he struggles to keep his expression neutral.

Lydia spoons sugar into her tea. "Mr. Wong seemed to think that he'd been mixed up with selling human remains."

"Nonsense!" says William. This is exactly the kind of rumor that Rawlings told him to quash. If word gets out there will be a terrible scandal for the hospital.

"He also asked me if he'd ever tried to blackmail you."

"What?" William's stomach lurches, recalling the terror he felt, right after Ambika's mangled torso had been identified, that the salesman would come forward and tell everyone about their affair. But there's nothing to fear, is there? Despite Rawlings's doubts at the time, there's been no criminal investigation.

He lifts his teacup. It's too hot to drink. "Why ask you about that?"

"People think we're close. And we are, aren't we?"

William shudders at this assumption. "We're not close, Lydia. I can't have you telling people that we're engaged, when it's not true."

Her face turns red, her mouth trembles. "How could you say that—after everything I've done for you?"

A chill across the back of his neck, telling him to run, run away now. "I've never asked you to do anything for me."

"All the things that could have caused you problems—I got rid of them."

He shifts uneasily. Something is coming, approaching the doors of his mind. Something that he forgot or overlooked. He's not used to being hunted like this. It's wrong, all wrong. Outraged, he says, "I don't have any problems!"

But she's not listening. "Haven't you ever felt that you can change things, control them, if you wish hard enough?"

William flinches.

"You do, don't you? I knew you would. No one else understands." She clasps his hand. Her fingers are cold. "Well, I have that power, too. You probably know about it, since I heard you were asking around about my fiancés."

Fiancés. "There was more than one," says William, realization dawning on him.

"Yes, I was engaged twice. Three times if you count intentions. They were all no good, though. I didn't know how to choose, you see. I had to get rid of them."

Is she saying that she's like him, filled with that dark ominous power?

William's hand is numb. Pulling it away, he tries to say scornfully, "Are you saying you can wish people dead?"

"Can't you?"

William has never voiced this to anyone, but at that moment, drowning in Lydia's frenetic blue gaze, he almost does. "Everyone's wished someone dead at some point, Lydia. It doesn't mean anything."

"I did it for you," she says. "That salesman. And those women who were so bad for you. Why do you associate with them?"

Horror grows tendrils of blackness, twisting through his stomach.

"First was that Tamil woman Ambika, the one you used to meet in the rubber estate. I told you I'd seen you going for walks in the morning, though you never saw me. She was quite unsuitable, of course, and people were starting to talk, even our servants at home. So I removed her.

"Then that salesman turned up again. I knew him when he was a patient here. From time to time, he'd come by and visit that little nurse. We'd chat a bit—he was quite a flirt for a local." She smiles. "He was asking about you, hinting that Ambika was your mistress. I had to stop him, too."

Frozen, William listens as her rosebud mouth keeps moving, words spilling from it. A cold narrow thread of reason tells him it's impossible. Nobody can arrange for a death by tiger, or make a man break his neck. Lydia is just deeply disturbed, he tells himself, trying not to panic at how much she knows about his private life.

"Lydia," he says firmly. "That's enough. You're imagining things."

"No, I'm not." She stares at him over the rim of her teacup. "I did everything for you."

"I don't owe you anything!" And now William is furious, his stomach burning with acid. Foolish, stupid, troublesome woman! If she goes around talking like this, it will only turn out badly for him. He takes a deep breath and swallows a mouthful of tea. It's bitter.

Two spots of red appear on her cheeks. "There's a plant, a tall shrub with flowers. It's growing right outside your house. People think it's beautiful, but they don't know how poisonous oleander is. If you make a strong tea from the powdered leaves, it causes dizziness, nausea, vomiting. Then fainting, heart failure, and death." She recites the symptoms as though she's learned them by heart. "My father managed a tea plantation in Ceylon before, where it's common for young girls to commit suicide by eating the seeds. I kept some with me when I went back to England. It was very use-ful." She takes another sip of tea. "When I came out here, it was easy to prescribe to people. I help at the hospital after all; the locals believe what I say. I gave Ambika a tonic for female complaints—she must have wan-dered out and died in the plantation. Though I didn't expect that a tiger would eat half of her."

"It didn't eat her," says William, his voice cracking with strain.

She ignores him. "The same thing for the salesman, though I told him it was stomach medicine. He vomited and fell into a ditch."

"And Nandani? Did you give it to her, too?"

"She was sitting right there, in your kitchen." Lydia turns her feverish gaze to him. "It was for the best. She'd already caused a scene, showing up like that at dinner."

William's hands are shaking. Bile rises in his throat. "I'm calling the police."

Is it disappointment, or triumph, in her eyes? "You won't do that."

"Lydia, I can't perjure myself for you."

"Then for Iris," she says, her eyes glittering. "I know what you did."

William's throat closes, bony fingers pinching it, squeezing the air out of him. "What are you talking about?"

"You drowned her, that day on the river."

That day on the river, the light slanting green and gold. Iris turning angry, the black mood coming down on her. Accusing him again in her unending jealousy, jabbing her finger in his chest in the way that absolutely maddened him in all their quarrels so that he shoved her, hard. Or did she trip and fall by herself? Even he can't remember, or doesn't want to.

"It was an accident!"

"She would never stand up in a boat. Not ever, no matter what you said." Lydia's not pretty at all now, not one bit. She looks like a witch, her eyes wild and cunning. "Iris had a bad sense of balance. We all knew that at school. Something to do with her ears."

"Lydia—"

"And even after she fell in, you didn't pull her out."

He'd thought he'd teach Iris a lesson, let her flounder for a bit before pulling her out. But she'd gone under very quickly, the heavy woolen skirts dragging her down. So fast that William thought she was playing a joke on him, holding her breath to pretend she was in trouble. Who knew that a person could drown so quickly, so silently, without any of the wild thrashings that he'd imagined? By the time he went after her, she was nothing but dead weight.

"Lydia!" He has to stop her, spewing out these hateful words.

"Iris wrote me letters. Lots of them. About you and how she thought you were cheating on her. I have a letter written right before she died, saying she was afraid you'd kill her."

Don't panic, William thinks, biting down. After all, that's what he did about Iris. *She was leaning over and then she fell in. No, we hadn't quarreled.* Still, there were whispers and rumors that followed him. The same insidious tale of betrayal and cowardice, enough to cut him at the Club, enough to drive him to another place, another country. He fights to control himself.

"She was hysterical, manipulative."

Lydia leans back. "You're right." There's a faint smile on her face. "But you might be charged, given the circumstantial evidence, if you went back home." Another sip of tea. "I've made it fair, haven't I? I've told you all about myself. Though unlike you, I can easily deny everything."

"What about the deaths of all those people? The salesman, Ambika, Nandani?"

"Why, you killed them. They were all in your way. I'll say you got rid of the women because you wanted to marry me, but I turned you down. The police are already suspicious about Nandani being in your house right before she died, and if they dig up the talk about Iris from back home, it won't look good for you."

Silence. He hears the pounding rush of blood in his head. If he springs up right now, he can catch her by her long white throat. Dig his thumbs in until she stops breathing. Why, why is this happening again? Her resemblance to Iris, the same sticky, hysterical demands. It's as though Iris has returned from the river and she'll never be satisfied until she drags him under.

"What do you want, Lydia?"

She's going to play her trump card, whatever it is. Stomach leaden, William knows that he's been completely outfoxed by her.

"I love you," she says.

He gets up. Circles behind her, his mind racing through different possibilities. Shove her forward, crack her head open on the coffee table. She's infected him with her madness.

"So you want to get engaged?" A gun accident then. Showing Lydia the Purdey. But he's already shot Ren accidentally. Too suspicious.

"Yes. I'd like that." She smiles, as though he's just proposed on bended knee. "I've already told the police, but it would be nice to make it official. We could have a party."

"I'll think about it."

"A toast then?" she says. William numbly picks up his cup and clinks it against hers. *Play along; buy some time*, he thinks, draining the tepid, bitter tea. No amount of milk and sugar can disguise the vomit rising in his throat as he forces it down.

A swish of skirts, that light scent of geraniums that he hates now. He shows her to the door. Good manners, even if it's killing him. Lydia pauses, her eyes bright. "After we're married, I can't be compelled to testify against you. Nor you against me. It makes it fair, doesn't it?"

William wants to scream, smack her head into the wall, but he says through gritted teeth, "Why do you care for me at all?"

"Iris introduced us back in England, though you don't remember. It was a party at the Piersons'; you liked me, you really did. Afterwards, you kissed me in the hallway. I couldn't stop thinking of you for days."

Memory. The ticking of the grandfather clock, that quick, feverish fumble in the darkness. He'd been so happy with Iris that day, her pert face never more alluring, that he'd cornered her, so he'd thought, in the hallway. And afterwards, there'd been days of brooding sulkiness. Iris complaining that he'd drunk too much that weekend, the accusations that he'd brushed off, attributing them to her neuroses, his aching head. He says with sharp, sudden understanding, "That was a mistake. I never knew it was you."

But Lydia doesn't care. She's gone beyond him. A dreamy look fills her eyes. "And then when Iris kept writing about how unhappy you were with her, I knew that something would happen to make her disappear. Because you and I are fated to be together: we even have the same name. The other night, at your party, when you wrote your Chinese name—I told you that I have a Chinese name as well. I was born in Hong Kong, you know."

What is she babbling about? Doesn't she have any sense of danger from him?

"My Chinese name has the same character—*Li* for *Li di ya*—as yours. It's one of the Confucian Virtues," she says.

Ren comes into the hallway to hand Lydia her hat and parasol. He stares at her, eyes huge in his small face. William thinks feverishly. Play along; he has always been able to manage. There'll be time enough to deal with her.

"We'll need more servants after we're married," says Lydia, looking appreciatively around the large, empty bungalow.

Over my dead body, thinks William. But he smiles and shows her out.

50

SHIN'S ARM WAS BROKEN. THE RIGHT ONE, AS HE POINTED OUT WITH rueful humor. My stepfather had broken the left one, and now it was my turn: a strangely fearful symmetry. I said I was sorry, resting my head briefly against his shoulder after all the uproar was over and we were finally alone. They'd put us into a private room temporarily, though the only serious injury was Shin's arm and some cuts and bruises.

"You're very lucky," said the local doctor who'd examined me. "The other chap broke your fall."

I fell silent at the mention of Koh Beng. My statement to the police about how he'd tried to kill me, as well as the whole business of selling fingers as good luck charms, made both the hospital and the local police look bad: the hospital for not keeping track of human remains, and the police for failing to prevent an attempted murder right after Y. K. Wong had been killed that very morning. Already, a rumor had conveniently spread that Koh Beng had gone mad and run amok. In the meantime, they'd been especially nice to Shin and me.

"Well, that's the end of my job," said Shin, gazing at the cast on his arm.

"Perhaps they'll let you do something else," I said.

"Don't be silly. I can't write, either, so no desk jobs."

It didn't matter. I was filled with gratitude to be sitting here with him, remembering how I'd thought we'd be sundered forever by death. But my joy was tempered with grief. What had happened to Yi? His last words, *don't forget me*, struck me as a plaintive echo of his previous lament: *I don't want Ren to forget me.* Was he still waiting at that empty station, or had he given up and gone onward, alone? Wherever he was, I prayed he'd find mercy. I owed him a great debt.

I released Shin's hand guiltily as yet another nurse came in. So many nurses had come by to visit, giggling and perching flirtatiously on his bed. I'd told the police that Shin was my brother, so I could only sit by and smile. It was all right; I was used to this.

"Why won't you let me set them straight?" Shin said, annoyed, after the last nurse was gone.

"Not now." We had to think things through. Figure out how to get around our parents first, and not have it spread as gossip. My mother would have a fit when she found out we'd been shoved off a building. A wave of exhaustion rolled over me; the hospital smelled like disinfectant and boiled onions.

"I'll come and see you tomorrow," I said, standing up.

He grabbed my hand. "Stay. They offered to keep you tonight for observation."

"There's nothing wrong with me. And I should tell my mother we're all right." The news had probably leaked all over Batu Gajah and possibly even up to Ipoh by now. Besides, the hospital made me deeply uneasy, though I didn't want to mention this to Shin in case he worried. When I gazed out of the window, I could see the distant roof where Koh Beng had tried to kill me.

"Then I'll go home with you," said Shin.

OF COURSE, THEY WOULDN'T LET HIM GO, CLAIMING SHIN'S ARM needed more X-rays tomorrow morning. They tried to keep me as well, though I demurred. It seemed less about our well-being than an attempt to keep things under control. The medical director had already come by, assuring us that the hospital had only the highest standards and was deeply sorry for the actions of an employee who'd had a nervous breakdown (that would be Koh Beng, I presumed), and we could only nod and promise not to talk about it until the police had cleared things up.

Matron herself came to see me off. Her tanned, angular face was thoughtful as we waited for the car that the hospital had provided to drive me back. "So what are the two of you—siblings or engaged to be married?"

I looked down. "We're stepsiblings, but we're not really engaged."

"Sounds complicated," she said, not unkindly. "I'll keep your secret, if you like. Good luck." She shook my hand. I liked her firm, no-nonsense grip. "You seem like a smart girl, and sensible, too. If you don't want to rely on a man, we might have space for you."

I thanked her, wondering why I wasn't as thrilled as I might have been. Perhaps the hospital had instructed her to offer me a job, to keep things quiet. I was tired. So tired that all I wanted to do was close my eyes, though I was afraid that if I did so, I'd find myself back in that dark river. And this time, there'd be no coming back.

THE NEXT FEW DAYS WERE QUIET. MY MOTHER AND STEPFATHER were surprisingly subdued about the whole affair. The hospital had already notified them in the blandest of terms: an unfortunate accident with a mentally disturbed individual. And of course, they would cover all medical fees and pay Shin's salary for the rest of the summer, though he was excused from duties. Although my mother exclaimed over my cuts, she was relieved that my face wasn't marked.

"A girl's face is so important," she said as she helped change the dressing on my side. "Imagine how upset Robert would be!"

"What does Robert have to do with this?"

I shouldn't have said that. Her face fell and that timid look appeared. "You're still friends, aren't you?"

"As much as we ever were." Which wasn't much, but I didn't have the heart to say so. I looked down, suddenly anxious. "Did you manage to make this month's payment?"

I hadn't given her quite enough money to cover the loan, but to my surprise, she said, "You mustn't worry about that anymore. Your stepfather paid it."

"All of it?"

She hesitated. "No. Shin gave me some money to help pay it down." I understood, without her saying a word, that it must have been terrifying to confess even that reduced amount to my stepfather.

"Was he furious?" I stared at her arms, her narrow wrists. She was wearing loose sleeves; I couldn't tell if there was anything amiss.

"He had a right to be."

"And? Did he do anything else?" Fury and despair were rising in me, choking my throat.

My mother looked down at the floor. I realized this was deeply humiliating for her. "I begged him. I cried so hard that I fainted." At my look of horror, she said quickly, "It was actually a good thing. It worried him, coming after the miscarriage. I suppose he realized it wasn't worth it. And I'm fine." A grimace. "He made me swear not to touch a mahjong tile again."

Catching my anxious eye, my mother gave me a warning look. This time, it was none of my business. I supposed that the scare over my mother's miscarriage might have softened my stepfather up. Made him realize that he might be widowed again. Still, it was a tremendous relief. That debt had been hanging like an anvil over our heads. My mother smiled weakly. "Perhaps I should have told him from the start. I'm sure Robert would be milder about things like that."

"Mother, does it have to be Robert?"

She must have heard the sadness in my voice, because she stopped fiddling with my bandages and hugged me. "No, it doesn't. As long as he makes you happy."

"Really?" My spirits rose. Why had I ever doubted her?

"Does Shin approve?"

"Of who?"

"Of whomever it is you like."

I couldn't stop smiling. "Yes, he does."

51

REN WATCHES HIS MASTER CLOSELY AFTER LYDIA'S DEPARTURE. DOES his stomach feel better after drinking the medicine? But William goes out to the veranda, tearing at his stiff collar as though he can't breathe. He sits there, motionless, head in his hands as somewhere out in the dense jungle canopy, a bird sings. It's a *merbuk*, a zebra dove whose soft haunting call echoes through the vast green space.

"*Tuan*, are you sick?"

William turns, face pale and beaded with sweat. He doesn't look well, but he smiles briefly. "You're a good boy, Ren. I've been thinking: would you like to go to school?"

Surprised by this good fortune, Ren can only blink and stammer. "Yes. But the housework—"

"You needn't worry about that. We'll be getting new servants anyway."

Does this mean that Ren has lost his job? "Of course not," says William, reading his worried look. "There'll be some changes; it can't be helped. But I'll make sure you go to school. It's the least I can do." He makes a wry face.

Ren understands about guilt and bewilderment. Yi hasn't come to his dreams anymore, not since the last time by the river. In fact, he can find no trace of his twin at all. That faint radio signal has ceased transmitting, or is it tuned to another station now, one that he can't hear? Whatever it is, he thinks of Yi with love and sadness. One day, they will be together again.

/////

DISMISSED, REN STARTS BACK TO THE KITCHEN. THEN HE TURNS. It's not his place to ask, but he gathers up all his courage. "*Tuan*, are you marrying Miss Lydia?"

A tilt of the head. It's hard to read his master's expression. "You don't like that idea?"

"She said her Chinese name was Li. Like yours."

"Does it make us a good match, then?" There's bitterness in William's voice. Ren wonders what the rest of that long conversation was about, the one that ended with Lydia looking so pleased and his master so ashen.

"I don't know," says Ren honestly. He's confused. Which one of them is the mysterious *Li* then? Or perhaps he's been mistaken and neither of them is. Pressing his fingers into the numb white mark on his elbow only makes him dizzy, the air grows heavy and dark. He remembers the filmy cobwebs clinging to Lydia that made him recoil. "She'll make things difficult for you, that lady."

William smiles humorlessly and says something about *out of the mouths of babes*. Then he announces he's tired and is going to bed. No need for dinner tonight. His feet drag on the stairs, like a man sentenced to death.

THE NEXT MORNING, WILLIAM DOESN'T COME DOWN. AH LONG, frowning at the untouched breakfast, cocks his head at Ren. "Go and see what's happened."

Ren climbs the stairs, feeling the smooth, cool wood beneath his bare feet. All the way up, like a cabin boy climbing the lookout mast. At the window at the top, he remembers how he'd thought of the white bungalow as a ship in a storm, the deep green jungle a rolling ocean. In it were all manner of strange beasts, including Dr. MacFarlane, roaming around in the form of a tiger.

Ren shakes his head; the image vanishes. Already it's receding, that dim fearfulness about his old master: the dark loneliness, the promises about severed fingers and digging up graves. Even his worries about forty-nine days have subsided, a calamity averted though if you asked Ren, he couldn't tell you what or why. Only that he's certain, down to his bones, that the finger has returned to Dr. MacFarlane. He has an odd vision—small and bright, like a fever dream—of Ji Lin on her knees, digging hastily with a spade. Dropping something in, then sealing it under the damp red earth. Whatever happened, he has faith that she wouldn't let him down. Though since he woke up in the hospital after Nandani's death, he can no longer recall these things well, as though the long night has ended and day has begun. A day that beckons with the promise of school. Excited, Ren quickens his steps. Dr. MacFarlane would have been pleased; he always meant to send Ren to school.

The door to William's room is closed. Ren knocks, then tries the handle softly. It's locked. Puzzled and a little frightened, Ren reports to Ah Long.

"Is he sick?"

"Might be."

Ah Long gets up. He rummages in the kitchen drawer, then together they ascend the stairs. The house is so quiet that Ren imagines that everything—the walls and the ceiling, the grass outside and the bowl-shaped whiteness of the sky—is holding its breath. No sound but the quiet padding of their feet and the thudding of Ren's heart. At the locked door, Ah Long stops and bends his ear to the keyhole. Nothing.

With a sigh, he reaches into his pocket and pulls out the enormous bunch of keys that he keeps in the kitchen drawer. He searches through them, counting under his breath. Takes one out and fits it to the lock. As the door swings open, he says sharply, "Don't come in!"

Frightened, Ren waits outside. He doesn't need to listen to Ah Long's hasty movements. Walking over to the bed, drawing back the curtains. That stillness is familiar to him—the one that tells him that the occupant of the room has gone away forever. And Ren, leaning back against the wall, feels hot tears stream silently down his face.

52

AND SO WE WERE BACK WHERE WE STARTED. IN THAT LONG, DIM shophouse filled with the metallic scent of tin ore and the dampness that seeped from the lower floor. Discharged from the hospital, his broken arm in a neat white cast, Shin had come home.

My mother was happy that we were both back, though I was due to return to Mrs. Tham's in a few days. I should visit Hui, too. Tell her that I'd quit the May Flower, though she'd probably figured it out by now. There were so many matters I wanted to discuss with Shin, but we had no opportunity. My stepfather's silent presence filled the front of the shophouse where he conducted business, and my mother twittered about, cooking our favorite childhood dishes, though I begged her not to strain herself.

"It's good that you're home," she said, fussing over Shin's arm.

That was one thing I was glad about at least, that she was so fond of him. Perhaps it would all come out right for us. After all, Ren had been discharged after making a remarkable recovery. And neither Shin nor I had died yet. I kept my thoughts about Yi to myself, hugging them like a sad secret. If the dead lived on in people's memories, then I'd keep him safe forever.

THAT NIGHT I SAT AT THE KITCHEN TABLE IN THE WARM POOL OF lamplight, rereading *The Adventures of Sherlock Holmes*. I'd loved it enough to buy my own copy from the secondhand bookstore, though Koh Beng and his string of murders had dampened my enthusiasm for detective work. Still, it was better than being left to my own thoughts. My mother and stepfather had gone up to bed, and Shin was out with Ming.

The reality of what Shin and I were doing weighed on me. What sort of future would we have? Perhaps in this life, Shin and I could only be siblings, false twins destined to be together, yet apart. It was so still that I could hear the clock ticking far in the front of the shophouse. A hollow chiming. Ten o'clock. The rattle of the front door. And now Shin was back, his quick familiar step walking down the long dark passageway, past the heavy weighing scales, past the first open courtyard with its piles of drying tin ore.

"Shin," I called softly, getting up.

It was dim in the corridor, where the yellow lamplight spilled from the kitchen. All my thoughts, my good intentions flew out of my head when I saw him. Wordlessly, I tugged him over to the table. He gave a sharp glance upstairs.

"They're asleep," I said.

We sat next to each other, demurely. I felt oddly shy, my pulse racing. How strange it was, to be sitting like this in my stepfather's house. As though everything and nothing had changed between us. If I closed my eyes, we could have been ten years old again.

"What shall we do, Shin?"

He curled his fingers around mine. The slant of his eyebrows looked oddly vulnerable. "First, we'll get a copy of your birth certificate. I've already got mine. Then we'll go and register our marriage."

"What?" I straightened up.

"My father said so, didn't he? When you're married, you're not his responsibility anymore."

"He'll kill us!"

"He won't. He set the conditions himself. It didn't matter who it was, as long as he had a decent job. Of course, he was thinking of Robert." Shin scowled. "Anyway, you and I aren't related, not even on paper. My father never adopted you—I checked."

I didn't know whether to laugh or quail at Shin's brazenness. "Are you sure you want to marry me? Aren't you still a scholarship student?"

"I've been planning this for years." He was utterly serious.

"What if I don't want to marry you?"

"You will."

His lips brushed mine. Lightly, but my legs went weak and a dizziness took hold of me. It was like a spell, a conjurer's trick that pressed the air out of my lungs. Shin looked at me triumphantly. I had that feeling again, of love and longing and wanting to smack him all at once.

"People will talk."

"Let them."

Soft, urgent kisses. The moist heat of his mouth, the delicate probing of his tongue. That fluttering in my chest again, like a bird that yearned to fly. Shin's good arm encircled my waist; I shivered as he pressed me, hard, against the chair. My breath came in faint gasps. Using his teeth and his good left hand, he started to unbutton my thin cotton blouse. I should stop him, I knew it, but my fingers slid through his hair instead.

"Don't laugh," said Shin in mock indignation. "You're the reason my arm is broken."

In answer, I pressed my mouth against his. We were so absorbed in each other that we didn't notice the creak of the stairs, and then my mother's horrified whisper.

What are you doing?

Shin's hand froze on my half-unbuttoned blouse. We sprang to our feet, a dull roaring in my ears. His face was crimson.

"Mother," I said.

But she wasn't looking at me. "How dare you touch my daughter!" Even then, I noticed she kept her voice down, hissing the words out.

"It's not his fault, it's mine!"

It was then that she slapped me. My mother had never hit me across the face before. Disciplined, yes, with a weak switch when I was smaller, though she was easily talked out of punishing me. But never like this: a blow that made me gasp. The strange and terrible thing was that all this took place in near silence. None of us dared to raise our voices in that hushed dark house. We knew what would happen if my stepfather woke up.

I gripped my mother's frail shoulders, then let go. If I wanted to, I could easily have shoved her back. On the rooftop with Koh Beng, I'd fought desperately, kicking and scratching. But I couldn't raise a hand to my mother. Neither could Shin. The two of us stood with bowed and guilty heads as she slumped suddenly, as if the life had gone out of her. "Didn't I raise you properly?" she muttered. "Why are you doing this?"

"I love him," I said.

"Love?" my mother said. "What were you thinking?"

She wept, then, in that dreadful, silent way that unnerved me. The way all of us had learned to cry in this house, without making a sound. Stricken, I found myself helplessly consoling her. It was always like this. No matter what happened, I'd try to save her. I glanced at Shin, signaling him to leave the kitchen.

But instead of heeding me, he knelt before her. I'd never seen Shin get on his knees to anyone, he was too proud, but now here he was lowering his head.

"Mother," he said. "I'm serious about Ji Lin. Please let me marry her."

At the word *marriage*, my mother's body arched in a rictus, as though she was having a spasm. Alarmed, I caught her in my arms.

"You can't get married," she said faintly. "You're family now. I absolutely forbid it."

ONE OF THE APPALLING YET CONVENIENT THINGS ABOUT BEING family is that you can trade dreadful accusations at night, then pretend next morning that nothing has happened. Because that's exactly what we did at breakfast. We all came down, quiet and somber, and my mother dished out limp, steaming hanks of noodles. The noodles were bland, as though she'd forgotten how to cook. Her eyes were swollen, but she told my stepfather that she hadn't slept because of a headache.

He grunted, and I hoped that he hadn't noticed anything. After all, he was a heavy sleeper. Shin and I sat, unnaturally still, like two cardboard siblings in a perfect cardboard family.

"I'm going back to Singapore at the end of the week," Shin announced.

My mother nodded. She bent over her tasteless noodles, just as my stepfather did.

"Ji Lin is coming with me," said Shin. "She can get a job there."

Now both heads went up.

My stepfather's eyes narrowed. "Why her?"

"The truth is, there was a murder at the Batu Gajah hospital on Monday. Another orderly was killed by the same man who tried to shove Ji Lin off the roof. The police asked us not to talk about it, but there's a scandal brewing. Why do you think the hospital is paying me for not working? In return, they've asked us both to leave the area."

"Is that right?" his father said.

I glanced at Shin. He was an inspired liar, mixing half-truths and facts. "Yes. It will be in the newspaper soon."

My mother let out an exclamation of horror, though her eyes filled with suspicion. I squeezed Shin's hand under the table.

"You can ask Robert—his father's on the Board," I said.

It irked me how anything connected with Robert and his family carried weight with my mother. I could see the confusion on her face.

"They've arranged a position for me at a hospital in Singapore, as a trainee nurse. I'll live in a dormitory." This was pure fiction now, but nobody was stopping me. "Shin can take me down, because Robert doesn't have the time."

Robert again. But my mother wasn't fooled, shaking her head vehemently. "No, you can't go!"

My stepfather said, "What does Robert think about this plan of going to Singapore?"

"He wants me to study and get proper qualifications. And less scandal is better for his family." Amazing how easy it was to lie when I really wanted something. I apologized to poor Robert in my head.

"If Robert thinks it's a good idea, then it's fine by me," my stepfather said. And at that moment I was glad, so glad that he was hard and unyielding, only valuing the opinions of men. My mother's protests were overruled; after all, she dared give no reason other than Singapore was too far away.

"Shin will take her down," said my stepfather. "And she won't be our responsibility for too long."

"But Robert's family is in Ipoh," my mother said. She glanced from Shin to me in anguish, and I wondered if she would betray us. If so, we'd all suffer. My pulse raced unevenly. Shin had his most wooden look on, though a muscle twitched in his cheek.

"They have a house in Singapore," he said, examining his noodles as though he couldn't care less whether he took me along or not. "I'm sure he goes there all the time."

My stepfather nodded. And so it was settled.

I SHOULD HAVE BEEN HAPPY. GOODNESS KNOWS, SHIN WAS. HE could hardly stop grinning as the days dwindled before our departure, though by unspoken agreement, we avoided each other completely. He bought railway tickets for us, and I went to see Mrs. Tham and clear out my room over her dress shop.

"Are you getting married?" she asked, as I folded the last of my meager possessions. No beating around the bush with her.

"No, I'm going to study nursing." I'd repeated this lie so many times that it almost felt real to me, though I had to remind myself that I had no job prospects and nowhere to live. Still, I was buoyed by a simmering excitement.

"A nurse," said Mrs. Tham thoughtfully. "I don't think you'll be good at that."

"Why not?" I was stung by this casual assessment; she'd been pleased enough with my dressmaking skills.

"You're bound to contradict the doctors. I think you'd better get married."

I bent over to hide my smile.

"What makes you think I won't contradict my husband?"

"Oh, you mustn't do that!" She looked horrified, though we both knew perfectly well who ruled the Tham household. "Listen," Mrs. Tham said, drawing close, "the secret to a happy marriage is to make him think it's all his own idea. And of course, you should dress well and look as pretty as you can."

She gave a dissatisfied sigh as she contemplated me. All her stylish work was undone, as I was wearing an old pair of cotton trousers and a worn shirt to pack. "Make sure you hang on to him—women will be over him like flies."

Mrs. Tham gave me a knowing look as she went out, and I wondered whether she was talking about Robert, or someone else. She might have found out that Shin and I weren't related; I wouldn't put it past her.

I SAW HUI, TOO. I COULDN'T EXPLAIN EVERYTHING THAT HAD happened because of my promise to the police and the hospital director, but I tried my best.

"You could have told me you were quitting. I had to find out for myself."

She was indignant and a bit hurt. I could only nod and say I was sorry. I really liked Hui—I'd never had a friend like her before, though I was afraid I'd sadly disappointed her by not sharing all my secrets

"Thank you for helping me with Robert," I said, remembering how she'd flung herself into the fray, when Y. K. Wong had led him to the dance hall. "Be nice to him if you see him again."

Hui rolled her eyes. "Rich young men are wasted on you." But she smiled at last.

THE CONVERSATION I MOST DREADED, HOWEVER, WAS WITH MY mother. There was no getting away from it; I could see it in her anguished glances, her trembling hands. Of all people, I'd hoped that once the shock was over, perhaps my mother would come around to it. After all, she loved both Shin and me—just not together. Well, there was a price to be paid for everything.

So I could only sit guiltily on my bed late one evening, after my stepfather was asleep, and let her scold me. Shin had, diplomatically, gone to Ming's. The sight of him nowadays seemed to infuriate her. He'd gone from favored son to her daughter's seducer, and nothing I said would change her mind.

"It's not right," she kept saying. "People will talk; it doesn't seem proper. And Shin's never kept a girlfriend long. What if he changes his mind?"

"Then I'll just make my own way," I said.

She threw her hands up. "A girl only has one chance to marry well. This whole relationship is a mistake! You're confused because you're fond of him, like a brother. Besides, at your age it all seems romantic." All of sudden, she fixed me with a horrified look. "You didn't . . . you haven't slept with him?"

Why did everyone ask about that—what business was it of theirs? But of course I knew why. Humiliating as it was, it was blood currency: a girl could still find a husband if she could prove her virginity, even if he were old and fat and ugly. "What do you think?" I said bitterly.

Her eyes clouded with doubt, and I felt betrayed. Finally, she nodded timidly. "Of course I trust you. But don't do it. Promise me! It gives you the option to change your mind. I don't want you to ruin yourself, throw all your chances away."

"Mother," I said. "Do you really hate Shin that much?"

"I don't. He's a good boy. Just . . . I wish he wasn't for you. I was afraid of something like this, but you were always hung up on Ming. And I thought it would pass when Shin went away. I didn't think he'd be so stubborn. Marriage isn't easy. It doesn't always turn out the way you expect." Her gaze slid sideways. "You know your stepfather has a temper."

"Shin's never raised a hand against me!"

"But he's still young." She twisted her hands. "You don't know what he'll be like when he's older."

Fair enough, I thought, struggling to be stoic, though I wanted to shout and protest she was wrong and Shin was nothing like his father. Most of all, though, I wanted my mother to forgive me, and bless me, and tell me everything would be all right, just as she had when I was little, and there were only the two of us in the whole wide world. But perhaps that was part of not being a child anymore.

ON SATURDAY, WE STOOD ON A PLATFORM AT THE IPOH RAILWAY Station. It was a beautiful morning, all white and gold. I had only a suitcase and a box, tied neatly with string. Gazing at the painstaking knots that my mother had tied, I felt a lump in my throat. My pretty dresses were packed away, and I was wearing one of Mrs. Tham's best confections since, despite my protests, she'd insisted on seeing us off.

It turned out to be a blessing that she and Mr. Tham came, because her chirping commentary made the goodbyes bearable despite the tears that threatened to fall from my mother's eyes. They'd brought an enormous bag of mangosteens and a tiffin carrier of steamed pork buns, as though we might starve before reaching Singapore. It would be a long journey south: four hours to Kuala Lumpur, then an overnight sleeper of eight hours to Singapore. A total of about 345 miles—farther than I'd ever been in my life.

As the train slowly pulled out, everyone began to wave frantically in some unspoken semaphore. Even my stepfather, usually so undemonstrative, raised a hand, though I couldn't tell whether it was directed at Shin or me. At the last moment, my mother ran up alongside the train. I was filled with sudden panic. Was she going to denounce us? But she simply pressed the palm of her hand against the window. I fit my hand against it, all five fingers. Then she was gone, blown past by the gathering rush of the train.

Goodbye, I thought, as their figures shrank, left behind by the steady clack of the wheels, the humming of the track. Goodbye to my old life, and hello to the rest of it, whatever it might bring. Excitement and melancholy knotted my stomach, and I thought once again of Yi, that small boy left behind on a railway platform. Had he really gone away? I had the odd certainty that the ties binding all of us had been remade in a new and different pattern. *I'll never forget you*, I promised. My fingers curled around the letter in my pocket. I'd missed my chance to drop it in the post box, but I'd do it when we stopped in Kuala Lumpur.

THE OUTSKIRTS OF IPOH FLEW PAST—COCONUT PALMS, WOODEN *kampung* houses on stilts, a skinny yellow Brahmin cow—until green jungle pressed in on both sides.

"I'll have to find a place to stay in Singapore," I said, recalling how we'd lied about a hospital dorm.

"That's easy," said Shin. "I've got some money saved up."

"But that's your savings. I don't want to use it."

"Why'd you think I've been working? I wanted to bring you to Singapore."

"Really?" My heart skipped a beat. All those long, lonely months when I'd waited for Shin's nonexistent replies to my letters.

"Though I didn't know if you'd come. You were stuck on Ming for years. I was afraid if he changed his mind, you'd go running to him. You've given me more trouble than all the other girls combined." His mouth twitched. "We need to keep you busy. Perhaps you can sit in on lectures."

"I'd like that."

Shin shook his head ruefully. "Why do you look so much happier about this than a ring? Please don't ditch me for a surgeon."

I shuddered. "No more surgeons."

"I'll borrow your class notes every night," he said with mock seduction. My stomach gave a little flip. If Shin kept looking at me like that, I was going to make a fool of myself, and he knew it.

"Shin." I took a deep breath. This was going to be difficult to say.

In answer, he traced the palm of my hand delicately with his finger.

"We can't get married." I stared straight out of the window. His finger stopped. "At least, not now."

He was silent for a long time. "Because of your mother?"

"No, we ought to think things through properly—it will be hard for you at school and work. People will talk. And I want to live on my own for a bit. Find a job, take care of myself. I don't want you to be responsible for me, when you're still studying. And I'm not ready to get married right away."

"How long?"

"I'm not sure."

"A year," he said without looking at me. "In a year and a day, if you haven't made up your mind, then you'll be mine."

"I told you there's no such thing as belonging to anyone!"

But he only said maddeningly, "There has to be a time limit. Otherwise we'll just go on and on like this. I refuse to play at being twins anymore."

A year and a day. It sounded like a dark path strewn with thorny vines and unknown beasts. Were we out of the jungle yet, Shin and I? I'd no idea of the terrain ahead, but perhaps that was all right. I had a sudden vision of high-ceilinged rooms, long sunlit hallways, and quiet libraries. The King Edward Medical College, of which I'd heard so much. Shin laughing across a table with a group of fellow students. Myself, getting on a crowded bus while balancing a box full of books. Frying rice in a cramped apartment kitchen, listening for familiar quick footsteps on the stairs. Shin and me, walking by a river in the cool evening air, eating fried bananas and arguing companionably. Strangely enough, in all these scenes I was dressed fashionably enough to please Mrs. Tham. The breeze from the open train window whipped my short hair and bangs. My heart soared.

"All right," I said, laughing. "Friends?"

Shin rolled his eyes, but stuck his hand out in the familiar gesture. "Your mother said some terrible things about me the other night. But she was right. I'm definitely going to seduce you."

53

WHEN IT'S ALL OVER—THE POLICE AND THE FUNERAL AND THE well-meaning rush of visitors—Ren sits on the back kitchen steps. The house is empty; there's only him and Ah Long left packing up the master's things. Not that there's much. William had very few personal effects though he had, in his characteristically efficient way, drawn up a will. Very recently, the lawyer said. Ren knows about lawyers; he remembers the one in Taiping who took care of Dr. MacFarlane's affairs, and how he'd grimaced at the mess of papers stuffed into the crannies of the old doctor's desk. But William's affairs are neatly arranged.

Heart failure was the official verdict. Miss Lydia made a scene at the funeral, crying and carrying on that she was his fiancée, which was a surprise to lots of people, including her own parents. Her grief and fury were astonishing. Embarrassing, even. She wanted everything that had belonged to him, but the lawyer said she wasn't in the will and a fiancée wasn't the same as a wife. The servants have spread the gossip through their swift channels, and everyone knows about this by now.

Ah Long sighs and shrugs. "Lucky he didn't marry her." The lines on his face are deeper and his wiry frame has shrunk. As he moves around the empty house, packing away the good silver and crystal to be sent back to the Acton family, his steps are slow and less sure. He doesn't seem to care about the bequest that William has made: *To my Chinese cook, Ah Long, a sum of forty Malayan dollars for his loyal service,* though it is a princely gift.

Ren doesn't have the heart to rejoice, either, despite the fact he, too, is mentioned. There's a scholarship fund for Ren to go to school, though the monies can only be used for education.

"I don't want it," he says to the lawyer's surprise.

"Why not?"

"I don't want to study. Not right now."

The lawyer frowns. "Why not wait? Give yourself time to think about it."

AFTER HIS DEPARTURE, AH LONG CALLS REN OVER TO THE FORMAL dining room, the table's polished surface marked by neat piles of unopened mail. They're all addressed to William and will be forwarded to his family.

"What is it?" Ren asks.

Ah Long holds up a white envelope. For a dizzying second, Ren wonders whether his master has finally received an answer from that lady Iris, the one that he wrote letter after letter to. But no, this letter is for Ren. His name is written on it as a single Chinese character. That's the part that Ah Long can, thankfully, read.

"For me?" Ren has never in his short life received anything like a letter, though he knows how to write one. Dr. MacFarlane taught him the format, when they were practicing dictation. Ren slits the envelope open carefully. Inside is a single piece of paper.

"Who's it from?" asks Ah Long suspiciously.

But Ren is reading slowly. It's short, no more than a few sentences, and when he's read it through twice, he tucks it away.

"From that girl," he says.

"The one with short hair, from the party?"

Ren nods, impressed by Ah Long's memory.

"What did she say?"

Ren hesitates. How to explain it, this reluctance to share her words? Simple ones, but private. "She said she'd always remember me." *And Yi.* "And that we'd meet again. There's an address here if I want to write to her, care of Lee Shin at the medical college."

Ah Long grunts. Somehow, he seems satisfied.

////

THE NEXT DAY, IN THE STILL, HOT AFTERNOON, AN UNEXPECTED visitor appears. It's Dr. Rawlings. Waving aside Ah Long's attempts to serve him tea, he sits at the kitchen table and studies Ren's forlorn little figure. "Do you have a place to go?" he asks.

A headshake. "I might go to Kuala Lumpur. To see Auntie Kwan—my old master's housekeeper." Ren still has her address tucked away in Dr. MacFarlane's carpetbag. With a pang of doubt, he wonders if he'll be a burden to her.

"Boy, stay with me," says Ah Long, in his gruff broken English. "I find another job."

Ren stares at him, astonished. Ah Long has never said anything to him about this, but there's a warm feeling in his stomach. As though a cat is sitting on it, with its furry, comforting bulk.

Dr. Rawlings inclines his head thoughtfully. "I have a proposal for both of you. I've a job transfer coming up, and my current staff doesn't want to relocate. I'll need a cook and a houseboy. It will be much the same sort of bachelor duties, since my wife and family are in England."

Ah Long glances at Ren and gives an almost imperceptible nod. "Thank you, Tuan. I think about it."

Rawlings nods, too, a storklike jerk. He also looks at Ren. "I'm not a surgeon like Mr. Acton was. I'm a pathologist and a coroner, which is an interesting field of study, though I understand if you find that frightening, after all you've been through."

Ren says seriously, "Will it be all right?"

"Yes. I promise that you'll have time to go to school. I heard you said no to the lawyer, but I think in a little while, you'll change your mind. Mr. Acton would have wanted it. He thought very highly of you."

Ren's face brightens. "Did he?"

"Indeed he did. He told me about your treating that girl Nandani's leg, and said you were a natural physician. You ought not to waste such a gift—you may save many lives in future."

Saving lives. Ren feels a bubble of hope. Yes, he would like that. "Where are you transferring to, Tuan?"

"Singapore," says Rawlings. "The Singapore General Hospital. I think you'll like it there."

Notes

WERETIGERS

The tiger has traditionally been revered across Asia. Ancestor worship in the form of tigers—the belief that the soul of an ancestor could reincarnate as a tiger—was common in Java, Bali, Sumatra, and Malaya, and though the ancestor form was considered "friendly," it was also feared as a disciplinarian.

Spirit tigers appear in many guises, including guardian spirits of shrines and holy places, corpses who transform, and entire villages of beast-men. Tigers, like humans, were thought to possess a soul, and were often addressed with honorary titles, such as "uncle" or "grandfather." In many tales, the true nature of the weretiger is that of a beast who wears a human skin—the exact opposite of the European werewolf. There is probably some connection to Buddhist and Daoist beliefs that certain animals could, by practicing meditation and magic, attain human form. Yet no matter how powerful they become, they are never quite human.

Shape-shifters, in particular, embody the tension between man and his beast nature. In most tales, the tiger acts in ways that people normally do not, expressing hidden or forbidden desires: the most basic of which is to murder people in their own houses. The weretigers of Kerinci were said to covet gold and silver, while southern China has a number of stories of attractive women who are tigers in disguise, and are only revealed when they start digging up graves to devour corpses, much to the horror of their husbands. More amusingly, in Pu Songling's story "Mr. Miao" (苗生), a stranger who joins a scholar as his drinking companion is so irritated by the poor quality of poetry recited at a gathering that he turns into a tiger and kills everyone (perhaps the ultimate literary criticism!).

MALAYA

Malaya is the historic name for present-day Malaysia. Colonized by the Portuguese, then the Dutch, and finally the British before independence in 1957, Malaya was a highly profitable source of tin, coffee, rubber, and spices, as well as home to the important trading ports of Penang, Melaka, and Singapore.

PERAK (KINTA VALLEY)

This book takes place in the state of Perak, most notably the Kinta Valley towns of Batu Gajah and Ipoh. One of the world's richest tin deposits, the Kinta Valley has been commercially mined since the 1880s. For more than a century, up till the 1980s, Malaysia continued to supply more than half the world's tin ore.

Kinta has a long history, having been settled since Neolithic times. As far back as the 1500s, the Portuguese noted that Perak paid its annual tributes in tin. During the 1700s, it was famous for its wild elephants, which were trapped and sold for the elephant armies of the Moghul emperors. The landscape is dominated by beautiful limestone hills, many of which are riddled with natural caves and underground rivers.

Ipoh, the largest city in Perak, was once known as the cleanest, neatest town in Malaysia. The center of commerce and prosperity that resulted from the tin boom, it's famous for good food and many historic buildings. As this book is set in a fictionalized Ipoh, I've taken liberties with certain landmarks, like the Celestial Hotel, whose construction began in 1931 but opened later. Likewise, although Ipoh had several dance halls, the May Flower is a figment of my imagination, inspired by Bruce Lockhart's account of a Chinese dance hall in Singapore in his memoir.[1]

---

1   Bruce Lockhart, *Return to Malaya* (G.P. Putnam's Sons, 1936).

BATU GAJAH DISTRICT HOSPITAL

Founded in 1884 on fifty-five hectares of land, the hospital is built in colonial style and laid out in a low gardenlike setting. The buildings have modernized since then, but a few of the original structures can still be seen. I took liberties with the layout of the hospital to add steps down the hill, a pathology storeroom, a cafeteria, etc., as well as the entirely fictitious hospital staff, imagining what it might have been like in 1931 based on old photographs of similar colonial hospitals and wards.

CHINESE NUMBER SUPERSTITIONS

Chinese have a great love of puns and homonyms. This fondness for wordplay, coupled with feng shui, has led to many superstitions around lucky numbers, lucky directions, and the orientation of buildings. There is the sense that by naming something, you imbue it with both positive and negative powers, and this is particularly true of numbers.

During the Hungry Ghost Festival, you'll see quantities of paper goods fashioned for the dead, which are meant to be burned as offerings. Every detail is considered in these replicas, including the appropriate license plates and house numbers. A model of a car, for example, made of paper stretched over bamboo or reeds and intended to be burned, will likely have a license plate with a lot of fours in it to signify that it's for the dead.

For the living, numbers that sound like lucky words are in great demand. Some people are willing to go to great lengths to secure lucky house numbers, license plates, and cell-phone numbers. The reverse is true, and sometimes a certain house number, like twenty-four or forty-two (which sounds like "you die" in both Chinese and Japanese), is worth avoiding in Asia simply because you may have a hard time reselling the property!

Interestingly, the number five is both lucky and unlucky, as it is a homophone for "negative/not." So a lucky number eight, which sounds like "fortune" becomes less desirable in combination with five as fifty-eight sounds like "no fortune." Similarly, an unlucky number can be flipped, so fifty-four sounds like "won't die."

Romanization of Names

In keeping with the colonial era, I've used older variants of place names, for example, "Korinchi" and "Tientsin" rather than modern-day Kerinci and Tianjin. Chinese personal names at the time were phonetically spelled, often at the discretion of whoever the registry clerk was, and also varied by dialect. Cantonese was and still is the dominant Chinese dialect in the Ipoh area, though Hokkien, Hakka, Teochew, Hainanese, etc., are also spoken. Since Malaysia is a multicultural society, most people can speak a few languages, including Malay, English, and Tamil or a Chinese dialect. I have kept to a Straits Chinese spelling of personal names, such as Ji Lin and Shin, which would be *Zhilian* and *Xin* in modern-day pinyin. Traditionally, Chinese family names are given first, as in Chan Yew Cheung and Lee Shin.

Acknowledgments

This book would not have been possible without the support and encouragement of many people. Many, many thanks to:

Jenny Bent, my wonderful agent, who believed in this book (despite its getting longer and longer as I continued to write!), and championed it all the way to finding a home. Amy Einhorn and Caroline Bleeke, my amazing editors whose insight and support made this book blossom. Many thanks as well to Conor Mintzer, Liz Catalano, Vincent Stanley, Devan Norman, Helen Chin, Keith Hayes, Amelia Possanza, Nancy Trypuc, Molly Fonseca, and the rest of the Flatiron team.

Dear friends Sue and Danny Yee and Li Lian Tan, who have been with this book and all its characters since the beginning, were forced to read multiple iterations, and spent many long hours discussing alternate endings with me.

Readers Carmen Cham, Suelika Chial, Chuinru Choo, Beti Cung, Angela Martin, and Michelle Aileen Salazar whose thoughtful insights were invaluable. Kathy and Dr. Larry Kwan, for your steadfast friendship and medical input on the treatment of tropical wounds. Dato' Goon Heng Wah, for his advice about shotguns used in British Malaya, as well as for estimating historic railway distances. I'm so very grateful for all of you!

My dear family who has supported me in all my writing endeavors, especially my parents whose reminiscences helped build the world of *The Night Tiger*. Also my children, who inspire me every day and help me see the world through a child's eyes.

And to James. First reader and best critic. Without you, beloved, I would not write.

Ps: 50:10

The Night Tiger
by Yangsze Choo

PLEASE NOTE: In order to provide reading groups with the most informed and thought-provoking questions possible, it is necessary to reveal important aspects of the plot of this novel—as well as the ending. If you have not finished reading *The Night Tiger*, we respectfully suggest that you may want to wait before reviewing this guide.

1. The novel's title evokes the story of the weretiger: "a beast who, when he chooses, puts on a human skin and comes from the jungle into the village to prey on humans." What is the significance of that Malayan folktale in the novel? What does it represent for the different characters?

2. Discuss the structure of the novel, alternating between Ren's and Ji Lin's perspectives. How do their narrative styles and worldviews compare? Do you prefer one to the other? How would the novel have been different had it only been from one perspective?

3. Discuss Ren's relationship with Dr. MacFarlane. Does Ren's desire to bring the finger to his former master's grave come from a place of love or fear? How is Ren's life shaped by the masters for whom he works, and how does he determine his own fate?

4. As a surgeon in Batu Gajah, William Acton straddles two worlds, that of the locals and that of the foreigners. What is his relationship to the local people, specifically the young women he sleeps with? Do you think his impact on the community is ultimately positive or negative? What does this novel have to say about race and class more generally?

5. Ji Lin is a more talented student than her stepbrother, Shin, but because she is a girl, she isn't allowed to continue on to medical school with him. How does this novel portray

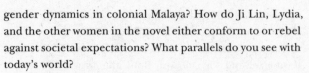

gender dynamics in colonial Malaya? How do Ji Lin, Lydia, and the other women in the novel either conform to or rebel against societal expectations? What parallels do you see with today's world?

6. At the beginning of the novel, Ji Lin leads two different lives—one as a dressmaker's apprentice and one as "Louise," a dance-hall instructor. What are the pros and cons of each role? Does she find a way to reconcile these two sides of herself by the end of the novel?

7. Ji Lin reflects, "When people talked about being lucky, perhaps they simply wanted to feel powerful, as though they could manipulate fate." Discuss the role of superstition in this novel, in which the supposed luck of certain numbers in Chinese tradition motivates many of the characters. What about in your own life? Do you consider yourself to be superstitious?

8. While speaking with Ji Lin about the other Confucian Virtues, Yi notes, "there's something a bit wrong with each of us." How do each of these characters—Ji Lin (knowledge), Ren (humanity), Shin (integrity), Yi (righteousness), and William/Lydia (ritual)—stray from their namesake values? At the end of the novel, are they more "right" or "wrong"?

9. In Chinese culture, the five Confucian Virtues are considered a matched set. Ji Lin reflects, "I had the odd fancy that the five of us were yoked by some mysterious fate. Drawn together, yet unable to break free, the tension made a twisted pattern. We must either separate ourselves, or come together." Discuss the tension between independence and dependence for these characters.

10. In his conversations with Ji Lin, Yi hints that the Confucian Virtue Li, meaning order or ritual, has been disrupted. What are some examples from the novel of characters, relationships, and other elements that are seemingly out of order or unconventional?

11. Discuss Ji Lin's relationships with the men in her life. How do her experiences at the dance hall shape her views of men,

in particular Shin? At the end of the novel, she wonders, "Had I managed to catch up to Shin, or had he, by playing a cool and patient game, ensnared me instead?" What does she mean, and what do you think the answer is? Do you think Ji Lin and Shin will ultimately get married?

12. Why do you think Yi disappears from Ji Lin's and Ren's lives at the end of the novel? What previously unfinished business does he complete? Discuss how the supernatural twines through this novel. Do you believe that the dead can continue to communicate with the living, as Yi does?

13. Although Lydia is proven to be a murderer, she also works hard to improve the lives of Málayan women. Does her charity work at all redeem her in your eyes? Do you think she is in part a victim of her circumstances?

14. The novel ends with Ji Lin, Shin, Ren, Ah Long, and Rawlings all headed to Singapore. What do you think the future holds for them? Are you glad the ending leaves open the possibility of a sequel?